Jade Lee

Dragonborn

LOVE SPELL NEW YORK CITY

LOVE SPELL®

March 2008

Published by

Dorchester Publishing Co., Inc.
200 Madison Avenue
New York, NY 10016

ISBN 10: 0-505-52754-5
ISBN 13: 978-0-505-52754-7

Printed in the United States of America.

10 9 8 7 6 5 4 3 2 1

Visit us on the web at www.dorchesterpub.com.

MORE PRAISE FOR JADE LEE!

DESPERATE TIGRESS

"Elegant complexity and beautifully rendered flaws in Shi Po and Kui Yu elevate the latest novel in Lee's series to a new plane of accomplishment. If Lee's skills continue to grow at this rate, it will be she who becomes an Immortal."

—*Booklist*

HUNGRY TIGRESS

"A highly sensual, titillating read."

—*RT BOOKreviews*

"*Hungry Tigress* is unusual and provocative...[and it] delivers a love story that all romance readers can appreciate."

—Romance Reviews Today

"Jade Lee is quickly on her way to becoming a unique and powerful voice in this industry."

—A Romance Review

WHITE TIGRESS

"An erotic romance for those seeking a heated love story."

—*RT BOOKreviews*

"Jade Lee has written a complex, highly erotic story...extremely sensual."

—*Affaire de Coeur*

"This exotic, erotic and spiritual historical romance is unique."

—Harriet Klausner

DEVIL'S BARGAIN

"Jade Lee has written a dark and smoldering story...full of sensuality and heart-pounding sex scenes."

—*Affaire de Coeur*

"A luscious bonbon of a sensual read—the education of an innocent: hot, sensual, romantic, and fun!"

—Thea Devine, *USA Today* Bestselling Author of *Satisfaction*

A New Fantasy Romance from the Creator of the Tigress Series

DISCOVERED!

As they watched, the dragon extended its neck, diving toward the city as a queenfisher would for its prey. It plummeted straight down. Straight at them.

All about, people screamed and grabbed their children. They trampled one another in their haste to escape while Kiril and his horse skittered to avoid a similar fate. And still the Copper came while Natiya simply stared, mesmerized. She felt the sweat of Kiril's body as he gripped both her and his horse. But most of all she felt her egg, wild and exultant inside her.

That's when she knew the truth. She knew who the dragon recognized, knew it was coming for her and the Queen's egg she carried. And somehow, from its place pressed deep inside her belly, the egg returned the call.

"Quiet!" she hissed to the egg. "You'll get us killed!" But the egg did not listen. It was screaming silently, creating waves and waves of joy—felt, not heard. And Natiya pressed her hands to her stomach trying in vain to silence it.

"Hold still!" Kiril rasped in her ear.

"I can't," she gasped. She barely had the control to look up, to see her death as the Copper shot like an arrow toward her.

Other books by Jade Lee:

TEMPTED TIGRESS
CORNERED TIGRESS
BURNING TIGRESS
SEDUCED BY CRIMSON (Crimson City Series)
DESPERATE TIGRESS
HUNGRY TIGRESS
WHITE TIGRESS
DEVIL'S BARGAIN

*For Pat Rouse for being such a great friend.
Thanks for all you do!*

DRAGONBORN

CHAPTER ONE

So young.

Kiril slipped silently through the stunning lakeside foliage, his grip tightening on his dagger as he studied the boy and wordlessly cursed what he had to do. The blond youth—Huet was his name—was about seventeen years old with the kind of face girls lined up to kiss. A smile at the right moment and this boy could have whatever he wanted. Many times at court Kiril had wished for a face like this.

Kiril shifted. Huet hadn't moved in twenty minutes but sat staring resolutely at the fire. Was he listening to dragonspeak? Dreaming dragon thoughts? It didn't matter. Kiril couldn't wait any longer. He had hoped to do this the easy way, but he couldn't stand it any longer. He had to finish this now.

He dove forward. Gripping Huet about a surprisingly muscular chest, Kiril pressed the dagger against the boy's slender neck.

"Where is it?" he hissed.

Huet didn't answer. He didn't even breathe.

"Do you know who I am?" Kiril tightened his grip, pressing down on the blade. A thin line of red appeared on the boy's creamy skin. "I am Kiril, the king's dragon-hunter. I

spare no one who congresses with dragons." The unfortu-
nate truth. "But I am tired tonight, and am prepared to for-
give. Give me the egg and you will live."

Still no response from the boy. For someone so
young, this one had nerves of steel. Unless . . . Was it
possible? Had Kiril been lied to? There was something
very wrong—

Faster than humanly possible, Huet swung around.
Kiril had been prepared, and yet he still couldn't
match the boy's speed. The youth shoved Kiril's dagger aside, spun past his campfire and grabbed a large
and obviously ancient sword. Kiril barely had time to
draw his own sword before his foe was upon him. Extraordinary speed. Lightning-fast reflexes. And *d'-
greth*, power in his stroke. Huet had a killing strike
with his blade.

Which meant a swordfight was the smallest of Kiril's
problems.

"It's not an egg anymore, is it?" he asked, already
knowing the answer. Dag Racho had sworn the demon
spawn wouldn't hatch for another week at least. "Where
is it, boy?" he demanded.

Huet wouldn't answer. He couldn't: He was dragonborn now. Huet—or *Dag* Huet now that he was
joined mind to mind with his serpent beast—was losing
his humanity by the second. His thoughts were completely consumed by dragon hunger, dragon power,
dragon evil. There would be no sparing him now.

Assuming Kiril survived the battle. He swung his
blade, parrying for all he was worth. The boy was in the
prime of his physical abilities; Kiril was old. Old enough
to wish he'd never picked up a blade at any rate—
dagger, sword or otherwise.

And bloody claw, this boy was strong!

Then it happened: He heard the sound. Dragons
were agile and deadly; they were *not* silent. He heard
the wings flap, felt the breeze on his back. Kiril wanted

to turn and face the real threat, but Dag Huet attacked with renewed ferocity.

The boy's blade had the speed of the wind. Thankfully, Dag Huet and his dragon were both young, newly dragonborn. That made Huet's movements jerky, his swings badly timed. It gave Kiril time to find an opening, some way to—

Too late. Dragon claws bit hard into his back, cutting through his leather and wire *loga* as if it were butter. The beast tried to pick Kiril up, but fortunately was too small to manage a man's weight. Dag Huet had the opportunity to slice off Kiril's head, but the boy was too new to being dragonborn to function as both man and dragon. He could be a dragon or he could be a man. Right now, it was the dragon's turn.

Kiril twisted, sliced his dagger across the dragon claws that held him. The skin was new and so very soft. He felt the spurt of black blood, and the wyrm's scream echoed through the small lakeside clearing. The claws straightened reflexively and Kiril was released—but not before he was thrown high into the air, across a jut of the lake.

At least he'd landed far away from his foe, he thought, grimacing. Bloody claw, what was he going to do now? He was paralyzed.

He looked up at the tree above him and realized with a distracted kind of fatalism that he was about to die. Here he was, Kiril, famous dragon-killer, lying like a discarded doll against a tree, numb from the neck down. Well, perhaps not totally numb. His hands had started to tingle and his legs were beginning to burn with pain.

Glancing around, he wondered how much time he had left to categorize body parts before he died. Dag Huet was the lesser threat. The boy had begun the long trek around the lake. Not even bothering to jog, the new dragonborn was moving deliberately, no doubt trying to remember how to walk. It would take him a while to get here.

The Sapphire dragon, on the other hand, was an immediate problem. It lived only to kill. Well, to kill and amass a fortune whatever the cost—but mostly to kill. That now its essence had a human component mattered only because it made the beast harder to destroy. Both dragon and Huet had to die at once.

A hoarse cry split the air, guttural and terrifying. From Kiril's crumpled position it was impossible to tell if the sound came from dragon or man, but it gave him hope nevertheless. The cry of a mature dragon settled deep into a man's bones, stealing the strength from limbs and reason from even the most seasoned of warriors. A dragon in its prime was impossible to kill; a man was defeated by sound long before the beast drew near.

But this cry had been loud and grating at best. This dragon was still immature. Like the boy, it was unseasoned and impetuous. Kiril could defeat it. At least, he had a chance if he could move.

The tingling in his fingers abated. Sensation returned slowly to his weakened limbs, and Kiril grunted as he struggled to stand. His knees quivered with pain, and his arm could not sustain the weight of his sword. The best he could do was lean over, gasping for breath as he braced himself in the cracked trunk of an aged tree.

Where was the dragon?

Shifting his gaze upward, Kiril swallowed, seeing the answer suddenly appear. What at one moment had been a tiny speck far distant, suddenly became an explosion of blue falling from the sky. The Sapphire was diving. Straight at him.

Kiril tried to straighten, but the shift in his weight caused a lancing pain in his knee. He staggered, gasping in agony, but a crazy grin split his face. Thank the Great Warrior Tiril the beast was still young. If the beast were a week older, Kiril would even now be engulfed in flame, cooked to toasty perfection in a delightful meal for man and beast. But the dragon was too young to have developed fire in his lungs, and so the wyrm would have to capture his prize and eat it raw.

Raw and still fully conscious.

Kiril gritted his teeth, trying to force his thoughts away from his imminent demise. He knew mindlock was the dragon's most potent weapon. But he was a trained fighter, a seasoned dragon-killer. He should be able to think. The dragon was still young.

And yet Kiril stood, waiting for his own death.

He had to move.

Move!

He closed his eyes, forcibly blocking out the terror. Then, with deliberate thought, he flexed his muscles, calling for them to contract, to shift, to move.

Tense hip. Lift leg.

Contract thigh. Extend leg.

Shift weight . . . land in pathetic heap.

That last had not been part of the plan, but somehow it worked. The Great Warrior Tiril must have been amused, because at the moment of Kiril's inglorious collapse the dragon's claws passed mere inches above him. Kiril felt the heated rush of air, gazed upward in horror at the serpent's glistening underbelly, then cried out in alarm as the tree above him splintered and cracked from the dragon's impact.

Stupid dragon. It had missed him and got the tree. A thick branch caught the beast square on the shoulder at the base of its right wing. Stunned from the impact, off balance and flailing, the dragon tumbled backward with a startled croak and crashed into the lake.

If he'd had breath to laugh, Kiril would have done so. Instead, he stared into the shimmering blue gaze of the Sapphire dragon and felt the mindlock seep into his bones. His mind slipped away . . .

Splat!

Icy lake water caught him full in the face. The dragon's struggles were drenching everything, Kiril included. He

jerked, reflexively turning his head and body away from
the icy spray, away from the dragon's gaze. He looked
down at himself. Drenched from head to foot, he had to
decide on his next move. He struggled up and fled behind the tree.

His next thought was to learn what exactly the dragon
was doing, but that was the surest way to lose control
once again. Instead, he closed his eyes and listened,
sorting out movement and proximity as best he could.
The beast was in the water, the wet slapping sound no
doubt its wings beating heavy and sodden against the
lake. A seasoned human controller would have sent his
dragon rushing to the shore, directing its muscle movements with clear deliberate thought. But Dag Huet was
too young to do this effectively—or perhaps even to see
his wyrm's danger. And that gave Kiril the time to act.

Pulling himself upright, he hefted his sword to use
like an ax. He cringed at the abuse of the weapon—it
was a family heirloom, the only memento he had left.
But dead men had no use for fine swords, and so the
exquisite blade became a tool to hack down a tree.

Fortunately, the parts of the tree not broken by the
dragon had been softened by age and disease. Though
thick and ancient, the core was wormy and soft. If Kiril
had not spent a year logging, he never would have
known where and how to strike. But he had, and he did.

Even in his weakened condition, he finished the job
in just a few quick strokes. Then he dropped his sword
into the mud, thinking only that this plan had to work:
He had to topple the tree or he was a dead man.

He still did not look directly at the dragon hatchling,
but the flailing sounds had grown more distinct. Rather
than the frenzied splashes of before, now he heard more
purposeful movement. The beast had probably managed to work its legs underneath him; it would be mere
seconds before the beast managed an ungainly leap
into the air and escape. For Kiril, it was now or never.

He grunted as he pressed his weight into the ancient wood. The rough bark bit into his flesh, scraping his hands bloody, but he barely noticed except to note that his grip became slick. He pushed and heaved, and yet all his strength accomplished nothing. The tree would not budge.

Did he need to cut the trunk more? Had he misjudged? Where was his mistake? Doubt assailed him as he scanned the ancient tree. No, he had done everything correctly. He was sure of it. This would work. It had to.

And his faith was rewarded. The tree began to fall.

But was it in time? Just as the wood gave way, Kiril heard a sudden explosion of water—the hatchling thrusting upward from the lake. The sound was unmistakable, as was the deluge of lake water that once again doused Kiril, chilling him to the bone.

Then came a heavy thud, the crackle of snapping limbs combined with a startled cry and the slap of displaced water. Kiril knew he'd won when he heard the burble of sound as the Sapphire continued to cry underwater. Turning his head, Kiril finally risked viewing his handiwork.

Stretching across the water, half submerged, was the ancient tree, branches broken, leaves falling to cover the churning water. Somewhere beneath the quivering wood was the dragon, kicking and flailing beneath the massive tree's weight.

Another sound rent the air. Less than twenty paces away, Dag Huet screamed in horror, clutching his head to block out the dragon's terrified thoughts. Even the most seasoned dragonborn could not control a wyrm in full panic. Dag Huet didn't stand a chance.

In the lake, the dark water churned as the dragon heaved and flailed to no avail. The tree was too heavy, the mud too thick, and the water too much an encumbrance for the beast to survive. Beside the lake, Dag

Huet mimicked his dragon's death throes, twisting and contorting, his human mind totally overwhelmed.

Kiril turned away from the youth, unwilling to look. His eyes fell on his abused family sword. With sluggish movements, he pulled at the hilt, dragging the weapon out of the mud. The cuts in his back burned through his mind as full sensation finally returned to his body. He simply closed his eyes and breathed through the pain, waiting until it faded to a dull scream. Fortunately, he had the time. It would take long minutes for the Sapphire to drown. Long minutes as the boy struggled to breathe for his beast, his childish mind twisted, his youthful body wracked with pain as the serpent died.

Too long.

Stumbling forward, Kiril crossed the mud until he knelt beside Dag Huet. Again he noticed the clear blue eyes, soft downy hair and freckles that had no doubt delighted a generation of girls. Kiril saw again how angelic the boy truly was, and he felt like a hideous monstrosity beside him.

If he could, he would have spared the boy. He would have separated Huet's mind from the dragon's, leaving the boy scarred mentally and physically, his capabilities no more than those of a toddler, but alive. But it was impossible. The mind connection could only be severed before the dragon hatched. Once the serpent crawled out of its egg and into the boy's hands, Dag Huet's fate had been sealed. This youth would die at the same instant as his dragon. And the reverse.

In the lake, the dragon's movements were slowing, each churning wave a little less high. Soon it would cease struggling.

Kiril raised his sword, unable to stop himself from looking into the boy's eyes one last time, and was shocked to see lucidity within. Beside him, the lake stilled as the dragon lost consciousness.

"Why?" the boy asked.

Kiril blinked. Huet knew why. Everyone knew why.

The youth continued, "Dag Racho is evil. I could . . ." He dragged breath into his lungs. "I could have stopped him."

Kiril nodded, unable to deny the accusation. Dag Racho *was* evil. But Kiril worked for him, and had since he was a boy of twelve.

"I would have made things different," the boy whispered.

Kiril closed his eyes, then plunged his sword down. He knew without watching that he had accurately pierced the boy's chest, deftly cleaving his heart in half. Then, eyes still tightly closed, Kiril listened for the end. It came as expected, the rattle surprisingly gentle. Dag Huet was dead.

Suddenly overcome with weariness, Kiril's hands slid away from the pommel of his sword, which was stuck firmly into the ground. His eyes opened to scan the water, confirming that the only ripples came from the wind.

He looked back at the boy, feeling a physical pain as he scanned the angelic face. It hurt to take it in. It hurt to see the water and the blood and the muddy ground. It hurt, but he looked nonetheless. It hurt, too, to remember the boy's words, but he did anyway.

Dag Racho is evil.

Yes, Kiril's mind answered. Dag Racho is evil. "But so were you," he whispered.

He pushed to his feet, more than weary, but still determined to give the boy a decent burial. He couldn't fault the child for hope, for the naive dream that the Emperor could be defeated. Perhaps their ruler could be killed, but not by committing the same sin that had created the monster in the first place. Nothing good ever came from joining one's heart and mind to a demon.

"All dragonborn are evil," he said aloud, repeating the phrase over and over, just as he had at the age of nine when first dragged to Dag Racho's court to pay for his uncle's crimes. Then he fell silent, even those words cut off as he looked at the boy.

Pain welled up inside him again. How he despised himself for this, for what he had done. But to not act would have been far worse. So, with a grunt of effort, he took the boy's sword, stabbed it into the ground and began to use it as a shovel.

It was many hours before he finished. He worked sluggishly, like a tired old man. He buried the boy. He could do nothing about the dragon, but he made signs warning passersby that the water had been fouled by dragon. And then, after it was all over, he left. There was still one last task for him to achieve.

One more. One more dragonborn to kill. One more child to murder. One more naive hope to dash. And then it would all be over.

If he'd had the strength, he would have smiled. As it was, he could only groan.

CHAPTER TWO

"Natiya! Side room."

Natiya turned, a look of dumbfounded amazement on her face at her employer's demand, but she didn't get a chance to respond as the grime-caked customer at her side took exception to waiting another second for his drink.

"Natiya," he said in a gritty voice. "My ale. *Now.*"

She turned and slammed the tankard of ale down in front of the burly dockworker so hard that it sloshed in his lap. Personally, she thought it could only help wash away the caked fish smell on his clothing, but he took exception. He grabbed her wrist with a half bellow, half roar, and she shoved him away with a glare.

"I know, no tip. Somehow I'll survive," she drawled. The comment infuriated the brute even more, and Natiya was almost pleased to see him stand, fists at the ready. She was feeling just cranky enough to enjoy a bar fight. But then his friends grabbed him, pulled him down, and shoved their ales into each of his fists.

Natiya sighed in relief.

Much as she hated to admit it, she was never irritable enough to enjoy a bar fight. She was tired, hungry, and achy in places she couldn't even name. Still, That Part of her truly wanted a release, an outlet for her anger and frustration.

"Natiya! Side room now!"

That Part of her swiveled and found its target: her boss, innkeeper Talned.

"No dancing today! You agreed!" she called out.

Apparently, Talned had his own set of annoyances to release. Slamming down a couple of tankards on a tray, he glared at her from beneath bushy eyebrows. "Don't flatter yourself. The customer don't want your skinny ass pirouetting before him. Now get in there or get out!"

Natiya was unimpressed. Talned threatened to toss her out at least twice a day. But as this was threat number three, she knew he was reaching the limits of his tolerance. She might be his best dancer and a favorite among his customers, but four threats and she would be out on the street.

Sighing, she wove her way through the crowded inn, swerving past grasping dockworkers while forcing a smile for the soldiers, because they were the truly dangerous ones. Even she was nice to Dag Racho's men. Those who weren't ended up as dragon food. Fortunately, the fort had scheduled evening drills, so the military was blessedly thin tonight. Which meant she got the night off from dancing, to rest muscles that were overworked. Unfortunately, she still had to slop ale for the crowd. That, and serve whomever had booked the side room.

She frowned as she slipped into the hallway, her curiosity piqued. The side room was used for many purposes, only a few of which required a dancer. It offered privacy and, since the entrance was hidden in the rear, anonymity.

But if she wasn't requested as a dancer, then why was she needed? Monik was the prettier of the inn's two barmaids, and so she usually functioned as waitress for the private-room customers. Monik was also the most accommodating of Talned's employees. She would be the one in demand if the customer requested sexual favors. In fact, Monik was sweeter, kinder and less violent than Natiya, so all the usual possibilities were removed. What was going on?

Opening her mouth, Natiya inhaled deeply, tasting the air for anything unusual. Nothing.

She tried to force herself to relax. "*D'greth*," she cursed. "It's nothing. Relax." But she couldn't shake the feeling of doom. Knowing full well that she was growing more paranoid by the day, Natiya straightened her shoulders and faced the door. "You can handle anything," she told herself. "Anything."

And with that she shoved open the door.

The room was medium-sized, cozy enough for a clandestine rendezvous but large enough to accommodate a meeting of military and civilian enforcers. Her gaze quickly swept the room, cataloguing the cheery fire, the tray of sweetmeats, and dual goblets of fine wine. Clearly a seduction.

Natiya sighed, wondering how many times she would have to go through this scene. Despite her reputation as a hellcat with no sexual interests whatsoever, man after stupid man thought they could change her mind. She was on the verge of walking out when a familiar head popped up from behind the couch.

"Come in, come in! And shut the door. You're letting in a draft."

Natiya's mouth went slack. "Uncle?"

"You were expecting someone else, mooska?"

She shook her head, still caught up in shock. "No. Yes. I mean, I thought you were in the Sarent Mountains."

He grinned, motioning with one hand for her to shut the door while beckoning her further inside with the other. "I was, I was! Beautiful place, that. Awe-inspiring if you forget the armies—ours and theirs." He shook his head and sighed. As they both knew, Dag Racho's wars made business difficult for a trader. "But the view, Natiya—it leads a man to think."

Natiya almost smiled. When Uncle Rened thought, life quickly became more complicated. But complicated wasn't necessarily dangerous, and Natiya had always loved the way his mind worked. She shut the door with a firm push and grabbed a handful of sweetmeats as she advanced.

"You look tired," he said as she approached the fire. "And skinny." His smile widened. "A little less work, a little more pampering, and you could be a beauty to rival the greatest jewels in the land."

"You sound like you're buttering up a customer." She narrowed her eyes, inspecting Rened as openly as he had been watching her. As sturdy as ever, her uncle was thick-boned, thick-set, and jovial as always. Though his hair was thinning, his eyes remained sharp, his hands firm and his mind quick.

"I brought you new books," he said as he pulled out a stack of three well-worn picture books. "Children's books. In Sarcenti. So you can learn the language."

Inside her, her secret bubbled up with delight. "I haven't read anything in that language," she breathed as she held the books with reverence. "Thank you!"

"You and your books," he laughed as she curled against the cushions and began to read. "You are like your parents in that."

She smiled and forced herself to close the book. Reading was for alone time in the quiet of her rooms.

"Where is your pipe?" she asked. One of her secret pleasures had been sneaking downstairs at night to hide in the shadows, listening to his grand plans and smelling the tangy odor of his pipe.

He grinned, pulling it out of his pack. "I kept it away so as not to offend your delicate sensibilities."

She laughed. "I have no delicate sensibilities, as you well know."

"Tamara did try," he said, and lit the pipe.

Natiya nodded, inhaling deeply of the smoke, remembering her aunt with a rosy kind of fondness. "I came to you too late for that." She had moved in with Rened and Tamara after her family died when she was eleven. She'd remained with them until her dancing apprenticeship began at thirteen. It was the only respectable job available to a girl orphaned by her parents' treason.

A sudden burst of angry voices from outside intruded on the pleasant atmosphere of the room. More soldiers released from night duty. Out of habit Natiya looked toward the sound, knowing that Talned would not let her remain in the side room for long no matter how important a trader Rened was or how much her uncle had paid for the privilege. "I do not have much time, Uncle. Tell me quick. What is it that you have been thinking?"

He shook his head, his eyes sparkling in the firelight. "Always impatient."

"Always working."

"Ah, but that can change." Rened leaned forward, and Natiya matched his posture, actually tingling with anticipation to learn what her uncle's latest scheme was. He was a genius at turning a profit despite Dag Racho's iron grip on all business ventures. She was even holding her breath.

"Marry my son."

Natiya still held her breath. She couldn't exhale. In fact, she couldn't do anything but stare. Of all the devious plots, of all the convoluted manipulations he had described to her over the course of his years as a trader, this one was the most mind-boggling. Finally, her body demanded she draw breath. It came as a gasp, then rushed out again with a word. "What?"

"Marry Pentold."

She laughed; she actually laughed. She could see the hurt on her uncle's face, but could not restrain herself. "He is my cousin! You are my uncle!"

He leaned back, deftly choosing a few sweetmeats and pushing them on her. "Not by blood. Surely you know that."

Natiya looked away. Her parents and Uncle Rened had been neighbors, not true relatives. At his urging, she had always called him and Tamara aunt and uncle. When her family had died in dragon fire, it was the most natural thing in the world for her to move in with them; they were family, the only ones she had left.

Except that they weren't; they were merely neighbors. Even if somewhere deep down inside she had always hoped, had always wished that they were related by blood. It hurt to hear him say so bluntly that they were not kin.

Then she felt him touch her. His thick, callused hands covered her own, surrounding her in his warmth as they had when she was a small child. "But we can be related. I can be your father in truth. Marry Pentold."

Much as she didn't want to, she withdrew her hands from his tender hold. "Uncle . . ." Her voice faltered. What could she say that would not insult him or his son?

"Wait. Listen a moment before you decide. Surely you can give your old uncle that courtesy?"

She sat and wrapped her arms around her knees, looked into the fire and felt a heaviness settle upon her. Still, she spoke the words he expected, each heavy upon her tongue. "Speak, Uncle, and I will listen, but it will not change my decision."

He hesitated a moment, no doubt surprised by the flatness of her tone. Only she knew how impossible the suggestion was. Even though he had known her all her life, some secrets remained untold. Even to him.

"Pentold is devoted to you," he began. Then he reached out, pulling her chin sideways so that she looked directly into his eyes. "If you want flowers and poems and protestations of love, then I will send him."

She shook her head, barely preventing a shudder. The last thing she wanted was for Pentold to suddenly act the lovesick swain.

"I thought not. Pentold is my poet, and I adore him for it. Every family should have one such as he. But you, Natiya, you are of a more serious mind. Flowery language means little to you unless it is followed by substance. Advantage." He drew himself up proudly. "In this, you are like me."

He paused, waiting for her acknowledgment. She gave it to him—a curt nod, because everything he said was true.

"Very well," he continued. "I will give you advantage. First, Natiya, he wishes to marry you. Honorably. Honestly. And none could gainsay or mock it. That shall be my gift to you, for no one will go against my will. You will be his wife in all honor and truth."

Natiya stiffened in wariness, knowing what was coming as much as she knew he must say it.

"What better offer could you hope for, Natiya? You are a dockside dancer."

"The best dancer in the province!" she blurted before she could stop herself.

He nodded. "Yes, you are. But eventually your youth will fail. An injury perhaps. Or maybe just the passage of time. There will be younger dancers, sweeter to the customers than you. Prettier dancers . . ." He sighed, then went on, pushing forward in the name of brutal honesty. "Then what will you become? Concubine? Mistress? Whore?"

Unable to sit any longer, Natiya stood, pacing to the fire then back again. "Grandmother was a dancer, and she married honorably."

"And hated every moment of it because her husband was cruel and vicious."

Again, Natiya had no response. Everything he said was true.

"Think, girl. Pentold adores you. He will spend his inheritance pleasing you, and his aged years writing sonnets praising you. He is not violent, and his worst vice is a love of cats. What better mate could you hope for?"

Natiya looked down and noticed the sweetmeats still in her hand. She ate them out of habit, knowing it would be a long while before she found the leisure to fill her belly. But even as she chewed, she tasted nothing but bitterness. Marry Pentold? The very thought made her sad to the point of illness. He was no match for her now. What would happen to him after the Hatching?

And yet, for all that, she still considered. As Pentold's wife, she would not have to work at this wretched inn. She could lie in a soft bed and eat sweetmeats to her heart's content. She would have perfumed baths and a husband who brought her flowers in the morning, poetry in the afternoon, and would be grateful for the slightest attention in the evening.

"Why?" she asked. Why was she considering this? What was Uncle's advantage, for he never did anything without that.

He shrugged. "If you were someone else, I would spend many days convincing you. I would flatter you and tease you and make you work for your answers. But because you are not, because I raised you as one of my own, I will tell you the truth."

Natiya straightened but was not fooled. Despite his words to the contrary, she knew his honesty was as much a stratagem as the sweetmeats and proffered wine. He knew that brutal honesty had a better chance of success with her.

"You are the finest dancer in Dabu'ut. Perhaps the finest in all of the Emperor's realm."

Natiya nodded, knowing his words were truth and not flattery, but feeling flattered nevertheless.

"I am a businessman saddled with a poet for a son whom I must support for the rest of his days. What value does he present except in the woman he attracts for a mate?"

"You underestimate Pentold." She said the words reflexively, without thought, because they were polite, not because she believed them.

"Perhaps. But you, you I do not underestimate. You are smart, capable, and you dance like the dragon fire, mesmerizing enough to rob a man of his reason."

Natiya shook her head, finally understanding what he wanted, but not why. "Uncle," she said with asperity, "you are the richest merchant in Ragona. Even with the Emperor's taxes, you find a way to survive. What need have you of a distraction to your customers? You are a fearsome negotiator without a dancer to fog their minds. And even if you were not, why would you embark upon such a path now?" She took a deep breath. "Uncle, you are growing old. How much more gold must you amass before you take a well-deserved rest?"

He stared at her, then burst into laughter. The booming sound filled the room, warming Natiya even as it confused her. "Child, I am not that ancient! And resting is for those who dislike what they do." Once again, he reached out and took her hands, clasping them as warm and firm as his bearlike embrace. "I amass gold because I enjoy it. I negotiate because that is exciting. But more than that, I trade because it is my life's blood."

Natiya sighed. "Very well, but it is not mine."

He grinned. "Perhaps not. But then, perhaps it will be, if you were to try it."

"Uncle . . ." she began, her voice low.

He waved away her protest. "Dabu'ut is changing. Have you heard news of the new governor?"

Natiya nodded. He was the Emperor's dragon-hunter. Young and handsome, but with a dark scar in a hidden place, and an even darker heart.

Her uncle grinned, as if reading her thoughts. "Do not believe everything you hear. He is a smart man, intent on changing this land, changing how life is lived within all of Ragona." He leaned forward, his voice low. "They say he wants to end martial law, take away the curfew, pull back on the military's power."

"Will he cut taxes?" she asked, already knowing the answer.

"Well," her uncle hedged. "As long as Racho has someone to fight—"

"There will always be taxes to support the military." She shook her head. "The governor is doomed to fail. Nothing will change as long as Dag Racho's Copper dragon flies."

"Perhaps and perhaps not. Either way, I intend to master this newer, freer lifestyle. But to do so, I must accomplish two things." He leaned forward, and his eyes appeared to dance in the firelight. "I must bring to my side every advantage I have." He pulled her hand to his lips, kissing it with courtly formality. "And that means you."

She nodded, accepting the compliment for what it was. "And the second?" she prompted.

He sighed, letting her hand drop to his lap. "I must find a way to occupy Pentold. He pesters me to distraction with one nonsensical idea after another." He looked at the fire and sighed in frustration. "Do you know that he wants me to finance a playhouse? With him as playwright!"

Natiya cringed. A playhouse was something that romantic men would finance, that poets dreamed of and actors worked at. Her uncle was none of those things. Worse, the government would never allow anything so uncontrollable. The last playhouse had been burned by troops more than a quarter century before.

"A new wife will occupy him nicely," Rened said.

"And you believe I will steer him from his wilder thoughts and into more productive channels."

Her uncle grinned. "That is my fondest hope."

Natiya couldn't help but return the smile. "Uncle, I have no wish to be Pentold's nursemaid."

Rened pushed the wine into her hand. "Come now, Natiya. It is not such a bad bargain. A lifetime of security. A husband who adores you. A father-in-law who recognizes your value. Some would say it is an excellent bargain."

"Some would say it is better than I deserve," she returned quickly. "But I am not some people."

"But you are considering it, yes? I see that light in your eyes, and I know you see the wisdom of this." He leaned back, his face alight.

Once again, Natiya had no ready response. She could not tell him that her secret made his suggestion impossible. And also, she wanted it: the security, the peace, the settled life. How she longed for such simple things.

You are worth more than he offers.

The voice came unbidden, as it always did, but Natiya appreciated it nonetheless. It always spoke with reason. "I am worth more than this," she repeated out loud, not realizing how her uncle would interpret it.

He exploded upward, his face darkening as she had not seen in a long time. Not since the shameful waste of her family, her home and their library in dragon fire. "Natiya!" he bellowed. "You forget yourself!"

She looked up, cringing inside, straight-backed and steady on the outside. But for all that, she did not know what to say. She did not know what she wanted.

You are worth much more than he offers.

She closed her eyes. The voice was correct, but she could not tell her uncle that. He did not know. Then a sudden noise in the hallway distracted her, saving her from answering her uncle. The noise was the sound of heavy, rushing feet, a quick knock, and an even more hurried push as the door to the side room burst open and—just as quickly—was pulled shut.

It was Talned, looking as frazzled and excited as she had ever seen him.

"Natiya! Quick!" he gasped. "You must dance."

Natiya groaned, feeling herself slip into the familiar pattern again. "You promised, Talned. Not today."

The bald man rushed forward, shoving aside furniture in his haste to chastise his employee. "You will dance today. Now!"

She could only look at him in confusion. Something momentous had happened. And something momentous in Dabu'ut usually meant soldiers, danger and dragon fire. "Talned . . ." she began, only to be cut off by a furious slash of his hand through the air.

"Now!" His face twisted in fear, not anger.

Natiya bit back a sigh. She knew she would not win this argument. "Fine."

"Dress! Go! Dance!"

"I said, fine." But she looked in worry to her uncle. What could have happened to send the usually unflappable innkeeper into a terrified tizzy?

Rened merely shrugged, his expression unreadable. "As long as you work for him, you will always be at his beck and call."

Natiya didn't respond. She could tell by his flat expression that she had offended her uncle deeply. Perhaps even irreparably. But there was nothing she could do about it now. And no chance she could accept Pentold as a life mate. Not with her secret.

So she turned away, feeling more lost and alone than ever.

"Go! Go!" Talned was waving her on, actually pushing her when she moved too slowly. In fact, she would have stumbled if her uncle had not distracted the innkeeper.

Tugging backward on Talned's arm, Rened asked the one question that Natiya hadn't dared ask, not with the innkeeper in such an agitated state: "Whom does she dance for?"

The answer came quickly, and with a tremor of excitement or fear; she couldn't tell which.

"The new governor."

Natiya tugged at a loose string of beads on her dancing costume. She would have to repair it tonight before it came apart. In fact, she thought, looking sourly at the entire bodice, there were quite a few places that needed repair.

Someday she would be able to afford all the beads and jewelry she wanted. And a seamstress to sew them into her clothing. But for now, she needed to take more care with her two costumes.

"Ooh," crooned Monik, coming around the corner beside her. "What a lovely red jewel," she said, pointing to the ornament in Natiya's navel. "It would go perfect with my costume. And I have a gold piece that would complement that dress so much better."

Natiya's hand covered her abdomen reflexively, not needing to look down to remember the brilliant, shimmering red stone that flashed there. Then, realizing what she had done, she slowly lowered her hand. "That's a good idea," she said slowly, "but I just glued this one in. It'll have to stay for a bit. But we'll discuss a trade later."

Monik's expression turned sour. "Oh yeah, I forgot. You don't share."

"That's not true," began Natiya, but Monik had already flounced off.

She doesn't matter, came the voice, and Natiya nodded in confirmation. It was true. Monik didn't matter. She was an average dancer with less intelligence than the dock workers she serviced. Still, Natiya thought with a sigh, it would have been nice to have a friend.

I'm your friend. The only one you need.

Before Natiya could respond, Talned came scurrying over. "Are you ready? He's right over there."

Natiya peered through the curtain, not needing the
innkeeper's extended finger to spot him. It was not that
the new governor was so very handsome. Dark hair, tall
stature, hauntingly clear blue gaze—those were mere
physical attributes that would tempt a lesser woman.
His shoulders were wide, his clothing immaculate, and
his hands steady. Very nice, but she focused on his
hands and her breath caught in her chest. His fingers
were long and tapered. Elegant. Almost refined. And
more importantly, they were quick and sure as they gestured whenever he spoke. That was it. That was what
made her heart beat faster and her eyes linger on the
sight of him.

Confidence.

She supposed someone who killed dragons had the
right to be secure. His every movement, even the way
he breathed, was flush with assurance. And from the
way everyone in the room deferred to him, they felt it,
too. This was a man who would be obeyed.

Then he looked up. He had been drinking ale, and
she had been fascinated by the splay of his long,
tanned fingers about the tankard, noting the calluses
typical of a man who used a sword. Until he set down
his drink, his gaze wandering almost casually about the
room. Until it landed on her.

Instinctively she drew backward, deeper into the
shadows, making sure she was hidden by the curtain. It
did not change a thing. Though he could not see her,
she could feel his gaze on her, steady, heavy, seeing too
much. Yet she knew it was impossible.

Nothing is impossible in a land of magic.

Natiya winced at the oft-heard admonition, but did
not respond.

Why do you look just at him? See everything.

Obediently, Natiya scanned the room, taking in the
drunken revelers scattered about, Talned and Monik
in hurried conversation in the back, the covetous

glances of men and women alike as they gazed at the new governor.

Everything.

Natiya sighed, knowing what the voice wanted and slowly shifting her gaze to see. The governor had a companion. A woman. Brown hair, dumpy, well-manicured, and dressed too beautifully for a common tavern.

The men watch her.

Yes, Natiya thought sourly. They watched her too-ample curves accented by her tight-bodiced gown. Lord, she jiggled every time she breathed. And now she was leaning toward the governor, touching his arm with casual intimacy and speaking to him in an undertone.

Don't turn your head away, Natiya ordered the woman silently, and happily, the woman didn't. Narrowing her gaze, Natiya watched the woman's lips, reading the words as easily as if she'd heard them whispered into her own ear:

"I'll never understand your . . . plebeian tastes," the woman said.

Natiya stiffened, feeling the insult even though she had to search her memory for the meaning of the word. Plebeian. Peasantlike. Lower-class.

Far from being insulted on his people's behalf, the governor merely smiled. His words were equally silent, but also easily read from his lips. "You know why I am here."

"I never know," returned his companion. "Nor do I care to learn."

Neither do I, Natiya thought as she turned away, focusing on readjusting her clothing. So the governor had another purpose for being here? No doubt to find a prettier whore to grace his bed. Well, it wouldn't be her.

You are angry. Why?

"Because I don't want to dance. Not now. Not ever. And certainly not for the likes of him." She muttered the words aloud, using the sound to reinforce her ill humor.

You are lying. You always want to dance.

"I'm tired." This time her words were a peevish complaint.

What are you hiding from me?

Natiya sighed. She hated it when the voice got this demanding. There was never any judgment in its tone, merely a steady and insatiable curiosity. It wanted to know. It wanted to understand. And Natiya struggled to answer honestly.

"That woman," she whispered silently. "She is rich."

You will be rich one day.

"She is dark-haired and curvy. Voluptuous."

The physical is not important.

Natiya grimaced, knowing the voice would not be still until it had a label, a name to put to the unaccustomed emotions flowing through her.

"I am envious of her."

But she has nothing you envy. Wealth and physical form are unimportant. Power is important. Power will get you everything you desire.

Natiya shook her head. "You do not understand," she said. Then she finished her thought silently, knowing the voice would hear what she dared not say out loud: *I envy her the man.*

Why?

Because the man has power, and she has him.

Could not he have her? Must it be she who has possession?

Natiya shrugged. To be honest, she could not believe that the man was the woman's puppet. Most likely, it was he who toyed with her. Still, she thought in response, sometimes access to power is enough. If she were this woman, she would not squander the opportunity. She would study and learn and use the man until she had gained all she could from him. Until she understood him.

Mercifully, the voice remained silent, no doubt studying her thoughts as Natiya wished to study the man. But both were denied the opportunity because, at that moment, the musicians began to play.

"Time to dance." She didn't need to speak the words; the timing was obvious. Yet it was a ritual with her, something she always said before the first step, before even her first dancing breath. And the sound of the words reminded her that this was a task now before her, a persona she donned for the benefit of others.

At least, that's what she told herself.

She began haltingly, sliding slowly out of the curtained alcove, moving awkwardly because she truly was tired, and she hated being forced to dance. Merely for emphasis, she shot both her uncle and Talned a scathing look, one filled with anger and resentment.

Rened responded with a self-satisfied smirk. He knew she was angry, and he mistakenly believed that this enforced activity would bring her one step closer to marrying his son. Talned simply jerked his head toward the governor, telling Natiya to dance for the dignitary and no other. As long as Dag Racho was Emperor, insulting any branch of the government— even a governor bent on reform—could make one dragon-bait.

The music began in earnest.

She intended to dance badly: It was the only way to prove to Talned that he could not command her, that when he forced her to dance against her will, the result was ugly, stilted and ungainly. *Eyes open. Body stiff.* These were the orders she gave her limbs. These were the thoughts that she chanted over and over in her mind.

The music turned, the melody began, but she heard only the beat of the drum. The low *tum* was steady, merging with her thoughts, adding tempo and cadence to her chant.

She turned, and the coins and beads of her costume shifted as well, adding another sound. The steady *ting* was a necessity, demanded of all dancers. But for her, the adornments were tactile, the heavy tap of jewelry against her skin an echo of the drum.

Eyes open. Body stiff.

Tum. Tum. Tum. Tum.

Her hips shifted. Her back arched.

Eyes open. Body stiff.

Tum. Tum. Tum. Tum.

Her head fell back as her shoulders swayed. Her arms curled with the melody, lifting and moving, adding form and depth to sound.

Eyes open. Body stiff.

Tum. Tum. Tum. Tum.

The words of her chant had no meaning now. She heard only sound, felt only the beat while she explored the true expression of muscle and sinew.

Stretch, pull, arch, breathe.

All was one. The sound, the movement, the breathing, even her vision melded color and light into a kaleidoscope of harmonies. Dance steps disappeared from conscious thought. Her training faded. The hours of repetition and study meant nothing to her here; all was life and movement and joy.

Joy.

The music swelled. Did she lead it now? Did her feelings pull the harmonies with her? It didn't matter who led and who followed; they had joined, and the beat pulsed on. As Natiya gave form and expression to sound.

Tum. Tum. Tum. Tum.

Joy!

CHAPTER THREE

Kiril set down his tankard untouched. Great Unity, the girl could dance!

She had started out stiffly, obviously angry with the innkeeper. Her fury had radiated like the sun, and Kiril had been surprised by it. The dancers of his acquaintance welcomed the opportunity to show off their skills and, more to the point, their assets to a wealthy customer. The other wench, Monik was her name, had proclaimed her interest by all but stripping before his very eyes. So when the innkeeper had mentioned his best dancer, Kiril had considered feigning an illness just to escape what would no doubt be an oppressively grotesque display of feminine harlotry.

But disappearing early would not only have been rude, it would also have defeated his primary purpose in coming here: to meet the local population and show himself as a friendly peer who happened to govern them. He wanted to say as loudly as possible that he was nothing like their last money-hungry, power-drunk brute of a governor. And so he had stayed, barely noticing the mediocre music or the girl's obvious hatred.

To make matters worse, she was blond. Who had ever heard of a blond dancer? Truthfully, there were probably many, but those so cursed dyed their hair. Failing that, they at least wore a wig. But this dancer obviously scorned such convention, deliberately flaunting her pale tresses as openly as she displayed her fury.

Then, *d'greth*, she began to dance in earnest.

She had begun slowly, as if unwilling to surrender to the lure of the music. But who would deny such a gift? Even the drunks about the room had ceased imbibing long enough to watch.

For a bare moment Kiril tried to analyze what made her movements so compelling. There was skill, surely, but he had seen dancers with greater practice, greater training. It wasn't in the way she twisted or shifted before his eyes, her movements almost serpentine in fluidity. No, though mesmerizing to watch, the attraction did not lie in her sheer physical performance.

Then his mind began to falter, conscious thought slipping away as he gave himself up to the pure joy of watching. The music, the dance, the girl herself; all combined to express an emotion he had rarely seen, much less felt.

What was it? He couldn't even give it a name.

Sufficiency, perhaps. He doubted the girl even remembered she had an audience. And happiness. Her expression was rapturous.

Joy. That was it. Simple, pure, unadulterated joy. *D'greth*, when was the last time he'd felt that happy?

She took a leap into the air. He was so caught up in the dance that he fully expected her to sprout wings, taking the explosion of power and movement into the air. But she didn't have wings, and so she fell, plummeting to the floor in a dazed heap, as though she too were surprised by her lack of wings.

The tavern was silent, the musicians done, and as one, dancer and audience took a breath, all simultaneously returning to reality.

Then came another explosion: a roar of deafening

applause, whistles and cheers. For a moment Kiril envied these men, knowing that for them, the dancer's performance was routine. The innkeeper said she had danced here most of her life. What would it be like to know, at the end of the day, that such awesome beauty awaited? One need only step down the corner to the local tavern. No wonder this inn was thriving.

Kiril took a deep breath, startled to realize it was his first in many minutes. In fact, his dizziness came as much from lack of air as from the woman still on the floor by his feet. Without thought, he left his seat to crouch beside her, gently lifted her up in his arms.

Tiny was his first thought. She weighed next to nothing. But through the thin barrier of her costume he felt the hardened muscles, the strength and the power of a body that could perform such miracles.

"I can stand on my own, thank you very much."

Her cold words jolted him into awareness. Sweet Amia, he had been standing with her in his arms for who knew how long. He felt his face flood with heat, and the shock of that sensation made him drop his arms as if she were no more than a sack of meal. Fortunately, she was lithe and found her feet as easily as any wild animal. And like any wild animal, she turned to flee.

Fortunately, he was regaining control of his thoughts. Quicker than she could run, he extended his hand, catching her arm. And though he tried to be gentle, his urgency to keep her near him made his grip tighter than he'd intended.

"Don't go," he urged.

She stood still, her expression wary, her gaze locked not on his hand where he gripped her wrist but directly at him. On his eyes.

She herself had the most marvelous eyes. Pale. Changeable. They matched perfectly with her blond hair and fair complexion. And once again, they were angry, blazing challenge at him for daring to touch her. He felt their impact as a physical blow. No doubt this was how she kept the local populace in line. Otherwise, she would likely be mauled at the conclusion of her first dance.

But he had not become a dragon-killer without obtaining some skill. No human could match a dragon for power in their mesmerizing gaze, and as potent as this girl was, she was nothing compared to the creatures he had already defeated.

Instead of releasing her, he drew her forward, urging her to sit with him, talk with him, anything that would keep her by his side a little longer. His attraction was not physical, he told himself, it was intellectual. What type of creature, what type of woman could dance like that? She had to be extraordinary.

"I'm sorry, my lord."

Kiril blinked. That comment came from the innkeeper as the man rushed forward, stupidly trying to interpose his body between the governor and the dancer. Kiril ignored him, his entire being focused on the woman.

"My lord!"

Kiril blinked, frowning as he turned to the irritating man. "Talned?" His voice fairly dripped with rancor, completely at odds with his plan to befriend this influential businessman.

"My pardon, Your Lordship, my greatest apologies. You must understand how awkward this is for me. She . . . we . . . I have a rule. No man may touch the dancers. Not when they are dressed as such. Else all the girls, their very lives are at risk. Please, my lord." The balding man reached out with thick hands and gently tried to ease apart Kiril's fingers where he gripped the dancer.

Kiril stiffened, angry beyond measure that this man sought to interfere. "I am the governor," he said stiffly, then marveled at the idiocy of his words. Had he not spent years fighting those who believed their mere titles gave them power over others?

"Yes, yes," said the innkeeper, bowing his sweating head twice before speaking more. "And as such, I must beg of you to set a good example. Otherwise, I fear for Natiya's safety." The man glanced sideways at the girl, his expression clearly nervous.

At that moment, Kiril's mind registered two very distinct facts. First was that the woman's name was Natiya—a beautiful name that should be sung by birds. In fact, he remembered abruptly, he was here searching for a girl named Natiya.

The second fact was much more compelling, coming to him in a flash of insight that made him smile. The innkeeper was afraid, not of him, but of Natiya. The look he gave her was positively pleading. But what hold did she have that would reduce her employer to such desperate straits? Did he fear she would quit, taking away what was undoubtedly a key source of income for him? Or was it something else?

Kiril did not speculate for long. Much to the innkeeper's obvious dismay, the girl chose that moment to speak. "Governor or not," she said, her voice caustic, "you are all men bent on rutting, and I'll not be touched by a one of you." Then she twisted out of his grip and stalked away, her head held high, her body rigid with disdain.

"Oh my lord, oh Your Lordship, great sir, my apologies. She has such a temper. Especially after she dances. Monik, more ale for the governor. My lord, please accept . . ." The man droned on and on, nearly apoplectic in his mortification. Now, as he bowed and scraped before him, Kiril understood the man's terror: that the girl would open her mouth and dispel the magical moment her dance had created, insulting the new governor in the process.

Kiril turned his furious gaze on the man, his hands curling into fists. Talned had been right to fear.

But then another sound penetrated Kiril's thoughts. Laughter. Loud, high-pitched squeals of humor that sliced through all thought and brought his head snapping around to his companion. Sabina was laughing. Not only was she laughing, but she was holding her ample sides to contain her mirth. Tears rolled down her cheeks. Her bosom jiggled as wave after wave of loud guffaws burst from her.

"Bina," he snapped. "Control yourself!"

Far from having the desired effect, his words elicited additional gales of laughter.

Kiril bit his lip. There was nothing to do but fold his arms in a semblance of dignity while waiting out her perverse sense of humor. It felt like an eternity, but eventually she settled enough to form words.

"Contain myself? Myself? Kiril, you were about to hit the man. Hit him! And why? Because a woman had the audacity to tell you to keep your rutting hands to yourself!"

Again she dissolved into laughter.

Abruptly, the reality of the situation sunk into his dazed mind. She was right. When trading on his title had not worked, he had actually been about to hit the man— hit an innocent innkeeper! And why? Because some dancer had tossed him aside like so much rancid meat.

He stared at his fists, still clenched in anger. The innkeeper slipped backwards, his bald pate glistening with sweat.

"My lord—"

"No." Kiril's single word was harsh. Then he took a deep breath and continued in a more measured tone. "My apologies to you and to the dancer. I understand your rules and will of course respect them." He glanced sideways, seeing Sabina's disdainful smirk.

"He will, or he will forfeit his every cent to me," she said, her voice casual as she pushed away from their table and stood.

The innkeeper shifted, rushing to assist Sabina with her chair. "My lord?" he asked.

Kiril shook his head. "Nothing. Merely a wager, nothing more."

Sabina smiled, but her voice kept its hard edge of cynicism. "As delightful as this evening was, Master Talned, I believe I have had quite enough entertainment. Don't you agree, Kiril?"

Kiril bowed politely, knowing that any other response would be to invite forfeiture of his bet.

The innkeeper was quick to assist. "I shall have your carriage brought round immediately." Then the nervous man bowed twice before rushing away.

All around them, the inn's patrons returned to drinking and muttering amongst themselves. They, too, realized that the show was over. They would get no more entertainment from their newest governor. Of course, many kept an eye on Kiril just in case they were wrong.

"A dancer, Kiril. One dancer tells you to keep your hands to yourself, and you throw it all away." Sabina's voice was bitter, filling the dark carriage with her disillusionment.

"Do you wish to leave my employ?" Kiril's voice was equally acerbic, though his tone held self-disgust, not anger.

True to form, Sabina took her time responding, allowing him to fret over her decision. *D'greth*, he couldn't lose her now, not after just gaining the governorship. It would destroy him, and well she knew it.

"No. Not yet. But—"

"Then the wager is not forfeit," he interrupted. "And we will speak no more of it."

She spun in the confined carriage, her ample body straining the ties that bound her bodice. "Dragon's eyes, Kiril, we *will* speak of it, and we will speak now! Have you forgotten what is at risk here? You can have everything. Do not throw away your wealth, your power, *d'greth*, your very ideals for a common tavern dancer!"

"There was nothing common about her!" he retorted hotly.

"There never is," she replied just as quickly. "At least not until after her legs have spread and you are pulling on your pants."

Kiril winced at her crude statement. "Vulgarity ill becomes you."

"As it does you." She leaned back, her expression softening on a heartfelt sigh. "Kiril, this has nothing to do with the dancer. I don't care if she was the most voluptuous whore in all Dag Racho's kingdom."

"She's not a whore. She refused me, remember?" His words were mere reflex, a muttered complaint to stave off the coming lecture. And true to form, she ignored him, knowing his words for the distraction they were. But when she spoke, it was not the lecture he had anticipated but something else entirely.

"My skills are prized the kingdom over. There is no one with my financial ability this side of the three seas." She paused, waiting for him to comment. He did so quietly, warily.

"I know."

"I could share my bed and my talents with kings, lords, any man I wish."

Another pause, and again Kiril responded, "I know that."

"But I choose you. Do you know why?"

This time he didn't answer. He had asked himself this very question a thousand times, sometimes of Sabina herself, yet he never received a clear answer. Never, at least, until now.

"I stay because I believe in you. I know what you wish to accomplish. For yourself. For this land. I stay because you will make Ragona a better kingdom."

He looked away, humbled by her faith, seeing now that a lecture would have been far less painful than this bald statement.

"Do not throw that away."

"On a woman?" he asked, wondering just where she thought the pitfalls were.

"Lust. Greed. Envy. Fear. Shall I name more sins? You have always been moderate, Kiril, levelheaded in your virtues as well as your vices."

Kiril was silenced, abruptly realizing that all the time he had spent studying power and the court, she had spent studying him. She likely knew more about him than he did himself. Given that, he could not easily dismiss her opinion.

"Do not throw yourself into a grand passion."

"Any?"

She smiled. "Only a cool head can face a dragon's fire."

He groaned. "Don't quote platitudes at me."

"Very well," she said as the carriage drew to a halt before the governor's mansion. "Then listen to this. If you become intemperate in any form, whether over a woman or gambling or even food, then do not think I will hesitate—I will call in our wager and leave you penniless."

Kiril straightened, hearing the seriousness of her threat. "That wager called for me to forfeit my ideals, to throw away all I believe in for the exercise of power. Sabina, I am not a corrupt courtier using my power to satisfy—"

"Your own lusts?" she interrupted, her brow arched in skepticism.

He looked away rather than admit how close he had come to breaking his own rules. What was it about that girl that drew him so powerfully? Had he been be-spelled?

"Tread carefully, Kiril, because I am watching you," she said. "Lose your way now, and I will take every cent, every cloth, every morsel. And then I shall leave you be-cause you will have betrayed us both."

She swept from the carriage, her words ringing loudly in the gloom.

Kiril whistled as he sidestepped a puddle of slime in the street. The air was ripe with pitch and fish, two oily scents that tended to cling to the skin, befouling what-ever they touched. They mixed with nauseating effect with the vapor from the slowly cooling meat pokoti he held in his hands, and he prayed the odor wouldn't destroy the taste of the best flat-bread in the entire province.

The wind slapped his gray homespun coat against his legs, the coarse fabric making his skin itch even through the heavy wool of his tight-knit trousers. But he contin-ued to whistle, startled and annoyed with himself for the joy that bubbled inside him.

He was happy. On this miserable, cold, foul morning, he was happy. Why? Because he had discovered where the dancer lived and was bringing her a present. Well, a present and a threat, but he hoped that the former would soften the latter.

He pushed through the door of the boardinghouse where the barmaid Monik claimed Natiya slept alone. It only cost a few coins, and the girl had given him exact directions to the dancer's room, and then had provided a lot more. Things like Natiya's favorite pastime: eating. Natiya's favorite gift: food. Natiya's favorite color: any-thing reminiscent of food. She eats like a gremblin, the woman cursed. And then, most valuable of all, the woman told Kiril her real name: Natiya Draeva. A little more digging had revealed the dancer was probably the only surviving child of Samuel and Amaya Draeva—dragon scholars.

Imagine the luck. The very girl he sought when coming to this damp, ugly province was the very girl he wanted most to know better.

So he whistled as he walked to the spice-baker, buying the man's largest and most portable meal. And he hummed as he climbed the stairs to her bedroom door. And he grinned as he banged on the thin wood. Then he stood there like an idiot with a cooling pokoti dripping into his hand because no one answered.

He frowned, his tune abruptly stopped. She couldn't be gone already. Monik had assured him that Natiya did nothing outside of dancing except sleep and eat, alone in her room in this boardinghouse.

He banged on the door again, cursing under his breath as the spiced sauce dripped through his fingers.

Then he stopped. Had he heard something? It was hard to tell; there were so many noises in this decrepit building. *D'greth,* he swore he could hear every crying child, every screeching fishwife, even every netted fish as the morning's catch dropped onto the dock. But he couldn't hear if Natiya was inside her room.

He thought about kicking the door in. The boards were certainly flimsy enough. Then he caught himself, cursing again the strange fascination that gripped him. He had never, ever lost his reason over a woman, certainly not a dockside dancer, no matter how skilled. He needed her for an entirely different purpose—one that didn't currently involve kicking down her door and scaring her half to death.

Certainly that method had its place. Indeed, that was the threat part of this morning's work. But for the moment, he intended to catch the dragonfly with honey, not vinegar. Assuming his charm worked, he wouldn't even need his threat. And if this morning's work found him climbing into bed with the delectable dancer, then it was all in service to his king.

Or it would be if she ever opened her door.

He banged again. Then did it once more for good measure, his fist making loud echoes in the tenant house despite his intention to remain unobtrusive. And then, dragon's egg of miracles, he heard it. Her voice. It came as a low sound he barely understood: "I'm coming."

He leaned forward and shamelessly pressed his ear to the door, fearing he would hear a man's voice inside with her. He heard nothing but her and some banging, followed by the very same curses he'd just used. My, the woman had a warrior's vocabulary.

Suddenly the door hauled open and a tiny fist flew out at him, barely missing the pokoti.

"Here, you bloodsucking worm. Take it and let me sleep."

Kiril looked down to see a small pile of coins clutched in a tiny fist. "I assure you," he drawled, "no payment is required." Then he used his shoulder to push the door open wide enough for him to see Natiya, her hair in a wild tangle about her head, her lithe body shrouded in a ragged sleep shirt that ended just above her knees. He grinned, knowing now that she was definitely alone. No woman dressed like that when she took a lover to bed—though, perverse man that he was, he found her attire especially sexy, as it would take less than a moment for him to rip the thin fabric from her body. Or it would if he didn't have a dripping pokoti in his hands.

He felt his hand clench slightly as he fought the urge to toss the hot item away. Fortunately, he remembered his purpose and his gentlemanly upbringing, even if he'd rarely had cause to use it. He extended the hot pie to her, noting how her nose seemed to twitch with the scent, her drowsy eyes widening.

"I'm sorry if I woke you," he lied. Indeed, he had specifically planned to catch her before she was awake and could marshal sharp wits to her defense. "But I brought breakfast as a way to atone."

Her clenched fist slowly dropped to her side. "I thought you were my landlord."

"A little behind on the rent?"

She shrugged as she carefully dropped her coins back into a tiny purse she held by her side. But even as she handled her money, he noticed that her eyes never left the food extended toward her. In fact, she looked like she might even be leaning a little closer to him.

But even though she stared at his offering like a starving dog, she shook her head, slowly inching backward. "Please. It's bad for me to be seen with you. Thank you . . ." She almost choked on that part. "But no."

Fortunately for him, her tiny shuffles backward gave him room to step fully into her tiny room, quietly shutting the door behind him. "No one knows who I am," he said, keeping his voice low and soothing. Then, before she could object further, he pressed the pokoti into her hand. "Please. Eat. You look hungry."

"I'm always hungry," she groused, but she took the food nevertheless. He could tell she wanted to refuse him. She didn't trust his motives or his food, but she was clearly hungry. In fact, he was surprised he hadn't heard her grumbling stomach through the door.

So while she gobbled down the pokoti, all the while watching him with wary eyes, he surveyed her surroundings, noting how very much they seemed to fit her. Tiny and spare, her room revealed no concession to comfort or leisure. She had a pallet, a washstand without adornment beyond a pitcher and a bowl, and a small, closed wardrobe, which presumably held all her worldly goods. What lighting there was came through a dirty window that looked out on the street below. A single chair sat beneath it, as if she sometimes climbed up on it to look out; but no other form of entertainment revealed itself.

In short, like the woman, the room was compact, efficient, and gave absolutely nothing away. He narrowed his eyes, looking deeper into the shadows beneath her bed. Were those books? By the Father, there were dozens of books secreted away under her bed! How he itched to know what she read. He couldn't see the titles from here.

He turned his attention back to her, watching her finish off the pokoti with amazing speed. Then he watched her flush with embarrassment as she suddenly stopped licking the sauce from her fingers before slowly lowering her hands.

"I apologize," she said, her words somewhat stilted, as if she were forcing herself to act more politely than usual. "My manners are hideous. I . . . I did not eat last night. And after dancing . . ." She let her voice trail away even as she crossed to her washstand, carefully turning her back to him as she dropped her coin purse someplace he could not see.

"Surely Talned knows he must feed his dancers," Kiril commented, not from any desire to know, merely a wish to keep her talking. "Does he not tell the kitchens to—"

She released a sharp bark of laughter as she poured water into the bowl. "Talned knows we will eat all his profits if he is not careful. I do not fault him for his stinginess." She carefully wet a cloth to clean her face and hands. "Monik and I still manage to take a little here and there. Only last night . . ." Her words trailed away and he watched her bite her lip, no doubt startled that she was talking to him so easily.

But then, that was exactly why he was being so charming: so she would talk easily with him. With that thought in mind, he leaned back against the door, purposely appearing as nonthreatening as possible.

"Only last night," he finished for her, "you had not intended to dance. But you did. For me. And because of that you did not get any dinner."

She did not deny his words, but focused on her toilette, each movement slow and careful. He knew she was thinking, but could not begin to guess what choices she pondered. So he continued babbling, trying to distract her from her wariness.

"I am pleased, then, to repay my debt to you this morning. Or perhaps that wasn't enough. Are you still hungry? We could go out for more . . ."

She set aside her towel, still remaining tightly controlled as she shook her head. "You should go now," she said, her voice a low warning. "I thank you for the breakfast, but I cannot give you what you want. I will be no man's mistress, least of all yours."

He pushed off of the door, but did not approach her. He had expected as much, and yet, still the thought irritated him. Did she think him so single-minded? "What if I told you I did not come here to make you my mistress?"

She did not retreat but stood her ground, arching a single eyebrow at him to emphasize her disdain. "I would tell you that there is a scent a belly-horned man exudes, a kind of perfume that proclaims to all with noses exactly what interests him."

He straightened, flushing slightly as she called his bluff. Yes, he was belly-horned, as she so crudely put it, but she could not truly know that beneath his heavy clothing. "You have a discerning sense of smell if you can detect a man's scent over that lot." He waved his hand toward the nearest dock where boat after boat was just beginning to off-load the morning catch.

He meant to challenge her, wondering if she would back down. She merely arched a single well-sculpted brow at him, managing to maintain her dignity while refusing to banter with him. And he found himself admiring her ability to remain immune to his usual tricks to get a woman to talk.

Clearly, he needed a new approach as his usual flirtation games were not working. So he decided on honesty.

"All right, then, I do not deny that my body hungers for you. That much was obvious last night." He still felt the burn of embarrassment at how easily his flesh had betrayed him. "I assure you that was highly unusual for me. And even despite my"—he swallowed—"my lust, I am not ruled by my appetites, and you have value beyond your dancing skills."

He watched her grow still at his words, like an animal freezing in fear, waiting and watching for the predator's next move. He took his time, knowing that his next words would strike terror in the heart of any sane man.

"You have knowledge that the Emperor wants."

She gasped, flinching backward, her hand automatically covering her belly. He frowned, his gaze focusing on the movement. She couldn't be pregnant, could she? He replayed the movements of her dance last night. No, her belly was as flat as the bread she had just devoured. Flatter and stronger. But couldn't a well-toned woman be pregnant for months before any man became aware of it?

He decided to keep a closer eye on her body, watch for further signs of a child. Meanwhile, she curled her hand into a fist and slowly drew it away from her abdomen.

"I have nothing the Emperor wants," she hissed.

Well, no love lost there, he thought to himself. The little dancer was clearly no fan of her ruler. But then, that was not a surprise.

"But you do," he countered sweetly. "Or more importantly, he thinks you do."

She shook her head, and he could feel the panic within her for all that she fought to contain it. "He cannot," she whispered. "I know nothing."

Kiril felt guilt cut a tiny fissure in his control. She was just a dancer, after all, a woman struggling to survive as best she could. She was not up to the usual court games. Besides, hadn't the girl already suffered enough?

Unfortunately, he couldn't allow himself to feel tenderness toward her. He had come to the province especially to find her. Had gone to Talned's specifically to hear word of her. That she had appeared before him, and as a dancer no less, had simply been dragon's luck.

So he continued to play her, allowing his expression to slide into one of rueful neglect. "I told him you know nothing. Those were my very words," he lied. Truthfully, Dag Racho knew nothing of the girl's relevance to his plans. "But you are Natiya Draeva, aren't you? The only surviving child of Samuel and Amaya Draeva . . ." He drew out his next words as the damning evidence it was. "The dragon scholars."

She didn't respond, but he could tell by the way she paled that she was indeed the woman he sought. So he stepped forward, dropping his tone and his demeanor into the threat it was.

"Dag Racho thinks you hide something from him."

CHAPTER FOUR

*Why are you afraid? He has said nothing but the truth.
We do hide from the Emperor. Everyone hides from him.*

Natiya closed her eyes, shutting out the world, wishing
she could shut out the egg's voice as easily. But it was always there, always questioning. It didn't understand that
they hid a bit more than unreported taxes or a son who
was unfit for soldiering. If anyone discovered she incubated a dragon egg, they both would be killed immediately and very probably by the man who stood in her
room being so charming. Damn the man for having the
Emperor's ear. Damn him, too, for being their new governor. And damn him most of all for being ruled by his
belly-horn just like every other stupid man.

Because she had no doubt that was the real reason for
his presence here. Dag Racho had no reason to fear her.
If he had wanted her dead, he would have killed her
years ago when his dragon unceremoniously ate the rest
of her family before firing their home. That she did indeed possess secret dragon knowledge had been carefully hidden. That she even now plotted the Emperor's
downfall: mere coincidence.

The simple truth was that the governor wanted to
bed her, so he had asked a few questions, somehow

stumbled upon her true ancestry, and was now trying to use it to frighten her. Hell, a child could see through the ploy.

But that didn't make the situation any less dangerous. Any focused attention—and from the land's greatest dragon-hunter, no less—could expose her secret. But how to remove him?

She briefly toyed with the idea of giving him what he wanted. She could bed him, she supposed. Monik told her it was a simple matter of spreading one's legs and moaning a lot; no more, no worse. It couldn't be that bad. Indeed, she thought as she glared at her adversary, there could be worse men to initiate her into coupling. He was handsome, powerful, and—most important— clean. And lately she admitted to a curiosity, perhaps even an interest, in the things that Monik participated in so freely. Best of all, she doubted that the governor's attention would remain on her for long. Once she gave him what he wanted, that was.

But her stomach twisted at the thought. Any type of intimacy was too great a risk. She carried a dragon egg, possibly the greatest dragon egg found in the last century or more. There were ways, her father had warned her, ways to tell who incubated an egg and who did not. But he had died before she learned what they were. There was no way to tell if she could keep her secret during such intimacy. Which was the reason she refused every possible friendship, every possible intimacy since she'd begun dancing. The risk of discovery was too great.

So she shook her head, finding her strength with the movement. "Dag Racho doesn't want me. He doesn't even know about me," she stated flatly. "You are merely trying to frighten me so I will bed you." Then she lifted her head, allowing him to see the tears that shimmered in her eyes. That had been the first thing she learned from watching Monik: some men are more easily manipulated by tears than curses. And from the way the governor shifted awkwardly from foot to foot, he was one of them.

"Can't you bed someone else?" she asked, the question an honest one. "Why focus on me?"

She watched him swallow, his movements shaky as he abruptly pulled out his sword. She tensed, prepared to jump for the window and from there into the street. But before she could do more than gasp, he held the sword before him, pommel first. "I swear by the only thing I hold dear, I swear to you that this is not a ploy to get you into bed. We think you know something—about dragons—and neither I nor Dag Racho can afford to leave you be."

She frowned at him, seeing earnestness in his expression and his rock-solid stance as he held his sword before him. He truly meant what he said, and that thought threw her into an even greater panic. What did they think she knew?

She had no answer, and so she stalled for time, reaching for the first question that came to mind. "What thing?"

He stared at her, clearly frustrated. "A dragon thing. That you hide."

She shook her head. "No. What thing do you swear by? What do you hold most dear?"

He frowned, pulling his weapon closer to his chest. "My sword, of course. What else would a warrior treasure?"

She could think of a thousand things. A belly-horn, for example, as rutting seemed to dominate most men's minds—certainly every soldier she'd ever met. But he appeared so genuinely confused that she couldn't stop her smile. "Of course. I didn't understand."

"It's a family heirloom. My great-grandfather had it made, and it has been passed down through generations to me."

"I see."

"It's got jewels in the hilt, loga filigree throughout, and it cuts through bones like butter. It's an exquisite blade."

"I believe you."

He abruptly sheathed his sword, clearly insulted. "Warriors *always* swear by their swords. What else would we swear by?" Then he paused, readjusting his clothing so that it hid his scabbard as much as possible. "What do you swear by? What do you hold most dear?"

Knowledge. Ask him to teach us something.

She mentally silenced the voice inside. Its thirst for information was insatiable. Meanwhile, she decided to answer the governor with a partial truth, and one that he could have guessed anyway. Let him think their sudden accord had relaxed her guard. "My legs," she said. "Without them, I can't dance."

"And without my sword—"

"You would still be the greatest dragon-hunter in the land, and still our new governor. And Ragona is filled with swords you could use."

He smiled. "True." Then he remained where he was, standing tall and proud in her tiny room, like a huge statue to Dag Racho's evil, oppressive government, for all that he smiled, trying to make himself appear harmless. "Natiya, I wasn't lying. We need to know what you know, what you have learned from your parents about the dragons."

"If Dag Racho had wanted information on dragons, he should not have killed all the dragon scholars." She turned her back on him, letting him see her anger in her rigid stance and clipped words. "I have nothing for you or my parents' murderer."

She hoped he would leave then, hearing the finality in her words and attitude. She hoped, but she did not expect. He hadn't become governor by taking no for an answer. Still, it was with considerable surprise that she felt his touch on her shoulder. She had not heard him approach, and with her dragon-enhanced senses, she should have.

But she hadn't, and so she was surprised when she felt his warmth on her shoulder and smelled his scent surround her. It was a clean scent, not polluted with perfumes or the spices of necromancers. Soap. Fish from the docks. And man. The very same scent that he had left on her skin yesterday when he held her, the one that had surrounded her as she slept last night, and the one that caused a pooling of liquid in her bones. She didn't understand it, and she didn't want it. Especially since she most certainly liked it. What was happening to her that she actually liked a man's touch? A man's scent?

"Natiya—"

"Don't!" she ground out as she shrugged him off her shoulder. "Don't hurt me like this."

"I'm trying to help you," he spat, and she could tell by his frustration that he meant it. "You have held off Dag Racho for now, but he will come for you. He has already begun questioning and torturing all those with ties to the old scholars. He will come for you eventually. He is desperate."

His words sent shivers down her spine, but that did not stop her words. "Then he should not have killed—"

"The scholars. Yes, he knows. But that doesn't help you now, does it?"

She shook her head, drawing her arms tight around her belly. "What do you want from me?"

"The hatching grounds, Natiya. Where are they? We know the dragons left their clutches in the caves all along the coastline, but we cannot find them."

"Maybe they don't exist."

He laughed, the sound bitter and hard. "He doesn't believe that. And what Dag Racho believes, he will find a way to prove." Though she had stepped away from the governor, she felt his hands return to her shoulders. Two hands this time, slowly sliding down her arms, drawing her backward against him. His touch was gentle and comforting, and it soothed her fears.

She wanted to push him away, needed to stay distant from his touch, his scent, even the sound of his voice, but she couldn't. Or rather, she didn't. She liked the man's touch. She enjoyed the feel of large, callused hands gently caressing her. And even if she didn't, the egg certainly did.

Of all the dangers inherent in her task, this was surely the worst: the egg's insatiable curiosity. Natiya had never felt a man's arms around her before, not with such care and tenderness. She had never experienced it before, and so the egg demanded that she succumb to it, sending wave after wave of desire coursing through her. *Experience this*, it whispered into her mind. *Allow this*.

So she did. And worse, the governor began speaking, his words like tiny pebbles dropped one by one into her heart, causing ripples to echo throughout her entire body.

"You are not the only one to lose your family. The Emperor killed mine as well. Dag Jaseen was my cousin."

Her body jolted in shock. He was related to Dag Jaseen, the last dragonborn to challenge their ruler? The battle was said to have lasted days, but in the end, Dag Jaseen had lost. "But Dag Racho ordered all Jaseen's kin executed."

She felt him nod, his chin moving lightly against her temple. "All save one. His youngest cousin, who would be raised in the Racho court to serve as a reminder of what happens to any who challenge the Emperor."

"You?" she asked.

"Me." She felt a shudder flow through him into her, and she wondered at its cause. Was he remembering his cousin's death? The loss of his great family? Or perhaps he recalled the bitter aftermath when all he knew and loved was gone, and he became the plaything of an evil court.

It will not happen to us. We will win.

Natiya closed her eyes, knowing that the egg merely repeated what she had said to it so many times. They would not lose. They would destroy Dag Racho and his evil forever. And yet, she knew Dag Jaseen had thought exactly the same thing.

Suddenly the memories and the fears became too much. Spinning around in his arms, she shoved at his chest with all her strength. Caught unawares, the governor stumbled backward. But true to his athleticism, he did not move far.

"Why do you serve him?" she demanded, hating the way her voice trembled with the question. "He is evil and cruel. He killed your family! And yet you serve him with all your strength. Why?"

"For the same reason you dance for drunken louts night after night. Because I have to. Because he is stronger, and I am weaker, and this is the only way I can survive."

"By doing his bidding like a lapdog? By killing the very people who could save us from him?"

The governor's eyes darkened to granite. His voice sounded clipped and hard. "Have a care, dancer," he warned. "You speak treason."

"He killed your family!"

"And he will kill you if I do not find those caves. My parents are dead. So are yours. Now, do you wish to live or not?"

She stared at him. Truly, she was tempted. She knew where the clutch-caves were located. She'd walked to them at least a dozen times with her parents. And one more time alone, after their deaths. She knew as well that the most valuable egg—the queen egg—was gone from the caves, for she held it tight in her navel. What would it hurt if she gave this man what he wanted? He would search the caves and find nothing.

She shook her head. "I know nothing," she lied. In truth, she knew that once she gave the tiniest bit of information, Dag Racho would hound her until her death. He had done it to others—other scholars, friends of her parents, even students. Paranoia ruled the Emperor. Thus, paranoia was the only way to survive in Ragona. It was best if she kept silent.

As if guessing her thoughts, the governor sighed, reaching out with a single hand to stroke her cheek. "Do not lie to me, Natiya. I am trying to help."

"You are saving your position and your life."

He shrugged. "That, too. But I truly am trying to make things better. For all of us."

"I know nothing," she repeated. "I was a child interested in dolls, not silly stories about dragons."

His hand fell heavily to his side, and yet she still felt his strokes as a tingling across her cheeks. "He will come for you. Soon. I will not be able to stop him. Think beyond the present moment."

She felt her legs go out from under her, collapsing her backward against the washstand. "Should I run?" she wondered aloud.

"Where would you go?"

She bit her lip. Nowhere—she had nowhere to go. She could not even risk trusting Uncle Rened, for the wealthy merchant had great ties to the Racho court. And after the insult she had dealt him last night, he would quite likely turn her over to the Emperor simply to buy court favor. No, she had nowhere to go.

"Stay with me," the governor urged. "We can search your memories together. Maybe there is something you have forgotten. Something that would show the Emperor that you are trying to help. That you are no threat."

"I don't help murderers."

He sighed. "Do you know any other way to survive?" He reached forward, clasping her hands in his. "When the soldiers come—and they will come—what else can you do?"

She shook her head and reluctantly withdrew her hands from his. "Quite likely die, for I know nothing." She searched his face, looking for some hope, some answer different from the future he had already described.

Why do you look to him for hope? Aren't we the only hope?

She didn't know how to answer the egg, especially since it was right. She would get no help from this man. As governor and Dag Racho's dragon-hunter, he was the last person she would ever trust. So she walked away from him, dropping wearily onto her pallet.

"I must dance tonight, and I can't do that unless I get some more sleep. Thank you for the breakfast, Governor. I am sorry I cannot help you further."

He didn't say anything at first, merely watched her with an infinitely sad expression etched onto his face. Then, eventually, his shoulders dropped the tiniest fraction and she knew she had won.

"Contact me," he said softly. "If you think of anything or need any help, send me a message. I will help you any way I can."

To which she could only reply, "Thank you."

"It will not be enough," he warned. "Not unless you take the initiative. Do not let Dag Racho find you first. Otherwise, he will always believe you're hiding something."

"I'm not," she repeated wearily, desperately trying to suppress her fear.

"But he will not believe you. And he is the ruler of this land." The governor paused, as if waiting for her to change her mind. She almost did. He looked so kind, his expression so sad, that she was tempted despite all logic. But before she could make up her mind, he spun on his heel and left.

Natiya knew he watched her dance.

She would have known he was there even if he hid himself in the back room and watched from one of the darkened alcoves. But he had not. Talned had walked him to the center front table, chatting up the new governor as much as he dared. But apparently the dragonhunter wasn't very talkative, for Talned soon slunk away. Monik had equally little success, for it seemed the man wasn't very hungry either. She served him a bitter dakla and watched him from the sidelines as he nursed his drink and kept his attention on the curtain. It was as if he knew Natiya stood right behind it, watching him.

Perhaps he did. Perhaps he felt the same itch on his skin that she felt on hers. Perhaps her scent followed him, clinging to his clothing and hair, just as his scent tormented her. And perhaps her words, her attitude, her very image had rooted in his thoughts just as he stood like a large statue within hers. Indeed, she could barely think without bumping into him.

Should she eat before work? The pokoti he'd brought her for breakfast still lingered on her tongue.

Did she have enough money to pay rent *and* buy thread to fix her costume? He had nice clothing and lots of coins to buy food. What would it hurt if she allowed him to spend some of it on her?

Was Dag Racho truly rounding up all the people connected with dragon lore? Or had that been said simply to frighten her, to gain power over her?

And why did she like it that the governor made his interest in her so obvious? That he sat at the center table, clearly waiting for her? Why was she so illogical as to thrill at this tangible draw between them when she needed to keep quiet, remain hidden, disappear in

darkness only to rise again with dragon fire? She could
soon burn evil from the world, if only she remained hidden a little longer. A year, maybe two . . .

She had no answer, and in truth, she discovered she
did not need one. The feelings were real, her attraction
nearly overwhelming. She knew the egg enhanced her
hunger, wanting to experience these new sensations,
these new feelings. So the why of her choices didn't
matter. Only the what.

What would she do now? Trust him with useless
secrets—tell him the location of the clutch caves—in
the hope of fooling Dag Racho that she gave over everything? Or say nothing, run from her attraction, and continue as if the governor had never spoken to her, never
seen her, never tempted her with his words? What
would she do?

She would dance.

That's all. Dance. Move. And certainly not decide. Not
until later. When she had time and space to sort
through things. For now, she danced.

Except, it wasn't her usual dance. Her usual dance
began with the beat flowing through her body until her
heart picked up the tempo and the pace and the purpose of the music. But this time she felt a second beat—
not just from the drums. She felt *his* heart beat, his
tempo, his power. And when she merged with the music, he was there as well, adding another layer to her
movements, another reason for her dance.

His reason. His purpose. His presence.

She danced for him and for his seduction; there was
no other way to define it. Where before she had danced
for herself, for the simple joy of creating form and
movement out of sound, now she danced for him,
stretching her body toward him, pulling her shoulders
up and away to tease him, arching her back to tempt
him. And when the beat increased, so did his breath.
When the music swelled, so did he. And she. Until with

a final crash of cymbals, she collapsed at his feet, breathless, ecstatic, and completely overwhelmed by what she had done.

So, too, was he, for they looked at one another in mutual shock and hunger, and something she could not define.

"Well, well," drawled Monik from the side. "Little Natiya grows up."

"No," she gasped, startled by her own vehemence. She didn't want to feel lust or passion, didn't want to care for any man, woman, or child. Loved ones died, leaving her lost and alone except for the egg. But her thoughts were drowned out by the explosion of noise from the other customers. All about the room coins were drawn out of purses and pockets, hefted aloft, waved in frenzied demand. Where before they would simply have thrown them toward her, now patrons held them out, asking her to come to them, to take the coins herself.

She shook her head in confusion. They had never acted this way before. For some of the other dancers, yes. Monik, certainly. But not for her. And now she did not know what to do.

Hide.

She nodded at the egg's suggestion. It wasn't truly a suggestion, merely an echo of what she had always done. Whenever she had become confused or disoriented, she hid herself, waiting until the terror passed. It was what she did when Dag Racho came for her parents. It was what she did when customers became too demanding and followed her home. It was what she had to do now.

She scrambled backward, ignoring the men, ignoring even the governor's outstretched hand. Her only thought was escape, and so she did, not even stopping when Talned tried to help her. She dashed from the stage and then through the back door. She ran all the way to her home, slamming her feeble door behind her as she stood shaking and confused.

What was happening to her? Why was she changing? What would she do?

She had no answers to her questions, no one to guide her. And so she collapsed onto her pallet, drawing her knees against her eyes in a useless attempt to stop her tears.

Dragon's teeth, she cursed into the blackness; she felt so alone.

They came for her that night. While she slept, beset by fitful dreams full of throbbing drums and aroused flesh, they came for her. Her door burst open and her room filled with large, sweaty men. She had no time even for a scream before a hand smothered her mouth and cold steel pressed against her flesh.

Then she was tied, bagged and carried away, her only protest the soft whimper of a frightened child.

CHAPTER FIVE

Natiya's mind was numb with terror.

She sat on a stone floor slimed with filth, thick and oily and fouled with human waste. No air stirred in this blackened dungeon. Sounds came, too: a skittering of vermin that made her skin crawl, the sobs of the wretched and the giggles of the insane tightening her belly against the nausea that roiled inside her. The steady drip of water made her shiver with chill.

And yet, for all that, she did not move, did not think. Indeed, she barely felt at all, so caught was her mind in the grip of dragon terror—remembered, not present. She heard her father's scream just after Dag Racho's Copper wyrm roared through the night sky. The tremors that wracked her body were the echo of soldiers' booted feet as they tore through her home while she crawled away, slinking out her window and then across the yard only to bury herself in the gap underneath their neighbor's porch. And the air she tasted was hot and burnt and filled with the loss of everything she once knew and everyone she loved.

Why do you live in the past?

The egg had been persistent with its questions: Why had soldiers grabbed her from her bed? What did they want? Where was this place, and who were the people trapped in it with her? The questions continued, but they had no power over the memories that locked tighter than any bars around her consciousness.

Why do you live in the past? This question came most often of the egg's repetitions. *Why do you live in the past?*

She finally found an answer: *to prepare for what is to come.*

Death and dragon fire?

Yes.

Why would a dragon kill his queen?

Because he is evil. And because I have failed.

The egg stopped speaking after that, clearly trying to understand. It did not, of course. No more than she did.

She knew about death, of course. No one could live in Ragona without knowing soldiers lost in battle, friends who'd disappeared without a trace in the night. How many times had she heard dockworkers talk of petty thieves caught and eaten by the Copper dragon as punishment?

No dragon will kill his queen.

Natiya did not bother to argue with the egg. She did not know what would happen to her, how she would die; she only knew what she remembered, and that was terrifying enough. She tried to distract herself. She tried to think of Uncle Rened, but she knew he had left yesterday on another trading journey and would be gone for many months. Talned and Monik would not help her. They were as powerless as she. And the governor . . .

Naitya sighed. She would not hope for help from him. She did not trust him, nor did she trust the things he did to her. It was because of him that she no longer felt normal inside her own skin, because of him that she had run home like a frightened child to cower in her pallet where the soldiers had found her.

So she sat on the filthy floor, immobilized by terror, until a man with an iron sword and a perpetual scowl unlocked her cage and hauled her out by her arm. She stumbled after him, fighting his grip out of reflex rather than intention. But he was encased in hardened leather, and she naked except for her dirty sleeping tunic. All her struggles gained her nothing but bruises, until she was unceremoniously dumped into another stone room, this one with a scarred black wood table and a soldier behind it staring at a single sheet of paper. A torch burned fitfully in a wall sconce, its flame echoed in the man's scarlet uniform. Even his hair was red, and whenever she looked at him, she remembered the dragon fire that had engulfed her home.

"Natiya Draeva," he said without even bothering to look at her. "Daughter of Samuel and Amaya Draeva, dragon scholars." His voice was as dry as ash, without inflection or pity. He did not seek confirmation to his words, merely stated them as if he recited a list of supplies to purchase. Or prisoners to execute. "You have been brought here to share knowledge of the dragonborn. Of their life and death and purpose under Dag Racho's most glorious reign. Refuse to cooperate and you will be killed. Acquiesce, and you will be released unharmed."

He was lying, she knew. No one taken in the dead of night to the Kotoni dungeon ever returned alive. And yet she could not suppress a surge of hope at his words. If she pretended to cooperate . . .

She pressed her lips together. It was too late for that. Any hint of secret dragon knowledge would surely damn her completely. Better to maintain her ignorance. Better still to maintain a terrified silence she did not need to fake.

"What do you have to say?" he asked.

Nothing.

She remained silent, though her hands trembled where she crouched on the floor. She could not trust what this man said, dared not even listen to his lies, for she was not smart enough to spot the traps. Her only hope was in remaining silent, focusing only on the egg and its approval of her decision.

Say nothing.

"Natiya Draeva! What do you have to say?" At least this time the soldier was looking at her, his black eyes narrowed in anger.

She shrunk into a tinier ball, feeling a growl build up inside her. Where such defiance came from, she did not know, even though it was only a useless sound, powerless and animalistic. But she felt it nonetheless and held it back, used it instead to consolidate her strength.

The soldier frowned at her, clearly confused by her defiance.

"You would do well to cooperate with me. Do not wait until the Emperor himself comes to interrogate you. There will be no leniency then, I assure you."

Natiya felt her lips thin into a grimace. Dag Racho would come here? To interrogate her?

Far from striking fear into her heart, it brought her a fatalistic sort of peace. She would at least be able to look into the eyes of her enemy before she died. She would have her moment to see him, face him, and damn him with her final breath. She would not cower in hiding as she had so many years ago. She would not bury herself in the dirt and sob out her mother's name. She would face him upright and die.

Or perhaps, if she grew strong enough, delayed long enough, her egg would hatch and she would be able to kill him.

It was a vain hope. The hatching process took time. Longer still to bond with the newborn dragon. Neither she nor her dragon queen would be allowed within a fire plume's distance of her enemy. But she did not focus on that. Instead, she drew her fantasy around her, using it to steel her spine. She would face Dag Racho on her feet, cursing him with her last breath.

With that thought, she straightened her body, coming to her feet with a dancer's grace.

"Excellent," the redheaded soldier responded, though his voice remained flat. "What do you know? I will record it."

Nothing, the egg said silently.

Natiya remained frozen, and the soldier slowly began to understand her plan. She would not speak, so he stood as well, hissing and spitting threats at her. She still did not speak, and so he raised his fist, shaking it before her fixed gaze. He let the blow land, and she did not avoid it. And even then she said nothing.

Until the door flew open, and *he* walked in.

She sensed him immediately, even before he entered, but her attention had not been on the things outside of her body and mind; she had been focused inward, on the egg. Now, as he strode in, his body taut, his gaze quick as it darted about the room, she realized that she had felt the hum of his sword long before. And he'd broken her concentration, so she was fully aware of him as he took in her swelling cheek, her tattered shirt, her bare and dirty feet.

"Out!" he growled at the redheaded soldier.

"Governor, you have no authority here. She is Dag Racho's prisoner—"

"Do not anger me, Lieutenant," he interrupted. Then Natiya watched in amazement as the governor appeared to grow taller, his face darkening as he glared at the other man. "I am the Emperor's dragon-hunter. All things dragon go through me." Then he narrowed his eyes, his voice dropping to a near whisper. "I wish to speak to her alone, that is all."

The soldier appeared to consider his options, glancing first at her, then back at the governor. Finally he nodded. "Five beats. No more." He paused at the door, one hand on the knob. "This is a courtesy only. You have no authority here." Then he waited for the governor's nod. It was slow in coming, but eventually there came a dipped chin in acknowledgment.

Natiya's heart sank. The governor had no authority within Kotoni dungeon. This was a military facility controlled by the Emperor and the true power in Dabu'ut. Still, she was grateful for the few moments' reprieve when the door finally shut behind the lieutenant. But that was nothing compared to what she felt when the governor stroked her face, trailing a single finger across her swelling cheek.

"Does it hurt?" he asked, then grimaced. "Stupid question. Of course it hurts. But other than that . . ." His gaze once again devoured her entire body. "Have they done other things? Hurt you in other ways?"

She didn't answer. Indeed, her mind felt slow and dumb; her mouth spoke of its own accord. "You didn't tell me Dag Racho would come tonight. That they would take me from my bed. That—"

"*D'greth*, Natiya! Do you think I knew? Do you think I would have allowed this?" He made a helpless gesture at the room, the walls, the prison.

"You have no authority here. No way to stop it." Her words were a statement, not a question, but hope flared in her heart that she was wrong. Perhaps he could help her somehow. All she needed was a few more months . . . maybe only weeks for the hatching and bonding. Right now the egg was hidden as her belly jewel: small, red, and completely uninteresting. But soon—she didn't even know how soon—it would start to grow. It would swell rapidly, like a baby in her belly but outside, attached to her through her navel. She would pretend it was a pregnancy and disappear to the clutching caves. It would hatch there and they would bond. She didn't know the details. Dag Racho had long since destroyed all history of dragons. The last scrolls had burned in her parents' home. If only the governor could get her out of here.

"I . . ." He shook his head. "I am new as governor. These people—these soldiers—were here long before me and will remain long after I am gone." He stepped closer, rapidly pulling off his cloak before wrapping it around her. She hadn't noted his clothing before, but she saw it now: simple traveling clothes, warm and lush. Neither too rich nor too coarse, they seemed to mold to him and blend him into his surroundings, as if he intended to hide.

She frowned. "Were you leaving?"

"I was on my way to the capital when I heard. I came directly here." He sighed, pulling her deeper into his arms. She went willingly, allowing herself to relax into his solid support. "Natiya, you must tell them what you know. It's your only hope."

She shook her head, already firm in her resolve. "I know nothing."

He stroked his cheek across her hair, his words a gentle breeze of worry across her ear. "They know you went with your parents. You walked with them to the clutching caves."

"I was a child. I do not remember the way," she lied.

He pulled back, gazing into her eyes, his own filled with worry. "Try to remember. Your life is at stake."

She sighed, at last speaking her fate aloud. "My life is already forfeit. No one comes out of this prison."

His grip tightened against her arms. "Some do. And I will help you however I can, Natiya, but you must trust me." He stared hard at her. "Do you trust me?"

"Of course." When had she learned to lie so easily?

"Then tell them what you know."

She turned away from him, the words mere whispers, but she knew he would hear them nonetheless. "Nothing. I know nothing."

They remained silent then. She knew he was studying her. She felt the prickle of his gaze upon her back but she did not move. She was too weary.

"You have already given up," he said.

Had she?

"You have been taught since birth that there is no hope. It died with your parents, and now you are lost."

No. She was a fighter. She would hatch her egg and kill Dag Racho.

"And yet you will not help us. You will not tell us what you know."

She turned to look at him, wanting to see his face as she struggled to understand his words. And as she moved, he watched her and flatly stated his conclusions.

"You fight out of habit, defying others because it is easy to say no. Even when it means saving your life, you still cannot allow yourself to say yes to anything."

She wanted to look away, to stop her ears and close her mind, but she could not. What he said rang too true for her to deny.

"What will it take, Natiya, to make you save yourself?" He reached out, once again stroking her cheek. "Not threats. You are not a crude woman in any sense of the word." He sighed, cupping her chin as he lowered his head toward her. "Oh, Natiya," he whispered. "I am trying to help you." Then he kissed her. He pressed his mouth to hers, using his tongue to stroke the seam between her lips. She did not know what to do or what he wanted. And yet, her body did. As his tongue tingled across her lips, she let her mouth drop open. Without her conscious decision, her hands rose up, feeling the muscles of his arms and his chest, stroking every sinew through the soft fabric of his shirt.

He pulled her closer to him, deepening the kiss, invading her senses along with her mouth. It was as if he entered her in all the most basic of ways. His scent filled her lungs, his hands caressed her skin, his taste was in her mouth; and most devastating of all, his words echoed in her mind.

What will it take, Natiya? Say yes.

She said something then. She did not even know what it was. It came out more as a whimper or a groan of surrender. Or perhaps it came from him. He had invaded so much of her, she could not separate herself from him in her mind, and that more than anything made her hands curl in panic.

What was happening?

He must have sensed the change in her, the tension that knotted her shoulders and stiffened her spine. And yet, when he pulled back, she clung to him, perversely wanting him closer.

"What do you want from me, Governor?" Was that her voice? All breathy and soft?

"Kiril. My name is Kiril."

She nodded, her gaze trained on his face, her body still achy and jumpy from what they had just done.

He groaned as he looked down at her, the rumble of sound transmitting easily into her body. His hands tightened on her shoulders. "*D'greth*," he cursed in an undertone. "You are such an innocent."

"No . . ." she murmured, though she didn't even understand what she was denying.

He slowly, carefully, set her away from him, gently tightening his cloak around her. "I will do what I can, Natiya. But it would be so much easier if you would talk to the lieutenant. Tell him what you know."

She closed her eyes, wishing she could stay immersed in these last few moments. But she could not, and he had already stepped away from her.

He sighed when she remained silent. "You will tell him nothing. You do not trust him."

She glanced up, seeing his grim expression, the regret in his eyes, and the tightness around his lips. "I don't know anything—"

"Don't lie to me, Natiya. Lie to them if you must, but not to me." And with that he hauled open the door, nearly bowling over the lieutenant who stood framed in the opening. Kiril frowned at the man, and his words came out like hard chips of ice. "Do not touch her again."

The soldier straightened, his eyes narrowing in anger. "Dag Racho approves of my interrogation techniques."

"Dag Racho is not here." Kiril leaned forward. "I am."

The man shrugged, as if the governor's statement were of no concern, but Natiya saw the hitch in his movements, the strain in the gesture. The lieutenant was not as sanguine as he pretended. But she had no time to consider that as Kiril gave her one last look.

"I will return soon," he promised; then he spun on his heel and left.

Natiya watched him go until the lieutenant slammed the door, blocking him from view.

"Natiya Draeva," he snapped, drawing her attention back to him.

She turned, looking at the young man, startled not by him but by the change within herself. Instead of the dull fatalism that had gripped her earlier, she now felt alive, curiously alert as all her senses continued to stretch beyond herself, beyond these walls, as if they wished to follow Kiril instead of remaining here.

She felt her lips curl into a smile, amazed by this feeling of . . . what? Life? As if, for the first time in many, many years, she had suddenly woken up.

"Natiya Draeva," the man snapped. "Tell me how to find the clutching caves."

"I cannot help you," she answered honestly. And then she closed her eyes, returning to her former stance of saying absolutely nothing. But instead of concentrating on the egg, her thoughts remained focused on four other words: *I will return soon.*

He did not return soon. "Soon" for Natiya meant the time it took for her to serve three customers and take orders for three more. "Soon" was the time between hungry and famished. "Soon" was before the lieutenant became furious.

Natiya was taken back to her cell after the lieutenant had hit her in places that would not be seen, after he had touched her in other ways that made her bare her teeth and growl like an animal. He did no more than touch, and that only briefly. Then he stood back and left the threat hanging in the air: He could do as he liked with her, for she was Dag Racho's prisoner and he was her interrogator. Then he sent her to her cell so that she could think about being more cooperative.

She thought about "soon" instead, and what that word meant to the governor.

As it turned out, it meant after the noon meal. The prisoners did not get any. The meal was for the guards, who ate with noisy relish in a room right next to the cell corridor. It was a petty torment for petty minds, but Natiya was no different from the other prisoners. Like them, she stood next to the bars, sniffing the air as if she could fill her empty belly by scent alone. She even closed her eyes, using her dragon-enhanced senses to try and identify what they ate.

She could not, for the food disappeared too quickly into the men's mouths. But as she opened her eyes, she saw Kiril striding down the corridor, his booted feet clipping at the heels of the guard who walked too slowly before him.

"Where is she?" he demanded.

"Here," she answered for the man—a boy really, with greasy blond hair and shoulders too thin to fill out his uniform. Kiril pushed him easily aside as he rushed to the bars.

"Are you all right? I swear I tried to come sooner. Did they hurt you? *D'greth*, this place stinks."

She smiled at his quick flow of questions, amazed that she could find humor in this place when her life—even outside these walls—was so humorless. "I am fine," she lied. In truth, she was hungry, cold and wet. Her other pains—from both the lieutenant's blows and too many nights dancing—simply merged into an ever-present ache, which she had long since learned to ignore.

"Open these bars," Kiril snapped to the guard.

The boy pursed his lips, clearly unhappy with the command, but he was not as strong in character as the lieutenant. In the end he ordered Natiya back, away from the bars. Then he quickly unlocked her cell. "You'll have to go in there with her," he mumbled.

He needn't have said it; Kiril was already inside, wrapping her in his arms. She went willingly, closing her eyes as she absorbed his heat, his strength.

Why do you rely on him? the egg asked. *We have always depended on our own strength.*

Natiya didn't answer, not knowing what to say. She knew only that it was heaven to rest against his chest, to hear the steady beat of his heart, to feel the supporting circle of his arms.

Behind her, the guard shut the cell, relocking it with a quick turn of the key. And then he turned his back on them, staring into the cell across from Natiya's, as if that would afford them some privacy.

Kiril pulled back from her, studying her face as he spoke. "The lieutenant is very angry. I fear for you." He bit his lip, his eyes skating away from hers. "I tried all morning to find a way—"

"But you have no authority here. I know." She knew he would not be able to help her. She'd known it all along, and yet somehow she had allowed herself to hope. To . . . rely on him. She turned away, silently cursing her stupidity. The egg was right. She had pinned her hopes on him instead of relying on herself. Hadn't she learned that lesson a long time ago? Her only hope lay in herself.

Then she felt his hands on her shoulders, gently turning her back to him. "Don't despair," he whispered. "I have—"

A trumpet blast cut through the air and his words. Once. Twice. Thrice. Kiril frowned, looking first at her, then at the guard who had turned at the sound.

"What is it?" he asked.

The boy didn't answer, but another prisoner did, coming to his feet to push his face against his own bars. "It's a summons. To assembly." Up and down the narrow hallway, all the prisoners shifted or spoke or jeered, each adding his opinion about what was happening.

Meanwhile, down the corridor, the other guards were rushing, banging chairs and cursing each other as they scrambled to right their clothing, find their gear and run to the courtyard. All the while, the boy guard stood, fidgeting in nervousness, his dilemma clear: he was called to assembly, and yet he could not abandon his post. Not with the governor here.

Kiril stepped forward, his expression kindly. "Go," he told the boy. "We can go nowhere. You have locked us in." Then he yanked on the bars for emphasis. They were truly trapped inside. Together.

The boy made his decision quickly, already moving down the hall. "I'll come back for you as soon as I can," he promised. Then he was gone, and Kiril frowned after him, his eyes darting between the now empty corridor and the window slit far above their heads. He could see nothing of outside, but he kept looking, his expression more and more troubled.

"Kiril?" Natiya asked. "What is it?"

"There was no assembly planned for today. I know. I checked."

"What does it matter?" she asked, not understanding his concern and feeling more interested in what he had been about to say before. "Why shouldn't I despair?"

He turned to her then, after one last glance down the corridor. "Because I have the keys." And with that he pulled out a ring of keys identical to the one the boy had worn.

"How?"

He grinned and made quick work of opening her cell. "Do you think his are the only set? There are others, easily obtained by someone with quick fingers and the nerve to barge into rooms where he's not supposed to be."

"Someone like a governor?"

He didn't answer except to flash her a quick smile; then he rushed to the corridor, looking to each side before gesturing to her. "It's clear, but we haven't much time."

She was beside him in an instant, gripping the hand he held out. But she didn't move when he tried to pull her down the hall. He glanced back, confused.

"Natiya?"

"The others. What about the other prisoners?"

Kiril's eyes narrowed, his gaze hopping from her to the pleading wretches behind her. "I cannot release everyone. I don't know what they've done."

"They are military prisoners, Kiril. What could they have done except run afoul of the Emperor?"

"Plenty," he snapped. "And they are not all military prisoners."

"I did nothing but read books," cried one prisoner, his cultured accent giving support to his words.

"I stole bread," said a woman. "I was hungry!"

One by one they called out their pitiful crimes. They could be lying, but Natiya couldn't simply ignore them. "Please," she said to Kiril. "You know they're telling the truth. Real criminals are given over immediately as dragon food." She stopped speaking as they both heard the sound of running feet from the corridor to the right. "Kiril, please. Besides, it will help to cover our escape."

He bit off his curse, then quickly tossed the keys into the nearest cell where an old man crouched in his own filth. "Now come!" he ordered her, and together they flew down the left corridor.

She moved as fast as she could, her bare feet skidding on the stone floor. He moved with one hand gripping her arm. With him as her anchor, she never fell. He moved with assurance, taking turns and stairs through the fortress without pause except to listen for soldiers in the hallways. Twice they had to hide: once in a doorway, the other time pressed into the shadows, holding their breath in order to remain silent. Fortunately, both times the people passing nearby were too intent on their tasks to pay much attention to their surroundings. Finally Kiril dragged her behind a tapestry, muttering under his breath as he fumbled against the wall.

"Someone's coming," Natiya whispered, her senses straining.

"Got it!" he returned, and even in the dark, she knew he was grinning.

Then she felt a rush of cold, damp air. She pulled back, instinctively disliking the feel of a yawning, black maw somewhere directly ahead. But she was given no time to think as Kiril drew her forward, still gripping her arm.

"There are stairs right here. Going down."

Here, at least, her bare feet helped, and she curled her toes around the edges of narrow stone steps. She extended her left arm, feeling the chill wall to the side, and began to descend. He followed, his breath exhaled in short, controlled bursts as if he were in combat. Then he released her, and she stopped.

"Kiril?" she whispered, hating the panic that gripped her at his abandonment.

"One moment," he said, his voice a disembodied ripple of sound. Then she felt more than heard the thud of a door pulling shut behind them.

"What is this place?" She spoke in an undertone, disliking the way her whispers seemed to hiss back at her from the darkness.

"Dag Racho's business often requires secrecy. This is just one of the many hidden ways in and out of his fortress."

"Makes it a lot less of a fortress, doesn't it?"

She could hear his chuckle as he once again found and took hold of her arm. "No one has dared attack these lands in one hundred years. Our Emperor has more need of secrecy than defense."

"And yet you still serve him," she said, her tone more bitter than she intended.

"And so I'm still alive."

She heard him fumbling in the wall beside her, and then suddenly the light from an oil lamp cut the blackness. Her eyes adjusted quickly, and she saw a long passageway extend before her. Despite her earlier fears, the tunnel was actually quite clean, with iron hooks and more lamps dangling at regular intervals.

"We must hurry. This is a well-traveled secret passage."

"Then you should have taken me on a less-well-traveled one," she returned.

He shrugged. "That one is a lot harder to find."

She glanced at him, wondering how a new governor would know these things. Then she remembered: he was the Emperor's greatest warrior. Of course he would have come here many times on secret business of one kind or another.

"Come," he urged, picking up speed. "It is not much farther."

She kept pace with him, mentally calculating distances. "This must go under the entire courtyard."

"It ends in the stable of the Open Maw inn. My mount is there."

She nodded, recognizing the name of the largest and most luxurious inn of the city, famous for the number of dignitaries who stayed there. No doubt because of just this reason: It gave direct and secret access to the fortress and whatever business was inside.

They were through the exit within moments, sliding into the stables as if they belonged there. Kiril took her directly to his mount—a large, mottled beast of unclear ancestry and ugly appearance. Natiya stared at it in shock.

"It has no hair!" She glanced at the other mounts in the stable. All of them were large, stately beasts with matted fur toeholds and finger grips. They had full cushions of fur that likely felt as soft as the finest down, but his creature was bald! "How will we sit on it?"

"I had a special saddle designed," he said. The beast nuzzled his master's shoulders. "And hair is decidedly dangerous for a dragon-hunter." Then he reached down, grabbing his strange saddle with ties that gripped the creature's belly instead of weaving into the fur. The leather was worked with tiny filaments of silver in ornate patterns, and Natiya felt a strange power coming from it. But she had no time to ask as Kiril reached inside the saddlebags and pulled out clothing, which he tossed to her. "There's an empty stall over there. No boots, I'm afraid, but the socks will keep you warm."

She held the clothing, lifting it up to her face to feel the velvety fabric. It was the finest cloth she had ever touched. "I will get them dirty," she said; then she felt her face heat, knowing how stupid a concern that was.

Fortunately, he didn't comment except to gesture to the other stall and whisper, "Hurry."

She nodded and ducked away, quickly donning the loose trousers and pristine white shirt. His clothes, obviously, for they were cut for a man and wrapped around her like a pale echo of his arms. The attire was much too large on her frame, but it would keep her warm, especially as the velvet jacket wrapped fully around her. *D'greth*, his clothes felt good. Oh, what would it be like to live in such finery every day? And to not even think about it?

She closed her eyes, inhaling deeply. She smelled the stable, of course, and the lingering filth of prison that still touched her skin and hair. But mostly she smelled him. He wore no perfume, so none scented his clothing. Instead, she sensed him—strong and dark, like the dragons he hunted.

And with that thought, her eyes shot open and she quickly returned to the business at hand. He had already climbed atop his strange mount, the stall door open as he exited. Seeing her, he leaned forward and extended his hand to her, but his words were for his animal. "I've brought a friend today. This is Natiya. We're going on a trip together, and I'm afraid you'll have to carry us both. And yes, she's heavier than she looks, but even that isn't so much."

"What?" she said, unsure she had heard him correctly.

He glanced up in surprise, then flashed her a lopsided grin. "I make it a policy never to lie to Mobray."

"But you lie to people?"

"Of course I do. I was raised in the Emperor's court." And with that, he grasped her hand, lifting her up in a single, powerful movement. She settled awkwardly on both his lap and saddle at once.

"Isn't your family name Mobray?" Why would he give his own name to such a haggard creature as this mount?

He didn't answer at first, too intent on guiding the beast out of the stable, casually flicking a coin to the stable boy who had just now noticed their presence. Then, when she'd nearly forgotten her question, he answered, his voice low and intent. "We Mobrays may not look like much, but we're strong and smart. People laugh at us all the time, but this I swear, Natiya, we will have the last laugh."

She did not doubt him. The intensity of his words radiated like an oft-spoken vow, one mumbled beneath one's breath, but all the more powerful for its softness. She now knew Kiril hated Dag Racho almost as powerfully as she. And more, that he had plans; probably complex, devious ones. That thought alone made her smile.

With luck, Kiril's plans would keep Dag Racho busy, taking attention elsewhere while she quietly hatched her egg and grew strong enough to gut the Emperor and his thrice-cursed Copper dragon. And with that thought firmly fixed in her mind, she relaxed back against her rescuer, feeling the tension of the last twenty-four hours melt away.

She was free from prison. Her plans were still feasible. All she needed to do to see them put into place was to hide somewhere and await the hatching.

"Take me to the edge of the docks," she said as he maneuvered them out of the inn yard. "I can make my way from there."

"You cannot go back to your room. It is not safe there."

"I know," she answered easily, though in truth she was already mentally listing all the supplies she would need and where she could get them. It was many days yet before the hatching. "I have friends."

"Don't be a fool," he answered curtly. "You have no friends except me."

She stiffened, insulted, and twisted as much as she dared on her precarious perch. "I am not a fool, Governor. Do not presume that your kindness today has—"

"Kindness!" he snapped, pulling on the reins. "Dag Racho is searching for you, Natiya. Do you honestly think Talned will help you? Or Monik? Who do you know who can stand up for you against the Emperor?"

She bit her lip, mentally reviewing her options. They were picking through the midday traffic, moving as fast as they could through the clogged streets. And as she looked at her familiar world, the truth of his statement crashed down upon her. None of her friends had the spine to stand up to a drunken soldier, much less the full weight of the Emperor. "No one," she breathed. "Not a one."

"Wrong," he snapped, the word sounding like stone splitting in two. "I have just done it. But that lieutenant is no fool. He will know I got you out of there—"

She shook her head, denying his words even though in her heart, she feared he was right. "I was just one of many prisoners to escape."

"You are the one Dag Racho wants." Then, as if to emphasize his words, a dragon's cry split the air. Indeed, she had known a dragon approached. Her egg had felt it, and she through it. But she had been consumed by her escape, too distracted to consciously understand what the tremor of recognition meant.

Until now. Until she heard and recognized the cry of Dag Racho's Copper.

Kiril heard it as well. Indeed, all the city must have heard, but he was the one who identified it. "That is not an attack cry."

Natiya didn't respond, was too focused on the dark brown speck in the air. Especially as it grew larger and larger with alarming speed.

Another dragon cry tore through the air, to be followed by a heated plume of fire sizzling the clouds.

"That is a recognition cry," Kiril murmured, frowning as he, too, watched its approach. "But Dag Racho was not to come here, not for many days." He shifted uneasily in his seat. "And who would the lizard recognize?"

Kiril clearly had no answer. She could tell by the concentrated frown on his face that the Emperor's presence was both a surprise and a discomfort to him. As they watched, the dragon extended its neck, diving toward the city as a queenfisher would for its prey. It plummeted straight down.

Straight at them.

All about, people came to the same conclusion. One by one they gasped, abruptly turning away from the spectacle of a dragon in full attack. They screamed and grabbed their children and goods. They trampled one another in their haste to escape, while Kiril and Mobray skittered and pranced to avoid a similar fate.

And still the Copper came while Natiya simply stared, mesmerized by the awesome sight. Distantly she heard Kiril curse as he tried to both control his mount and move them out of the square, away from the fortress. She felt the sweat of his body as he gripped both her and his horse. But most of all she felt her egg, wild and exultant inside her.

That was when she knew the truth. She knew who the dragon recognized, knew it was coming for her and the queen's egg she carried. And somehow from its place pressed deep inside her belly, the egg returned the call.

"Quiet!" she hissed to her egg. "You will get us killed!" But the egg did not listen. It was screaming silently, creating waves and waves of joy—felt, not heard. Natiya pressed her hands to her stomach, trying in vain to silence it.

"Hold still!" Kiril rasped in her ear.

"I can't," she gasped, for the egg's shrieks were growing more intense, reverberating through her entire body. She barely had the control to look up, to look death in the face as the Copper shot like an arrow toward her—larger and larger in her field of vision—while inside, the egg's screams built and crashed through her mind.

The Copper stopped. Natiya did not know how it did it, except that with a full spread of its wings and riding the invisible waves of the egg's power, it pulled back and floated in the air just above them. Then, with a deafening roar, it belched a fire plume, heating everything around it in a flashpoint of blistering agony.

Everything, that is, except Natiya, Kiril and his mount. All around them, wood burst into flame, metal glowed bright hot, and unprotected people screamed at their death. But Natiya and her companions were protected by the egg. The queen egg absorbed all that crackling energy into itself until it throbbed with life. Natiya writhed and screamed, knowing if she did not escape soon, the egg would hatch right here, right now. But she could not control her body, for it was in the egg's grip. All she could do was mentally scream out her fears. *Not here! Not now! Not yet!*

Fortunately, Kiril understood the danger. He could not know the cause, but he knew to push his mont to run. The way was cleared before them, still smoldering from the dragon fire. And so Mobray kicked into a gallop, flying through the city streets. Kiril leaned forward, pinning Natiya between him and Mobray's neck, his harsh breath rasping in her ear.

For Natiya, all these things remained in the background, distantly felt and even more sparsely understood. Her eyes were filled with the sight of the Copper in full spread, giving honor to the queen she carried. And above it, she saw a rider: Dag Racho, his wiry body and pinched face awash with heat and exertion as he tried to control his dragon mount.

Natiya could see him for only a moment, a split second when the Copper's wings had pushed down and before Mobray ducked between buildings too tall to see around. But in that second, she and Dag Racho found each other. Their gazes locked, their breaths caught, and they both understood.

Natiya knew that here was her enemy—a dark and twisted mind so evil that it killed not for food, but for pleasure. And she knew, too, what it thought, what it knew:

Dag Racho knew she incubated a Queen.

CHAPTER SIX

Kiril slowly straightened, at last relaxing his death grip on one terrified and squirmy dancer and one exhausted horse. They were well out of the city now and into the Clutching Mountains. Thankfully, some rock or metal in these mountains confused dragon senses, so Dag Racho would not easily find them here. Unfortunately, they were still out in the open, easily spotted if the Emperor wished to pursue. So Kiril kept to the woods as best he could and tried to fade into the traffic from the few farming towns that clustered along the road. They stood out more and more as the tiny villages became less and less prosperous the farther they went from Dabu'ut.

He glanced at his fellow travelers along the road. There weren't many, but he knew their numbers would soon increase. As word spread about Dag Racho's latest display, people would be fleeing the city in droves. Kiril still wondered what that had been about. Dag Racho was cruel, certainly, never truly caring whom he hurt in his quest for power, but he had never been careless with his dragon. His sense of self-preservation was too strong for him to endanger the flying lizard, for if the Copper were hurt, then Dag Racho himself would also be in pain, also be vulnerable.

So, why take his Copper into that steep dive, saved only by some miracle of flight? Both Dag Racho and his lizard should have buried their heads at least two spans deep in the city's foundation. How the creature had managed to stop like that, Kiril would never know. And then it had released a fire plume uselessly into the air, as if it were a display meant to impress. But that made no sense. Who in Dabu'ut could Dag Racho want to frighten?

Kiril had no answers to his questions and no way to find them right now. He had a task to complete with a terrified dancer. His best hope was that Sabina would ferret out the truth when he returned. And that bothered him more than anything else—this reliance on Bina as his sole source of intelligence. A lack of information in Dag Racho's court could spell not only disaster, but death. Only a fool relied upon a single person.

Thank the Father, his magic had protected them. At least he didn't have to deal with painful burns and bleeding sores right now. All that money he'd spent on fire protection—for his weapons, his mount, and himself—had finally paid off. He had never truly believed in the magic, but he had faith now. Though he'd felt the heat, not even his hair had been singed. And Natiya was equally unharmed.

Kiril had no explanation for that. The magic was for himself and his things, not for the people with him. He could only surmise that she had benefited from proximity. She had been on his lap, held fast between his body and his mount's for all that she had tried to run away in her panic. Thankfully, he was stronger, and she had remained in his protective circle. Who knew what would have happened to her if she'd escaped his hold.

He glanced down at her now, seeing her pale face as he cradled her limp body. She had the look of a woman in shock, and he could well understand the feeling. He leaned down and tucked her tighter against him.

"You know," he said, "many men freeze at their first sight of a dragon. Baby dragons even. A mature Copper is a terrifying sight. And today . . ." He shook his head. "That was truly unusual."

She didn't answer. Indeed, he wasn't even sure she heard him. He kept speaking nevertheless, hoping his tone might sooth her.

"There is no shame in your fear. Just try not to panic next time. I promise you, your safest place is with me." He tried not to wince as he lied, and he was sure he kept his expression flat, but inside he cursed himself. Natiya's safest place was as far from him and court politics as she could run. But she didn't know that, and he couldn't tell her. He needed her too much. Now that Dag Racho was in Dabu'ut, the pressure increased a thousandfold. Kiril had to find that egg now before the Emperor did. And that meant he had to get Natiya to lead him to the Queen's clutching cave.

"How are you feeling?" He shifted her again in his arms, hoping the movement would spark a response in her.

"Am I too heavy for you?" Her voice was thick with disuse, but he heard her clearly enough.

"I like holding you," he answered truthfully. "But how are you feeling?"

She shook her head, and he wondered what that meant—that she didn't know how she was feeling, or she wouldn't tell him? He sighed. At least she was talking to him. That was more sign of life than she had shown for the last hundred beats. And, better yet, she appeared to be looking around, seeing her surroundings for the first time.

"Where are you taking me?"

He smiled. He had been waiting for the question. He was lucky that it came when she seemed too weak, too defeated to argue. "Actually, Natiya, you're taking me. To the clutching caves. I know they are in the northern mountains. Tomorrow morning we will be near enough for you to guide me."

She let her head drop back onto his chest. "I don't know where they are."

"You are a *wanted criminal*, Natiya," he said, investing his voice with all the worry within him. In truth, he exaggerated the danger. Dag Racho was likely too busy to worry about one lost pawn in a complex political game.

"He will not stop until he finds me," she said dully.

Kiril hated the sound of dread in her voice, knowing he had put it there. Even so, he pressed a gentle kiss to her forehead, hoping she understood his gesture as one of tender concern. "There is hope, one way to avoid him."

She nodded, seeming to accept his statement without question. "Hide."

He released a dramatic sigh. "For how long? He has a dragon's memory, Natiya, that forgets nothing." He shook his head. "You must try to think beyond the present moment. Your only hope is to help me. We must find what the Emperor wants before he does."

"Why?" She shifted uneasily in front of him, unaware that every time she moved, she set fire to parts of him all too aware of her presence. "Why does he want the clutching caves?"

"He doesn't. He wants the egg that was found there: a golden egg. A Queen."

She released a soft laugh. "But if it was found, it is no longer there."

"True, but that is where I come in." He inhaled deeply, letting her scent fill his mind with pleasant fantasies. "Once I am in the Queen's cave, once I find where the egg sat, then I can use my sword to find it."

Natiya tilted her head back to see him more clearly. "How?"

He looked down at her, seeing her sparkling light eyes, her lush pink lips. He even had an excellent view of the soft white skin below her neck. What was it about her that drew him? From the moment he'd seen her, there had been a pull between them. No, more than a pull, it was a physical ache that dragged his every thought to her. It was a power he usually only felt in battle, but this time it consumed him as a man for a woman.

He moved before he realized what he was doing. He dropped his head and kissed her. He pressed his lips to hers, tasting her as he had wanted to for so long a time—at length and at leisure. She murmured a sound, neither protest nor hunger. Simply a gasp of surprise like fire in his blood.

He released the reins. Mobray would follow the track. Indeed, Kiril and Mobray had taken this route to the mountains many times in search of the Queen's cave; he need not concern himself with direction. Which left his mind and both hands free for the lush woman in his arms.

He deepened their kiss. Her gasp had allowed his tongue entry, and now he penetrated her mouth with a fervor that stunned him, especially as her head dropped back against his supporting arm, giving him greater access, greater depth.

His free hand moved without his conscious direction, caressing the long column of her throat before pushing aside the collar of his jacket that she wore. She had raised her own hand and now began to mimic his motions. Her tongue touched and teased his. Her fingers stroked his hair, his neck. And all the while, his free hand delved down and along her collarbone, slipping beneath the loose fabric of her shirt until he held the soft, perfect mound of her breast.

She shivered in his arms, unconsciously moving against his hand, his arms, his loins; and he tightened his grip, squeezing and molding her nipple to further the sensations—or that would have occurred if his mount had not chosen that moment for a good scratch.

Kiril cursed, suddenly occupied in keeping Natiya balanced while Mobray decided to scratch against a tree. She, of course, helped out by twisting forward—away from him—leaning forward over Mobray's neck, murmuring soft words into the beast's ear. Mobray quieted immediately, and Kiril was able to guide him back onto the track from where he'd strayed. But when the beast was finally headed back the way he should, Natiya rigidly refused to sink back into Kiril's arms.

He sighed. Sometimes rescuing beautiful dancers just didn't pay off. Then again, he thought with a slight smile, they had a long way to go and plenty of time for Natiya to relax again.

"How?"

Kiril blinked, wondering if he had heard his companion correctly. "What did you say?"

She straightened, twisting the tiniest bit to look over her shoulder. "How do you find dragon eggs?"

"That's a long story," he said.

She shrugged, turning back to look at the road ahead. "We have plenty of time."

That they did. So he gently settled his free hand on her thigh, letting it rest there as if he'd casually dropped it. And if the movement of his mount slowly shifted his hand higher, that wasn't his fault, was it? He was involved in telling his story.

"Did you know," he began, "that dragons are magic? Their eggs can change color and they have intelligence long before they are hatched. They speak to their bonded partners and to each other in ways that we cannot hear." He paused, wondering what she was thinking, but also taking a moment to enjoy the ripple of her thigh muscle beneath his hand. She was certainly aware of his touch, but hadn't rejected it.

"Go on," she prompted.

He nodded, recalled to his story. "Dragon blood is equally magic. Anyone who touches it absorbs some of its power."

"What power?"

"Resistance to fire, for one. But more importantly, an extra sensitivity or perception. Metal, too, can sometimes absorb this magic, if it is soaked long enough."

"Metal things like your sword. And the silver decoration of your saddle." She turned again toward him. "You have soaked them in dragon blood."

He smiled, though her expression was appalled. "Natiya, I am a dragon-hunter. My sword and I have swum in the creatures' blood. I have smelled it, swallowed it, breathed it, been baptized in it . . . That is what it means to be a dragon-hunter."

"You sound as if you have no love for the task."

A humorless chuckle wracked his body. "Oh, no," he said, his words more an extension of the tremor than actual thought. "I have a great love for the task. I will not rest until I have buried my sword in the last of the evil beasts."

"Dag Racho's Copper?"

Kiril didn't answer. She was right; but to tell the truth would be the highest form of treason.

"But it is the Emperor who is evil," she protested. "Not the dragon."

Kiril shook his head. "Nay, it is the beast who corrupts. By all accounts, Racho was an honorable man. It is only after he became Dag Racho that his thoughts turned to conquering and hoarding."

He felt her body stiffen. "Nay," she said, though he caught an echo of doubt in her voice. "Dag Racho has changed the accounts. He would have us *believe* he is a holy man ruling us with justice and mercy despite the evidence of our own eyes."

Kiril could not refute her claim. Indeed, he was sure the Emperor had done exactly what she claimed. "Nevertheless, I know the beast corrupts."

"How?" This time she twisted fully in her seat, turning to directly search his face. "How can you know that?"

"I have seen it."

She frowned when he would not say more. And then abruptly he saw understanding light her eyes. "Dag Jaseen. Your cousin."

He nodded once but did not say more, and in the end she returned to looking out over Mobray's ears.

Kiril sighed. This was not the way to gain her trust. And this simmering hunger for sex distracted him too much. Then, to his surprise, she asked another question, a strange anxiety in her voice.

"So, you can talk to dragons?"

"What?" He frowned, wondering at her question. "No. Only the bonded can."

"But you said you can feel things. Because of the dragon blood."

"Ah," he returned, at last understanding. "If I concentrate, I will be able to feel the dragon egg. Especially if I hold my sword and take my time." Natiya's body tightened. He could feel the anxiety rolling off her, but he did not understand its source. Unless . . . "Do not be afraid," he soothed. "The power is too weak to call to Dag Racho. He will not find us by my sword. But . . ."

She shifted uneasily. "But what?"

"But I will feel the egg, Natiya. If I am standing in the Queen's clutching cave."

"By holding your sword?"

"All I need do is find the nest and stand there. It takes a while, and I must have absolute silence, but eventually I will feel the egg. It is a kind of tug inside. A desire to go one direction, and down that path will lie the egg."

"You must be in the caves to do this?"

"Sometimes, if the egg is very close, I can find it just by holding my sword."

Natiya shook her head, the movement distracted as she obviously fought to understand his words. "You carry your sword all the time. You held it out in my room back in Dabu'ut."

"I must be concentrating," he said. Then he waited, thinking hard as he studied her. It was already getting dark. Thankfully, they would make the inn soon. But before they arrived, he needed to talk to her about something. And yet, he hesitated, unsure how to broach the subject. She was obviously young and inexperienced, and though that added to the excitement, it also complicated what should be a simple matter.

"Natiya, do you know what happens between a man and a woman?"

He felt her start of surprise all the way down to his toes. But he felt it more in the part of her still pressed intimately against him, and he was hard put not to groan.

"I know," she answered, her voice tight, her attitude . . . insulted?

"Of course you do," he said, trying to gentle his voice. "You work in a tavern. And I grew up at court, so I suppose you and I had the same early education."

"I doubt tavern brawls are part of your experience."

"You'd be surprised what courtiers fight over and how. And you'd no doubt be startled to realize that they often rut in public as well, just as in your tavern's back room. Couples, threesomes, orgies of ten, maybe twelve. By the time I was fourteen, I had seen it all. In fact, some people made it their express mission to make sure I saw much more than I should."

He could tell he had surprised her. And more than that, she seemed interested, her body relaxing as she allowed herself to turn—not quite to look at him, but so that she could better hear his words.

"I didn't participate," he continued. "I was fortunate in that I had a protector of sorts. You may remember her. Sabina, the woman who was with me that first night I saw you dance."

"Your lover."

Did he imagine that her voice was clipped, even a little angry—or better yet, jealous?

"No, Sabina has much better taste than the likes of me."

Natiya arched a single eyebrow at that statement, but she did not comment. Too bad, he thought wryly, because right then he desperately needed some gauge as to how she was reacting to his words. But all she gave him was a view of her profile and the feel of her muscular body taut with some unnamed emotion.

"Sabina once told me—actually, it was in the context of a wager, but that's not important now—she once said there would come something to tempt me. A woman, probably, who would obsess me as no other. I would think of nothing else, dream of nothing else, live and breathe and scheme only for this woman." He glanced away, remembering the moment and the cold implacability in Bina's voice, as if it were a foregone conclusion that he would fall prey to the same vices so grossly displayed in Dag Racho's court.

"You don't believe her, do you?" Natiya challenged. "You think her silly for even suggesting it."

He glanced back at her, realizing belatedly that how he handled the next few moments could very well determine whether he accomplished all he planned, or whether Sabina was right and he was no more than a belly-horned man with no brain beyond that which led his lust. He took a deep breath, unable to change course. "I laughed at her when she said it. I was twenty-eight years old and had long since proven myself an exceptional hunter and a stable, temperate man. A man needs a logical mind and a steady hand to fight as I had. As I do. And I wagered everything I have on that stability."

He glanced at her, wondering if she understood. But instead of watching the emotions shift in her eyes, he saw the white flesh of her chest peek out as his jacket slid open.

Abruptly irritated with himself, he turned away, pretending to focus on guiding Mobray. She spoke, interrupting his confused thoughts.

"But, things have changed."

He sighed. "Things have changed." He looked at her then, not doing anything to hide the lust that continued to course through him. He let the hunger shine through his eyes, and from where his hand rested on her thigh. He slid it higher, pushing closer to where he wanted to be. She clenched, as he knew she would, gripping his hand like a vise, and yet her actions only served to feed his hunger.

"I want you," he rasped. Then he swallowed, forcibly bringing his thoughts and emotions under control. "I cannot explain it, but the moment I saw you dancing, maybe even before you entered the room, I felt the pull. *D'greth*, Natiya, I have never felt this . . . this . . ."

"Obsession."

He flinched, not liking the word but forced to agree. "It has never been like this before. I am consumed by you."

He saw her swallow in fear, then abruptly she began to twist off her perch, trying to escape the lumbering Mobray. "I will go. We need never see each other again."

"Wait!" he cried in panic, grabbing her. One hand clamped down on her leg, the other suddenly gripped her shoulder. He was careful not to hurt her, but he would not release her: She needed to understand that.

"Wait, please," he said again, trying to moderate his tone. "It is not that easy, but neither is it so complicated." He took a deep breath. "I swear by my sword, Natiya, that I will not hurt you or force you, but please just listen to me."

She did not respond. Like a trapped animal, she held absolutely still, her eyes wide.

"My feelings have never been this . . . intense before, but they are not unfamiliar. No man can reach my age without knowing lust, hunger, the need for a woman."

She shrank from him—not physically, but he felt it nonetheless. She drew into herself, tucking her thoughts and feelings tight inside.

"Do you know why people couple?" He reached forward, touching her face even though he knew she did not want it. He did so anyway, because he wanted her to understand. And because he needed to touch her. "Because it is pleasurable," he said.

Though her eyes were wide, her body frozen, he began to caress her. First, her face. Then he stroked his fingertip across her lips, pressing slightly inside so that he could feel her moist heat. His belly tightened, but he forced himself to go slowly, to accustom her to his touch as his fingers continued their leisurely stroke. He let his hand trail away from her mouth, slowly stroking across her chin and down the side of her neck. He watched what he did, seeing her pulse leap beneath his fingers, her skin heat to a rosy hue wherever he touched.

Her eyes were growing heavy-lidded, though he knew she still felt wary: Her body remained too tense to be anything else. So he moved with excruciating care as he once again slipped his fingers beneath the collar of her shirt. He heard her gasp and feared she would draw away. She did not. And so, taking it as a sign that she was ready—or at least not going to fight him—he once again stroked lower. And lower. He moved in a lazy horizontal pattern while her breath became stuttered. His own throat grew dry with desire.

Thank the Father that his clothing was so loose on her, because—an eternity later—he once again touched the hardened tip of her breast. And when she did not fight him—he doubted she even breathed—he allowed himself to open his fingers, turning his hand until he cupped her in his open palm.

"I should not do this," she whispered.

He knew she was not speaking directly to him, but he challenged her nonetheless. "Why not? It feels good, doesn't it? You like this, don't you?"

She closed her eyes, her face flushed. "Yes," she whispered, as if she could barely admit it to herself.

"It is merely lust, Natiya—a body's need, neither good nor evil. It simply is. A pleasure like a good meal, nothing more."

She shook her head: a quick jerk of her chin. "It is too dangerous."

He leaned forward, touching his lips to hers but no more. "That is where you are wrong. There is no danger in this. The danger is in denying the power of our bodies. The danger is in fighting these feelings so much that it clouds our thinking about other things." He released the reins, this time seeing that they were riding on a straight track with few trees and no people. Mobray would not interrupt them again.

So he extended his tongue, touching her lips, smiling when he felt her gasp. Then, with a firm stroke he shifted his hand so that the shirt and jacket slipped open, baring her right breast to his view.

D'greth, it was beautiful. It was full and peaked, rosy in hue and perfectly suited for his kiss. And so he did. Though he strained in the saddle, he leaned down, drawing her nipple into his mouth. She cried out in surprise, but he was prepared and held her fast as he swirled his tongue around her tender flesh.

He moved too fast. He knew it, but he could not stop himself. Even as he tasted her, rolling his tongue around the hardened pebble of her nipple, he knew he was pushing too hard. And so he was not surprised when she shoved him away.

"No!" she cried, and she struggled to dismount.

Once again, he was prepared; he simply held her still, even as he straightened away. "Very well," he said, as if his entire body weren't throbbing with a painful desire. Then he released his grip on her, when it became clear that she was not going to run—when she realized he would not force her. He would never force her.

She spun away from him, turned her back to him and held herself stiff. He knew she would tire of that position soon, so he waited, guiding Mobray with what little of his mind and body was not completely and totally focused on her.

He kept silent and relaxed, though it nearly killed him to do so. He took some comfort in the knowledge that he had confused her—that she was intrigued rather than horrified. Intrigued even though she clearly expected him to insist, to take what he wanted despite her protests.

"I will not force you, Natiya," he said. "I merely wanted you to feel a tiny bit of what you could be experiencing, of what we could share together."

"I cannot," she replied, though the words sounded hesitant. "I should go away."

He sighed, but also noted that she made no move to run. "That is what I am trying to tell you, Natiya. You are a fire in my blood," he said honestly—bluntly. "I want you to the point of obsession. I told you, it has never been like this for me. I have never been this possessed by a woman. But even though it is new, I recognize it. I know how to end it."

She swallowed. "By . . . taking me?"

"By enjoying you. Just as one would enjoy a fine meal, Natiya. We can share this passion, enjoy it, relish it. Together. And after it is done—"

"You will be satiated."

"We will be full together. And happy." He leaned forward slightly, letting his breath heat her neck. "I'm certain you only know a little of what we can do," he said. "I swear I will make it a delight for both of us."

She was weakening. Her spine was growing less rigid, her body becoming a bit more slack as she leaned ever so slightly closer to him. "What if I become pregnant?"

He paused, startled but pleased by her question. "Do you not know how to prevent it? The ladies at court—"

"I know. Monik showed me."

He smiled, purposely adopting a casual tone. "We will be stopping soon. There is an inn nearby with a discreet innkeeper." He saw her glance around, as if just now noticing that it neared dusk. "For the rest of the way, why not relax against me? Think about what I have said."

She frowned, and at first he thought he had failed. But all too soon her spine softened and she leaned back against him. He pressed his lips against her temple, the gesture tender and soothing even as his free hand slid around her belly.

He felt her stomach muscles quiver, her toned dancer's body betraying every shiver of sensation. Then he dropped his head to her ear, stroking it lightly with his tongue.

"I want to touch you, Natiya," he said. "You will enjoy it. However, all you need do is tell me to stop and I will. But allow me this, at least, for rescuing you from prison. Let me touch you as we ride to the inn."

He waited for her agreement, though it took all his control to do so. And when she finally dipped her chin in acknowledgment, it was all he could do to continue to move slowly. He let his hand slide down her leg, stroking the soft fabric of her trousers before slipping underneath the shirt. Then, as he gently directed Mobray with one hand, the other slipped up her thigh, barely brushing across her hip before flattening against her belly. She whimpered in protest, and he knew he could not move his hand where he wanted. So he slid it upward instead, moving over her belly jewel, the hard nub firing in his mind with an eroticism he had not expected.

Biting his lip, he somehow managed to control himself. But only barely. And so, with more speed than finesse, he lifted his hand until he cupped her breast. She gasped and grabbed his hand, holding him still. He could feel the furious beat of her heart beneath her tender flesh.

"Tell me something first," she said, her voice breathy.

"Anything."

"How do you kill dragons?"

He frowned, startled. Many women were excited by bloodthirsty tales, but he had not guessed her to be one of them.

"How do you avoid the fire?" she pressed. "And their claws?"

Her heartbeat was steadying beneath his palm, and her grip on his wrist was easing as she grew accustomed to his hand. "It is not a pretty thing," he answered, understanding now that she needed time. "Are you sure you want—"

"I want to know," she insisted. "How do you kill them?"

"Poison," he answered, and felt her start in surprise. "It is the only way with a mature dragon. But that is why I hunt them young. If I can find them as an egg or before the fire develops—"

"Then it is easy to kill them."

"Killing is never easy," he returned. "Or it shouldn't be. My best skills are as a tracker of eggs."

She was silent a moment and her grip eased even more. He didn't dare move his hand yet, though his thoughts were almost totally consumed by the desire. He waited, annoyed by how much control was required for this simple act of patience.

"Don't you find them beautiful?" she whispered. "Mama once told me that the eggs can glow just before hatching. That magic is something beyond understanding. It fills your body with peace, security. Even love." He heard the yearning in her voice and knew that, like him, she ached from loneliness. Like him, she craved the simplest touch out of friendship without compulsion.

And so he moved his hand. Though his mind burned with the need to possess her, he shifted until he tucked his hand around her waist, pulling her into a gentle hug. "Once, when I was young, Dag Racho brought me to meet his Copper. I had never seen one so close before. He was huge."

"Awesome beauty," she whispered, and he knew she was thinking of that moment in the city and the Copper's plume of fire bursting just above them.

"Terrible beauty," he agreed. He returned to his story: "I think the beast tried to speak with me then, back at court. I was allowed to touch it, to feel the heat of his skin, the hard ridges around his eyes and even the beginnings of the soft underbelly. I felt his magic enfold me in warmth, just like you said. Only it felt sad as well. So very sad."

She twisted slightly to look at him in question, but she didn't speak.

He shrugged, wishing he had better words to explain. "I was half in love with it just from that one touch. The magic was so strong." Even now, the memory slipped into his thoughts, dark and insidious. "Mind to mind, thoughts to thoughts."

"To never be alone," she whispered, and he knew she understood. "I want to hold a baby dragon," she added. "They are said to look like funny chickens, with leather-like feathers, but when they look at you, all you see is love."

She was romanticizing the beast, just as everyone did. Everyone who didn't know better. "Then I saw it eat, Natiya. The blood . . ." Kiril swallowed, wishing he could forget the screams and the mess. "I was sick for three days just from the smell."

Natiya frowned, but her hand stroked the back of his wrist in comfort. "All things eat. And all beasts are messier than humans."

He shook his head, tightening his hold on her. "It was my cousin. Five years old, a little girl from my mother's side. She remembered me, but there was nothing I could do. It ate her like she was a sheep."

He shuddered in memory, and she twisted to look at him fully. He closed his eyes rather than allow her to see his tears. How foolish that, after all this time, the memory could still shake him, but it was like a living thing inside him, still screaming. Still dying.

Natiya touched his cheek, a tentative brush that he felt all the way to his toes. He turned his face into her palm because he could not stop himself. And in time, his breath steadied, his thoughts shifted to better things: her.

"Why do you blame the dragon?" she asked, before he could stop her with a kiss. "Dag Racho controls the Copper's food. Dag Racho chose the victim."

He took a deep breath, releasing as much anger as he could before he spoke, tucking his fury away into a tiny compartment of his mind so that he would not frighten her. "They are one and the same, Natiya, bonded and intertwined so that there is no separation. The beast eats with casual disdain. The man laughs as his dragon is satisfied." He pressed a kiss into her palm. "You do not know how the beast twists a man. It starts as an egg whispering poison into his mind. Quiet and slow, the corruption eats away until all that is left is a beast in a man's form."

She shook her head, pulling her hand away from his mouth. "No. No, it is not like that. The man retains his goals, his plans." She swallowed. "Maybe it is the man who corrupts the dragon."

He focused on her, knowing he had to disillusion her. He had seen this kind of dragon worship before; it was built on ignorance and lies. "Many years ago, I learned of a scroll. It was written before Dag Racho was born and described the bonding process in detail—its risks and its purpose."

She straightened, her eyes bright with interest. "What did it say?"

He shook his head. "I don't know. Racho found it before me and had it destroyed."

"But the man who had it?"

"Killed."

"The place it was hidden—"

"Burned to ash by the Copper."

She grimaced and slumped back down. "He destroys everything," she said angrily. "Burns it, kills it. Like the people in the square—burned for no reason." She shot him a heavy look. "But it is not the dragon. It is the man."

Kiril shook his head. "They are one and the same."

When she didn't answer, he tucked her back more tightly against him. His hand still spanned her waist, idly stroking the smooth skin just below her ribs. "I did learn something, though, from that man's daughter."

She looked up. "What?"

"I helped her escape over the mountains," he said. "To a country where dragons are just a legend. In gratitude, she told me everything she remembered."

"What?"

He smiled wistfully as he pressed his cheek to Natiya's forehead. "She didn't know much. Only that her father said it wasn't supposed to be like this. That the bonding process was supposed to last for only a short time."

"How long?"

He shrugged. "I don't know. Not the century and a half that Dag Racho has been in power."

"But then, is there a way to end it? Does the dragon die? The man?"

"I don't know."

"How do we know if it is coming? *Why* does it end?"

"I don't know."

"But—"

"Natiya!" he interrupted. "I don't know. And the Copper killed everyone who might."

"No," she answered with a huff. "Dag Racho has."

He didn't respond. They both knew what he would say: that their Emperor and his dragon were one and the same. But he didn't want to repeat the argument again. Instead, he pressed his lips to her temple, feeling a sweetness enter his soul. It was her, of course. It was having a beautiful, feisty, and intelligent woman resting so contentedly in his arms.

"I could ride like this for days," he whispered, startled to realize that he meant it. She didn't answer except to relax a little deeper into his hold.

He meant to remain like that until the inn, meant to relish the quiet novelty of a woman without demands or ulterior motives. But in time, the lust once again took hold. The more he rested—his hand against her waist, his wrist across her belly jewel—the more his thoughts turned to sex.

Unable to deny himself, he lifted his hand to her breast. She didn't stop him this time. Indeed, she breathed deeply, pushing herself into his cupped palm.

"You can tell me to stop," he whispered, all the while praying that she did not.

"I know," she answered. And when she said no more, he took it for permission.

Within moments, his other hand had delved quietly inside her shirt. Soon he touched both her breasts, stroking them, molding them, toying with their hard peaks while she trembled in his arms, her head dropping back against his shoulder as she exhaled tiny gasps of delight.

CHAPTER SEVEN

Natiya could barely stand. In the time it had taken to reach the inn, Kiril had done things to her body that made her mindless with hunger. She knew he was using her, knew that the things he said were merely words men said to convince a woman to spread her legs. But, *d'greth*, it didn't matter. Those words were effective.

She knew he had told her things he never shared, and that made her soften toward him. Then he spoke honestly about his feelings in a way no man had ever spoken to her before: as an equal and a willing participant. He talked of his obsession with her, and she leaned back against him, making sounds that had never before passed her lips. She ached and wanted in a way that terrified her. There was so much at stake, so many worries; and yet when she felt his arms surround her, she didn't care.

At the inn he became discreet, gently easing away from her and refastening her clothing. Before he did, she hadn't even realized they'd arrived, and heat burned in her face at the shame of it all. Why, oh why, had the dragon egg chosen now to exert such a powerful hunger within her? But even as she mentally chastised the egg for its dominance, she knew she lied to herself and to it. The egg always hungered for new experiences; it always wanted to do more, to know more. Before now, she had been able to control the drive, control its curiosity. But not now, not this time.

Why? Because this time there was her own curiosity as well. For many seasons now she had wondered exactly why so many souls spent every waking moment consumed with the search for a partner. And if not for life, for the night. What did Monik know that Natiya did not? What did she *feel* that Natiya did not? Until now, she had resisted her curiosity. The danger and the fear had been too great.

But, now Natiya knew. And Kiril promised there was more and better to come. Except they arrived at the inn and she would have to stand and think and move her body when all it wanted was to return to his arms, his touch, his wants.

He was kindness itself as he helped her off his strange mount. Indeed, he treated her like a true lady as he held her arm, supporting her when her wobbly knees could do no more than quake.

The innkeeper obviously knew him. He did not even blink when Kiril ordered their best room and a hot bath for the lady. Then, as the man escorted Natiya upstairs, Kiril promised to bring food and better clothes as soon as possible.

Through all this, Natiya remained silent, her body straining for him, her mind spinning with thoughts too scattered to knit into coherence. *Stop this!* she ordered herself. She was not some mindless beast in heat with no thought except rutting. Something had changed. Dag Racho knew the truth now—that she incubated an egg—and would surely spend all his energies on finding her. But even more than that, something else was different. She had changed, or the egg had changed, or perhaps both at the same time. She needed time to think, to sort through what had happened—what was happening—

and to plan the next step. Rutting was a distraction. A powerful one, but a distraction nonetheless.

As she soaked in the hot bath, she decided that there would be no more touches from Kiril. Not until she had some answers. Not until she planned her next course of action. No matter how much she lusted—and indeed, she now could at least label the feeling—she would not give in.

She rose from the water, abrading her skin with harsh strokes of the towel as if she could wipe away the memory of his hands as easily. She could not, of course, and to make matters worse, her mind was so occupied with thoughts of him that she did not realize the change. Indeed, if it had not forced her attention, she would not have seen it.

The egg had grown. Not only grown, it had changed colors and now glowed in the darkness. No longer appearing a small red jewel, the egg was orange in color, and larger. It more than filled her navel, and it pulsed. There was no other word for it. Natiya pressed her hand to the egg. Indeed, it throbbed; she felt a tiny beat against her palm, and a deeper, stronger pulse against her womb.

It was the cord that bound them, extending from the egg, through her navel, deep into her body. That was how she fed the egg and how they were bound together. She knew from her parents' studies that the egg could burrow into a person anywhere—an arm or a leg—and grow from there. All it took was a steady hand to cut the egg out when it was time. She had chosen to press the egg to her navel, and now the cord that bound them throbbed like a heartbeat.

And she'd thought Kiril's touches had created this sensation! Except, she thought, frowning, the egg had not been like this before. Certainly it had been as usual in prison. And then . . .

The Copper. She knew the Copper's plume of fire had

been for the egg—a show of power, perhaps. The egg had taken that fire and used it somehow, used that energy to grow and change. It had absorbed the Copper's—

Adulation.

Natiya froze at the egg's remark. Adulation? She did not even know what the word meant. When had the egg ever known what she did not, said anything that she had not taught it?

The Copper knows me, and offers respect.

How do you know this? Natiya demanded, but the egg did not answer. Not out of petulance, she realized, but out of confusion: It did not know how it knew; it simply did. And that was all it would say on the matter. The Copper's fire had been a show of respect.

I used the fire to grow. The Copper has need of me now.

Now? she asked the egg. *What need does it have? What will you do?*

The egg did not answer. She did not think it knew. Very well, thought Natiya, staring down at her belly. Things were changing. She'd already known that. The egg was growing a mind of its own. This was not all that startling, she told herself. For many seasons now her egg had talked to her independently, thought on its own, even if it mostly echoed back what she told it. It simply had additional information now. Additional input. That was all to the good, right? New information was useful.

She thought the words, believed them even, but she could not control a tremor of panic along her spine. What was happening to her? Was she being corrupted by the egg like Kiril said?

She dressed quickly, pulled on Kiril's trousers and shirt, doing her best not to relish his scent now mixed with her own. She closed her thoughts to the memories, but in her efforts she became careless. As she drew the shirt closed, the fabric brushed across her nipple, and the resulting fire made her gasp in stunned shock. In her belly, the egg twisted and burned, adding to the hunger, magnifying it in pulsing waves that went straight to her womb.

So, she thought, with a kind of dull understanding, the egg took what she felt, the sensations she enjoyed, and magnified them. The effect had never been this powerful. Or had it? Perhaps there had been other times, other moments when her joy seemed magnified, her pain more deeply felt, even her sorrows and frustrations seeming out of proportion to the event. Could that have been the egg? Possibly, but it was hard to tell. Hard to separate what had been her thoughts and feelings and what had been the egg's. They were one and the same, intertwined. That was what it meant to be dragonborn.

Except, the dragon had not hatched yet.

Her hands froze, Kiril's jacket pulled onto only one shoulder. In one thing the egg had always known more than she. In one answer, it had always remained consistent. When asked, it had always said that it would hatch this coming cold season—some weeks from now.

Slowly lowering her hands to cover her belly, Natiya shuddered. *How long?* she thought to the egg. *How long until the hatching?*

Soon.

How soon?

Less than two weeks.

Natiya felt her knees hit the floor as her body crumpled. Less than two weeks? But she wasn't prepared. She had no place to hide. No place to complete the hatching and then the bonding.

The Queen's clutching cave.

Natiya nodded. Yes, they were near the caves. She would lead Kiril there, then disappear. She knew them as well as anyone. There were hundreds of caves. She could pick one—any one—and hide until she was ready.

The Queen's clutching cave.

The image came strong and clear. The egg wanted to be in its own cave, the one where it had been laid. But they couldn't go there. That was the one place Kiril wanted, the one place he searched for. And it was the one place that would allow the dragon-hunter to kill them when they were most vulnerable. They couldn't go there.

The Queen's cave. Soon.

Why?

Soon.

Before Natiya could ask more, Kiril walked into the room. She spun around, clutching her clothing tight, panic making her heart pound. Then she remembered, he didn't know; he couldn't know. She was fine, safe for now. He didn't know.

He looked at her warily, bowls of steaming meat stew in his hands. His smile was warm, gentle even, as he extended the food. "I'm sorry if I startled you. I knocked, but you didn't answer. So I came in."

"I-I was thinking." She reached out, taking the bowl from his hands, careful not to touch him. She pulled the food closer, inhaling deeply. It smelled heavenly, and the egg twisted hungrily in her navel. "Thank you," she managed to gasp before eating. She tried to go slowly, but suddenly she was famished. She couldn't devour the stew fast enough, and he watched her with a chagrined expression.

"I'm sorry. I should have realized you were starving."

She shook her head, trembling as she tried to control her need. "I didn't know . . ." she whispered. Then her bowl was empty, as was her flagon of ale. And still her hands shook with hunger. "Is there more?"

He nodded slowly, pushing his own bowl toward her. "Have this. I'll get another."

She should have refused. She intended to; she was a woman, not an animal—there was no need for her to fall on his food as if she were a starveling. Except, she couldn't stop herself. She took his bowl from him, barely restraining herself from snatching it out of his hand. Meanwhile, he took her empty bowl and left the room, an anxious expression on his face.

It took less than a beat for her to finish his food. And his ale. And the pitcher of water as well. Then she began pacing, the egg twisting in her belly, demanding more. Always more. Food, touch, hunger—all desires merged together until Natiya thought she would go mad.

This was not her. This was not the way she acted. And into this madness came the memory of Kiril's words. *The beast corrupts. I have seen it.*

Natiya dropped down onto the large bed, feeling her shoulders slump. Could it be possible? Was she changing? Was the dragon corrupting her? She didn't know. She didn't think so, but then again, how would she? She tried to remember herself as a child, before she had decided to carry the egg. She had been so young and so angry. Her only thought had been revenge. How would she know if the egg corrupted her?

She needed more information. She needed to know what Kiril knew—what had happened to his cousin and how, all the details that she'd never considered. But how to get the information without arousing his suspicions?

Kiril returned to the room with two more bowls of stew, and the innkeeper's daughter's boots clutched under one arm. All in all, things were going well. Though the news of Dag Racho's strange behavior had not yet reached this sleepy village on the edge of the Clutching Mountains, other news had. His promotion to governor was well known, making interactions with the innkeeper a great deal smoother. Requests—such as for boots—were filled with speed. And bird messages were dispatched without

demur. The innkeeper also informed him that the cold
season seemed delayed this year. The mountains were
easy travel right now.

But best of all, Natiya was ready. After her bath, she
would fall easily into his arms, and tonight he had no
doubt he would be able to slake his overwhelming
hunger for her. He could hardly take the stairs fast
enough.

He pushed open the door, saw her curled tightly
against the bed's headboard. Her knees were to her chest
and panic flared briefly in her dark blue eyes. Anxiety
rolled off of her in palpable waves, and then, abruptly, it
disappeared. She took a deep breath, obviously struggling to control her fear, and then she straightened, her
every move regal.

D'greth, she was impressive. Perhaps when this was
all over he would keep her as his lover. With a few lessons and the right clothes, she would be quite an asset
at court. He would be an envied man.

Meanwhile, he smiled warmly at her, extending the
boots. "The innkeeper's daughter is about your size. Try
them on and see if they fit."

She nodded and took the boots. He watched like a
lovesick boy while her dainty feet slipped inside, his
body clenching with an absurd desire. How ridiculous
that he would envy a pair of boots for being so close to
her, but he had been mad for some time—even ready
to take her hours ago on his mount! The sight of her slim
white ankle slipping inside the dark fur made his mind
spin with fantasies.

"Thank you," she said softly. "You have been most
kind." Even her voice was enticing, all the more so
because it sounded as if she hovered on the edge of
control.

Kiril grinned, allowing her to understand some of his
thoughts. "Perhaps we can find a different way for you to
thank me."

She knew what he meant; he could see it in the way her eyes widened and a shiver trembled through her body, making her breasts jiggle in just the right way. He would have reached for her then, despite his intention to go slowly, except she gestured to the bowls of stew still in his hands.

"Is that for me?"

He looked down and flushed. Some seducer he was, standing in the middle of the room like a servant. "Yes. Of course. Here."

She nodded as she took the bowl, and as before, he could only marvel at the quantity she consumed. But this time she ate slowly—with dignity—though her face was flushed with embarrassment.

"I must seem like a beast to you, eating so much and without manners. Truly, this is so unlike me."

He grinned, finding her nervousness sweet. He would take great delight in showing her that she had nothing to fear from him. "A lot has happened in the last day," he answered gently. "Yesterday you were dancing as usual. Today . . ." He let his voice trail off, thinking not about today but about tonight.

"Tell me about Jaseen."

It took a moment for her words to penetrate his fantasies. He had been imagining other words on her lips, other requests. "What did you say?"

She looked up and he saw desperation in her expression. "Please, tell me about Dag Jaseen."

"Why?" He had not intended to sound curt and angry, but he was having difficulty reconciling his plans with her question.

"Please. I need to know. I need . . ." She took a deep breath. "I need some time." She looked at him, probably not realizing her heart shone in her eyes. She was terrified.

He felt his eyes close momentarily as he cursed himself. Of course she was terrified. She was an innocent.

He paused to wonder how a dancer could remain so pure. She was clearly terrified of any intimacy. Surely there was a reason for such fear. Fortunately, the best way to discover her secrets was to push their relationship further.

He smiled as he extended his hand. "You needn't be afraid, Natiya. I swear it shall be—"

"Don't touch me!" She scrambled backward, away from him, but she did not curl again into a tiny ball. This time her feet were close to the floor, her body tensed for a leap toward freedom. If he did not move carefully, she would bolt. And then it would be a long, cold night as he went in search for her.

He eased himself down onto the edge of the bed opposite her. "Whatever you say, Natiya. I promised I would not force you, and I meant it." He took a deep breath. *D'greth,* this lust was becoming an irritation. He had to find a way to release it or he would go insane. Unfortunately, the only way to do that was to soothe this virgin's fears. "We can speak of my cousin if you like, but there are many more pleasant things to discuss—"

"Dag Jaseen. Please. Tell me about him."

Well, he had walked right into that. He sighed, reminding himself to be patient. "Very well. But not Dag Jaseen." He swallowed, still finding it difficult to even say the monster's name. "I will tell you about my *cousin* Jaseen. The man before the change."

She nodded, and he was pleased to see her relax slightly. But then she looked at him, and he knew he had to start talking. About Jaseen.

Stifling a curse, Kiril crossed his arms, feeling his irritation grow but unable to stop it. When he spoke, his words came out without inflection, like stones dropping from a great height to land with a dull thud in the room.

"Jaseen was my cousin. My father's sister's only son. He was nearly eight cycles older than me." Kiril reached out for his ale only to find that the flagon was empty. "He had fiery red hair and freckles everywhere, which Aunt Marta hated but he thought was funny. What need did a warrior have for clear skin? And that, of course, was what I found funny." Kiril fell silent, his mind whirling back to a hot day spent wandering through a cool forest.

"I don't understand." Natiya's words were soft, interrupting his reverie.

"What?"

"Why did you find his spots funny.?"

"Huh? Oh, no. Not his spots. That he thought he'd be a warrior. He just didn't seem like one. Even I—so many years younger—could see that he wasn't a fighter. Jaseen was the gentlest soul I knew." Kiril readjusted his position on the bed so he could lean against the headboard. "We spent a lot of time there. My father and uncle were plotting, I suppose, but all I knew was that I got to run around the woods with Jaseen. It was great fun." He smiled. "*He* was great fun, always laughing, always happy. He taught me everything I know about the forest—where to find food, what the animals do, how to track them. He talked about the souls of the birds and the wisdom of the trees. Once he even talked to a water spirit."

Kiril twisted the empty flagon in his hands, remembering too much of his laughing cousin. "We never hunted. He knew how, of course, but even eight cycles younger, I was better at it. He just didn't like killing anything, even fish. And since he could always find berries and roots, why hurt something else?"

Kiril looked down at his palms, seeing the hard calluses there, knowing they came from steady work, hard study in the ways of wielding a sword. In the ways of murder. What would Jaseen have thought of him? he wondered. A dragon-killer? He curled his fingers into his palms, pushing aside the memories with steady effort.

Then he looked up at Natiya, felt the lust heat within him at the sight of her unbound hair, her freshly scrubbed face, and for once he didn't fight it. How much better to focus on a beautiful woman than the ugly past. Except, she would not let the subject drop.

"How did he change? What happened?"

"He got the thrice-cursed dragon egg, that's what." He turned away, clenching his teeth but forcing himself to explain. "I'm not sure why my father and uncle picked Jaseen. Probably because he was the right age. I was too young, the others too old. Plus, Jaseen took after his father—large-boned with thick muscles. A warrior's body containing a poet's soul. So they gave him the egg."

Unable to sit still, Kiril reached for his bag and pulled out a thin spool of white loga. The metal thread had not been cured in dragon blood, so it didn't matter what he fashioned out of it, merely that it kept his hands busy as he spoke.

"Jaseen wore the egg on his right bicep. His egg was dark green—like jade—and he had it worked into a warrior's armband along with the family crest." He looked at his own arm, knowing underneath his clothing he had a dark tattoo—a black stain fashioned as an armband but in truth a picture of a dragon. That had been Dag Racho's big joke the first year Kiril was brought to court: tattoo a fake warrior band across his arm, make it look like Jaseen's Platinum dragon, and immediately all would know exactly who and why Kiril was tolerated there. Everyone in Dag Racho's court who saw it—and Kiril was never allowed to hide it when there—would know him to be the last survivor of Dag Jaseen's failure.

"What happened?" Natiya pressed, and he spared a moment to wonder at her insistence, then immediately dismissed the thought. She was probing because he disliked it. She wanted to test how far he would go to please her. But she needed to understand that these painful memories did not come freely, so he raised his banded arm and gestured to her. "Come closer, Natiya. I don't want to have to shout my family history across the room."

He wasn't shouting, of course, but his ploy worked. She climbed fully back onto the bed, settling on her knees at the furthest edge of his reach.

When he would have drawn her closer, she shrank back from him. "Not yet," she said, fear still skating along the edge of her voice. "Tell me about how Jaseen changed."

He nodded, knowing he could press her no further just yet. So he sighed, dreading the return to the memories that hovered as always at the back of his mind.

"The egg was a boon—at first. Jaseen grew stronger. Faster. His sword arm became more confident, his actions more assured. He seemed to have the senses of the creature—better smell, better sight, better . . . everything. But he also developed a taste for meat."

Natiya straightened. "Surely he ate meat before."

"Of course he did, but not often. He didn't like it." Kiril grimaced. "In fact, he often slipped his pieces to me under the table."

"It is no crime to like meat," she laughed.

Kiril shook his head. "No crime. That came later." He focused on his hands, letting his fingers twist the metal strands of loga however they willed. "He changed, Natiya. I cannot say it more plainly than that. Where before he was kind and gentle, he became brutal and cruel. He started collecting things. It didn't matter what, so long as they were valuable. I once gave him a piece of jewelry—a family brooch, tarnished and worn. He said he would have it reset for me, put the old stones into new metal of my design, and then I could give it to my mother for her birthday."

He fell silent, remembering the betrayal.

"He stole it, didn't he? Gave you a fake."

Kiril nodded, unsurprised that she had guessed what happened; no woman could live on the docks and not learn about such fraud. "I saw the exact same piece years later adorning the breast of Dag Racho's mistress. He had taken it from Jaseen's hoard." Kiril released a bitter laugh. That treasure hoard had been worth thousands, hidden in the bedroom of a boy twenty-two cycles old. "That is what the egg does: It overwhelms a man's mind and creates a monster."

"Do you think me a monster?" Her voice was small. Afraid.

He frowned in confusion at her pallor. "Of course not."

"But I like meat. And jewels. And in my bed I have hidden all my wealth. Or I wear it on my costumes so that it is close to me."

He leaned forward, tugging on her arm until she rested beside him, still facing him, her long legs tucked beneath her. "That's simple practicality. Where else could you put your coins safely? And I am sure you need meat for your dancing. Fruits and grasses are all very well, but meat fills the belly like nothing else." Then he smiled, remembering her room. "And I have seen your wealth, Natiya. Books and books, stacked in neat rows beneath your bed. What do you read about, I wonder?"

She shrugged. "Everything." Her gaze slipped to where her fingers toyed with the fabric of the coverlet. "I hoard those books like treasure."

"Jaseen committed crimes because he was . . . evil."

"How?" She leaned forward, and he extended his free hand, resting it along her thigh while she focused on her questions. "What did he do?"

"You must understand. A dragon lives only to possess. It doesn't matter what, only that he has, that he *takes*." He looked down at the twisted loga in his fingers. He had fashioned a shimmering white dragon with out-stretched wings—beautiful to behold, but created of twisted metal with cuttingly sharp points. "It is a fire that possesses the mind, making the bonded think of nothing else. Of no one else."

"What did Jaseen *do?*" she pressed.

Kiril looked into her eyes, wishing he could make her see the truth. "He took a woman, Natiya. The man who would not fish because he could not bear to kill, that man took Sabina in the most brutal of ways."

Kiril watched her eyes widen, but even so he could tell she did not comprehend. Not really. "You mean, like you intend to take me," she said.

He jerked back, cut his palm on his own sculpture. "Of course not!"

"But you said I am your obsession. That you want me with a fever you cannot explain."

"You would be willing!" he snapped. "The experience would be pleasant. It would not be rape."

She nodded, straightening her spine and staring at him. "And if I said no? Indeed, I have said no, but you still look for ways to persuade me, to use my body against me."

"That's not true!" he cried. "I have told you, all you need say is no."

She looked down at his hand where it had slipped to the inside of her thigh. "I have said, no, and yet you continue. Didn't I tell you not to touch me no more than five beats ago?"

He snatched his hand back, glaring first at it, then her. Why was she being like this? "It is different with a dragonborn. *They* are different."

She shook her head. "I think you damn Jaseen for the wrong reason. I think the failing was not in the dragon, but in the man. What he did may have been harsher because he was stronger, but the evil lay not on his arm but between his legs."

Kiril's hands became fists, crushing his sculpture, which sliced deeper into his palm. "He was evil, consumed by the dragon."

"He was consumed by rutting—just like you," she countered. "What possessed him was his prock—just like you."

"That is not true!" he bellowed, throwing away his wire creation hard enough to mark the wall where it struck. "It is the dragon that is evil!" He said the words, even believed them. But her implication hung in the air between them.

Just how far *would* he go to possess her? He had not yet forced her. So far she had been amenable to many of the more subtle and pleasurable ways to entice a woman. But if those ploys failed? He had already called her his obsession. He had already admitted she fired his blood as no other woman ever had. What if she said no? Even now, wasn't he belly-horned with hunger?

"I would not force you," he repeated firmly, more to himself than her.

She scrambled off the bed, leaning over to lace her boots. "Then let us leave now."

He blinked. "What?"

"Let us leave this large room with its soft bed and perfumed sheets. Let us go to the Queen's clutching cave now, before the cold freezes the entrance."

"You know where it is?"

Her gaze flicked over him, then darted back to her boot laces. "Yes."

"You will take me there?"

She nodded—a quick jerk of her chin. Then she looked up. "If you are not a man ruled by his organ, then you have no need of this bedroom."

"And what of sleep? Have I no need of sleep?" he rasped, even as he fought his own reaction. He was angry. More than angry, he was furious at her suggestion that he was no better than a dragon-possessed man. And yet, if she was wrong, why wasn't he jumping for joy? She was offering to take him to the clutching cave. To the Queen's cave, which up until now she hadn't admitted existed. He ought to be rushing her out the door before she changed her mind. And yet here he sat, in the middle of a large, soft bed, wondering why they could not stay the night. Or the hour. Just long enough for him to remind her how good it felt to be touched. So that he could . . .

He grabbed hold of the sheet, tearing off a strip of the white fabric so that he could wrap it around his wounded hand. His movements were harsh and violent, making him flinch. And yet he welcomed the pain, knowing that the sharp stab of sensation cleared his thoughts.

Was she right? Was he a man controlled by reason, or a beast bent on possession? He could not be the beast. But honesty forced him to admit he didn't qualify as a thinking man just then either; his reason had deserted him the first moment he had seen her dance.

Natiya pushed open the door, headed down the stairs to the main inn floor.

"Where are you going?" he demanded. Any moment when he could not see her was a physical pain to him.

"I am leaving," she called back.

He nearly tripped in his rush to her side. "Why?" he asked stupidly.

She shook her head. "To be honest, I don't know. Dag Racho hunts me. You search for the cave. I should be running away from all of you. And yet, I cannot deny its draw."

He frowned, trying to make sense of her words. It was some moments before he realized the truth. "You want to find the egg," he accused. "You want to bargain with it for your life." He grabbed hold of her, his bloodied hand staining her shirt. "You are thinking of your future.

That's good, but you will not be safe without me. Not when bargaining with Dag Racho."

She jerked out of his grip. "I am not safe *with* you."

"Of course you are," he lied. Then he took a deep breath, struggling to find a logical solution. "Is it far? Can you make it on foot?"

She shook her head, and he read frustration in the movement. "Not before it freezes."

"Then you need Mobray. And me."

She pushed away, descending the last of the steps. "I need a mount, not you."

"You need food, blankets, *and* a mount. I have all three. And I am willing to take you there."

She didn't respond, though he saw her shoulders droop in silent acknowledgment. So in her moment of vulnerability, he reached out, stroking her cheek with studied care. He did not intend to do this; indeed, his mind screamed at him that it was a false move, a stupid, useless gesture guaranteed to undermine his position. And yet, such was her power over him that he could not stop himself. He had to touch her.

"Need we go tonight?" he coaxed. "The room is paid for. And I need—"

She slapped his hand away with a strength borne of fury. "It is *not* the dragon that is evil. It is your prock. A plague upon it." And with that, she stomped away.

Kiril stared at her retreating form, the ashes of his plan lost upstairs along with the dirty bathwater and torn sheet. She was right. He knew it, and yet his mind reeled from the truth. He was ruled by his prock and the woman for which it lusted.

What was happening to him? Where was his control that could break a dragonspell? Where the body so honed it could withstand a dragon's attack with honor and strength?

Gone. Because of a woman and his prock. The very thought sickened him. And yet, he had no way to stop himself, no way to abandon her or his quest. He needed to get to the Queen's cave, and Natiya was the only one who could lead him. Therefore, he needed her.

But he would be damned if he needed to rut with her. Damned if he would force the woman. Damned if he allowed the fire in his blood to rule him. And so he stomped after her, his body still hungry, his mind dark with frustration.

Part of him warned that this was no state in which to embark on a night's travel, much less a night in mountains soon to be clogged with ice and snow. But he had no choice. And worse, he didn't care. She was going into the caves, and he would be damned indeed if he let her escape him. Because, after all his curses, after all the lectures and admonitions his mind screamed at him, one thing remained unshakably true: He was still belly-horned for her, and no amount of logic or fear would keep him from her side.

If she was leaving, he would be at her side.

CHAPTER EIGHT

Natiya's fury took her all the way out through the inn-yard and into the stable, but by the time she reached Mobray's stall, it had already petered out. True, she was furious with Kiril, but with distance from the over-whelming man, she could look at the situation more logically.

So, Kiril wanted to rut. Didn't every man? So he'd focused entirely upon spreading her thighs as opposed to someone else's. He was neither the first nor the last man to want her, at least for the moment. Eventually he would tire of her refusals and leave her alone. That made him no different from any of her other admirers.

Except, he *was* different. He had broken her out of prison. He had treated her gently, respectfully; and in her experience that made him unique among men. And far from stopping her from using her mind, he was constantly challenging her to think more, to plan ahead, to reason out her options.

But what really confused her was that, for the first time, she wanted him as much as he seemed to want her. He didn't even have to touch her. As a dancer, she was familiar with every ache her body could experi-ence. He made her flesh respond in entirely new and devastatingly intriguing ways. She wanted him to touch her and do all those other things Monik talked about.

She leaned wearily against the stall door, reaching through to stroke Mobray's nose, feeling an odd kinship with the bald creature. How often did Mobray feel buffeted by forces he could neither control nor understand?

Two days ago, her only concern had been whether or not she could afford another costume. Within the last forty hours she'd been kissed, imprisoned, rescued, and now hunted. Worse, her egg had changed, growing larger and suddenly insistent that they travel immediately to the Queen's cave. Why? She didn't know. But the egg insisted, and she found herself powerless to deny it. Worse, her only bulwark in this storm was a man who seemed to increase the storm's power and fury.

She felt her body tense, felt the moisture of desire. She didn't have to turn to know that Kiril had joined her in the stable. His presence affected her so strongly that even the egg seemed to vibrate with his every breath.

He made it to her side, a heavy satchel slung across his back. "You're still determined to go?" he asked, his voice resigned. "We can't wait until morning?"

"Now," she said, the word ringing clearly despite her doubts. Why the egg insisted it must go now, she hadn't a clue. But the urge—no, its demand—was undeniable. The egg needed to be at the cave quickly. Immediately, if possible. Even the wait to saddle Mobray made it twist in irritation.

Kiril did not complain. He merely dropped his satchel at her feet before going in to saddle his mount. He was clearly peeved, no doubt because of her refusal to lie with him. But at least she'd gotten an answer as to why Dag Jaseen had failed.

No, Jaseen hadn't been possessed by an evil dragon egg. The man had failed because he was a man and subject to all men's failings. They wanted. They rutted. And they usually didn't think beyond that. Thank the goddess

Amia that she didn't have the same problem. She only wanted revenge on Dag Racho. She would make him pay for his crimes, and then the rest would fall where it may. As for rutting—she'd lived this long without it; she could go a while longer. Or so she hoped.

"Hand me the bag," Kiril said, his voice sharp and cold.

Natiya grabbed it, taking a moment to look inside. She saw food, water, a fire staff, even cleansing cloths for wounds. He appeared to have thought of everything, and she cursed her own stupidity. *D'greth*, she was unprepared. She would probably have just set out, not even thinking to grab more than a loaf of bread on her way through the door.

What else didn't she know? What other skills did she lack? If nothing else, the last forty hours had told her that she was woefully unprepared for some of the challenges ahead. And yet, she saw no way to deal with her ignorance. Hatching time was fast approaching, and she would simply have to make do.

With that grim thought in mind, she stepped back, allowing Kiril and Mobray to exit the stall. Moments later Kiril pulled her up with him, placing her once again half on his lap, half on the saddle. She went easily, settling too happily into arms. But that, too, was something she could not change. Her body was already humming in anticipation, her breasts growing heavy with longing, but she had no choice. He was her only means to the Queen's cave. They exited the stableyard quickly, but once away from the stable lights, the night closed about them. The three moons were small these days, making the darkness inky black.

"Here," Kiril said as he lighted the fire staff. "You'll have to hold this. I've got the reins."

She took the heavy rod with both hands, bracing it against her leg. The yellow light from its tip illuminated the path ahead, but it also functioned as a beacon for anyone in the sky: Dag Racho would have little difficulty finding them. She spared one last moment to try and reason with the egg. *Certainly,* she thought to it, *we should wait the night—*

Now, was its only answer. So she sighed, relaxing back against Kiril's steady warmth. He felt as solid as any rock, and she could not resist smiling slightly. It was ridiculous to feel safe in this position—with this man— but she did. And since she had no choice, she decided to enjoy the sensations of his arms around her, his large hands resting lightly on top of her right thigh. Then, just as her eyes began to drift shut, his voice rumbled through her entire body.

"What path do we take?"

"Go east through the Wiaken Pass. There is a path just beyond."

"How old were you when you last went there?"

"Eight. Maybe nine," she lied. In truth, she had been fifteen and running from Uncle Rened.

"How sure are you of this path?"

Positive, she thought. But for his benefit, she shrugged. "It was a long time ago, but I think that's the way."

Apparently, that was all he needed to know. He spoke his commands to Mobray, and soon they were moving through the night toward the Wiaken Pass.

"Tell me about the cave. What do you remember?"

Natiya shifted slightly, readjusting the firestick but mostly wanting to feel the contours of his body against hers. She seemed excruciatingly aware of his chest against her back, his hips and belt hard against her buttocks, and his corded thighs cradling her against the front ridge of the saddle. "I remember the air mostly. Cold and wet, and yet there was a tang in it that seemed to tingle against my skin." She wet her lips. "I could almost taste it." She sighed. "I suppose that doesn't make much sense."

Kiril shook his head, his voice a low thrum against her back. "All clutching caves are like that. I cannot explain, either, but I know what you mean."

"I didn't understand it, but I think my parents did."

"Why?" His voice tightened with intensity. "What do you think they knew?"

She shrugged—again, not because she needed to express her confusion, but because she liked the feel of moving against his body. "I don't know. They just seemed to spend a lot of time in there and were happier when we returned." The memories were tangled in her mind, confused and faded with time.

"What else do you remember?"

"Nothing." Unfortunately, that was true. Once one knew the path to the cave, the rest was no more than common knowledge. A dragon's nest was obvious—no more than a small circle of eggs on a pillow of spongy effluvium surrounded by a circle of stones.

"Were there markers along the path? Could anyone find it given basic instructions?"

"No and no. I remember because . . ." Her voice trailed away as she tried to isolate exactly why she did remember.

"Because?" he prompted.

"I don't know." She sighed. "I just remember, that's all."

"Did you play in the caves?"

She felt herself smile. "Always. My family used to tease me, saying I was dragonborn." She twisted, looking up at his face as she shared her memories. "They said I was conceived in a clutching cave, and born in one, too." She leaned back, relaxing into his heat once again. "They were dragon scholars, remember? They spent many years in or around the caves when my brother and I were little. They only came back to teach at the university and so I could go to school."

She felt him nod, his chin rubbing in gentle strokes across her temple. "There is your answer, then. I have told you that dragons are filled with magic. If their blood holds special properties, doesn't it make sense that the place where they mate and bear their young would also hold great power? Without even thinking about it, you probably attuned yourself when you were young."

She hadn't considered that, but as soon as he said it, she knew he was correct. And even if she herself hadn't, the egg echoed his sentiments. Then the oddest thought popped into her mind, and since she was so relaxed, the words found voice even before she recognized the question.

"How did your family find an egg? Where did they get it?"

She felt him inhale, a sharp intake of breath before he finally released it in a slow, controlled whisper of air.

"You don't want to tell me, do you?" she guessed.

He sighed. "I have grown up in court, Natiya, where information is more valuable than gold loga. But there is no reason for you not to know." Still, he didn't immediately answer, and she was forced to twist, looking up into his face.

"Kiril?"

"They got it from your parents. How do you think I knew who you were? You were very young, no more than five, with short cropped hair and a penchant for stealing my soldier toys."

"I did not!" she exclaimed. Or at least she had no memory of such an event.

"Oh yes, you did. I believe you wanted to play school with them, taking my best wooden archers and punishing them when they couldn't spell words correctly." He chuckled at the memory, and she smiled along with him. "You had short dark hair and a perpetually dirty nose from all the places you kept poking it into."

"What a rude thing to say!" she returned, pretending to an insult she didn't feel.

"I was eight, and you were a royal pain."

"And all the while our parents were plotting . . ." Her voice trailed away in confusion. All this time, she'd thought them innocent victims of Dag Racho's dragon purge. To find out now that they had been involved in a conspiracy felt profoundly unsettling. She couldn't even say how, only that she did not like her view of the past altered.

Kiril did not comment, but she felt his displeasure. He thought them fools, that the whole attempt to destroy Dag Racho had been ill-conceived from the beginning. And given that both their families had perished, perhaps he had the right of it. But if they had been wrong in their plans—her parents were dragon scholars, and his a great political family—then what chance did she have, a lone woman with no training at all? The very thought gave her shivers. Especially since she had no way to change course.

"Are you cold?" he asked, tightening his arms around her.

"No," she answered truthfully, then hugged his arms to her chest. "Just haunted by memories I'm not sure I understand."

She felt his smile against her cheek. "That, too, I understand."

They both fell silent, more in accord than they had been since that first night in the tavern. But as they continued along the path, Mobray's monotonous rhythm merging into the inky night, Natiya felt melancholy build. She missed her family, even her little brother. She missed the life she had once lived. She no longer even knew if her memories were correct, and so she missed the security of those as well—the certain knowledge that her innocent parents had been wrongly destroyed.

She still believed in her task, and yet . . . Loneliness ate at her.

"Kiss me, Natiya. Please." His words trembled with an ache that echoed her own. Loneliness, grief and pain were all wrapped together in his request, offering her the simple relief of his touch—the only relief possible at the moment, and she welcomed it with open arms.

Their lips touched briefly, then separated as Mobray shifted his gait to accommodate the rising terrain. But the change was subtle, easily adjusted to, and soon their mouths connected again. Connected, deepened, and began a dance she was all too familiar with by now.

Pulling away, she turned to look out beyond the halo of firestick light. "I do not want to kiss you," she said to the enveloping darkness.

"I know," he answered, his voice equally flat. "I don't want to desire you either."

"I cannot stop these feelings."

He stroked his cheek along the side of her head. "I must have you, Natiya. I do not know why, but the need grows stronger and stronger with every breath, every touch."

"I know," she responded, not because of his words but because she felt an answering tide within her.

"I am a man, not a beast!" he said, his words angry.

"I will not be had by any of you," she returned, equally firm. And yet, for all their words, their hands had not been idle. His curled around her stomach, inching higher as they sought her breasts. Hers twisted her around so that she could look at him while she worked her fingers between the buttons on his shirt.

Moments later, his groan signaled a surrender—for both of them. Their mouths met and clung once again. Within her she felt the egg begin to stir, vibrating with an energy that could have come from it or from her. She didn't know and didn't care; all she knew was that it fired her senses, pushing her to greater hunger, greater need.

His shirt buttons were soon undone. Her breasts were exposed to the cold air only to be warmed by his large hands.

"Turn around," he urged. "Face me and put your legs on either side of my hips."

She shook her head, her words slipping out between kisses. "I'll fall."

"I'll hold you."

"It's too unstable. The ground is uneven." But even so, her legs were shifting, trying to maneuver.

"Mobray's very sure-footed."

"The firestick is falling!"

"I've got it."

"Amia!" she cried, invoking the goddess as he rescued the stick but lost her. She tumbled backward, falling off Mobray to land painfully on the very rocky ground. She knew the truth then; it came in a flash of the blindingly obvious as she watched the firestick twist and careen above her. She heard Kiril's curses as he struggled to control Mobray, the firestick, and the saddlebags that had come undone with her fall, all the while trying to see if she was hurt. She knew the truth then and accepted it with a liberating fatalism.

They were going to rut together, she and Kiril. Not just once, but likely many, many, many times. Despite the Emperor who hunted her. Despite the risk of discovery that her "belly jewel" grew and pulsed in a way that no cold stone could. Despite her resolve to keep everything the same until she understood the reasons behind and consequences of every action. Despite it all, she and Kiril would become lovers.

"Natiya! Are you all right?"

She laughed, feeling the humor shake through her like a small echo of the tremors deeper within. She laughed long and hard, and also with such joy that tears streamed from her eyes.

"Natiya? What is happening?"

She didn't know, so she couldn't answer. Or perhaps she did, because something else had just become blindingly obvious.

"I just figured out why my parents liked going to the caves. And all this time, I thought it was for scholarship."

He was silent for a long time as he stopped Mobray, resettled the bags, then dismounted. "They are clutching caves. The . . . sexual magic would be strong." He moved to her side.

She smiled, coming to her feet in a slow, languid movement. She glanced to the side, seeing Kiril swallow convulsively as she stretched her arms high above her, her naked breasts thrusting forward in the chill air. His gaze was riveted to her, his prock obvious even through the layers of his clothing.

How wonderfully powerful I feel, Natiya thought with surprise. How easy it was to reduce a strong, competent man into a mesmerized slave. "So, it is only the caves, you think?" she asked sweetly. Coyly.

Abruptly he turned away, his hands fisted and his shoulders rigid. "Dragon magic," he cursed, spitting the words out like bad meat. "Of course."

She felt her arms slip down as she stared at his back. "You don't like dragon magic?"

He lifted his chin but did not look back at her. "I use dragon magic. I will not be used by it." Then, before she could ask for more information, he spoke again, his words hard and cold, aimed at himself, not her. It was as if he were issuing orders to his own body. "I am a dragon-hunter. I cannot be vulnerable to dragon magic in any form."

"But this—"

"Dragon magic," he continued, "is evil magic. It undoes the mind. It turns warriors into beasts. I will not allow it." Then, without hint or warning, he spun around, grabbing her firmly around the waist and lifting her onto Mobray's back. He grabbed the firestick, using it more as a walking stick than a light source as he gathered the reins and began to pull Mobray and Natiya forward.

"Kiril?" she asked when he did not join her on his mount.

"I will walk for now, Natiya."

She stared at him, seeing the absolute determination in his heavy footfalls, his firm stride. She could hardly believe it, but the proof walked angrily by her side. The very moment that she finally succumbed to his seduction, to the sensuality that still shimmered just beneath her skin, was the very moment he resolved to disdain her. She ought to be thrilled—at least one of them remained rational—but instead she felt a childish irritation cutting at her. As if he had suddenly taken away her toys.

"And Natiya?" he said.

She straightened, hope sparking within her. "Yes?"

"Cover yourself. It will be even colder in the caves."

Kiril was losing the war. He knew it with absolute certainty, but he couldn't summon the will to care. In fact, he was having trouble remembering exactly why he was so intent on *not* bedding Natiya. She was beautiful, absolutely willing—or would be with a little encouragement—and yet he was stomping in front of his mount like a man on a forced march. What was wrong with him?

He didn't have to wait long for his answer. All he had to do was close his eyes and see Sabina as she had looked when Jaseen had finished with her. It had been near hatching time, so the magic ran strong within him, and like all the women, she had been entranced by his golden beauty, his rippling muscles and his sweet, innocent smile.

Kiril was eleven and already feeling betrayed by the cousin who had once been his friend. Not because of the brooch; it would be years before he learned of that small deceit. But because Jaseen's laughter mocked instead of expressed joy. His words cut rather than instructed. And he had no time for a young boy except to expose Kiril's ineptness at swordplay, at learning, at everything. And he was especially cruel when girls came by to watch.

So when Jaseen came for swordplay lessons from Kiril's father, Kiril-the-boy slunk away in a self-pitying temper rather than remain close by to see what the dragon egg had done to his cousin. So no one had been around to protect Sabina.

Kiril slammed the firestick into the ground, extinguishing the light, which was no longer necessary to cut the dawn mists. They were well into the mountains now, but they still had many hours left to travel before they reached the Wiaken Pass. Behind him, Natiya drowsed on Mobray's back. Ahead of him lay rocky terrain, sparse vegetation, and cliffs riddled with clutching caves. But with him—inside him—was the constant image of Sabina as she had appeared that day.

The sounds were what drew him from his tree fort. The woods were never very thick there, the underbrush long since cleared away by students who ran or wandered through the greenery. More than one couple had exchanged illicit kisses against the trees, so Kiril was used to hearing giggles and soft moans echoing all the way up to his tree fort.

But these sounds were different. Grunts—guttural, animal sounds mixed with muffled sobs. On some level, Kiril must have understood what was happening, because he brought his sword with him as he crept from his play-place, but nothing prepared him for what he saw: Jaseen, his pants down to his ankles, contracting his buttocks with brutal force as he lay on top of a bruised and bloody Sabina. Kiril had called out—a stupid, childish mistake. He should have just chopped the monster's head off right then and there, but he had cried out—thereby alerting the beast—before he rushed forward, sword upraised.

He knew Jaseen's reactions were quick—knew it, but had not truly understood how a dragon enhanced a man's fighting skills. In the time it took for Kiril to rush to Sabina's side, Jaseen had lifted himself off her, readied himself, then smashed his fist directly into Kiril's face. Kiril went down like a stone only to have Jaseen follow.

His cousin's blows were brutal, punishing enough to break bones, but still Kiril fought as best he could. He'd kicked, struck, shoved, but in all that, Jaseen was only playing with him. They both knew Kiril could just scream—loud and long—and someone would come help. Someone who could have stopped it. But Jaseen had never allowed Kiril the breath, and Kiril had been too young to know how to prioritize energy, how to protect his ribs long enough for a single long bellow for help.

Jaseen could have killed him then, probably would have but for Sabina. She could have run or screamed or done something, anything that would have saved herself. Instead, she threw herself onto Jaseen, raking her nails across his face as she pulled him off of his cousin. Then when the monster turned back to her, she had negotiated not for herself, but for Kiril's life.

Yes, in the end he had lain on the ground, seven ribs broken, the bones of his sword arm snapped in two, while Jaseen returned to Sabina. The bastard spread her legs and took her like a beast in the field. Kiril tried to move, tried to help her, but the pain was too great and he'd passed out.

Hours later he'd awoken in his room, encased in healing plaster, his mother sobbing silently by his side. Jaseen had been spirited away for the hatching. That was the reason for his behavior, they told him. And as for Sabina, her parents had already taken her away on an extended holiday. Kiril didn't see her again until after the dragon's birth, after the fight and the murder of his entire family, and long after he had been brought to court to serve as a living example of what happened to those who challenged Dag Racho.

"Slam that fire staff any harder and you'll break it."

Natiya's soft words startled him, and he spun around, one hand already drawing his sword. She didn't even blink as she watched him with large, wary eyes. She waited until he relaxed, slowly returning his sword to its scabbard; then she spoke.

"What were you thinking?"

His first thought was to lie, to make up something she wouldn't question. But before he could bring a convenient excuse to mind, his mouth was already forming an honest answer. "About Jaseen. About dragon magic."

"About why you suddenly hate me."

He frowned at her. "I don't hate you."

"No. Just the dragon magic. But right now, it amounts to the same thing."

"Of course it doesn't." He stopped, turning to look fully at her. "Why would you think that?"

He watched her sigh, felt his body tighten at the delicate rise and fall of her breasts. When she spoke, his attention riveted back to her face and her words.

"Dag Racho is my enemy now. How many people, do you think, have survived as his enemy? How many live for more than a cycle?"

Kiril didn't speak. They both knew the answer was zero. No one lived long once Dag Racho declared them an enemy.

"I know this . . . lust . . . is dragon magic. I know it, but I don't care. I want to enjoy myself once before I . . ." Her voice trailed off, but he completed the thought for her.

"Die? It may not come to that—"

"Before things change," she interrupted. "We will get to the cave soon. You will find your lead on the Queen egg, and then your need for me will end."

Given the way his body hungered, he sincerely doubted his need for her would ever end, but he didn't say that. Indeed, he was too busy damning himself for his own deceit. The danger to her was real, though exaggerated for his benefit. "There are ways to avoid Dag Racho. I could help you."

Natiya shook her head. "The Emperor knows who I am now. He will not stop until he finds me."

Kiril frowned. He heard the certainty in her voice and grieved that he was the one who had put it there. "You are too young to believe you will die tomorrow."

"I will take what pleasure I can today and leave death until then." She looked at him boldly, her eyes open, her posture awkwardly seductive. She was clearly unused to playing the game between men and women, and yet his body reacted as if she were the most seasoned courtesan. Until he looked into her eyes and saw a worldliness at odds with her sexual innocence. She had obviously come to a decision and was now simply waiting for her path to play out.

"Natiya, there are ways to escape the Emperor," he said.

She smiled. "Did I ever thank you for my escape? Will you be in much trouble for it? Will they know it was you?"

"I will be fine." He shrugged to cover his uneasiness. "There are ways for a governor to cover his tracks."

"Kiril—"

"No more," he interrupted. Then he stepped forward, touching her because he could not stop himself. He reached up to stroke her cheek, but she leaned forward, and without even realizing what was happening, he found himself kissing her. Well-schooled in kisses now, she opened her mouth, teasing him with her own tongue when he was reluctant.

D'greth, she tasted good. His hand tightened, pulling her closer. She went willingly, leaning forward into his arms. He didn't remember setting the fire staff aside, but all too soon she was fully off Mobray and he was staggering slightly as her full weight landed upon him. Exactly as it should be, he thought. Pressed fully against him. Beneath him.

She was already on the hard ground and he kneeling above her. His hands were on her breasts, and behind him, Mobray was snorting and pushing at his rear. The beast wanted a treat for all his hard work, and Kiril kept the sweets in his back pocket.

"Mobray," he muttered between kisses. "Not now."

But his mount was determined, butting his head against Kiril's leg, his hip, and then one last time, hard, against Kiril's rear. Kiril overbalanced, dropping his shoulder and all his weight onto a sharp rock.

"Mobray!"

Natiya, of course, was giggling. Kiril at last saw the humor of the situation, and he too began to chuckle. And with the laughter came a release from the dragon magic. Or at least enough focus for him to stand. With one hand, he gave his mount the treats. With his other, he assisted Natiya to her feet. He didn't dare look at her, though, or they would be back on the ground. Keeping his gaze trained on the path ahead, he quickly mounted Mobray.

"My eyes feel on fire," he lied. "I need some rest. Will you lead Mobray for a bit while I take a nap?"

Peripherally he saw her press her lips together in resignation, her hands already busy returning her clothing to order.

"Kiril—"

"You will not die, Natiya," he swore. "There is time yet for you to find real love. Let us not cheapen you by giving in to false dragon magic."

She faced him then, refusing to move until he looked at her. Even so, he kept his gaze trained to the side of her face, at a point just above her right shoulder.

"This is real," she snapped. "Real feelings. Real need. If you do not want me, then just say—"

"You know that's not true." His prock was like a living thing, practically dragging the rest of his body behind as it sought out her body. How real was that?

"What I know," she returned, "is that you are a stubborn, foolish man who will not take the gifts you are offered."

He laughed at that, the sound harsh and bitter. "You are right, Natiya. I will not take any gift from the flying serpents. If that makes me foolish, so be it." And with that, he folded his arms and shut his eyes, pretending to sleep.

Eventually he heard her huff her disgust and begin to walk. He trusted her to lead them safely, honestly, to the caves. Indeed, he believed the need was so strong in her that she would go there with or without him now. Such was the nature of dragon magic. For whatever reason, it drew her to the clutching cave—probably because the Queen egg, wherever it was, was nearing hatching. Someone somewhere in the world struggled with an egg the size of a child's fist attached to his body. It would be unwieldy, but it offered such promise of power that few men could resist the temptation.

It was said that the caves burned with an unholy light whenever an egg clutched there finally hatched. When Jaseen's Platinum had hatched, his clutching cave lit the shoreline like a beacon.

Since Natiya was attuned to the cave, it did not surprise Kiril that she was drawn there. No, what worried him was what would happen after the hatching, after the cave's magic finally faded. How would Natiya feel about him then? About what they both wanted to do? The thought of her hatred—especially if they succumbed to temptation—kept him firmly settled on top of Mobray, his hands fisted where he tucked them tightly against his chest.

He would not touch her. He would not succumb to the magic. He would not have her hate him.

With those thoughts firmly settled, Kiril bent his mind to the task of sleeping. He failed, of course. No man could sleep with a belly-horn constantly poking him. But he tried nevertheless.

An hour later, he grunted in disgust at himself. "Tell me about the books you read," he said.

She jumped, obviously startled by his sudden words. She glanced over her shoulder, her eyes sparkling blue fire in the morning light. "You're awake."

"Never slept. The dragon magic irritates me." Which was the polite way of saying he was too aroused to rest. "Tell me what you read all alone in your bedroom."

She turned away from him. "No dragon scrolls, if that's what you mean. As you know, Dag Racho burned all of those long ago."

Yes, he knew. He recalled well how, after Jaseen's attempt on the throne, the Emperor had decided that no one would be allowed dragon knowledge. It wasn't just Natiya's family who perished that night: All the dragon scholars were destroyed, along with their families and all their worldly possessions. Whole universities had been burned, thousands of students disappeared, entire libraries were engulfed in flames. One night, one dragon, and it was all gone. It had taken Kiril weeks of dedicated searching—and a bit of luck—to discover that the merchant Rened didn't have a sister who'd given birth to Natiya. The "niece" he raised was really his neighbor's child, and one of the few survivors of the dragon purge. She only lived because the merchant had protected her so well. And because she was young and female, and therefore of little threat to the Emperor.

"I wasn't looking for dragon lore," he groused, though a part of him had hoped she knew something. "I wanted to learn about you. What do *you* read?"

She shrugged, the graceful movement seeming resigned, as if she agreed to talk only because it would
pass the time. He didn't care so long as she spoke. If he
couldn't have her body, at least he would have a little
piece of her thoughts.

"I read about foreign countries, mostly. Places Dag
Racho's terror doesn't touch." She glanced back. "Do
you know there are countries where there is no curfew?
Where it takes twelve people to agree before a man can
be sentenced to death? Where people do not disappear
at night never to be heard from again." Her face took on
a wistful expression. "I read about that a lot. I read
about a country far to the east where laws are created
by a group of people, not a single Emperor."

He looked at her, his estimation of her intelligence
rising by leaps and bounds. Clearly there was more to
this little dancer than met the eye, but then he already
knew that. "How do you find such books, Natiya? And
are they written in a language you can read?"

"Uncle Rened travels far and wide." Her voice turned
light and dreamy. "He goes to a place called an open
book market. Imagine! An entire market devoted to
books from everywhere." She shook her head. "If I had a
dragon, I would fly there every day."

"You would have to teach your dragon not to blow
fire and burn it all up."

She laughed, and the sound lifted his spirit. "My
dragon would not burn up things. My dragon would be
a good dragon who helps people."

There were no such beasts, he thought to himself. But
he dared not voice it for fear of breaking the spell. Instead, he leaned back, watching her carefully. "But the
words, Natiya. Can you read—"

"I am good with languages," she said in Common, the
tongue of merchants. Then she loosened her grip on
the reins and allowed Mobray to walk ahead a bit so
she could speak to him without craning her neck. "Tell

me about the places you have visited," she said. "You must have gone everywhere."

He shook his head. "Not everywhere. Probably not as far as your Uncle Rened, but I have seen many strange things."

"Tell me!"

He had her full attention now, and he was stunned by how heady an experience it was—and on a level completely different than the physical. Was dragon magic strong enough to make her attractive to his mind as well? He hadn't thought so, but then again, there was a great deal about dragons that no one knew. No one alive anymore, that is. Either way, it made no difference. He could not resist talking to her, and so he began to share his tales.

"Many years ago, I heard of a dragon egg smuggled across the border to the south."

"How did you get past the border guards?" she asked. "I hear the Pitswains are more territorial than a marshrat."

He grinned. "You have read about them, haven't you? Well, did you know . . ."

And in this manner they moved through the first half of Wiaken Pass and onto a side track invisible if one did not know where to look.

CHAPTER NINE

"We're here."

Kiril opened his eyes. He'd known they were close for an hour or more. They had spoken for hours, their understanding of one another growing with every shared story, every lively discussion. He was still in awe of the mind hidden beneath her surly dancer persona. *D'greth,* she was brilliant! And so beautiful that he'd had to curl himself around his fists to keep himself from touching her. In the end, he'd shut his eyes and pretended to sleep rather than torture himself with the sight of her.

Looking at her now, he saw that she, too, was suffering. Her body was flushed, her dark red lips parted as she panted. She'd unbuttoned her shirt almost to her waist, leaving her flesh open to the cold air, but it obviously did little to cool the fever.

Their eyes met—hers from in front of Mobray, his from his perch atop—and they shared a moment of silent accord. This hunger, this drive was unnatural, but neither of them could deny it. All it would take was one movement, one accidental touch, and he would be on her like a ravaging beast. Like Jaseen on Sabina.

He spared a moment to wonder at the strength of the dragon magic. He had been in clutching caves before, but never a Queen's, and never one flushed with power as the hatching drew near. The power was incredible, overwhelming. It—

His thoughts were cut off as Natiya began to walk away.

With firm movements and hands that shook, she pushed aside a thin sanga bush, its pink-petaled flowers breaking in her grasp. The perfume it released was heady, an intoxicating sweet musk scent. Or perhaps it was Natiya he smelled, for she too gave off a scent that slipped into his mind, curling into his imagination like a serpent. He knew exactly where the scent would be strongest on her, and he wondered what exactly she would taste like there.

She had to work hard to get past the prickly leaves, and as he watched, her shirt caught on one of the broken branches. She tried to free herself, but then, with a sailor's curse, she simply shrugged out of the fabric. She spared one moment to look back at Kiril, her white shoulders and pink, pointed breasts gleaming in the afternoon light. They were trembling with the force of her breath, and he heard himself growl with need. The sound was bestial and should have served as a warning, telling him more clearly than anything that he was out of control. They both were. But it was too late, and the magic too strong.

"In here," she said, her voice husky and low. Then she ducked her head and slipped into a dark tunnel opening.

He followed her, shucking his coat and shirt as he went. Even his sword lay abandoned by Mobray, his only thought to follow her into that moist, dark place. He knew the ocean was close. Indeed, all clutching caves had to be accessible either by air or water, else how would the dragons find their way inside in the first place? But this was the back entrance—the human entrance—and he pushed inside without care or thought beyond reaching Natiya.

The tunnel was short, quickly opening into an expansive cavern. To one side, he saw the remains of the clutch—empty now. Way ahead, the sea opening had teeth of ice, but the sun shone through with a beauty that should have been astounding. Instead, he saw Natiya, her back to him as she stretched her arms out as if embracing the light. She seemed to be humming, her entire being vibrating with the sound, which the cavern picked up and echoed through his body, his mind, his soul. It made his hands shake as he pushed off his trousers. Even his boots lay discarded.

He barely felt the cold against his feet. His skin seemed to be on fire for her, but more than that, it felt sacrilegious somehow to enter this cavern while covered. He approached Natiya from behind, the humming echoing louder and louder. He gave no thoughts to his actions, only did what his body demanded. What the magic demanded.

Stepping behind her, he grasped her breasts with both hands. They were full and pointed, and as he felt them, she arched into his hold, dropping her head onto his shoulder and pressing her hips backward against him. Together they made sounds, hungry, needy moans that rolled through his senses like a tidal wave.

He let his hands slip down, across her flat belly, outlining her overly large belly jewel, which seemed to throb with her—with him. Then with both hands he pushed her thighs apart, letting his fingers dip into her moisture, and she purred with contentment. There was a scent—a thrilling, musky scent that was all hers—but when he touched her it became all-consuming, as if it had sunk through his skin into his very blood.

With a growl of hunger he pushed her forward. She went willingly onto all fours like a beast before him. Part of him somewhere objected. Part of him had wanted this to be beautiful and tender. But he had no restraint, and she was pushing back against him.

After that, he had no control at all. Grabbing hold of her hips, he sunk himself into her, mounting her like the dog he was. He barely felt the barrier of her maidenhead rip. Mostly he heard her gasp in surprise, but it was too late and she felt too good. He pulled out only to push into her again and again. Around them the cave continued to pulse with its own eerie light, and around him she became unbearably tight.

Sweet Amia, she was tight. And he was hard. He rammed into her again and again while her body tensed beneath him. He heard her gasp, her body quivering like a bowstring released. And then, goddess, she climaxed.

Her body gripped his prock until he nearly lost consciousness. Her grip was that tight. And then she began undulating, her whole body milking him. It was a climax, and yet it was more. So much more. He heard her scream, and his own roar mingled with the sound, echoed in the chamber. Still he rammed into her while she writhed beneath him. His release finally quaked through him, bursting him open while she continued to contract in wave after wave of ecstasy.

It had taken only moments, and yet they were the best damn moments of his life. And still she did not stop. When he stumbled, falling backward in his exhaustion, she followed him. How, he did not know, but she did, spinning around to straddle him with a quick, urgent motion.

The ground was sandy and surprisingly soft, but her thighs were hard where they gripped him. She looked down, her eyes reflecting an eerie light, and she kissed him deep and forcefully. She was the one who pressed his hands to her breasts. She was the one who pushed herself down onto his again ready prock.

How he was ready again, he hadn't a clue. Probably the dragon magic. Whatever the reason, he thanked the Father that he was. She slid around him, breaking her lips away from his enough to command, "More."

So he gave more. While she bucked atop him, he pushed into her. Her first climax was fading, the contractions slower, and she whimpered in frustration. He released a breast to sink a hand lower. With his wrist twisted awkwardly, he pressed his thumb into her. She growled in pleasure or need; he wasn't sure which. But he knew she arched into his hand even as he pulsed up into her.

Then it came upon them again: the rush and the explosion, again detonating in their bodies while the hum, the damn hum pushed him to greater depths, greater lengths of stamina and hunger and animal passion than he had ever imagined possible.

How long did they couple? They rolled around the cavern floor, joined over and over. He could not get enough, and she was insatiable, her climax unending. And whenever she began to flag, all he needed to do was press a finger into her or shift his hips against her, and it began for her again. And for him.

For them.

Delirium. Rhapsody.

Ravishment.

At last exhaustion claimed them both, and they collapsed, still joined, still pulsing, still reeling as the cavern hummed, unconscious.

Kiril woke to the sound of giggles. Not nice ones, not even soft, sweet, womanly ones, but coarse, male giggles. He jolted upright, but his body ached from head to toe and he collapsed backward with a soft moan. Dimly he realized he still cradled a soft, warm woman—Natiya—on the sandy bed that was the clutching cave. His sword was outside, lying on the ground along with most of his clothing. He was naked, as was she, the cool air drifting gently across their skin. He opened his eyes.

The giggling had come from soldiers. A dozen of them, all smirking, but nonetheless alert as they held their swords in their hands. He could tell by their uniforms that they were Dag Racho's personal guard, and he knew without looking that they were seasoned soldiers of unimpeachable loyalty to their Emperor. All around them the clutching cave continued to pulse with a yellowish-orange light. Then, just to his left, he heard a snort like the exhale of a great bellows, and his blood grew cold. It couldn't be, although he knew it was.

Twisting slightly, he saw the great Copper dragon lounging nearby with the large mouth pulled open just enough to reveal a grin of blackened teeth. Nearby stood Dag Racho, sword sheathed, his manner tense with excitement.

Not a good sign. In fact, a very bad sign, especially as the man sauntered forward, his eyes gleefully trained on Natiya's naked body.

"You're even better than I thought. Excellent work, Governor. Excellent work indeed."

Kiril resisted the urge to cover Natiya. It would be a silly, useless gesture, especially since he had nothing with which to cover either of them. Even so, he glanced down, looking for something, some way to ease her humiliation.

That's when he saw it: large and planted in her belly, a golden yellow-orange shape that pulsed, creating the light that reflected through the chamber.

The Queen dragon egg! Natiya had been the bearer all along.

He saw his own stupidity in a long series of flashes, a litany of failure. It had begun when Natiya first danced before him, her tiny red belly jewel flashing as she undulated with unnatural grace before him. No wonder he and everyone else had been mesmerized. Her dancing had been dragon-enhanced.

The second thought centered on his lust for her, unnatural and all-consuming—like in battle, he had once thought to himself. Except, he had never fought a female dragonborn, and so he had confused the energy of dragon-battle with lust.

How could he have been so stupid? He had held her, touched her, stroked her in every way possible, and yet he had never noticed how her belly jewel had grown. He had ascribed their lust to the nearness of the caves, to her attunement created when she was a child, his from battle and dragon blood. And yet, it had been beyond that. If he had spent two beats thinking, he would have realized it was more than simple nearness to the caves. Many souls lived near the caves. They did not go mindless with lust. Not unless they were a dragon-bearer near to hatching.

Natiya was stirring, and Kiril was fast running out of options. Dag Racho would surely kill her now. She was the last threat to his power. Kiril winced at that, but saw no way to avoid it, no way he could save her.

He had to focus on what he could do. Did Dag Racho know the danger the Queen egg posed to his own Copper? Could Kiril take the egg from her body while Dag Racho and his men were here? He needed that egg—or at least the pieces of it—for his and Sabina's plans. But wouldn't one of the guards be bright enough to wonder why Kiril collected the scattered remains of a dragon egg?

Meanwhile, the hatching magic was still moving full force. Natiya stretched languorously along his side. Still nestled against her bottom, his prock leaped to attention, if in fact it had ever been fully asleep. To his dismay, Dag Racho growled, a low sound echoed by the Copper, then echoing throughout the pulsing chamber. And all the while the soldiers shifted uneasily, no doubt feeling their own interest peaking, though clearly less strongly than for Kiril and the Emperor.

Kiril had to get Natiya out of there. He had to have time to think and to separate her from her egg, even though he knew it was already too late. No, with the hatching process started—though it still might take many days—Natiya was too bound to her egg to be separated. The umbilicus would be too buried in her body. It would kill her now to rip it out. And he could not see her die. Also, the thought of her violation—for surely that was what Dag Racho intended—made him growl his own warning of bestial territorialism. His body tensed as he shifted away from Natiya, readying to fight his Emperor.

All around him, the soldiers stared at him in shock. They had never seen anyone openly defy Dag Racho. Certainly not one in so vulnerable a position. Dag Racho, too, paused, though his expression was one of malicious delight.

"A fight?" he said. "Little Kiril, you do surprise me."

And at that, Natiya abruptly leaped to her feet, taking everyone by surprise. While Kiril was on his back, still growling at Dag Racho, she had been merely pretending to sleep. So she sprang to her feet, neatly avoiding the soldiers, who were caught flat-footed. But the Copper was not so dazed, nor so small. He easily blocked her exit while the now-alert soldiers closed in from behind.

There was nowhere for her to go, no way for her to fight. But she did so anyway, and Kiril admired her for it. He admired her so much that he intended to leap to her aid, though it was suicide for them both.

He never got the chance. More than one sword teased his throat, his belly, his bare ass, before he could do more than roll to a crouch. Meanwhile, Dag Racho continued to giggle—a low and nasty sound like a parody of his own Copper.

Kiril froze, unable to do more than watch helplessly while Dag Racho waved his men backward. Natiya was caught between the Copper and Dag Racho—the bastard Emperor's exposed prock clearly leading the way. She spun around, facing her oncoming doom, her eyes wild.

Then she saw Kiril, who tensed again. Their gazes met—just for a moment—and an infinity of agony passed between them. There was nothing he could do to save her; the soldiers wouldn't even let him stand.

The Emperor shifted, drawing his sword with the ringing sound of metal on metal. His blade was a heavy, jewel-encrusted monstrosity that only a man with dragon strength could wield. At least Natiya's death would be quick.

Kiril's thoughts spun, his soul twisting in pain as he tried to think of something to do, some way to save Natiya. But the soldiers were taking no chances and their blades still pressed against his skin. He couldn't so much as twitch without being impaled. And all the while, the Emperor's sword was raised higher and higher.

Kiril watched as Natiya tensed, though there was nowhere for her to go. Even if she avoided the blade, one quick burst of fire from the Copper and she would be engulfed in flame. As would Kiril and most of the soldiers, though only Kiril seemed aware of the danger.

Dag Racho had reached full extension, his sword tip seemingly kissing the cavern roof. And then, abruptly, the Emperor dropped to one knee. He bowed his head before Natiya, his every gesture . . . reverent?

Kiril blinked, not believing what he saw. But the sight remained: Dag Racho on one knee before Natiya. Even the Copper had lowered its head. The soldiers, too, seemed equally baffled; and then, once again, Kiril understood. Too late. Too slow.

"You're not going to kill her," he muttered to himself. And Dag Racho's next words confirmed it.

"Normally I would not take anything touched by a servant," he drawled, his tone low and husky. "But I understand about the hatching lust, indeed I do." He reached out, stroking his hand down Natiya's belly while her stomach rippled, the egg's light shifting weirdly through the cavern. "I understand," he crooned, "and I swear you will be satisfied, my Queen. But not here. Not now." He glanced disdainfully back at Kiril and his men. "It is too open." Then he abruptly pulled off his cloak and wrapped it around Natiya's nakedness.

She meant to struggle. Kiril could see it in her eyes, but Dag Racho's sword remained within a baby's breath of her neck. Any untoward movement and she would be skewered. So she stayed frozen and afraid while Kiril crouched on his knees.

Moments later, Dag Racho had her mounted before him on his Copper, a possessive arm wrapped around her waist, already fondling not her but the golden egg. Then, as the Copper began to turn, Dag Racho spared a moment for Kiril.

"My thanks, dragon-killer, but your services won't be needed this time." Then he grinned. "I cannot blame you for enjoying your pursuit, but you need not have gone through the ruse of imprisonment and rescue. Given time, she would have come to me." He nuzzled her neck while Natiya shrank away. "A woman needs her mate."

Kiril slowly straightened, pushing the swords away. Dag Racho allowed it because he had a harsher fate in store. Kiril could see it in the malicious gleam of his eyes as the Emperor continued to speak—casually—making sure Natiya understood exactly what had happened.

"Isn't it ironic that he orchestrated everything—your arrest, your escape, even that cozy little inn last night—all so he could gain your trust. And why? So you could lead him here, of course, so he could find the egg. And all the while, it was right here." He stroked her egg, pulling her tightly against him. "Tsk, tsk, dragon-hunter. Such effort and yet so blind."

Kiril watched, his heart sinking into his stomach as comprehension slipped across Natiya's features. Her eyes widened, her lips parted, and she shook her head in denial. "It can't be true. All the things we said. All the things we shared . . ."

He met her anguished gaze, and his hands tightened to fists. It had all been true—or almost all of it. The tales he told her, the confidences he whispered: they had been real. His feelings were real! But if he said that aloud, his life would be forfeit. Dag Racho killed anyone who was not completely loyal to him. If Kiril showed the least bit of allegiance to Dag Racho's new "queen," he would be dead in a heartbeat. The best he could do was raise his hands and shrug. "I serve my Emperor," he said.

"It was all a trick?" she gasped. "You never cared for me . . . at all?"

"Do not feel bad, my dear," the Emperor interrupted before Kiril could speak. "He is legendary at court for the women he has seduced. Were you truly under the delusion that he loved you?" He gave a dramatic gasp. "He did say he loved you, didn't he? Or were you not even worthy of that petty lie?"

Kiril jerked forward, despite the cut of at least three blades. At that moment he intended to rip the man's arrogant smirk right off his face, no matter the cost. But the soldiers were efficient. A single punch to his kidney and he dropped to the ground. Then once again, the thrice-cursed Emperor spoke.

"Tell her, my dragon-hunter. Tell her the truth. You owe her that, at least. Tell her that she meant nothing more to you than her knowledge of the Queen's clutching cave."

Kiril swallowed his own bile. He knew Dag Racho's game, even if she did not. He had to echo exactly what the Emperor said or he would die. The bastard wouldn't even have to give the order. His men were trained to re-act instantaneously if Kiril said anything but what he had been told to say.

He nodded.

"Say it aloud, dragon-hunter," Dag Racho said, his voice low with deadly threat. "And say it to her face."

Kiril lifted his head. He had no choice with a blade beneath his chin. He almost took the coward's way out, almost dove forward onto the sword rather than speak the lie. But suicide would not help Natiya. With his death, she would be completely alone. So he said the words. He looked into her eyes and uttered all he had been ordered to say. "It was a ruse, Natiya. It was all a lie."

He watched in despair as the light faded from her eyes. A dark fury slipped into her expression, and he nearly cried out at the sight.

"Well, my Queen," Dag Racho purred. "What shall we do with him? Do we reward him for his perfidy? For be-traying one so innocent as you? Or—"

"No." She did not let him finish his question. Kiril looked up enough to see her face shift from angry to im-placable as the beast inside her took over. Kiril watched it happen and felt the tiny spark of hope die within him. But still it hurt to hear her say it. Worse yet, it ached to know he deserved it.

"Kill him," she ordered; then she turned away.

Dag Racho laughed in appreciation, sparing one last moment to glance at the soldiers of his personal guard. "You heard my Queen," he said. Then he grinned. "You need not even make it fast." And with that, his Copper burst into the air, flying over the water with firm, elegant strokes. As if in a last good-bye, the beast released a plume of fire, either out of respect or merely showing off for the Queen, Kiril didn't know, nor did he care. He had his own problems now:

A dozen seasoned soldiers with orders to kill, and him stark naked in the middle of it all.

CHAPTER TEN

Some cages were better than others, Natiya thought as she sank into the steamy heat of a perfumed bath. From the moment she'd opened her eyes to see Dag Racho and his Copper breathing down on her, she'd expected a quick and fiery end. Instead, the Emperor had flown her to his palace, fed her a feast and set her up in lavish quarters the likes of which she never dreamed existed. He'd also posted guards for her "protection," warning her that men in the court would want her dead.

She didn't believe him, of course. So the moment the Emperor had left to attend matters of state, she had set about subverting her keepers. They wouldn't leave her rooms when she wanted to rest. They allowed her to change her clothing behind a privacy screen, but they wouldn't leave her bedroom. They did, however, agree to let her have a hot bath in seclusion.

She'd quickly entered the huge tiled room, stripping off the cloak as she went. Then she'd turned to stare at the waterfall, greenery and lush towels heated over a vent in the floor. Natiya hadn't even known that such things were possible. A quick glance had told her there was no escape from the bath except back to her bedroom, and so she'd succumbed to temptation and sunk down into hot, wet heaven. She even had food available: a tray of fruit within easy reach from the edge of the pool. She was starving, of course, and soon she was swallowing tiny madda grapes with her eyes closed, while thoughts of cages and guards faded away.

An image of Kiril surfaced quickly in her thoughts, but she resolutely pushed it aside. She would not think of him naked and surrounded by swords. She would not dwell on the fact that she'd known not to trust a governor and a dragon-hunter. And yet, when he'd looked at her so sadly in prison, when he'd folded her in his arms and then found a way to escape . . . But that had all been a lie. *He* was the one who had put her in prison in the first place. And it didn't matter now because he was dead, dead, dead!

She cut off a sob and submerged herself totally. The heat enveloped her and the water cleansed her thoughts, or so she pretended. Then, when she surfaced, she resolutely pushed away all thoughts of Kiril, his betrayal, and—*d'greth!*—what they had done together. She would not think at all. For the moment, she would lie in her bath, eat sweet grapes, and . . .

Think about the sharp prick of a knife at her throat. Natiya froze. The blade tickled cold against her throat. She didn't open her eyes, but she could feel the icy press of steel, especially as it differed so radically from the steamy heat of her perfumed bath.

If she could have, she would have sighed. Even though she sat frozen in a jewel-encrusted tub, part of her still registered shock that Dag Racho had been right. He had warned her that many at court would want her dead. But she had sent her protectors away, and now the blade began to press harder against her neck.

"Do I have your attention?" a female voice hissed against her ear.

"Yes," Natiya answered equally softly, opening her eyes, turning ever so slightly to see a dark-haired woman crouching beside her. Natiya frowned, wondering if she knew the woman. She certainly seemed familiar enough. Then the dragon egg flashed her a memory of Kiril and this woman sitting at the table that first night Natiya had danced for him. What was her name?

Sabina.

Natiya would have nodded, but with the blade against her throat, all she could do was stare at the dark-haired woman and wait. Fortunately, the longer this went on, the more chance that a servant or the guards would discover what was happening.

"Where is Kiril?" Sabina's voice was a low hiss of deadly intent, but her gaze hopped around, betraying her nervousness. She was not a woman used to violence.

Natiya waited. *Now.* Sabina had looked to the door—only for a moment—but that was all Natiya needed. She had discovered in the last few hours that her reflexes were even faster now; whether because of the egg's maturity or because she wasn't dancing three shows a night, Natiya didn't know. Neither did she care. What mattered was that it gave her the speed required to grab Sabina's wrist, enough to wrench it and the dagger away from her throat.

Less than a beat later, Sabina was flat on her back, a dripping Natiya pinning her to the cold, wet tile. Only then did she bother answering Sabina's question.

"Kiril is dead. I gave the order myself."

She watched Sabina's eyes go dead, and she knew the woman had been expecting this answer. Knew it, but had apparently hoped for something different. Yet even as she lay there, her eyes draining of life, her spirit would not give in.

"How could you do that?" the woman whispered. "He was our only hope."

"I make my own hope. And he was a liar." He had lied to get between her legs, and she had allowed it. She had believed he was different, and she, who had kept herself closed and contained for so long, had opened up to him.

Which made her a fool. That more than anything else fueled her hatred. And while Natiya was filled with self-loathing, Sabina found the strength to fight back. Twisting hard on the tile, Sabina shoved her captor backward. Natiya could have countered the move, but she had no heart to hurt another woman duped by a skillful liar. So she sat back, sinking onto her heels as she watched her adversary.

Sabina scrambled for her dagger, words boiling out of her. "Of course he lied to you. It's the only way to survive in Ragona. You were using each other. You never would have gotten to the clutching caves without him."

Natiya didn't answer except to flinch at the woman's words.

"But I know him. He cared for you. He probably even warned you."

"He had me arrested!" Natiya shot back, rather than admit that Sabina was right. Kiril had warned her. And if she doubted her memory, the egg was right there with another flash of recall, this time of Kiril in her bedroom, his hair slightly askew, a rogue's smile on his face.

Neither I nor Dag Racho can afford to leave you be.

She was not stupid. She'd known then that he had been warning her, telling her that both men would do anything to get to her secrets. Already weary of her own thoughts, she sighed. "He is dead," she said. "There is nothing either of us can do to change that now." Then Natiya stood, pulling a silk robe about her.

"How?" Sabina pressed. "How did he die?"

"A dozen of the personal guard with orders to kill," Natiya responded flatly, unwilling to admit that she too wondered if he could have escaped. "He was unarmed." And naked after their lovemaking.

"I will kill you for this." Sabina's voice had settled into an equally flat statement of fact.

"Why?" Natiya asked, genuine interest prompting her question. What were these two to each other? "You were not lovers, so I have killed no one important to you. He said he does not even support you with money since you have your own. What does he mean to you?"

Sabina stared at her, those dark eyes widening in horror and disgust. "You are a beast," she breathed softly. "The dragon has already taken you. Or perhaps there was nothing there to begin with."

Natiya reared back in shock, stung by the words without knowing why. "No—," she began, but Sabina gave her no time.

"He could have saved us all," she breathed, her body shifting as she adjusted the dagger in her palm. "Until you." And with that, she lunged.

Natiya had expected it. Indeed, she was already tensed, preparing for the attack, but she never got the chance. Two guards leapt between them, catching Sabina in mid-swing, restraining her with brutal force. Natiya frowned, annoyed with herself for not sensing their presence, for being too preoccupied with thoughts of Kiril to hear their approach.

Meanwhile, Sabina screamed and fought, her furious cries echoing off the tiles. It did no good. She was no match for the men, who quickly dragged her away. She was gone before Natiya could figure out what to say. What to think.

"She doesn't know, does she?"

For the third time that day, Natiya flinched at the surprise presence of another soul. She didn't need to turn, though, for she recognized Dag Racho's voice. And more than that, she felt his presence—a nervous crawl on her skin.

She shuddered, pulling the robe about herself to cover the gooseflesh. "How . . . ?" Her voice trailed away, unsure how to phrase her question.

"How did I sneak up on you unawares?" he asked calmly.

She nodded.

"There is a way to mask the dragon inside you, a way to hide from others, even those with their own dragons. You will learn it in time." He smiled as he spoke, and she was surprised to notice how handsome he appeared. Though he was accounted over a century old, he seemed nearly as young as Kiril. His body was lean and strong, though less angular, more soft. Perhaps it was the clothing he wore—soft velvets in golden hues—but he appeared celestial. And when he smiled, his teeth shone like polished pearls and his hair glinted reddish-gold in the fading sunlight. He looked every inch an Emperor, and Natiya felt a stirring of desire.

She knew that it was the hatching time that sparked such feelings in her. They were a pale comparison to the overwhelming hunger that had driven her to Kiril, but she recognized them nonetheless. So she stepped away from Dag Racho in an effort to diminish the lure.

She saw annoyance flash briefly in his eyes, but it was quickly suppressed as he settled on a bench near the bathing pool. "So, what shall we do with the impetuous Sabina?" He smiled, inviting Natiya to join him in this discussion as though he truly valued her opinion.

Natiya did not trust him. This man was evil incarnate. He had ruled for a century with a heavy fist. He had killed her parents and destroyed everything of value.

Except, right now, he seemed . . . nice. She bit her lip, completely confused. "What doesn't Sabina understand?" she asked, referencing his earlier comment.

"Hmmm?" His gaze slid leisurely from her stomach to her face. Natiya flushed, her hands instinctively slipping to cover the egg and her now swollen belly.

He grinned, as if he found humor in her movement. "She doesn't know that you intend to kill me." He arched a single sculpted brow at her gasp. "That is why you incubated the Queen, isn't it? To come and destroy me? Revenge for killing your parents."

Natiya glanced around, searching for anything—a weapon, a means of escape. Nothing. Nothing was at hand, and soldiers right outside. With her dragon-enhanced abilities she might be able to avoid two, maybe three of them, but she doubted she stood a chance against the entire regiment of castle guards.

Dag Racho's laughter cut through the air, warm and filled with good cheer, abruptly interrupting her thoughts. "Relax, my dear, I have no intention of harming you. Would I have fed and bathed you, set you up in my private quarters if I planned to kill you?"

"These are your chambers?"

He grinned. "Yes, my dear. My private bath. And my bedchamber is that way." He waved negligently to the wall opposite her bedroom. She didn't see a doorway, but she knew from her escape from prison that doors could be easily hidden.

She tensed her shoulders, preparing herself for anything. "What do you want from me?" she asked, hating the way her voice trembled.

"Don't worry," he answered. "I have no designs on your virtue, such as it is." Then he grinned. "At least not until we get to know each other a little better. Debauching the innocent lost its appeal a few decades ago." He winked at her. "Though every once in a while, as a change of pace . . ." He let his voice trail away before abruptly bursting into laughter that filled the room. "Oh, you should see your face, my dear. I do believe your eyes are the size of that egg you carry."

Natiya felt herself flush again as she looked away. The Emperor was nothing that she expected, and she wasn't sure how to proceed.

"Perhaps you should get dressed. I have ordered clothing placed in your bedchamber. I have some business to attend." He sighed. "It is the little details that are so bothersome, you know. Constant and unending." He glanced up with a smile. "But I have cleared the rest of my schedule so that we may dine together."

She shook her head, reluctant to spend more time than necessary in the Emperor's confusing presence. "I already ate."

He chuckled. "Yes, I know. But as I recall, I was constantly hungry before the hatching. And belly-horned, but I suppose you already know about that."

Natiya felt her hands clench, though in anger or mortification, she didn't know. "I have no wish to bed you," she snapped, avoiding her confusion by rushing headlong into anger. "And I will hurt you if you try to force me." She lifted her chin, looking directly into his flat gaze as his grin slowly widened.

"I'm counting on it," he drawled, a low, sinister sound that sent chills down her spine.

She swallowed, tensing for an attack when—abruptly—he once again burst into laughter, all vestiges of the threat gone.

"I am joking, my dear! Ah, please allow an old man his sense of humor." Then he stepped toward her, stopping only when she began to shy backward. "Come, come, I simply wish to get to know you. We will share a meal and some conversation. I promise, nothing more."

"I don't believe you," she said, though in truth she didn't know what she believed anymore. Kiril false and the Emperor kind? Nothing made sense.

"Such honesty," Dag Racho said, admiration coloring his tone. "I had forgotten how refreshing it is." Then he shrugged. "Well, no matter. I have to eat, and you have to eat, if not for yourself, then for the Queen. Go. Get dressed." He motioned her off to her bedchamber. "We will talk more later."

"Not with the guards in my room."

He shrugged. "Very well. They will watch from just outside your door. But do not go beyond these rooms.

Not until I am sure you are safe." And with that, he turned and left the bath. She watched long enough to see him exit into the hallway with all her guards. Then the door shut and she was left alone.

She walked slowly, cautiously into her bedroom. Like everything else, it was luxurious. The bed was huge and covered in silk. The bedposts had gold with bronze filigree trailing beautifully throughout. A huge closet was made of the finest black . . . she didn't know what. Not metal, not wood, but some combination of both, and inside it hung a dizzying array of dresses. Ornate, subtle, warm or the sheerest gauze—she found all types, each with a relaxed waist for her growing belly.

Turning slowly around, she realized she had everything she had ever wanted in her most decadent fantasies. And yet, she felt empty and tired. Food had not helped. The bath had not helped. She doubted even sleep would make her feel better.

Yes, inside she still felt empty, even as the egg she carried continued to pulse and grow with alarming speed. Thankfully, it was not ready to burst out of her. Once they'd left the Queen's cave, the need—even the size of it—had shrunk. Not greatly, but enough that she noticed. It wanted to be born in the cave.

She still talked to it, still communicated thoughts, opinions and interpretations, but now it remained noticeably silent. She decided that was perfectly normal: The egg seemed mostly to reflect back her thoughts, and since Natiya could not sort through her experiences, the egg had no opinion to reflect. It had only images and memories over which the egg seemed to mull, with annoying frequency. As soon as Natiya found a moment's respite from her conflicting emotions, the egg flashed her a memory: Kiril with a tender smile and even more tender touch. Kiril in her bedroom, speaking calmly, respectfully to her, and then letting her decide her course. Kiril, his face twisted with worry, as he stormed into her interrogator's room.

Except, it had all been a ruse, Natiya reminded herself. A big, fat lie. He was the one who'd had her arrested, not Dag Racho. He was the one who'd ordered her stolen out of bed and dragged into that dungeon. And he was the one who'd created the very interrogation from which he rescued her. That's what Dag Racho had made clear on the flight to his palace. And even had he not said so, she had seen the truth on Kiril's face.

D'greth, she had been such a fool! To think that anyone, even a governor, could orchestrate an escape from prison. She was glad—ecstatic—that the foul creature was dead. And even more thrilled that she had been the one to order it.

And yet, as soon as she thought that, the egg flashed her the image of his face: the anguish in his eyes when she had been caught by the Emperor, and the absolute fury of impotence that he could not protect her. She tried to tell herself that his expression was just another one of his lies. She could not know what he thought, could not believe anything he said. And yet, the feelings had seemed so true.

She sighed, once again turning toward the flowing gowns hanging before her. She selected one of deepest brown, soft enough to be fur but light enough to feel like a second skin. She chose it not for its beauty, but because it was simple and would not confine her too greatly if she needed to run. And for her feet, she found a pair of slippers. Not the sturdy boots Kiril had obtained for her, but delicate slippers meant for a lady.

She slipped them on her hard and callused feet, sighing with joy. She had never possessed anything so fine. Indeed, she thought the footwear an exorbitant waste of money. What use were slippers that would tear at the slightest pebble, that offered little in way of protection or warmth? Their only value was in looking pretty—for a short time—and for feeling like the gentlest of clouds when she walked on the flat stone corridors of a castle.

A silly waste of money, and yet, she had secretly coveted slippers such as these all her life. Now she had an entire wardrobe full of them. It left her feeling stunned and overwhelmed. And secretly so gleeful she took an experimental twirl just to see how they would feel to dance in. Glorious. They felt glorious.

But the joy of her dance soon faded, and she found herself by the window, staring out at a sunset that painted the sky in shimmering colors. Her muscles twitched with the movement, unused to remaining idle for so long. She had been in this castle for less than a day and already she missed dancing. She missed the outdoors. *D'greth*, she even missed Talned's filthy dockside bar.

If only she could wander outside, could move beyond the confines of this opulent room. She stepped to the door, pulling it open only to see four guards turn and smile at her. The nearest stepped inside.

"How may I help you, Empress?"

She blinked. "Empress?"

"Is there something you need? I shall send for it immediately."

"N-no, no," she stammered. "I thought I would walk a bit. Ease the strain—"

"Apologies, my lady, but it is not safe. You must stay—"

"But I wanted—"

"—inside. For your own safety. I will send for someone to read to you. Would you like that?"

"No. I want to take a walk. You can accompany me, if you like." She smiled as winningly as possible, hoping to find an opportunity for escape. If he were one to be swayed by a smile. If . . .

"Gravest apologies, but I cannot. The Emperor would feed me to . . ." He didn't have to complete his sentence; they all knew that the Copper had large food requirements.

"But—"

"No, my lady." Then he paused. "Should I send someone—"

"No. No, thank you." Then she backed up and firmly shut the heavy door. She barely restrained herself from kicking it in frustration. Instead, she whipped around and went back to the window. Then she leaned forward, wondering if she could fit through.

No. Even if she could get her shoulders through, her belly was too large. And besides, she was nearly at the very top. Without a dragon to fly her to the ground, there was nowhere for her to go.

So she was stuck inside a plush bedroom with nothing but her thoughts and her egg for company. Once she would have thought this heaven. Now, she very much feared she was going mad. One day cooped up in this room and she . . . what?

She was suddenly looking forward to dinner with Dag Racho.

Natiya belched loudly, then pressed her hand to her mouth in mortification. "I am so sorry," she breathed, appalled by her rudeness. It had been so long since her parents or Uncle Rened had tried to instill polite behavior in her, she struggled to remember how one should behave among the upper class.

"Not at all, not at all. My chef is from that northern land we discussed earlier. And there, such actions are considered a compliment."

"Really?" Natiya asked, intrigued. "Well, then I . . . I hope he thinks . . . I mean . . ." She swallowed, hating that she felt so awkward in such lavish surroundings. "The meal was divine. Thank you."

The Emperor grinned. "I shall make sure he learns of your appreciation." Then he nodded to one of the burly guards who doubled as their waiter. The man disappeared, leaving no fewer than five other guard-servants spaced discreetly about the small dining chamber.

"Thank you," Natiya said out of politeness, but also out of true gratitude. The food had been the best she'd ever tasted, even surpassing Uncle Rened's table when he entertained wealthy customers. Her every need—whether for wine or a clean lapcloth—had been swiftly and respectfully met, often before she even realized the lack. And best of all, the conversation, like her companion, had been fascinating.

The Emperor had begun by complaining, albeit mildly, about the difficulty he faced in establishing trade relations with the northern country of Gambolt. He even asked her advice on the best plan of attack when dealing with northern thieves. She hadn't ever heard of any northern bandits. Uncle Rened had said nothing about roving bands of murdering thieves, but the Emperor was certain they existed. And when she pressed for details, he painted an ugly picture of death and destruction that she had no ability to counter. Without actually traveling to Gambolt, she couldn't know if the country was on the verge of civil war or invasion. And so she gave a simple, noncommittal answer, and then was stunned when he appeared disappointed. But his good humor quickly returned as he began asking simple questions about her life, seemingly fascinated by daily life on the docks.

It was a heady experience for her: having a man, especially so powerful and handsome a man, hanging on her every word. He listened attentively, pressing her for details when she skipped over things, sympathizing when she recounted even the slightest hurt or misunderstanding—which had naturally come often, given her secret. But he understood. He, too, had worked hard to hide his own egg so many cycles ago.

She knew he was merely gathering information, learning about her in the easiest of ways. But he was so charming and skillful that she found herself talking even when she resolved to change the topic. In the end, she wondered why she was so uneasy. After all, there was little to say about her life beyond dancing, serving drinks and hiding the egg. But his charm and wit had her revealing details about her life that went far beyond what she normally told anyone.

So when she at last rose up from the table, she felt sated, content and bizarrely guilty for enjoying the evening so much. In truth, she was reluctant to see it end, especially as her only other option was to return to her empty bedchamber and her thoughts.

"Please, could we not walk around the castle some? I am so weary of my bedchamber."

He turned, blinking in surprise. "Of course!" he responded congenially. "I had forgotten how the hatching time makes one edgy. I remember feeling trapped inside, as if the very walls were going to fall upon me."

"Exactly!" she whispered, realizing how perfectly he summarized her feelings.

"Then we must stroll the upper grounds. Besides, the Copper has been anxious to see you." He extended his arm as if she were a true lady, and Natiya blushed as she delicately placed her fingertips on his sleeve.

He was warm, of course, his body radiating an unnatural heat that was part of being dragonborn. But she found she liked the physical sensation of power that she got whenever she came near him. How much stronger it was when she touched his arm, and how delicious a feeling.

Natiya smiled as Dag Racho's guards fell into place around them: two in front, two beside, two behind. It made for a wide and rather ridiculous party, and the Emperor winked at her as if to share his amusement.

"They get upset if I go anywhere without them," he confided in an undertone. "Truly, they can be annoying, but they have their uses."

She frowned as they began to climb stairs that led to the highest floor of the castle. "But surely you can tell them to go away. If you wish for privacy."

He shrugged, the gesture resigned. "Danger lurks everywhere for a man such as myself." He turned and looked earnestly at her. "And for a woman like you."

She began to object, but he stopped halfway up the stairs and pressed a finger to her lips.

"Hear me out. We have power, you and I. Power that everyone would take from us if they could. And then they would abuse it, my dear, visiting horrible death and destruction upon these lands." He shuddered. "I have seen it, sweet Natiya. I was raised in it." Then he looked away, quietly climbing the rest of the way to the open roof. "They would abuse the power, and I will die before I see that happen again."

His voice had the low throb of a vow, and Natiya looked at him in stunned surprise. He must have realized the shock that echoed through her, because he turned to her, smiling ruefully at her expression.

"I forgot. You think I abuse the power, don't you?"

"Of course not," she responded quickly, because he so obviously wanted her to say just that. But then he shook his head, denying her very words.

"Of course you do. Why else would you have incubated an egg except to wrest the power from me?"

She opened her mouth to deny it; though how she could reasonably deny the truth was beyond her. It didn't matter in any event, because he kept speaking, forestalling her words.

"It's only natural. I killed your parents." He sighed. "I know you will not believe me, but truly it was necessary. They—"

"Were plotting against you. They gave the Platinum egg to Dag Jaseen."

He raised a single eyebrow and turned to her. "So you know."

She nodded. "I learned it from . . ." She couldn't say Kiril's name.

As if reading her thoughts, he nodded. "Of course. Kiril would know."

"Not everything," Natiya countered. "He thinks that all dragons are evil. He truly believes this."

"I know," Dag Racho said mournfully as they crossed the last threshold onto the roof. There, framed in stately glory before them, sat the Emperor's Copper dragon. The beast's eyes glittered like jewels, reflecting the brilliance of a hundred lightstaves. His wings were behind him, but as Natiya approached, he began to unfold them.

She had never been this close to a dragon before. The Copper was huge, standing three times her size, his wingspan over double that. And as she watched, he tensed on powerful legs before springing into the sky, a plume of fire heralding his flight. The wind from his massive wings nearly knocked her off her feet, though Dag Racho, she noted, stood rock solid.

Swiftly the Copper was lost in the night sky, only the occasional trace of fire marking his flight. Indeed, she would have lost interest were it not for her host's face. His eyes were closed in ecstasy, his lips slightly parted. His face was turned up, as if to the wind, and his shoulders were pulled back, his arms twitching beneath his thin silver shirt, as if he, too, flew.

As if . . . Well, of course he *was* flying, she realized with shock. Dag Racho was bonded to his dragon. That meant, if he chose, he could experience every sensation of the Copper's amazing flight. And she would, too, in less than two weeks when her Queen hatched. She would be able to fly.

The thought was as astounding as it was riveting. It would be like dancing, only better. It would be boundless and joyful and everything that she loved about dancing except she could do it in the sky!

"A hundred cycles, and I still love it," Dag Racho murmured by her side. "Just as you will, a hundred cycles from now."

She looked at him, searching his expression for signs of deceit. She so desperately wanted his words to be true, but she had lived in the shadows for so long; it hardly seemed possible that she could ever soar openly into the skies.

"Watch," he ordered, his arm pointing to the sky. "He's coming back."

And indeed the Copper was. At first she had no guide to his location beyond Dag Racho's outstretched arm. But then she saw a dark smudge blocking out the stars. The inky cloud seemed to grow larger and larger until suddenly it was lit by one last stream of fire, revealing the Copper in all its glory. She gasped, stunned by the display. Her egg, too, seemed to appreciate it, twisting and pulsing with a kind of happiness Natiya had never felt from it before.

Then the Copper spread its wings, extending its powerful claws before it dropped back down to the stone roof. She expected to feel the thud of impact as the huge creature landed, but there was no sound, no vibration. He had landed as light as a feather with barely a breeze against her face to mark his presence. The Copper stood facing her, eyes once again glittering from the lightstaves, and slowly lowered its head before her feet.

She held her breath in awe. Unable to stop herself, she reached out and stroked his nose, feeling the cool scales and thinking them the most sensuous texture in the world. That was when she heard the noise: a low rumble that throbbed through the stones at her feet.

"He's purring!"

"Of course he is. He knows his beautiful Queen."

She turned to her host, seeing his smile and gentle expression, and she felt such an overpowering wave of love, it nearly buckled her knees.

"Kiril is wrong," she said with absolute conviction. "They aren't evil. They're wonderful."

CHAPTER ELEVEN

"And what about me?" Dag Racho asked, his expression almost sad. "Am I evil?"

Natiya hesitated, unsure how to answer. At one time, she had certainly thought he was. But now? She didn't know, and so she sought to divert the topic. "How did you find the egg?" she asked. "Where did you hide until the hatching?"

"Ah, well, that is a tale and a half. Are you sure you want to spend so much time with such an evil man?"

She flushed, stroking the Copper's nose in her nervousness. "I am beginning to rethink my earlier opinions," she said slowly.

Once again his laugh startled her, filling the night sky with the sound—both gay and somehow infinitely sad. And when he was done, he grabbed two cushions and dropped them beside his dragon. "Well, that is something, I suppose," he said, as he offered her his hand.

She went willingly, settling down on the cushion right behind the Copper's left haunch.

"Lean back," Dag Racho urged as he sat and rested his head against the creature. "We like you there."

She did as she was told, feeling the dragon's heat enfold her from behind, while beside her, Dag Racho radiated his own type of heat. It was not sexual, although she could easily interpret it as such. It was more a banked intensity, as if at a moment's notice he could suddenly scorch someone with his fire. She knew it was silly, and yet she could not shake the feeling, though he did no more than smile drowsily at her. There was a danger about him that both thrilled and terrified her. So she remained wary even as the gentle thrum of the Copper's heartbeat tried to lull her.

"How did you get the egg?" she pressed, when it looked like Dag Racho was relaxing into sleep.

He took a deep breath as his gaze focused on something far away. "My parents were academics." He glanced at her. "We have that in common, you know. Except mine studied the sea. My father studied plants, my mother the sea creatures, and so we spent a great deal of time on the shores near the clutching caves."

She nodded, understanding what he was getting at. "You found the clutch."

He shrugged. "Actually, my sister did. She thought they were pretty stones, but I knew what they were."

"How many eggs did you find?"

"Five or six. But my Copper was the best. Sarah took the Coral."

"And the others?"

He shrugged. "We smashed them."

Natiya flinched, horrified at the thought.

He sighed, as if understanding her emotions. "You have to understand how different it was back then. I was only ten, but we all had suffered. Dragonlord after dragonlord fought over the smallest things. If the land were to survive—if the world were to survive—the other dragonlords would have to be defeated. I was only ten, but even then I understood."

"And so you incubated your Copper, and your sister a Coral. What did your parents think?"

Again, his shrug was casual. "They didn't know for

many months. And by the time they discovered, it was too late. We both had already bonded with the eggs. To separate us then would have meant disaster."

Natiya frowned, matching his words with what she already knew. "But that's not true. It takes at least a cycle before separation becomes dangerous."

He grinned, as if pleased that she'd questioned him. "Ah, but you see, my parents didn't know that." He leaned forward, touching her arm in his earnestness. "Even then I knew what I wanted, knew what it would take to get there." He sighed. "Well, perhaps not everything, but I knew enough." His grin abruptly returned as he looked out into the blackened world beyond his castle. "And I was right. Look at everything I have achieved."

She didn't answer. Her eyes were busy watching his face, gauging his shifting moods and trying to guess what he wasn't telling her. She didn't know, of course, and more than that, he had the air of someone sharing a secret—as if he had waited for many cycles just to talk to someone, to tell someone his tale.

He glanced at her, shaking his head. "You don't know, do you? I forget how young people really are these days. Everyone who remembers my time died long ago, and you children don't remember how terrible it was."

She had no choice but to agree. "I'm sorry. I was only an average student, and history never seemed that important."

"But it is!" he exclaimed. "It will show you, it will tell you . . ." His voice trailed away.

"What?" she wondered. But even as she asked the question, she knew the answer: History would tell her what he had achieved. So she touched his hand where it lay on her arm. "I was a silly child. Please, will you tell me now?"

He brightened at that, his smile warming. Behind them, the Copper rumbled a contented purr. "Are you sure you want to hear such a dry, boring tale of cycles gone by?" His response was a token protest that Natiya was happy to brush aside.

"Of course I do. Please, tell me what you did."

He grinned, obviously relishing the telling. "I was young when I found the egg, but I rapidly grew, as did the egg. Ah, it was a dark time, all those years ago. We heard daily reports of dragons eating children. Babies by the dozen. Of the crops destroyed by dragon fire, of the acres and acres of farmland fouled by the beasts. And with every report, I swore I would see it change. I vowed with every breath that I would end the destruction."

"And you did," she said, caught up not by the tale but by the animation in his face, the light that seemed to glow from inside him as he spoke.

"It was my dream, and yes, I have seen it fulfilled. But it cost me greatly."

She nodded, though in truth she could not imagine the price he had paid. She only knew of the secrecy and daily fear that came with incubation. "How did you hide the egg?"

"Ahh," he said with a sweet smile, "that was the easiest part of all. As I said, my parents knew what we were doing—my sister and I. When the time came, they simply went on one of their research trips near the clutching caves. My Copper was hatched there."

"Did . . . did it hurt?" She hadn't meant to ask that, but the words slipped out, and his eyes softened as he turned to her.

"It is not painful so much as . . ." He wet his lips, searching her face for something. Whatever it was, she apparently didn't have it, because he soon patted her hand. "I will help you through. Truly, it is much easier—much safer—with someone who understands."

She nodded to cover a tightness in her chest. The hatching was fast approaching, and she was not at all sure she wished to be around Dag Racho when it came. But if he were the only one who truly understood the process, then where else could she go? Who would help her? Her only thought was Kiril. As a dragon-hunter, he probably understood more than most exactly what was in store. Except, he was dead. By her own order. So she had best learn as much as she could from the only other person who would know.

"Please tell me about it," she urged.

The Emperor shook his head. "It is not a tale I wish to recount tonight. Suffice it to say that . . ." He sighed. "Well, my parents did not survive. They did not know how violent the hatching can be. How difficult." He twisted to stroke the side of his dragon. "But I had my Copper, and we did just fine together."

"I am so sorry. That must have been terrible for you both."

"Hmm?" He turned back to her, but his gaze lingered on his dragon.

"Your sister. At least you had your sister."

He frowned. "Oh yes. Well, she had her Coral, but that is a much lower dragon, you know, nothing like the metals. My Copper." He focused on her. "Your Golden Queen."

She nodded, uncomfortable with the way his gaze caressed her. It was so soon after Kiril and she . . . She pushed away the memories. She simply wasn't comfortable with sexual overtures of any nature, and so she shifted position, gently easing her leg away from his touch even as she kept her eyes trained on him. "Tell me more about after the hatching. They say it takes a while for the man and dragon to adjust to one another."

His eyes flashed a moment in frustration, but it was quickly covered as he reached out, this time to stroke her cheek. "My dear, you know—"

She caught his hand, startled by the heat that abruptly arced between them when their palms touched. She gasped, trying to pull away, but his grip was strong, and he held her hand in place—palm to palm—while his eyes seemed to blaze.

"Please," she whispered. "I'm so confused."

His eyes seemed to gentle, but he still held her hand imprisoned. "I know you are," he said softly. "Just give it a moment. We must become accustomed to one another."

Inside her belly, the egg twisted, seeming to churn and move. She felt her stomach muscles contract, trying to fight the egg's agitation, but its contortions were too strong.

"Let it happen," the Emperor urged.

She had no choice; she couldn't pull away no matter how much she tried. Power—she had no other word for it—pulsed between their palms, and she heard her breath come in stuttering gasps. Her body tingled with the energy coursing through her, and one look at Dag Racho's face showed her that he, too, felt the waves that crashed through her body. Behind them, the Copper also tensed, his tail and wings twitching, his body beginning to undulate. She watched in frightened horror as Dag Racho's prock thickened inside his pants, the bulge clear even in the shadows of the Copper's wings.

Then Dag Racho leaned forward, his hot breath fanning her cheeks, sending ripples along her neck and shoulders. "I know it is too soon for you," he rasped, "so I will not take you now. But we are fated to be together, Natiya. My Copper. Your Gold. It cannot be any other way. You need to understand that."

She did. She did understand, and if she didn't, the clench of lust that twisted with the egg in her belly more than explained matters. They were two dragonborn—male and female—and the draw between was undeniable.

"Not now!" she gasped, planting her feet and hauling back on her arm. Her move was abrupt and violent, but even so she sensed that she did not escape of her own power. The Emperor released her, allowing her to scramble backward only to be caught between the Copper's foreleg and belly.

"As I said," Dag Racho continued, his breaths absolutely even, his expression completely calm, "it is too soon for you, but I have been so worried for so long. You cannot know what fear I labor under daily." His shoulders drooped slightly as he looked at her. "And you cannot remain a child forever, especially since the hatching time approaches. Natiya, you must see that we will be mated. For the good of the land I serve and for your own safety."

"How?" she whispered, fighting to calm her racing heart. The power had lessened the moment their hands separated, but its aftereffects remained like tiny rivers of fire still burning in all parts of her body—some areas more than others. She swallowed, forcing herself to focus on her questions. "How is this for the good of Ragona?"

He sighed as if he were looking at an especially stupid student. "You cannot wish to return to the dark days of the dragonlords! Even my fight with Dag Jaseen devastated the area for two cycles. Some parts are only now returning to their full crop production. You cannot want that. Think of all the people who will starve in another dragon war."

She looked away, her mind in turmoil. She didn't want that. She couldn't want that. But Dag Racho was evil. He needed to be overthrown. And a war . . .

"There are other ways, Natiya. A dragon is a powerful weapon. And a Queen almost matches my Copper. Think what would happen if we joined together. No country would dare attack us—"

"None attack now."

"Exactly!" he said as he straightened to his full height. "That is because of me. Because I ended the dragon wars of a century ago. I ended the rampant greed, the destruction, the violence that tore Ragona apart until even the invaders didn't want it." He leaned forward, passionate in his vision. "But we are no longer a poor country. Our lands are fertile, our cattle fat. Many amass armies even now. Those druting Gambis to the north for one. Only my Copper keeps them at bay, and not for long."

He dropped to his knees, reaching out for her. She shrank away, so he did not press her. Instead, he slumped back onto his heels.

"I know I am pushing you too fast, but the need is urgent. Natiya, our two dragons—allied—will buy Ragona some time. But if you and I go to war, then the Gambis will sweep in and destroy everything while we are occupied with each other."

"How can you know this?" she asked, her voice high and weak.

"I have seen it with my own eyes. The Copper and I travel far and wide on his wings, and dragon eyes see much."

"An army on our border?" The very thought chilled her.

"A huge one. Poised to attack. Your native city—Dabu'ut—will not be the first to fall, but it will eventually. There is much wealth in any city next to a sea, and the Gambis will stop at nothing until they have it all."

Natiya bit her lip, imagining an invasion. She bore no great love for Talned or Monik, nor even for the many rough sailors that frequented the bar. But neither did she wish them to be slaughtered by an invading army.

"They won't attack if you and I join together. I think we have enough time for the hatching and then a mating, but not much more."

She felt her eyes clench shut as she tried to sort through his words. Could it be true? All her life, she had lived under martial law. Soldiers patrolled the streets, creating as much havoc as they ended. But they were manageable: If you knew how to stay out of their way and pay the right bribes, you survived. Some even thrived. What would happen if the soldiers disappeared? If they weren't around to prevent an invasion? She sincerely doubted the Gambis would accept a bribe. Rape and pillage was more their style, or so she had been told. The thought of the Gambis invading her home terrified her.

"There is more," he pressed. "Think of our children."

Her eyes flew open as she gazed up at him in shock. "Our children? Yours and mine?"

"New eggs. A new dragon clutch. To be raised under our tutelage, our guidance."

This time he did reach for her, grasping not her hands but her arms. She felt the power skate along her skin, but knew he restrained it this time, carefully managed the flow. And all the while he kept talking, kept trying to persuade her.

"An army, Natiya. An army of dragons—our children— guided by you and me. We can defend Ragona, keep everyone safe." His hands gentled on her arms. "Think on it, Natiya. We could do it together. You could be the mother of a new age, a golden age."

He waited, searching her face. She did not know what he sought in her expression, only that he grunted softly, abruptly leaned down and pulled her to her feet.

"Think on it," he whispered. Then, before he left, he once again reached out and stroked a finger across her cheek, leaving a trail of power. He touched her lips slowly and with infinite tenderness. "We are fated, Natiya. But more than that, our joining makes sense. Simple, logical sense."

He gave her one last speaking look before gesturing to his guards. Four stepped forward, coming to either side of her. She was being dismissed, the guards obviously there to escort her to her room.

"Wait!" she cried, giving voice to something that was only now seeping into her conscious awareness. "I keep feeling like there's something more to the bonding. Something I'm missing." She struggled helplessly with thoughts that weren't clear. "As if there's a purpose to humans and dragons. And an endpoint."

For a brief moment, a strange expression like terror flashed across his face. He masked it quickly, but she saw nonetheless. And then he laughed, loud and too long. "That is just your fear, little Natiya," he said when he could draw breath. "Dragons are like pets to us. Like very large dogs that can fly."

Inside her belly, her egg twisted in disagreement, but Natiya kept silent. She would question it later in the privacy of her own room.

Dag Racho stepped forward, patting her cheek in a condescending motion. "Dragons are our servants—nothing more, nothing less. Do not confuse the voice inside you as intelligence. Haven't you noticed how it echoes what you think and feel?"

She nodded slowly, using the motion to pull away from his touch. The power that always arced between them confused her. "It seems like the egg thinks what I do, only more so. It feels what I do—"

"Only it exaggerates it. Exactly! It is a magnifying glass for your thoughts and emotions, but it does not think on its own. We do. We control." Then he leaned forward, his entire presence expanding with threat. "*I* rule."

She frowned, her thoughts shifting until she saw a pattern in his words and actions. "Then . . . if you are afraid of assassination, you would feel that threat a hundredfold and surround yourself with guards at every turn. If there were bandits to the north, your dragon would magnify that fear, creating an entire country ready to invade Ragona."

His eyes hardened, and she felt anger roll off him in waves. "Experience and intelligence, my dear. Those things keep everything in perspective. And they are sorely lacking in you."

"But—," she began.

He waved her into silence. "Enough of this. You need rest. After all, you have a big day tomorrow."

She looked up at him, feeling more than dazed; she felt drunk with possibilities. "What?"

"Tomorrow your tutelage begins." And with that, he gestured. The guards took her arms gently, but no less firmly, and she was forced to go with them. At the last moment she turned, a question on her lips.

She never voiced it. The Emperor was preoccupied. He had another five guards around him, all assisting as he latched a strong iron chain around the Copper's neck. The dragon twisted, but not much, as he tried to face the Emperor. In fact, Natiya had the distinct impression the dragon wanted to touch his human— forehead to forehead—but she had no understanding of why. And there was no time to ask, for the guards led her firmly away.

Why do you sleep?

Natiya woke with a start. She winced as her back protested; she'd fallen asleep on the cushions near the window rather than in her bed, and with the extra weight of the dragon egg she felt fat, unwieldy and just plain annoyed.

"What do you want?" she groused to the egg.

Why do you sleep? There is so much more to learn.

Natiya sighed. At times the egg could be relentless in its quest for more information, more stimulation. More, more, more. Just when Natiya felt she needed less. Less confusion. Less doubt. And certainly less of this annoyingly huge bulk the egg created on her body.

"You've grown again," she grumbled at the fist-sized jewel in her belly.

The Copper feeds me power.

"Have you found out any answers?" she asked it. The moment she returned to her room this evening, she had begun questioning her egg. Unfortunately, it had only reflected back her own confusion. It thought there might be a purpose to the bonding, but it didn't know what. It maybe saw dragon-magnified paranoia in all of Dag Racho's actions, but maybe not. It didn't know, and so in disgust Natiya had sat on the window seat and tried to think. Sleep had claimed her instead.

Do not sleep again. We have to learn. Are there more books?

Perhaps, she thought back. This was the palace, after all. Wasn't there an entire library here somewhere? She pushed to her feet. She would have to be quiet, assuming the Emperor truly did sleep on the other side of the bathing chamber. After a minimum toilette, she tiptoed to her door and peered through the latticework. As expected, two guards remained against the door. They seemed alert, more's the pity, despite the late hour. But they were male, and since she had seen more than one pregnant former dancer, she had an idea exactly how to get just about anything she wanted.

"My lady!" one of the guards exclaimed, while both straightened to attention. "Is something amiss?"

She pulled open the door, abruptly thrusting her swollen stomach forward to exaggerate her bulk while simultaneously pressing a hand to her lower back. Then she waddled. It was a hideous movement, awkward and hard on the knees, but to the young men before her, it only meant one thing: cranky pregnant woman.

"Of course there's something wrong! I'm the size of a house, my feet are swollen, my head aches, and that flea-bitten mattress is lumpier than a rock quarry." Despite the vehemence of her complaints, she kept her voice low and raspy, as if her throat was hoarse from screaming. She was still desperately aware of the Emperor's bedroom nearby. "I need food. And a tonic. Now."

"Of course," the first guard answered, and bowed deeply before her. "I will get something immediately—"

"No, no!" she snapped. "Don't be an idiot. Do you know what foods I need to eat? What herbs turn my stomach? What smells?" She waved her hand in front of her nose and turned away from the second guard as if he had not bathed. He hadn't, of course, which made it an easier performance. "You." She pointed at him. "Back away. You foul the air." Then she turned to the first guard. "You. Show me the way to the library."

The smelly guard hastily jumped back while the other guard bowed. "My apologies, my lady, but if you would just tell me what food—"

She stepped forward, using her belly to shove him out of the way. He scrambled backward quickly, but she had been fast enough; she had managed to touch him, and immediately gasped in pretended pain, crumpling against the wall. Both guards rushed to assist her, but she batted their hands away with all the violence she dared. "Don't touch me!" she hissed. "You have hurt me on purpose! What's your name? I'm going to tell the Emperor! Ohhh!"

Then, just to cap the performance, she began to cry. She hated how pitiful and childish she sounded. Indeed, if anyone at home saw her, they would howl with laughter. This was not how she behaved. Ever. But these poor guards didn't know that. And so they fell over themselves trying to think of a way to help.

She sobbed unhappily. "Give me a cloth, buffoon!"

They did, and she blew her nose, then threw it at them in petty anger. "Take this away. It stinks! Oooh, you think I'm fat and ugly and completely insane, don't you?"

They blinked stupidly at her. "Of course not, my lady—"

"Shut up! Just shut up! I know you do. Oh, I need something to read, something that will calm my nerves.

That's all I want. Can't you please just take me to the library?"

"My lady, please." Guard One was practically on his knees before her, begging. "Please let us get a book for you."

She straightened, stamping her foot in impatience. "No! I want to pick it myself." Then she abruptly pointed at Guard Two. "You! Bring me some fruit. And soup. Hot soup. With anstou root in it. And you"—she pointed at Guard One—"you take me to the library."

"My lady," began the first guard. He spoke calmly, gently, indicating he was clearly a man used to dealing with irrational females. "The Emperor worries about your safety. It is dangerous to go about these hallways unprotected."

"Don't be ridiculous. Rachy and I already wandered about this evening." She sighed petulantly. "He said I could have anything I wanted. And I want a book! A good book. And I'm going to get one." She started stomping down the hallway—farther away from the Emperor's room. Both guards scrambled after her, but they couldn't stop her. After all, every time they came close, she complained of their smell. She wished she could summon up a good retch, but her stomach remained ridiculously empty.

"No," she suddenly snapped at Guard Two. "Your smell will foul my food. Don't you ever brush your teeth? You, show me the way to the libr—ow! Ow! Owwwww! Don't touch me! I'm all swollen, and everything hurts!"

She kept inching her way down the hall. If they tried to physically stop her, she simply crumpled in pain. She had enough achy muscles and swollen body parts to make this incredibly easy. Then she added a few irrational and contradictory demands, not to mention complaints that they hated her, and Guard One was all too willing to go get her food. Which left the other one—the one obviously unused to moody females—to lead the way while keeping ahead of her, supposedly to reduce his smell. She was fortunate that it was the middle of the night, otherwise there would be a much greater number of guards about. Plus, only the junior guards got night duty. That meant they were that much more nervous about waking their superiors.

Unfortunately, they weren't complete idiots. She had barely gotten down two flights of stairs before an older, obviously well-seasoned soldier appeared. She immediately dissolved into tears and whimpered that she wanted to go to the library. He rolled his eyes and agreed. Soon six guards accompanied her to a chamber filled to bursting with scrolls and tablets and ancient texts. Perfect!

Then the guards rousted a sleepy, ancient-looking librarian to help her: a man, of course, which made things even easier. She settled down with food to one side and all the books of the realm on the other—or so it seemed. Then she did her best to remember everything her parents had taught her about research. Unfortunately, it wasn't much. But what she did remember was that a true academic—or in this case, a true librarian—is never happier than when sharing his passion with another interested soul. And what interested her right then was history. Dag Racho's history. And just as she expected, the Emperor had a large enough ego to stock his private library full of his own self-importance.

She started with a child's text, as it was likely the fastest and easiest to read. It was also what the ancient librarian gave her. She read all about the dark days of the Dragon Wars, where one warlord after another fought to the near decimation of the land and population. Then a savior appeared. The picture showed a boy named Racho, a commoner and an orphan, digging through garbage to survive. Then one day two dragonlords were fighting overhead. Racho led a group of people into caves to protect them. And while he searched through the tunnels for food to share with everyone, he chanced upon a dragon clutch.

Only one egg lay in the clutch; all the others were dark, dead stones. But at that moment, the courageous boy took matters into his own hands. Vowing to protect the land and the people the dragonlords had forgotten, the boy incubated the egg. It took many years of hardship and deprivation, but in his struggles, the boy grew strong. In fact, the text suggested, he grew stronger, better and more understanding exactly because of his earlier deprivation. In the end, he arose on his glorious Copper dragon and in amazing battle after battle, he defeated and killed all the other dragonlords, thereby ushering in an era of peace and prosperity for all of Ragona.

Natiya struggled not to laugh at the obvious fabrication. To begin with, the Emperor himself had told her he was from a family of scholars and that he and his sister had found the eggs. She needed to dig deeper, but where? She sincerely doubted that Dag Racho would keep incriminating texts in his own library.

If only she knew what she was looking for. She continued to read, getting more and more advanced texts on the Emperor's battles, his early days of power and his later days of expansion. Thankfully, the egg was equally curious, equally insatiable, aiding her understanding when her reading skills failed her.

Until the Emperor himself walked in. "My dear," he drawled as he towered over her, "you need your sleep. Tell me you haven't been here all night."

Natiya had just taken a bite out of a huge reedfruit, and her gasp of surprise made the sticky purple juice dribble down her chin. She scrambled to clean herself even as the Emperor's booming laugh filled the large chamber. She glanced up at him, her face heating with embarrassment, and wondered if he had planned the timing just to make her appear foolish. In her years on the docks, she'd witnessed many such petty acts of cruelty, but there was nothing in Dag Racho's expression to indicate such meanness. Then again, his face tended to always look exactly as it did now: kindly, almost fatherly. Except when his gaze dropped to her full belly. Then she thought she caught a glimpse of hunger.

Or maybe it was just the shadows in the cavernous library. Natiya took a few moments to compose herself before smiling up at her Emperor, a slight challenge in her expression.

"I think you already know exactly how long I have been here, what I have eaten and which texts I have read."

His eyes widened a moment, and then his expression softened into a true smile. "I see you are clever. Excellent." Then his eyes became assessing as he settled into the chair across from her. "Tell me then, my clever Queen, what you have learned from these ancient tomes."

She glanced at the scattered stacks of parchment surrounding her, seeing the thin, weblike lettering cover the table that separated the two of them. Reaching through the piles, she pulled out the children's book with which she'd begun. Opening the pages to the colored picture of the young, sweet-faced orphan boy, she absently stroked his cheek while speaking.

"It would seem that you and these texts do not always agree," she said carefully. "Didn't you tell me you had parents and a sister?"

He nodded, and she could read nothing in the gesture. "Any other discrepancies?"

She almost laughed at that, but didn't dare push him too far. So she simply waved her hand over the entire table. "My lord, they are everywhere. Indeed, I am not sure any of these texts agree on anything. Take your sister, for example. She was definitely apparent in your early battles, fighting alongside you, though most do not label her blood kin. Then she simply disappears. Some say she was a myth; others that she died. Still others claim she flew off to parts unknown in search of conquest or fortune or simply a place to be at peace."

Dag Racho nodded, a sad smile on his face. "Many so-called scholars write what they want to be true, not what is truth. Others need to believe certain things just so they can sleep at night."

She nodded. "Your early years are fraught with bloodshed and terror such as I have never known."

"Such was the nature of those times." Then he grasped her hand, drawing her to her feet. "That is why you must rely on me for your information. I am the only one left who was alive during those times. I am the only one who knows the truth."

"But will you share it with me?" she countered, very sure he would not.

He shrugged, his expression a challenge. "That all depends on how quickly you learn." He raised her palm to his lips, blowing warm air across her skin before pressing a gentle kiss in the center. "And how much you please me."

She shivered; she could not help it. His touch still sent currents of power through her, and the heat he generated within her could easily be mistaken for passion. Indeed, she wondered if it was. After all, she only had her attraction to Kiril as comparison. Perhaps he had been infatuation, dragon magic as he called it, and Dag Racho was her true mate.

As if reading her thoughts, he stroked his palm down her belly. "You are still young, Natiya, so you question this passion between us." The egg responded to his touch, twisting within her, making her gasp. "I tell you it is rare. Extremely rare." He slowly released her, brushing his hand over her breasts before lifting her chin. "You must treasure what is between us, Natiya. Protect it, and I will fulfill your greatest desires." He leaned forward and pressed his mouth to hers, touching the curve of her lips with his tongue.

As always, a current passed between them. But once he withdrew, the power faded; the tingle quickly died, leaving Natiya to wonder what exactly made Kiril's touch linger in her thoughts long after he was gone from her.

"Come!" Dag Racho ordered before she could answer her own question. "You have much to learn before I introduce you to my underlings."

She fell into step beside him. Indeed, she had little choice as he pulled her along with him. "But—" she began.

"Hush. You must bathe first and attire yourself more appropriately." He flashed a grin. "After that, if you learn quickly, I shall give you a great reward." And with that, he handed her over to a contingent of guards. He gave them orders as to what she would wear, all the way down to the hosiery for her legs. He even told them the length of her bath. Then, without so much as a nod to her, he dismissed them all with a wave of his hand before sauntering off in the opposite direction.

CHAPTER TWELVE

Dag Racho was an exacting taskmaster. He spent hours with her, training her in history, deportment, statecraft, dragon care, and etiquette—everything and anything that would make her fit to stand by his side. That was his plan, of course, and the reason he had not simply killed her outright: he needed a female dragonmate. He spoke of their union frequently, of their future children, and of the dragon babies he would have under his control. Eventually, he claimed, he would lead an army of dragons to conquer the neighboring countries, which would finally make Ragona safe. That is what he said, and she could tell he believed it. Meanwhile, she struggled to hide her revulsion. More war? More soldiers? More dragons pouring destruction down on their neighbors? How could that possibly make anyone more safe?

Perhaps Kiril had the right of it. Perhaps all dragons had to be destroyed so that everyone would live in peace. And yet, that thought would not sit well either. Her egg was not evil; she was sure of that. And the Copper was definitely more than an achingly sad pet dog. Dragons were something apart from anything she had thought before. Something important. She just didn't know what.

How she longed for someone to discuss this with. She wished for a person who had seen more than she had read, who knew the court inside and out, and could give her new insight. And if he had large hands and a kind heart, if he risked everything to protect her, then all the better. In short, she ached for Kiril, the man she had ordered killed.

She still thought he was a liar and a cad—perhaps. If she allowed herself to believe he'd been true to her, guilt would overwhelm her. Had she really ordered his death in a fit of wounded petulance? What if Kiril's lies had been exactly what Sabina said: the only way to survive in Ragona? It made sense. If her last days were anything to judge by, Dag Racho did have absolute control over everything. He had brought her to witness the death of many prisoners. Indeed, it was a regular court event and the Copper's only source of food: men, women and children, eaten alive with only Racho's word to say that they deserved it. He called them criminals, conspirators, and traitors, and no one dared gainsay him.

What if Kiril had been forced into his lies to her? What if his deception, his time with her, had all been prescribed by Dag Racho? Then he would have been as much a victim as the people eaten before her very eyes. And perhaps those other moments—the times when they laughed together or touched one another— perhaps those had been the only real thing allowed between them. And she had ordered him killed.

As she turned her eyes away from the latest execution, Natiya vowed to never let emotion overcome her again. She would never again allow anyone—most especially Dag Racho—to manipulate her with such deadly consequences. She would never order anyone's death unless she had the weight of full evidence and a neutral party's assessment. It was the only way to be fair. And the only way to avoid the nightly travesties that Dag Racho visited on his "criminals."

So she vowed. And she mourned Kiril.

"Why do you watch that mountain?"

Natiya started, belatedly realizing that she had been once again staring at the mountain that crouched near the capital city. It wasn't all that unusual a sight. Behind her, the soldiers were cleaning up the last of the Copper's meal, the courtiers were disappearing as fast as possible, and she . . . she was staring out at a mountain. It wasn't even special. One need travel no more than a few delents to come to the beginning of the Clutching Mountains. The palace had an excellent view, of course, and Mount Rahot was the first of a long range that extended far to the north. And yet, night after night, she found herself staring not at the other peaks, but at Rahot's rounded top and irregular sides.

"Natiya?"

She flushed at the note of irritation in the Emperor's voice. After the Copper's meal, they began their nightly walk, a.k.a. interrogation. Matters of state had kept Dag Racho from being her instructor, and so he had delegated the task to various trusted servants. Until after dinner, that is, when they walked on the rooftop courtyard with his Copper, and the Emperor began quizzing her on what she had learned and how she had learned it. Until he ran out of questions or she grew tired—which she did more often of late—and they fell into silence. During this last silence, her gaze had once again been drawn to the mountain.

"It is . . . compelling somehow. I don't know why," she admitted.

"Think on it," he urged. "Tell me what you guess."

She stared at it, and began rattling off the facts she knew, just as he had taught her. "It is where you garrison your army," she said slowly. "It took many years to delve deep inside it to house your men." Or so she had been told. Then she frowned. "We are not at war, Emperor. Why do you keep such a large army?"

"We most certainly are at war. We fight thieves, brigands and all manner of criminals. Do you think a man could simply walk to market with his wares if the soldiers did not keep the peace? Do you think a girl could work her family's field without being snatched from beneath their very eyes? There are enemies everywhere, Natiya. Do not think they don't exist simply because my army keeps them in check."

"Ah, yes, the Gambis," she said, twisting to look at him more fully. "And the Sihotts. I understand they have made an alliance with the Gambis against you."

Far from being surprised by her recently learned knowledge, he actually smiled, pleased with her question. "Yes, they are dangerous barbarians, even more so now that their alliance has made them bold. Danger threatens from all sides, and I require more and more troops to defend our glorious country."

Natiya nodded, wondering if what he said was true, or if the truth was that it would take a larger army to conquer surrounding territories and the barbarians were merely defending themselves. Before she could think of a way to ask, he had shifted her body back toward the mountain.

"Do not change the topic, Natiya. Tell me what you see."

She looked again, trying to sense something with her dragon-enhanced abilities. What she saw was the mountain's relatively flat construction, its uneven sides, and the lack of sharp, jagged points so common among the Clutching Mountains.

"You *built* it," she breathed suddenly. "You constructed that mountain to house your army."

He grinned, nodding at her. "I took material from the Clutching Mountains, making sure it was rich in demoa metal." The obscuring metal that confused dragon senses.

"But why?" she asked.

"For you, of course!" Then he touched her again, caressing her dragon egg as he did so often now. "When you are dragonborn, you will understand how far ahead you can see and think. We are a long-lived race, you know."

"But it must have taken cycles to build. That makes no sense."

"Of course it does!" he snapped, but then he moderated his tone. "Can you not feel it? The pull, even now, of that mountain?"

She closed her eyes again, trying to block out the Copper behind them, the Emperor's hand on her belly, even the twisting antics of the dragon egg inside her. And then she felt the whisper, the draw, perhaps even the need to rest in the caves. In obscurity.

"We crave it, you know—the shield that demoa metal gives us." He linked her arm in his, drawing her away from his dragon. "It is only natural. The hatching is our most vulnerable time. Of course we would want to hide from everyone, even other dragons, at such a time."

Natiya sighed, knowing what he said made sense; and yet some part of her objected. Some part of her disliked the animosity he suggested. "Wasn't there ever a time when dragons protected one another? Instead of fighting?"

He laughed, long and hard. "Perhaps," he finally conceded, after he had wiped the tears of humor from his eyes. "But that was many generations ago. Long before my time even, when dragons existed apart from men— before the dragon bond was discovered and the first dragonborn became a dragonlord."

She stopped, turning to look at him. "A dragon can live unbonded? But how do they incubate? How do they hatch?"

He shrugged. "They can survive unbonded if lovingly tended by a parent. If the eggs are kept warm and protected from predators." He shook his head. "But remember, they are little more than large lizards with wings, creatures without thought or logic unless ruled by us. They would pillage unmercifully for food, laying waste with their fire and consuming whatever lived. It would indeed be a dangerous, ugly world if dragons were allowed to live uncontrolled. This is the better way, with a man ordering their thoughts."

She nodded, somehow saddened by his statement, but she could not deny the truth. Despite its intelligence, her egg had been childishly simple—reflecting whatever it was told, existing only to learn and absorb and act without thought or discrimination. Many times she felt the urges of the egg: primal forces demanding food or comfort or shelter no matter the cost. The very thought of a creature the size of Dag Racho's Copper acting without restraint made her shiver in horror.

She said, "I am very glad the unbonded dragons have all died out."

He didn't answer, and for a moment she wondered if she caught a flash of fear in his eyes. Her own egg—the Golden Queen—was by all reports the last egg in all the world. Even Kiril had confirmed it. But what if they were wrong? What if there were other dragons elsewhere, terrorizing good people in some far-off land? The very thought was chilling.

"Do you dream at night?"

Natiya started, once again aware that her thoughts had been wandering. She daydreamed so often now, it was becoming a serious irritation, especially for someone usually quite clear in her thoughts and direction. "Of course I dream," she answered, still flustered. "I thought everyone did."

"No," he bit out, irritation lacing his tone. "At night— here—are your dreams . . . vivid?"

She chewed her lip, once again looking away. She had indeed been dreaming strange things at night. Images filled with packs of dragons in flight, fire filling the sky as they fought or played or mated—she was never sure which. She often woke shaking and confused.

"You have been dreaming!" he accused.

She nodded. "I thought it was merely the approach of the hatching. The images are always of dragons, and so confused. I can never make sense of them."

He hunkered down, hunching his shoulders as he leaned against the stone wall. She mimicked his motion, tilting her head to hear his lowered voice. "I think they are talking to one another, at night when we sleep," he said.

She frowned, turning to face the Emperor directly. "Who?"

"My Copper. Your Queen. They talk at night. In ways men do not."

She frowned, trying to assess the possibility. The egg certainly communicated with her through her thoughts; but she had not believed it could speak this way to other creatures. To the Copper? The very thought terrified her. It would mean she had no secrets from the Emperor, for everything his dragon knew, surely Dag Racho knew as well. But one look at his face told her perhaps that was not true. Perhaps his dragon kept secrets even from him.

"If what you say is true," she began carefully, "then that is all to the good, is it not? No doubt your Copper is merely instructing my Queen on life and the human world. Just as you are instructing me."

He grimaced. "Perhaps."

She stared at him, trying unsuccessfully to read his mood. "What exactly do you fear?"

He straightened abruptly at her badly phrased question. "I fear nothing!"

Natiya looked away, sighing silently to herself. Of all the things the Emperor had told her, this was the most obvious falsehood. Dag Racho not only feared, he feared everything. Even his most trusted servants—the ones given the task to instruct her—were under constant scrutiny. Indeed, she sometimes wondered if her nightly interrogation was as much a way to spy on them as to see if she had learned her lessons.

And every person she met, including many she had not yet seen, came with a list of strengths and weaknesses, threats and exploitable assets. He would brief her on these things the night before she met anyone. To Dag Racho, no one was simply who they appeared. They were all harboring treasonous thoughts; they all looked for an opportunity to destroy what he had built. And why? Greed or stupidity ranked top amongst his explanations. They simply did not understand what he was doing, did not see the glory and prosperity he was bringing to the country. Or if they did, they did not care but would rather hog the glory, the wealth or the power to themselves. Time and time again the Emperor told her stories of how he had been betrayed by those closest to him. And so now he watched constantly, never at ease, always suspicious. But she'd never thought he would doubt his own dragon.

"You think they talk while we are asleep?" she asked to verify his earlier statement.

He nodded, his gaze darting to the side where the Copper reclined, tail tucked around him like a kitten, neck chain nearly hidden behind his left front leg. Then the Emperor turned back to her. "You must get up earlier," he ordered. "And I will go to bed later. If we do not sleep at the same time, they cannot talk." He stared at Natiya. "They do not tell us everything, you know. They are children hiding dirty secrets. It is up to us to keep them in line."

She nodded, as she knew he expected. "I understand."

"Good. Now go to bed. The guards will wake you early." Then, before she could turn away, he reached out, once again stroking and holding her egg. "A few more days, Natiya. Then I will take you to my mountain, and she will hatch and everything will be as I have planned."

She took a deep breath, using the motion to pull away from him even as she looked uneasily at the mountain. "How far inside?" She did not want to be inside the mountain during the hatching. She needed room. She needed air.

"The Queen needs a place to fly," he said, voicing her thought. "Have no fear. There is a chamber inside, very large. It will serve perfectly." Then he raised his hands, stroking her cheek. "It is necessary until you are stronger. Until you are ready." Then he grinned. "Our mating will be done in the open air."

With that final promise, he turned and walked back to his Copper, deftly avoiding the creature's outstretched head by walking to its side and petting it in much the same way as he often touched Natiya. He stroked its flank and murmured to it, but he never allowed the creature's head anywhere near his own.

Natiya watched until she could not stand it any longer. She was not ready for any of this: the hatching, the mating or any of the other things Dag Racho told her would soon arrive. Queenship. Children. A dragon army.

She bit her lip, trying to sort fact from fiction, future from fantasy. It was impossible, since her own source of information came from the Emperor himself. She had no way of knowing if his words were truth or clever lies. She had to find a way to escape, to choose her own path outside of his influence. But how? As the guards led her back to her bedchamber, she began to despair in earnest.

Then her gaze fell upon a book of poetry. The castle librarian had sent it to her, suggesting she might enjoy reading it. She did, as it nightly helped lull her mind to sleep: Poem after poem in awkward meter and even worse rhymes, all written in honor and praise of their glorious Emperor. She didn't know if the words had been ordered by Dag Racho or were simply the work of sycophants trying to buy favor. Either way, despite the poetry being utterly wretched, it gave her the most wonderful idea.

Turning to her guard—the smelly one from that first night—she demanded he call the librarian to her. Now, if only her memory was correct, for it had been years since she last saw her dearest childhood friend. And years as well since he had proclaimed his poetical passion to her. He could have changed his mind in that time. Any number of things could have changed, and that would make her entire plan a complete waste of time. Still, she had no other ideas, and so decided to see this through and pray it worked.

While she waited for the elderly gentleman to arrive, she opened all her poetry books while simultaneously cudgeling her poor brain into remembering everything she could about the ancient art forms. It wasn't much, but then, that was the whole point.

The librarian arrived with obvious haste. Sweat gleamed along his bald pate as he struggled with an armful of tomes. The guards, of course, did not help him at all, but merely stood watching his every move as he scuttled forward.

"My lady," he said, bowing deeply before her. "What may I do to help you?"

She smiled sweetly, doing her best to put him at ease. She needed him to be malleable. "I need your help, kind sir."

"Of course, my lady. Here, allow me to show you what I have brought." He bowed again, carefully spreading texts before her. She allowed him to describe them all in detail—ad nauseam—doing her best to nod where appropriate. But in the end, she pursed her lips in a moue of dissatisfaction.

"Those are excellent choices, of course. But what I need is something a little different."

The poor man looked up, his eyes growing wide as he began to sweat. She had seen the same panic on more than one servant in the castle; they were desperately anxious to please her, as if their very lives depended upon her mood. The thought gave her acute discomfort. Exactly what would happen to these people when she got what she wanted? What would be their fate when she finally escaped?

Her stomach twisted, but she didn't have the luxury of giving in to her compassion. Instead, she leaned forward, as if drawing the librarian into a conspiracy.

"I have a plan, but you must keep it secret."

Contrary to what she expected, the elderly gentleman widened his eyes in horror. Dag Racho had made her believe that secret plots lurked everywhere—even in men like this bookish old man. But the librarian's reaction was one of terror, not interest. Apparently, the wretch had no stomach for intrigue. Unless, of course, he was an excellent actor; in which case . . . She sighed. This paranoid conspiracy-seeking was beginning to give her a headache. Meanwhile, she patted the older man's hand to reassure him.

"I want to get the Emperor a present. For our . . . um . . ." What?

"A wedding present?" he offered.

"Exactly!" she exclaimed, though the very thought left a bad taste in her mouth. Pushing aside her fears, she settled onto the couch across from her guest. As she moved, she noted that the guard was listening with interest. No doubt Dag Racho would know of her "secret" within beats of her words. Which meant she had to be doubly careful with her performance. With that thought in mind, she picked up the book of poems that had so put her to sleep earlier.

"I wish to write a poem for the Emperor, glorifying all that he has done for Ragona."

The librarian nodded, his relief obvious. "Do you need help with your rhymes, my lady? I am accounted quite a good poet myself . . ."

She groaned internally. Just what she did *not* need: a self-styled librarian poet when she needed a specific poet. "Well, it is not so much the rhymes that have snagged me as the form. I want the work to be grand, like the Emperor himself. Long and overflowing, like his reign." She paused, waiting for the librarian to divine what she wanted. "Overpowering. Tempestuous." She was running out of adjectives. "Regal. Majestic." If only she could remember the exact name of the form. "Maybe even sublime."

"Epic?" he offered timidly.

"Yes! That is it exactly. But there is a specific form of the epic poem. One that is perfectly suited to my intention. What was the name of that . . ." And this was where she trod on thin ice. She thought she'd remember the exact form if the man said it, but she couldn't be sure.

"Well, my lady, do you mean the Traveling form? With love couplets?"

"No, that's not it." She bit her lip. At least, she didn't think that was right.

"How about the Romantic Quintet form, with alternating submissive and dominant cadences?"

"No, no, no!" Why would he not get off of the romantic forms?

"Ah, then, perhaps you mean the Strompatic form—"

"No—"

"Sometimes referred to as the Mythic form with alternating dragon tooth and claw couplets."

"That's it!" She was sure. That was the form her childhood friend adored, because of the dragon name. Now, if only she could be sure he had continued with his plan to become the only master of that ancient form.

The older man clapped his hands. "An excellent form! An excellent choice!" But then his expression saddened. "But my lady, that is quite a challenging format. And, um, you do not have much time." He glanced significantly down at her swollen belly. The egg had been growing like a stuffed pompet. Every day she was larger. "Perhaps I might suggest a simpler—"

"No, no!" she snapped. "It must be this. And it must be perfect!" She began working herself into a first-class temper. "The Emperor deserves nothing less. *I* will be satisfied with nothing less!"

"But—"

"Nothing else matters to me!" She began to tear up in yet another of her embarrassingly ill-tempered moods. Who'd known she was this good at being a pain in the ass? "And I must do it now, now, now! And you must help me!"

"My lady—"

"I cannot abide another moment of this! I simply cannot!" She glanced at the man and didn't need her dragon senses to know that his heart was beating erratically in panic. Sweat patches already darkened his clothing. He was ready to promise her just about anything so long as he was not personally responsible for the plan's success.

"But I can't—"

"You must! I order it! Your Emperor demands it!" Sweet Amia, she was tired of screeching.

The man swallowed, his skin becoming so pasty she feared he might pass out. Instead, he released a frightened squeak. "Help? From me? In the Mythic form?" He shook his head. "My lady, it is an extremely *challenging* form. Perhaps you would prefer a shorter meter, one that doesn't even require rhymes. I am quite proficient at—"

"Then send me someone who can!" She hoped he would leap upon this idea, neatly escaping the need to perform a task he was clearly unsuited for. Unfortunately, he didn't. He released a pitiful moan that drew her up short.

"But he is not allowed in your presence!" he wailed.

Natiya had expected as much, but she was not deterred. Instead, she maintained her pregnant-woman temper, huffing and pacing angrily about the room. "Not on the list! Of all the ridiculous . . . It is for a gift! Surely I am not a prisoner here?" She rounded abruptly on the guard, nearly slamming him sideways with the size of her belly. *D'greth*, when did this egg get so huge? "Am I a prisoner here? Am I?"

"Er, no, my lady," he stammered in an obvious lie.

"Then let this poet come to me!" She spun around, glaring first at the librarian and then at the guard. "See that he arrives tomorrow morning, first thing! Or I shall hold you personally responsible!" Then, after their faces drained of all color, she abruptly smiled prettily—and stupidly—at them, dropping her voice to a loud whisper. "And don't tell the Emperor! It's a secret, you know, for our wedding."

Then, while they stared dumbly at her, she waved them away. "Go now. It is time for me to sleep." She dropped onto her bed and made as if to strip naked right there in front of them. She had to restrain her laughter when the two scrambled like bunnies to escape her presence.

She had no doubt of what was about to happen. Her "secret" would travel up the official lines until it reached Dag Racho himself. She prayed his ego would be flattered enough by her plan to approve her poet consultant. She counted it likely for two reasons, his ego being the first. The second—and likely more key—reason was that working so hard on a poem would occupy her time while the Emperor slept. He would think her safely employed while she was not directly under his supervision. Especially if she did manage to create lines in the execrable form. *D'greth*! She hated poetry!

The real risk, of course, was that her poet consultant would not be the man she wanted, the one man in all Ragona whom she had ever trusted. Unfortunately, she had no way of finding out if her ploy worked. She simply had to wait and try to sleep. And pray she didn't dream.

It began as it always did: flying. Always flying. In the air above the clouds, through mist or brilliant sun or lightning storm. She didn't see herself flying; she felt it. The bitter cold, the clammy wet, even that stomach tickle that became a clench when a dip in the air became a dive and then a plummet.

And she loved it all, because she was insulated. A fire in her belly kept her warm and dry, and somehow she never vomited it up when the plummet took a last-beat shift, streaking her upward like an arrow shot from the Father's bow. She was a dragon in all its glory, and every breath, every movement, was pure joy. She was dancing with wings, and she laughed out loud, even though she knew she was sleeping.

But then the dream changed and evolved into something she'd never seen before. She was no longer flying, but sitting on a sandy floor in the corner of a shack. She shouldn't even call it a shack, for in truth it was simply driftwood stacked together, one piece atop another until it became a room: a fortress of driftwood, a place to hide in shadow despite the smell of dead fish and rancid seafung.

Except, it was no longer hidden. *They* had found him. Her older brothers. Or was she a he? By the name of Rashad. She did not know, and so she ignored it, settling into her hatred and pain like a frog on a toadstool.

Then she coughed. She did not intend to. In fact, she held it in as long as she could. But her clothes were wet where she sat on gritty sand, and her tears made her face slimy. Eventually she could not stop it; she coughed. That loud, rasping hack started in her stomach, making her sick. It built there, foul-tasting like bile, swelling within her until it had to escape, had to break free. And it did, violently, shaking her whole body as more coughs clawed through her throat, choking off her breath and making her spasm as she tried to contain them. In the end she lay shaking and gasping and even wetter and more miserable than before because she had fallen onto her side. Now her shirt clung to her tiny stick arms, giving her no warmth and no comfort.

And worse, they were coming. She heard them, just as they had heard her. They scrambled through the rocks and pushed into her fortress as if it were nothing more than driftwood stacked together among the craggy outcroppings that were once caves—which it was.

"Here he is! Hey, Wormy! He's here! Whatcha doing, Wormy?"

"He's hiding in the dirt like all worms."

"Hey, look, his pants are wet!"

"Wormy, Wormy!"

The taunts continued relentlessly, echoing in her head and her weakened body. For these were from her brothers, no less, the very ones who were supposed to protect her. But that, of course, was why they hated her so much. Not quite the oldest, she was still older than these two younger brothers. But they were bigger and stronger. They had never had this fire in their lungs or the worms they said ate her from the inside out. While they wanted to run and play with ease among the caves, his illness dragged them down and made them wait. When they were younger, his older brother carried him in a special chair, hauling him with grunts and groans along the sandy beach. But then his younger brothers grew larger, and they all had to take turns, pushing him off on the loser of their games.

It felt strange, being this boy in her dream, for Natiya was part of two minds—both the boy in pain and another mind that was not her own. The dragons? she wondered. Was she learning what the dragons shared with each other? She didn't know and had no time to understand. She was remembering things. She knew how the boy had hidden his brother's toys in his chair, stolen their treasures and kept them for his own. She knew, too, that all the taunts, all the ugliness, stemmed from boredom in this isolated stretch of sand and rock, and the constant struggle for attention from indifferent parents too absorbed in their work to care much about their progeny.

The dream could have ended here, rushing forward through cycles showing the way most siblings end their struggles: with maturity and time, most brothers cease pestering each other and spend more time hounding girls. Bit by bit, they find comfort in each other's struggles, strength in solidarity, and distraction in sex.

It should have ended this way, except for one thing: the treasure, the secret that brought him to his isolated fort to study, the means of his eventual revenge. A Copper dragon egg that he pressed deep into his belly and incubated there where no one outside of his family could see. That was the reason his brothers called him Wormy, that was the cause of the jealousy that now made them torment him. Because from the moment he pressed it deep into his belly, he'd known he would kill them all. He would have his revenge, and so he told them. He would make them pay for not playing with him, for not taking him places they went, for not loving and adoring him with the warmth they themselves all longed for.

Natiya wanted the dream to end there. She prayed for release from its grip, shaking with impotent anger at the wet ground and the cruelty of children. She wanted it to end, but would have remained there reliving each moment of humiliation rather than experience what was coming: the moment the family died. Not just the brothers—each and every one of them—but the indifferent father and too-tired mother as well.

The dream continued, scrolling through her mind no matter how much she fought. The egg hatched and the dragon-beast controlled Rashad's thoughts in a chaotic riot of pain and sexuality and rejection and fury. The hatchling was hungry. It needed food immediately, and the hunger clawed through Rashad's mind like a living thing.

Then the Copper saw something—someone—to eat, and simply did it. Rashad watched in horror and some satisfaction as his older brother fought and died. It was right, he decided; his older brother had tormented him. His older brother deserved to die to feed his Copper dragon's belly—his *own* belly. It was all twisted in his mind and he could not think clearly; but he knew that the larger boy had been the leader, the taunter, the one who had failed to protect his younger, weaker, sicker brother.

Sick no longer. Weak no longer. Rashad had a full belly and a satisfied smirk.

The others—parents and younger brother—died in the ensuing fight. Running to the cave, they had been horrified by the dead body, the blood and food smeared over his mouth—his dragon's mouth—their mouths. And so they had run, offering themselves up as further meals. It was right, Rashad decided, right and honorable that they should die in this manner, giving their lives to strengthen the greatest among them— himself. And also for his sister, who had a hatchling of her own.

Besides, they would have died in the next fight anyway. The local dragonlord had felt the births: Dag
Branth knew that two new dragons challenged his
reign. So he arrived quickly on a black dragon bent
with age and weakening. Sister and brother rose up together, easily defeating their enemy. And in the celebra-
tion afterwards, while parents and brothers still filled
their bellies, there had been little left to do—nothing
except grow, find strength in food and sex with one another while they prepared for the bloody war to come.

They were successful. They fought and murdered
and ate as they defeated one dragonlord after another.
No one had seen it done this way before: two dragons
cooperating, two dragonlords working in concert. And
bit by bit, the land fell to their control.

But there was a price for this cherished and holy
merging between man and dragon. One that Rashad
never expected. After a time—Natiya couldn't tell how
long—the Copper began to assert himself. *Enough,* it
said. *Finish it.* Rashad hadn't understood, but the Copper began to insist. It became willful and angry. The emperor's dreams became haunted by those words: Finish
it. Finish it *now.* Their bond became a war fought during sleep and in those rare moments when they
touched forehead to forehead.

What price? Natiya demanded of her dream. *What
does that mean?* Then she woke to a scream: a long
agonizing wail that was unending. And that was not
her own.

She shot to her feet, poised to run even before she
came fully awake. But where? The scream abated only
to be replaced by another sound, more wretched and
horrific than the first: sobbing. Deep, heart-wrenching,
terrible sobs, interspersed with words that she could
not understand.

A guard stumbled into her room, his eyes wide with
fear, his breath stuttering with frightened pants. His gaze

slipped through the bathing chamber to Dag Racho's bedroom, somewhere on the other side of a secret passageway. Natiya moved past the pool, looking for the door, dimly aware that she wore only her thin sleeping gown. Then she stumbled to a stop, not seeing the passage while the Emperor's keening cries continued on the other side of the wall.

She turned to the guard, completely at a loss. She saw him hesitate before making his decision. Apparently, it was to help her, because in two quick steps he was beside the wall, pressing one hand into a decoration that seemed to be more than simple art. She noted his hand position and memorized his movements, even as most of her thoughts remained on the man on the other side of the wall.

As she watched, a narrow hallway appeared behind a tall natsting fern. She moved as quickly as her bulk allowed, pushing through the short, dark hall before abruptly arriving in the Emperor's bedroom. He lay on his couch, apparently having fallen asleep despite the piles of documents that littered the floor beside him. He writhed on the couch, half sobbing and half screaming in pain, and she could not tell if he was awake or still caught within the memories their dragons shared.

That was what her mind finally grasped, now that the last of her "dream" had faded: What she had experienced, what she had "dreamed" was in fact Dag Racho's memories—or rather young Rashad's memories—of his childhood before his Copper dragon matured, before he became Emperor of all he surveyed. He had been a sickly child, tormented by his siblings. And somehow, some way, he had abused his dragon bond.

Natiya was not sure what to do. It had been many years since she had allowed anyone to act motherly toward her. Longer still since she had even pretended to such compassion within herself. But the man was in pain, his sobs softer now but no less devastating.

While she stood in indecision beside him, he abruptly turned, looking at her with eyes haunted by memories too heinous to speak out loud. "It's not true," he gasped, reaching out and grabbing her leg. "They lie. All lies," he whispered. Then he closed his eyes, curling in on himself as if trying to stifle the life that had once lived inside him.

Responding instinctively, Natiya dropped to her knees before him, pushing aside the documents that blocked her way. She reached out, stroking the hair off his sweat-soaked brow, wondering what to do now. It was all true, she knew; he was the one who lied.

"What does the Copper want? What have we promised our dragons?"

He didn't answer except to appear more wretched. "No, no, no," he repeated in an unending litany, and she heard an echo of the sad little boy he had once been. A child struggling from a disability, caught in a family starved for true nurturing in a time defined by brutal and selfish dragonlords. Rashad had earned her pity, and it was he that she stroked.

"Come to bed, my lord," she coaxed, trying to lift him off his couch. He was too heavy, of course. Nevertheless, he moved himself as he shook his head.

"I can't. The dreams. I can't."

"The dreams are ended for tonight," she said, sending a stern order to her own dragon egg to that very effect. "They will not talk more tonight."

"Promise?" he asked, his voice small and childish. Indeed, he seemed the boy again, his legs wobbly and his eyes pleading for . . . what? Not the truth, for his screams told her he had already run from that. Not for female attention either, for there was nothing sexual in his touch.

"Stay with me," he begged. "Don't leave me alone. Not alone." Then he buried his face in her chest and began to cry.

"I will stay," she promised. And she did. She pulled him to his bed and laid him down. Then she settled in beside him, curling her arm around his shoulders. And for the first time since she had known him, he did not touch her belly or the egg there. Instead, he curled his arms against his chest, his hands against his mouth while his head rested beside her breast.

"I hate being alone," he murmured. Then he fell fast asleep.

CHAPTER THIRTEEN

Natiya woke to a murky gray morning and a guard shifting nervously from one foot to the other beside the bed. She frowned at him, trying to orient herself, wondering why her fingers felt numb. Then she remembered a long night of holding Dag Racho while trying to sort through fragments of his memories. He still lay curled on her shoulder, his strange perfume clouding the air. Kiril's scent had been clean and masculine, as straightforward to her as Racho's was twisted. As if everything in the Emperor's life was contradictory, pain inextricably linked with pleasure, failure seeded inside his success.

She sighed, knowing that she made no sense this early in the morning.

"What is it?" she finally asked, keeping her voice low and muted so as not to wake the Emperor.

"Your poet," the guard mouthed. Then he jerked his head toward her bedroom, and Natiya understood. She nodded, waiting as the heavy man clumped out of the room through the secret passage back to her bedroom.

When she was sure the Emperor still slept, Natiya carefully shifted his weight off her shoulder and onto his pillow. Then she slowly slipped away to stand beside the bed, looking down at the powerful man resting there. As she watched, he sighed in his sleep, clutching her pillow, then wrapping himself around it. He looked like a boy aching for his mother or like a man missing his lover— she wasn't sure which, and frankly, given what she'd seen, the parallels disturbed her. Worse, she knew if she stayed with him, she would become both to this enigmatic man: his mother, soothing his fears, and his lover, because he wanted to father an army. Could she do that? Could she give her heart and her body to this man, accept the power that came with him, shape the policies of a nation, remake the world as they chose?

She bit her lip and turned away, knowing the image of her having any power to do good was simply that— an image, an illusion he spun for her sake. She sincerely doubted this man would ever release control to anyone. Looking about, for the first time she saw the clutter of his bedroom. It wasn't just the papers that lay about the floor, but the gems and artifacts scattered haphazardly on every surface. An ancient sword, rusted with disuse, hung next to a necklace of seashells such as a crippled boy might make. A diamond tiara was shoved into a corner, half buried by a badly folded tapestry of the finest silk, now moth-eaten and smelling of decay.

Mementos, every one of them. How she knew, she wasn't sure. Probably because the information was shared from the Copper to her Queen and then to her, usually in scattered bits of barely remembered dreams. But no matter how she gained the knowledge, she understood its significance.

What companions existed for a man who had lived over a hundred cycles? His contemporaries were all dead. All that was left to him were these moldy bits of fabric and strange artifacts—all disorganized, none truly cherished but none discarded. He kept them as he kept everything, because he needed to have them. Not to use them, just to have them.

As Dag Racho's Queen, she would be equally useless,

equally owned. Indeed, her mind flashed on the heavy chains that bound Racho's Copper. Her own chains might be prettier, certainly less obvious, but they would lock her down as surely.

No, she thought sadly, there was no place for her here. And so she would have to search for an escape. If only Kiril were here. He would know what to do.

She thought briefly of killing the Emperor here and now. The rusty sword was at hand, and any number of other weapons, for that matter. But even if she managed to chop off Dag Racho's head right now, the Copper would go insane. The human mind that restrained it would be gone, and in its place would be an unreasoning deluge of pain. And an insane dragon was not what Ragona needed.

She would have to wait until after her Queen had hatched. Until they were both ready to fight Dag Racho and the Copper. But first she needed to escape, and so she tiptoed to the secret passageway, sliding through the bathroom until she came into her own chamber.

She saw him immediately. Not the warrior she wished for, but a friend nonetheless. Tall, broad shoulders and dark hair like his father, though the skin was pale as befitted a man more used to libraries than outdoor markets. And when he turned, she saw the same smile, the same glorious love that she remembered from so many years ago. Pentold.

She leaned forward, about to rush into his arms then froze. A guard was inside the room, one she hadn't met before. He watched everything with flat, assessing eyes. So she tilted her head, narrowing her eyes as if searching for a memory.

The Pentold she remembered was smart when he applied himself, but more often he was caught dreaming, his hand on a book and his eyes focused vaguely on something leagues distant. Had he seen the flash of recognition in her eyes? Would he understand that she had to pretend to barely remember him for his own safety? Dag Racho would never allow him to visit if he believed Natiya held Pentold in more than just casual friendship.

Natiya frowned, moving slowly as she looked her childhood companion over from head to toe. His fingers were ink-stained, just as she remembered. And his clothing always had that slightly disheveled look, no matter how fine the cut or fabric. It was his face that had changed. It was no longer round in youth, and the bones had lengthened, drawing his face downward in sharp angles, his forehead higher as his hair was obviously thinning.

But what she noticed most was the way his eyes had changed. They had always been warm and open when they looked at her. At one time, she could read his every expression, almost his every thought as if it were her own. But not now. Now his eyes seemed hooded as they took in her swollen belly, her awkward gait. And then his gaze returned to her face, clearly searching her expression as carefully and thoroughly as she studied his.

She swallowed, hating to lie to her once best friend, but it was for his own safety. "Do I know you?"

He bowed deeply before her. "Pentold Marsters— poet, dreamer . . . and your one-time neighbor. How may I serve you, Lady Natiya?"

"Pentold?" she said softly, her eyes widening as if she had just placed him. "*D'greth,* how you have changed! I haven't seen you in"—she shook her head— "ten cycles at least."

"Eleven, my lady. And as for changes . . ." He glanced significantly at her large belly. "I am not the only one to have . . . grown."

She grinned at his understated humor. "Well, large is what I am. And unwieldy as a fat gommet. But the hatching time approaches, and I need your help."

Not by even a flicker of his eyes did he betray a sudden

wariness, but she felt it nonetheless. The egg was growing better at that, she realized—knowing people's moods and emotions by changes in their scent. It was a useful skill to have, Natiya thought as she ducked behind a screen to change her attire. She wanted to be out of both Pentold's and the guard's sight when she said her next line. After last night's revelations, she doubted she could keep her expression appropriately ardent.

"I want to give the Emperor a gift. For our wedding night."

"My lady, I am sure that your presence shall be gift enough for any man, including our leader."

"Spoken like a true poet," she said with a childish giggle, though, *d'greth*, she was tired of sounding like an idiot. As if in defiance of the very persona she was adopting, Natiya donned a flowing gown of deepest sapphire. Given her current size, it made her look rather like a large plumma fruit, but the color matched her eyes and the gown gave her room to move. "I wish to write a poem all about the glories our Emperor has bestowed upon Ragona. It must, of course, be an epic poem, with dragon meter and rhyme." She stepped out from behind the screen. "That is your speciality, isn't it?"

"Just so, my lady," he said. She caught a flash of pride in his expression, and she knew that he had indeed become a master poet, just as he had sworn long ago.

"I have made a start," she said, grabbing the parchment she'd scribbled on the night before. "But I'm afraid it is not very good."

"But one does not judge a gift from the heart."

She smiled. Pentold certainly had not lost his glib tongue. For all his daydreaming, he'd had the fastest excuses and the most amazingly twisted arguments whenever they were caught in mischief. She could have thought of no better ally.

Unless, of course, he was completely devoted to the Emperor. In which case, she was doomed. She had to be honest with him about her intentions. But first she had to get rid of the guard. So she gestured to a table, indicating that Pentold should sit. And as she moved to settle beside him, she banged into the guard, pushing him backward.

"Oh, please," she groused, "can you not move aside?" Then she wrinkled her nose, waving him outside into the hall. "Do you men never wash your uniforms? I swear I can smell horse dung and . . ." She hesitated. What was that smell? A bawdy house without the perfume? But that meant men alone or together . . . "Ugh! Go away! Outside!"

The guard had backed up as far as he could, but when she motioned for him to leave the room, he simply shook his head. "I cannot, my lady. For your own protection, I must remain here with you."

She groaned in true frustration. Dropping her fists on her now ample hips, she glared at him. "He is a poet, for Amia's sake!" As if Pentold were not large, strong and extremely dextrous with a knife. "And more than that, the Emperor is right on the other side of that wall." She pointed specifically for Pentold's benefit. "I assure you," she said with absolute truth, "that *he* can hear even the slightest noise from this chamber. I need only cry out and both he and you will come rushing to my aid."

The guard bowed most respectfully at her, and for a moment she hoped she had won the day. Then he shook his head. "The Emperor would also know that I had betrayed my charge to protect you with my life."

"But—"

"I shall not leave, my lady. Perhaps you should return to your gift."

Natiya bit her lip, seeing indeed that she would not hold sway with this guard. Damn, damn, damn! She had intended to be very careful in any event, but it made things much more awkward with a loyal guard in the room.

"Very well," she said, with little grace as she settled her bulk into the chair beside Pentold.

"You have done very well," her poet remarked as she gave him her attention. "But perhaps these adjustments would fit the meter better."

She glanced down at the parchment where he had written:

Are you truly well, Natiya? How can I help?

She looked up, grinning in thanks. "My, but that is just the thing! You are an excellent poet indeed." Then, before she could speak, she heard a noise from Dag Racho's chamber. Likely it was nothing more than the man snoring in his sleep, but she could not take that chance. Her time was quickly running out. So, looking directly at her once dearest friend, she decided to risk everything on the chance that he had not changed. That he would still brave anything and everything for her.

"I have just the idea!" she said, and she quickly wrote:

I cannot hatch here. I must escape. Soon.

"Oh," she moaned. "But then I need a rhyme for 'beneficence.' "

He nodded, his expression serious as he twisted the parchment to write on it. "That is a difficult task, my lady. But perhaps I could be of assistance."

She brightened. "Truly?" And then she looked down at what he had written.

Will you marry me?

Her heart sank to her toes. How had she forgotten her uncle's proposal so long ago in Talned's inn? He had wanted her to marry Pentold and had been quite eloquent on the matter, claiming that his son was still in love with her. She looked at her friend's expression and saw that Uncle Rened had not exaggerated; Pentold's eyes shone with a love that melted her heart.

She looked away, startled by the tears that blurred her vision. "No," she said softly, "that will not serve." Then she wrote:

It is much too dangerous.

"My lady . . ." Pentold began, and she could tell that he was about to waste time arguing. So she gave him the only argument that would hold sway for a man like him. And it was all the worse because it was true.

I do not love you. Then honesty forced her to add, *And you do not know how much I have changed.*

You love the Emperor? he wrote.

"No!" She gasped aloud.

Another?

She flashed on an image of Kiril standing naked, surrounded by enemies, and yet looking at her with his heart in his eyes. A sob caught in her throat. Had she killed the man she loved?

Beside her, Pentold bowed his head, and she saw resignation in the movement. It hurt her to see him so defeated, and it grew even more painful when she realized he would not help her escape now. In fact, she had just made a huge blunder. In her experience, spurned lovers did everything they could to harm the one they loved.

With a sudden anger, she grabbed the parchment and hurled it into the fire, watching the evidence of her request turn to ashes. "No, no, no! It is all wrong!" she cried. Then she felt his hand upon her shoulder, his long fingers gentle as they urged her to face him. She went slowly, dreading to see anger in his eyes. She was startled to see love still burning in his expression, only mixed with melancholy.

"Pentold?"

"Perhaps I should pen a few lines today. Just to help you get started," he offered. "I can bring it to you tomorrow at the same time. Would that serve?"

She bit her lip, afraid to believe he would still help even after her rejection. "Are you sure?"

He smiled, and she saw her childhood friend fully this time, appearing just as he had always looked: filled with mischief, cunning and such a romantic bent as to make her laugh. "Trust me, my lady. Allow me to show you what my feeble efforts can accomplish by tomorrow."

She smiled, feeling her knees weaken with a surge of love so different from what he wanted, but so like what they had once shared. "All my hope rests in your hands, dear poet."

He bowed to her then, so deeply as to convey great respect. And then, without another word, he turned on his heel and left.

Natiya was not one to trust solely in someone else's abilities, especially when her life hung in the balance. And yet, try as she might, she could think of no other escape except for one that Pentold might arrange for her. Everywhere she turned, she was surrounded by guards, given "lessons" by the Emperor's most trusted staff, or watched by Dag Racho himself.

With no other option, Natiya found herself relaxing. She did not fight the restrictions of the guards and the locked door. Instead she read, and when she could, she rested, knowing that in the morning the situation could look vastly improved. And truthfully, she enjoyed the feeling of simply laying her burden on someone else's shoulders. The egg was more than cumbersome now. It felt like a great big luggen beast wrapped around her body, and it made her damned tired.

So she was dozing when Dag Racho sought her out that afternoon. Her big feet were propped on a pillow while she stared out the window at that mountain that constantly drew her gaze. Her eyelids had slipped down, though, and Dag Racho came on her unawares. His touch woke her, firm and angry as he gripped her arm, then gentle as his other hand slid down to caress the egg.

"My lord?" she asked, as she set her feet on the floor, using the motion to draw her belly away from him.

"Were you looking at my mountain again?" His tone was strange, seemingly congenial, but there was an undercurrent of tension beneath, and she grew even more wary.

"I'm afraid I was looking at nothing more than darkness," she said.

"Yes, well, it won't be more than a day or two before you hatch." He smiled a kind of feral smile—both wild and civilized at the same time. But the emphasis was on wild, and so when he held out his hand for her to rise, she pretended exhaustion.

"Oh, my lord—"

"Do not seek to quarrel with me today, Natiya," he snapped. "I said, 'come.'"

He had not, in fact, said anything of the sort, but she knew better than to argue. So Natiya pushed to her feet, taking his hand when he still held it out before her face. Then, with a grip that could easily crush her hand if she struggled, he drew her out of her room, through the castle and then—eventually—into the courtyard.

"Where are we going?" she asked.

She didn't think he would answer, as he handed her up onto a large but docile horse, then mounted another himself. But, surprisingly he turned both their beasts—for they were tethered together—toward his mountain. "I thought you would like to see the inside of my garrison."

"I would, of course. But why?"

He flashed his pearly teeth at her. "Because I have something there which I think you would particularly enjoy seeing." And that was the end of their conversation as he kicked his mount into a fast trot.

His guards settled into pace around them. Natiya was not a skilled rider, and she needed all her concentration just to grip the hairy sides of her mount as the city streets flew by. She thought briefly of trying to escape, but discarded the thought. Even if she could safely jump from her beast to the ground, she would move too slowly through the crowded streets. The guards would be upon her in less than a beat.

Once again she found herself relaxing, enjoying the sights of the city on their too-fast, bouncy ride. She saw some rather impressive buildings, but mostly she noticed the people who scurried out of their way—a dirty, unkempt, resentful lot of pleasants.

How odd that after only a few days in the castle, her sensibilities had changed so much. Not so long ago she had been one of the unwashed. It was only with the presence of the Emperor's lavish bathing pool that she had been able to cleanse away her daily grime. Except, of course, there was no daily grime now that all she ever did was memorize lists of possible traitors.

And as for those who gave her dark looks, she didn't blame them. They had to scramble out of the way of the Emperor's procession or be trampled. Indeed, the guards took little heed if their mounts kicked through food, wares or the occasional unwary urchin.

"Perhaps, my lord, we should slow our pace," she suggested, "to allow your people time to move their things."

He glanced at her, clearly annoyed. "You shall not escape, Natiya, no matter how slow we go."

She wanted to argue that she had not intended to escape, although that would be a lie. And she knew that any protest on behalf of the peasants would be brushed off as a mere excuse. So she held her tongue, reminding herself that Pentold would visit in the morning with a plan for her escape. There was little she could do until then.

They made it to the mountain in a surprisingly short time, especially since they could not take a direct route but had to accommodate the clogged city streets. Indeed, the base of Racho's mountain was a good deal closer than she expected and a great deal wider. Which meant Racho's man-made mountain was huge.

"Does the mountain accommodate all your troops?" she asked, simultaneously awed and horrified by the thought.

He simply shook his head, and she was left to wonder if that meant the mountain housed things beyond his garrisons or if his army was indeed larger than she had at first thought. Larger than anyone could possibly guess.

Now that they marched through a huge practice ground, they could move faster. Except, ever contrary, the Emperor slowed them down. He smiled at his soldiers, beaming with pride as his procession meandered through men practicing with sword, crossbow, arrow, even strange balls caught in a hand net.

"They are quite skilled," she said truthfully. Indeed, she very much feared that this army could take down a Queen dragon if it had such a mind.

"We will go inside here," was his only response as he dismounted. Then his soldiers stood back, blocking the way as the Emperor assisted her off her mount. It was disconcerting how much he touched her, never letting anyone close. At first she had thought it kind, was even flattered at his attention and grateful that she was not mauled by any of his ham-fisted guards. But she was rapidly understanding how suffocating the Emperor's attention could be. So she shook him off, following his guard into a doorway built into the side of the mountain.

The first rooms were regular, the stone and wood clearly sectioned just as in any building. She found soldiers of all types here, gradually growing older and seemingly more dour as she moved deeper and deeper within the fortress.

As the stones grew rougher, however, the walls less finished, she began to feel a change in the air. It was not as stifling as she expected, but the weight of it pressed at her from all sides. She found it harder to walk, harder

still to breathe. And worse yet, she began to tingle.
From head to toe, but centering mostly around the egg,
she felt her body spark alive even as she felt compressed by the air and stone. She wanted desperately to
take a deep breath of salty sea air, but the ocean was
far, far away.

At last they came to a door made of heaviest stone,
wrapped in loga metal by the looks of it. Without even a
word from the Emperor, the guards melted away, taking
up posts back down the hallway while Dag Racho gestured her inside.

"What is this place?" she asked softly, hating the trem-
ble she heard in her voice.

"Prison," he answered with a smile. Then he pulled
open the door, allowing a foul odor to escape but nothing else. Not even light came from the darkened maw.
Then he pushed her inside.

She spun around, terrified that he meant to lock her
in there, but he remained in the doorway, casually lighting a lantern and then grabbing a set of keys before he
let the door swing shut with a ponderous thud.

"Why have you brought me here?" she asked. She
hadn't wanted to. Indeed, she knew she was giving
away her nervousness just by asking the question. But
the air was so close, the dark so thick, she couldn't help
it. She was more than nervous here; she was terrified.
And there was absolutely nothing she could do about
it. Except, of course, close her eyes and pray Pentold
found her a way to escape very, very soon.

"Come along, Natiya." Rashad's voice echoed eerily
in the gloom. Add to that the way the shadows writhed
from his flickering lantern, and she was hard put not to
scream. But she held in her fear, and soon found herself waddling beside him as they moved deeper into the
mountain.

She had no choice but to look around her. Her slippers were thin, and so she felt every pebble she stepped

upon, every skittering creature that brushed against her foot, every slimy puddle that seeped its way through the fabric to coat her toes. She had to look down to avoid the debris on the floor, but once focused downward she saw also the bars at either side of the path. And once she noticed the bars, she couldn't help but look at the creatures beyond—poor, pitiful wrecks that had once been people. Once, but not now. Men, women, even children, all destroyed in mind or body by the weight of their own filth and the darkness that surrounded them. As the lantern light neared each cell, they crawled to the back corners and crouched in the deepest recesses like spiders.

"What were their crimes?" Natiya whispered. She knew the answer even before he spoke. There was only one crime in Ragona.

"Treason," he said. Then he stopped, raising the light higher to shine on a woman and her slumbering child. That any child could sleep in such a place appalled her. That the mother slept too made her think that perhaps they were both dead, and better off that way.

Then, from her side, she heard the Emperor sigh. "This is an evil place, Natiya, but every land must have one. Evil must be punished."

"And is their only crime that they plotted against you? No murderers? Thieves? Prostitutes?"

He smiled. "They did nothing but threaten my plans, Natiya."

She swallowed, seeing the gleam of madness in his eyes. He was actually pleased to show her this abuse of power. He wanted to impress upon her that he could do whatever he willed to anyone in Ragona.

"How long, my lord? How long have these souls been in here?"

He looked at her and frowned, clearly unsure of the answer. In the end, he simply shrugged. "It varies."

"The longest?"

His answer was casual as he began to continue down the hallway. "Many cycles, I should think." Then he turned to her. "But the shortest is no more than an hour. Would you like to meet him? We could discuss his crime."

She felt a shiver of fear not at his tone, but at Dag Racho's flippant attitude. He could be talking about his breakfast for all that he seemed to care, and so she slowed her steps, turning to challenge him, to see perhaps if there was something decent still inside him. Something she could reach.

"If I discuss his crime with you, will it make a difference in his punishment?"

He grinned, as if he had been waiting for just this question. "Why, of course, my dear, of course. But first you must meet him."

He led her deeper into the mountain. In truth, she tried not to look at the wretches around her, but she could not stop herself. Nor could she stop the thought that if she lost her struggle against Dag Racho, at least she would die cleanly in battle. This endless incarceration in darkness would be infinitely worse, and her heart bled for the beings around her. It didn't matter to her what crimes they had committed. Surely a day here would be enough punishment for even the most heinous of sins. Thank Amia that in the morning—

Pentold. In a cell halfway down the line. His face was swollen, his clothing torn and bloody. His greater injuries took a moment longer for her to recognize. Though he tried to hide it, she could tell that one of his arms was broken, and his breath came in wheezing gasps, likely from multiple cracked ribs. Clearly he had not been taken willingly. And just as clearly, his captors had not yet broken his spirit, for unlike the other inhabitants, he faced the light openly, sneering at both Natiya and Dag Racho.

"He was caught bribing one of my guards. I believe he was trying to arrange for your escape." The Emperor sighed as he hung the lantern from a nearby peg. "Pity, really, for I understand he was quite a great poet." He turned to her. "Well, my dear, what shall we do?"

A flurry of responses flashed through her mind. The egg, naturally, was no help at all. It had never experienced anything like this and had no suggestions; Natiya would have to find her own answers. Still, she had done her fair share of bargaining in her past, and so she stepped forward, simultaneously coming closer to Pentold's cage and further away from Dag Racho. "You must release him, of course."

The Emperor laughed long and hard at that, the sound growing instead of deadening against the stone walls. Perhaps it was the metal that made up the bars, but his humor echoed back to her a hundred, then a thousandfold. When it finally faded, his jeers continued to sound in her mind such that she struggled not to clap her hands over her ears.

"Not him, my dear," he finally said, when he could catch his breath. "You. What shall we do with you for trying to escape?"

It took a moment for his words to make sense, but when they did she felt horror slip into her thoughts as easily as the slime had penetrated her slippers. "Me?" she said, trying hard to sound as casual as he. "But—"

"Pray do not be tedious and deny it. Of course you have been trying to escape. I would expect nothing less."

She bit her lip, looking about her, seeing the dark, hearing the moans mixed with insane laughter. She smelled the filth and even tasted the horror in the air. She experienced the prison as an animal would—as her dragon would—with all her senses, searching for a weakness, looking for a point of vulnerability.

And in all that place, she found only one opening—from Dag Racho himself. She smelled pride on him. Pride not in what he had accomplished—his capture of all these wretched people—but in her. For attempting to escape, for converting Pentold to her cause, for daring to challenge him. After all, what challenges remained for a man who had already conquered all that he could see?

She straightened. Well, if challenge was what he wanted, she would be sure to give it to him. She had been too long waiting on someone else, hoping for something else. It was time for her to take control.

"Release him, Rashad." She saw the Emperor's eyes narrow at the use of his true name, but she continued as if unaware of his irritation. "Pentold's only crime is that he loves me. And if you are to incarcerate every soul who loves the Queen, then even this mountain will not be able to hold all your prisoners."

"And why should I release your lover to you?" His words echoed in a kind of hiss that she found disconcerting.

"I said he loved me. I did not say I returned the favor." She sighed as she turned to Pentold, her expression gentle. "You are a fool, my old friend, to risk so much on a woman who cannot give you what you want."

Her friend shrugged, and she knew the gesture gave him great pain. "My risk was my own," he said.

She shook her head, already turning back to the Emperor. "Release him and all these people. Clean them up, get them some decent food and give them enough money for a full cycle's food and lodging. They have suffered enough for their crimes."

Dag Racho was leaning against the bars of Pentold's cage, his head tilted to one side. As he studied her, his attitude remained relaxed, even curious. "Why should I do that?"

"I told you. Because they have suffered enough."

"You do not know—"

"Nor do I need to."

He tilted his head toward the cell behind her. "What about *her*? Do you wish her to be released?"

Natiya twisted, looking over her shoulder to see a woman, obviously weak, her hair a matted shroud twisted about her face like rotting weeds. And yet, as she watched, the woman pushed herself to her feet, gathering a kind of dignity and beauty despite her condition.

"Sabina."

"She tried to kill you."

"With good reason." Natiya didn't dare look into Sabina's eyes when she spoke. She was ashamed to realize that she had allowed the guards to drag the woman away and not given her another thought since. Hadn't she learned as a child that even the smallest action had consequences? If not for herself, then for someone else? Someone like a small, young child, suddenly without family because her parents had found a dragon egg.

"Yes," Natiya said firmly, turning back to the Emperor. "Release her as well."

"And how do you intend to repay me for such beneficence, my dear? Why should I do these things for you? I assure you, their crimes have not been paid for. They should be thanking me that they still live."

This time, she was the one who laughed. "Let us not pretend. They live because you think they have value. Even I know that Sabina can take the meanest copper chamber pot and work it into a treasure fit for an Emperor. And perhaps you have no interest in Pentold's poetry, but he is the only son of the greatest merchant in Ragona. Perhaps his value lays there." She gestured to all the other cells and people who one by one were struggling to their feet as they listened to her words. "I do not even know these other souls' names, but I would swear they each know something or have something you want. I am most interested to learn what that is and how they would use it—"

"They would use it to destroy us!" he interrupted, but she waved the comment away.

"Are you so afraid, Emperor? Of this lot?"

His eyes narrowed, and he advanced on her. Not to defend his pride. That would be too easy. But to tower over her in a type of intimidation that—in this light and this place—was quite effective. "Do not try my patience with stupidity, little girl. I rule because I defeated the dragonlords. Because I formed a government and built a nation out of ragtag refugees. It is because of me that the land is now green and our people fat."

She looked at him, taking her time to notice his strength, his genuine pride in what he had accomplished. "Indeed, my lord, you have done much. But to what end?"

He blinked, clearly confused. "For safety, of course! So that what we have is safe."

"We *are* safe, my lord." She advanced on him, seeing if she could get him to understand. "These people, Rashad. Who are they? Are they the ones who steal and threaten the people of Ragona? Are they invaders from another land? Who do they threaten?"

"Ragona!"

"Ragona?" she challenged. "Or you?"

"We are one and the same!" he bellowed, abruptly shoving her away from him. His push was not hard, merely surprising, and she too ungainly to adjust. She stumbled backward, falling against the bars of Sabina's cell. Pentold surged forward, reaching for her despite his grimace of pain. There was little he could do, of course, but Natiya smiled at him. From behind, she heard Sabina step forward, pushing her hand out to help her regain balance.

All the while, the Emperor stood above her, his breathing loud as he struggled to control his emotions. Outside she heard the roar of his Copper, giving distant vent to the anger that Rashad could not contain. It was only his desire for Natiya's Queen that kept her alive right now. And so she banked on that, for that was all she—and those around her—had on their side.

"You should be more careful, Rashad," she said softly. "You might have hurt the egg."

Fear flashed in his eyes, but was quickly covered by a childish bravado. He squared his shoulders, smoothing his tunic with shaking hands. "You are unharmed. But let this be a warning to you, Natiya: Do not try my patience." And then, clearly gaining strength from his words, he folded his arms across his chest and began looking about him. "Now, as for these prisoners. You wish me to release them?"

She was balanced again on her own swollen feet, and she nodded, but was abruptly afraid that she had overplayed her hand. Would he kill them all just to spite her?

"I ask again: What shall you give me, my dear, to do as you request? How shall you pay me for my beneficence?"

"Oh, my lord," she gasped with mock embarrassment. "I am afraid you do not understand. It is *you* who must pay *me*. By releasing them."

He stared at her, clearly confused. If he were more in command of himself, she knew he would have laughed, his grating, derisive laugh that was both humiliating and irritating. She counted it a victory that he could only stare. So she pressed her point as quickly as she dared, letting her belly lead her closer as she spoke. As long as the egg was between them, he would be careful.

"You want the Queen, my lord. And the only way to have her is to have me. So, Emperor, exactly what will you pay to possess me? What am I worth to you?"

"You will give yourself to me if I release all these villains? Back onto the street where they will ravage and pillage—"

"*You* have ravaged and pillaged Ragona for the last hundred cycles, my lord, not these few. Let us abandon these games. And as for my price—I am afraid I am much more expensive than a few prisoners."

He inclined his head, acknowledging her words. But she also got the feeling he was playing her, or attempting. "Very well, my dear. I shall give you all the treasure you could wish."

She smiled—a natural, easy smile, for she had never wanted wealth or jewels. "I have no wish for trinkets, my lord. I want power."

"Ah. That is a great deal harder to give—and even more difficult to hold."

She glanced to her left and then back to her right, at Sabina and Pentold, knowing she could likely recruit both to her side, assuming she could gain their release. "Give me power. Leave the people to me." He didn't answer, and so she knew it was up to her to continue. "I am no fool, Dag Racho. Your army does not defend Ragona. It one by one conquers our neighbors. Very well, gobble up all the territory you wish. Rule your army however you want. Give control of Ragona to me."

"Ridiculous!" he snapped, his pride now taking control. "I am the Emperor—"

"Of an angry, wretched people." She gestured about the damp prison. "See the fruits of your labors, Rashad. Is this why you killed your family, lost all your friends and betrayed your sister?" She had been guessing about that, extrapolating from flashes of dream memory and what little the egg conveyed to her. At his flinch, she knew she had scored a true hit.

"You are not capable of ruling Ragona," he growled. "I am the Emperor. I release nothing to you."

He would not move on that point; she could tell that too much of his pride was involved. She would have to moderate her demand. "Very well. Leave me in charge of Ragona's justice. Allow me free rein over who is imprisoned and why. I shall hear the cases, I shall decide the punishments—"

"And make the laws?" he finished for her.

She nodded, and everyone waited while he appeared to consider.

"You would be my wife?" he asked, and she heard true yearning in his voice. "In all ways? You will love me, cherish me? Obey me?"

She bit her lip. Could she do that? Would she do it? "I cannot command the yearnings of my heart," she said. "But I will not betray you, and that, I believe, is more important."

It was, for he began to nod. But then Pentold stepped forward, gripping the bars of his cell with cut and bleeding fingers. "You cannot trust his word, Natiya. Do not—"

"Silence, droog!" Dag Racho slammed his fist against the bars, missing Pentold only because he pulled back in time. But the poet remained dangerously close, still within reach of the Emperor through the bars. And more specifically, well within reach of the sword Dag Racho always carried.

Natiya stepped forward, gently interposing her bulk between Pentold and the Emperor, speaking in a calm, almost congenial tone. "But I *can* trust him, Pentold," she said. This clearly startled the Emperor, because he leaned forward to stare at her more closely. She added, "And he knows why, don't you, Rashad?"

It was a random ploy. She'd hoped to get him to reveal one of his vulnerabilities by telling her a hold she had over him. It didn't work. He was much too smart for that.

"I am at a loss, my dear. I have only my word."

She sighed. "I can trust you because I am your Queen," she said. She leaned forward, touching his cheek with her right hand while the other slowly reached into his pocket and sought the keys he carried there. She let power flow between them, surging through her left hand while her other hand finally found cold metal. She pressed the keys against her palm and began lifting them away, holding Dag Racho's eyes as she worked, wondering if—or when—he would stop her. "He knows his people hate him. He feels them slipping away, and he does not understand why." She allowed her right hand to curve around his clenched jaw, caressed his cheek, his lips. "All Rashad ever wanted was love. He has brought Ragona a hundred years of prosperity, and still the people hate him."

He grabbed her left hand—the one holding the keys—and using his superior strength, pressed it against his thickened groin. Clearly, negotiations had an aphrodisiac effect on the Emperor. "And you," he rasped. "Will you love me? Do you love me?" She heard mockery in his questions, as if he already knew she did not—could not—and yet, there was longing there as well.

"I cannot order my heart. I have already told you that." She looked down at his sex, wondering if she could indeed give herself to him that way. She looked to her right, where Pentold once again gripped the bars as if he would break them. He watched her with his own longing, his own hunger, and her words came out without thought or volition. "You love me, Rashad, for the Queen I carry. You will give me power and a chance to shape the world in a manner of my choosing. This poet loves me, too, for the friendship we once shared. He is a good man who would give me everything." She felt a tear slip down her cheek, though she could not spare it a thought. "And yet for all that, my heart chooses a man who used me for his own ends. He only spoke lies, and even his caresses were manipulations."

"The dragon-hunter." She felt a change in the Emperor, a tension and a confusion as he struggled with her words. "But you ordered him killed."

She looked back at Rashad. "Like you, I am not ruled by love."

"Only by hate."

"And you by your fears," she snapped.

She and Rashad came to an accord at that moment: They understood one another at a level that went far beyond any exchange of material possessions. They knew the deepest terrors that haunted each other, and respected the power of those drives. Still, she counted herself the winner in this exchange, for whereas his fears were very real—his fear of loneliness and abandonment—her hatred was dead. It had disappeared the moment she ordered Kiril's death. And so Rashad had no control over her, for she had nothing left to hate beyond a lost dream.

"Very well," Rashad said, as he released her hand but kept the keys. "Make the laws, control the prisoners, play the beneficent queen. I wish to keep one prisoner, though. Just for me."

"No!" Three voices rang out: Sabina's, Pentold's, Natiya's own. She did not know who this prisoner was, but if Dag Racho wanted him, he had to be valuable. "No. All the prisoners, or no deal," she warned.

He nodded, as if expecting as much. "Very well. All the prisoners, Natiya, are at your disposal. But I think you get more than you bargain for. I have been ruling Ragona for a hundred cycles, and I believe you are unprepared. Like me, you will try to be kind, you will act with mercy and justice—and they will hate you anyway. The criminals will clamor loudly that you are evil and unnatural. The victims will claim you are weak and ineffective. And all about you will be leeches, sycophants and idiots. Truly, it is the idiots who are the worst, and there are a great, great many of those."

"Do not fear—," she began, but he cut her off.

"I do *not* fear, Natiya, because you are headed for a disaster bought by your own ignorance and naivete. And in the end, you will have no escape, nowhere to turn except to me and my army." He gestured about him, to the wretched souls all pressed against their cells, holding on to every word as tightly as they held the bars. "Here are the brightest of Ragona, the smartest and the most treacherous. Do not think they will thank you for their escape. They know you are mine, my queen, and they will rush home and begin plotting the moment they breathe clean air." He stepped forward, both hands cupping first her face, then trailing down her arms until he caressed the egg. "This will keep you safe for a time—a Queen dragon is an asset beyond the greatest army in the world. But in the end, you will come to me willingly because we are destined—"

She jerked away from him, speaking without thought. "No—"

He moved so quickly, her word was cut off on a gasp. "Yes, Natiya," he hissed in her ear as his hands suddenly roved freely over her breasts, her belly, and then delved deeper between her thighs. She could not fight because his grip was like iron. "You will give me everything." He abruptly tightened his hold. Pain shot through her from the press of the hard egg deep into her spine, the clawlike grip of his fingers as he burrowed deeper into her, and the binding of his arm across her chest. *D'greth*, she had never known anything this strong, this crushing. She couldn't breath! She heard screaming in the distance—Pentold, Sabina, all the prisoners—but the sound was fading as darkness ate into her vision. Then, he suddenly released her. She fell to the filthy floor while blessed air filled her lungs.

"Everything, Natiya. You will give me everything."

She shook her head, though the movement increased her headache a thousandfold. "Your threat means nothing," she gasped. "You need the Queen. Kill me, and you don't have her."

"After the hatching—" he began.

"Even you would not risk an insane Queen dragon. Especially you, since you would not be able to control her." She forced herself to stand, though her legs could barely support her weight. Then she faced him, her words choking her, but it was the only leverage she had. "Very well," she said. "I will give you my body and my loyalty. In return, I get the keys to all your prisons. I judge, I condemn."

He folded his arms across his chest. "I need two prisoners a day for the Copper's food." He smiled. "So will you."

She shrugged. "Our dragons will have food. I will see to it." What food, exactly, would be up to her.

He laughed, the sound harsh and grating. "Life has become somewhat tedious of late. I look forward to watching you struggle."

She held out her hand. "The keys, my lord."

He grinned and dropped the keys into the slime, continuing to lecture as if he could not stop himself. "Destiny is only as powerful as one's army, my lady. And I have something to show you exactly how inexperienced you are, how very much you are still ruled by your passions."

A cold shiver of fear slid down her spine. What had she missed? She was not given time to ponder, for the Emperor grabbed his lantern, stepping with long strides to the back of the room, to the very last cell and a dark figure standing against the bars. Lifting the lantern, he let the light shine fully on the man, the only man who could completely upset her every plan.

Kiril.

"Yes, my dear," the Emperor continued, his voice mocking. "The man you ordered killed, but whom I kept alive. The man who lied to you and used you in the worst possible way. He hates all dragons, you know, and despises the dragonborn even more. And you intend to free him." He held the light, making sure it shone on Kiril's face. Then he turned and walked back to her. "Do you know the moment when you will become a true

Queen, my dear?" He didn't wait for her answer, but said: "The moment you put him back here—this murderer of dragons—back into a cage where he belongs. You will not kill him out of passion or couple with him out of lust. You will think logically and clearly—like a Queen—and put him in storage—"

"In prison," she corrected in a harsh whisper.

Dag Racho dipped his head in acknowledgment. "For use when he is needed, and safely contained when he is not. Then you will be a true Queen." He turned as if to leave, but then stopped. "Oh, and if you give yourself to him in any way—a caress, a kiss, a touch of any kind—then our deal will be forfeit. You will have bargained all this for nothing."

She stared at him, horror seeping into her soul. "You cannot think to control my every action, to know—"

"I can, my dear," he said with absolute certainty. "I know everything. I hear from spies, from our dragons, from all kinds of secret magics everywhere. Touch him, Natiya, and I will know."

And without another word, he turned and walked away. He left her alone there with the keys and her criminals, allowing her to choose their fate and thereby create her own.

But what was she to do with Kiril?

CHAPTER FOURTEEN

Kiril watched the Emperor depart. He also watched Natiya hand the keys to Pentold, murmuring about releasing the other prisoners. He even saw Sabina press forward, watching for her opportunity to snatch the Queen egg as they had originally planned. But then she slid backward in disappointment as a half-dozen soldiers filled the hallway, reporting to their queen to serve as her assistants. Guards, more like, but Kiril barely noticed where they stood or what they did.

He was watching Natiya. He saw those other things as a warrior notices his surroundings: out of habit, not attention. His focus was fully and completely riveted on Natiya. She was nearing the hatching, likely no more than a day or two away; he had never seen a woman so near. Indeed, she was the only female dragonborn he'd ever heard of, and he was stunned by how . . . womanly she still appeared.

True, her belly was swollen as if she bore a child—or perhaps three human babes, for a dragon egg was that large. But her hair had a lustre and her skin a kind of glow that made one notice her. And in addition to the fact that her breasts seemed larger and her curves more pronounced, there was something else. Something vastly different in her carriage, in the way her eyes studied him, in her very demeanor.

It wasn't confidence, exactly, because he caught a flash of uncertainty in her eyes. Not even strength, because she seemed almost feeble in the way she waddled closer to him. So, was it faith? Hope? Determination? They all fit, and yet they did not seem quite correct.

He blinked, frowning as he fought for a label to attach to her. He could not. All he could think was that she was Natiya—strong enough to negotiate toe to toe with Dag Racho, the most powerful and dangerous man in the world. She might be uncertain of her path, but she seemed absolutely sure that she would prevail. And if she was wrong and failed, he knew she would accept the consequences with unflinching strength. He saw hope in her eyes and determination in her stance, and for the first time ever, he felt himself shrink under someone's regard.

Not even Dag Racho could reduce him to such a silent, deep feeling of shame. Natiya was someone he admired, someone he wanted to admire him. She'd said she loved him—and that he was a liar and a cheat.

He swallowed, appalled by what those words meant, by how much he must have hurt her, and by the knowledge that he had painstakingly earned each of those labels. He had indeed lied to her from the moment they met. He'd gone to Talned's inn specifically to search for her, doing everything he could to get her to trust him so that she would betray her every secret to him. Because he had thought she could give him a lead on the Queen egg.

Well, he thought wryly, stupidity had always been one of his attributes.

It didn't matter that he hadn't intended to hurt her. He hadn't planned on the lust that had burned—that *still* burned—through his body. But between his lies and the dragon magic, he had cheated them both out of a true relationship, possibly even a friendship. Because in the precious days they'd shared together, he had been intent on seducing her, not learning about her or getting to know her. So he had cheated them both, and for that he felt a shame that nearly brought him to his knees.

Still, she simply looked at him—and he at her—while all around them prisoners were set free. Guards grumbled, holding their swords at the ready, but they never made a move.

"Natiya," Kiril began, not knowing what to say or why. Merely that, after a week locked in this fetid prison, he wanted to say something beautiful.

"My dragon is not evil," she said, softly, her eyes never leaving his. "She . . . we are trying to do what's right." She looked about her, gesturing at the commotion behind them. "This could be a huge mistake, but I haven't got many options. I hope you understand that, and will give me—give us—a chance before you try to kill us."

"Did you mean what you said?" he asked. He hadn't intended to, but his words rushed out with a coarse burr. "Do you really . . . ?" He couldn't even say the word.

"Love you?" she asked.

He nodded.

She opened her mouth to answer, but no sound came out. In the end she simply shrugged, her whisper more defeated than anything else. "What do you want from me?"

Before he could find some way to answer, to express his regret for his actions, Pentold interrupted. He limped forward, his eyes darting with suspicious intent between Sabina—still waiting further up the hallway—and Kiril, who stood almost on top of Natiya, despite their being separated by the bars of his cell.

"Did you receive my books?" he asked in a bare whisper, and Kiril started at the apparent non sequitur.

Natiya, too, seemed thrown, and she twisted to frown at the poet. "I sent them through the castle librarian," he continued, pressing the cell keys into her hand. "They would have arrived a few hours ago."

Natiya shook her head. "I don't know. He was always sending me books."

Pentold touched her arm, gently drawing her away from Kiril. "Find them, Natiya. It's important."

"Why?"

Kiril saw the poet glance significantly behind him, subtly indicating the guards near Sabina, all of whom watched and listened with clear interest. They had been speaking in an undertone. Indeed, Kiril doubted that even Sabina with her excellent hearing could understand the words, but Natiya took the warning to heart.

She frowned at the soldiers and gestured them away. "What are you doing here? Go help the inmates find baths and see to their food."

The closest and burliest guard bowed with respect, but when he straightened he did not move. Instead, he smiled with false humility. "Apologies, my lady, but the Emperor ordered us to protect you with our very lives. Those other tasks"—he sneered when he said it—"have been given to new recruits."

"But I have no need for protection, sirrah," she said. "They are all gone." She gestured, indicating that the prisoners were all gone, and thus her reasons to fear.

Again the guard bowed, but Kiril recognized derision in the gesture. "Not *all* the prisoners, my lady. And even if the entire mountain were deserted, we would remain by your side. Your life is very important to the Emperor."

Natiya sighed. Kiril heard the sound distinctly, even though she was looking away from him. Then she turned back to Pentold. "I have done nothing today but buy a little time. Go, while you still can. Leave Ragona before the hatching."

The poet shook his head, grasping her hands and bringing them up to his lips to press fervent kisses along her fingers. "I will not leave you."

"You cannot help me, and it will hurt too much to see him catch you again. Do not make my work here for nothing." Then she leaned forward, and while Kiril clutched the nearby cell bars in irrational jealousy, he watched her press the tenderest of kisses to the poet's cheek. "Please, be safe. For me."

Kiril saw uncertainty in the way the poet would not look into her eyes as he tried to convince them both of a lie: "I can still help you. Even if I don't have influence, my father does—"

Natiya was not fooled. "That coin was forfeit the moment you were locked inside here. You cannot help me now." She lifted his chin, forcing him to look at her. "Please, my old friend, do not make me beg. Go. Now."

To his credit, the poet wanted to argue. He obviously searched his brain for a way to help, but they all knew he had already played out his hand. And so, in the end he bowed his head. "I would have showered you with riches, Natiya," he whispered. Then, before anyone could say more, he left.

Kiril watched the man go, knowing the poet for a better man than he. The poet had given everything he was—honestly—in the hope that Natiya loved him. All Kiril had done was use her.

But now was not the time for self-recriminations or self-pity. He straightened his shoulders when he wanted to drop to his knees and faced Natiya with pride, though he wanted to kiss her feet and beg forgiveness. And he waited—like a man—for her decision.

Fortunately for his pride, she did not make him wait long. She stepped forward, unlocking his cell with quick twists of her wrists. "You should run too, Kiril. He will try to use you against me." She paused, looking into his eyes, silently pleading with him to understand.

"I cannot let him do that. If he catches you, I cannot interfere. It would never end, and then I would have no power at all."

He paused, one hand holding the door of his cell open. "So you intend to stay. To . . ." He swallowed, furious with himself for struggling to voice the words when he had known it would happen. When he had, in fact, known it from the moment he first awoke to see Dag Racho holding Natiya. "You will join him. As his Queen."

"I hardly have a choice," she snapped, gesturing irritably at the guards. "He will not release me. So run, Kiril, and do not judge me before I have had a chance to make a difference."

He wanted to grab her, to take her with him and hide them until they could sort out their differences. He didn't truly think it was possible, but he wanted to try anyway, to find a quiet place to be with her outside of dragons and emperors and even Sabina, who was watching his every expression as if he were one of her accounting books. For a moment, Natiya caught his expression, matching his gaze for one, then two long breaths.

She felt the same way. She wanted the same thing. For the two of them.

He didn't know why the thought gave him such elation. It was impossible to start over, even if the situation were vastly different. And yet he lingered, wishing, hoping. The need to touch her burned hotter than dragon fire.

"Go, you fool!"

He could have resisted. She was not physically strong enough to force him to go anywhere, but he knew she was right, and so he left. He grabbed Sabina as he passed, knowing that they stood a greater chance of remaining out of the Emperor's clutches if they stuck together. But even as they hurried away from Dag Racho's cursed mountain, Kiril could not help wishing for what he could not have, and wondering at the fate of the woman he left behind.

Luckily, there was little time to think about that as he and Sabina hurried out of Dag Racho's mountain. The guards were offering baths and food, but neither he nor Sabina were tempted; they wanted out of the Emperor's influence as soon as possible. They had no money on them, so had to travel on foot. Fortunately Sabina knew a back entrance to a nearby bank—this was the capital city, after all; he would be surprised if she didn't know every banker and clerk within the city walls.

Less than an hour later, they had money and conveyance out of the city. Both knew it would be too dangerous to travel to their respective homes. They didn't even trust their friends right now, those few they had left. And so they could only rely on one another and the dubious anonymity of a closed carriage.

"*D'greth*, we smell," Sabina muttered as they wended their way through the clogged city corridors.

Kiril nodded, not trusting his voice or any part of his body right then. It had betrayed him too many times of late.

"So, what is the new plan?" she pressed.

He didn't speak, simply gazed at her dully, seeing only the gray outline of a lush, womanly figure. He barely noticed her ratty hair or filthy clothing. To him, she was simply Sabina, his friend and longtime companion, but also his mentor and his conscience. She had been there when he was first brought to court; quiet, withdrawn, watching him with large dark eyes. He hadn't known then how much she did to protect him, but looking back, he knew she must have risked much, sacrificed a great deal just to keep him alive and sane those first few years.

"Do you remember the first time I went against your advice?" he suddenly asked.

She answered immediately. "The hunting trip. Two soldiers—dragon-bearers you called yourselves—just across the northern border."

"You told me not to go. That if I once acted as the Emperor's terror droog there would be no turning back. I would be stained forever."

She smiled, her teeth a soft gleam of white in the carriage's gray interior. "I never thought you could be so good at it. You were so sweet, so young." She laughed softly. "And a really bad swordsman."

"I learned."

She nodded. "Yes, you did."

"But you were right." He knew he had startled her, but she didn't speak. And in the darkness, he felt more able to confess. "It was brutal, what I saw. What I did." He took a deep breath, remembering the blood on his hands, the smell of death. "I have done much worse since then. Killed in both harder and easier ways. But it all started then when you told me not to go. But I said I was a man and that men in Ragona were soldiers."

"You were right to go. You became the greatest dragon-hunter ever, and an even better man. You have exceeded everything we could have hoped for." She leaned forward, touching his leg, her hand a cool caress on his overheated body.

He shook his head, wondering exactly what he was trying to say. "I became what Dag Racho told me to become. I think he knew he had to turn my energies to his ends, bend my hate to his will, or I would forever be attacking him, trying to kill *him* rather than *for* him."

Sabina squeezed his knee. "And now you will do both." She sighed as she leaned back. "The question is, how?"

He shook his head, wishing he had something to do with his fingers. His hands felt empty without some strips of loga to shape. "You don't understand, Sabina. You were right. I should not have become a fighter. I'm . . . not suited to it."

He felt her study him but could not see her expression. Still, he knew her moods, felt the tension build within the dark carriage even before she spoke, her voice filled with venom. "It is the Emperor's bitch, isn't it? She says some lies about love, and you cannot think beyond your prock. Dammit, Kiril, she is a dragon's pawn! Evil—"

"We don't know that! We know only what we have been told."

"Were you *told* what happened to Jaseen?" she spat. "Were you told that he was kind and full of laughter before the beast took him over? Were you told what he did to me?"

"No!" he snapped, but then he moderated his tone, letting his doubts color his voice. "But . . . what if we're wrong? What if it is the man who shapes the dragon?"

"By all accounts, Dag Racho was a gentle soul before he was taken over. Look at him now," Sabina said.

Kiril all but laughed. "We cannot trust Racho's accounts of anything. Of course he would paint himself a sweet child. He thinks of himself as a kind Emperor."

Sabina glared at him. He could not see her in the darkness, but he knew she was furious. It hurt to feel her disappointment in him, but he could not change that. Natiya had sown doubts in his mind, and he could not proceed until he resolved them.

"What are you saying, Kiril? Are you saying that you think Racho and his bitch—"

"Her name is Natiya."

"I don't care if she's the goddess Amia, the dragon will turn her evil. And it is your job—indeed, it is your sworn oath to me—to kill her and Racho both. Do you forswear that oath?"

He looked away, caught by this life he had made.

"Do you?" she pressed, her voice harder. "Don't forget our wager, Kiril. It is not just a vow. If you forswear, then I receive everything. You will be left penniless—and you are already friendless."

He swallowed. "You would destroy me?"

There was no softening in her attitude. "You would destroy yourself."

"What if we are wrong, Sabina?"

"We are not—"

He did not let her finish but pushed on, wishing he could make her understand. "What if the dragons only give strength and power? Then the man shapes that power."

"You mean, woman."

"Fine," he said, irritated. "Man or woman. What if Natiya is good? She could be our greatest ally."

"She has allied herself with Dag Racho."

"She didn't in the jail. She negotiated for our release."

He heard a noise on the cushions of the carriage seat as Sabina, in her frustration, dug her nails into the fabric. But nothing in her voice betrayed anger, and she used flat, implacable logic. "Very well, Kiril. We will play this game even though we both know it is not true. Let us pretend that Natiya is a sweet and special virgin—"

"We need not be idiots," he snapped. She had been a virgin. But he had changed that.

"So, you slept with her. Damn, Kiril, you are such a fool."

He wasn't going to dignify that with an answer. But his face heated in embarrassment nonetheless. Sabina waited for a while, clearly hoping to goad him into revealing his actions at the clutching cave, but he would not budge. In the end she returned to her original tack.

"Very well. We assume she is a smart girl who has had a hard life. We can even admire her for taking matters into her own hands by incubating an egg, on her own, and keeping it secret for all these years. That indicates some measure of inner strength and intelligence."

He nodded. That was indeed a good characterization of Natiya.

"Has she told you why she did this? What is her goal?"

"She said she wanted revenge on the Emperor because he killed her family."

"And then?"

Kiril shrugged. "I don't know. She read a lot and had ideas about judges and a code of law, but she said nothing about ruling the kingdom." Even to him, that sounded ridiculous. No one gave up that kind of power when it was handed to them. And to have the only dragon in Ragona: that was just too much for anyone to lead a normal life, whether they wanted to or not. Where would she and the dragon live? Natiya had no personal wealth to buy cattle for it to eat, and no skills to procure such necessary wealth. She would be forced to drastic measures.

"We should help her," he said, desperately trying to convince himself. "Together we have enough honest wealth to maintain her dragon, and we can trade that to set up a peaceful rule."

Sabina nodded. "That would only work if she wants peace—and only if she would follow our leadership." Her tone was slightly mocking. "Does she seem amenable to things you say? Will she trust your word?" Sabina already knew the answer, and was forcing him to say it aloud.

"I have already lied to her," Kiril admitted, "even created an elaborate ruse pretending to break her out of the Dabu'ut prison. She will not trust anything I say."

"And I tried to kill her in her bath. We are hardly trustworthy—even if she were."

Kiril flinched at the image of the two women in combat. He had learned earlier the reason for Sabina's incarceration, and yet he experienced real pain at the thought of the two women fighting.

"No," he said softly, because he knew she would not continue until he acknowledged the truth. "Natiya will not take direction from us. But that does not mean she will not be a good ruler. There are others who will help her. The poet, for one."

"Who is halfway to Pajora by now." Kiril didn't answer, and Sabina folded her arms across her chest. "Very well. She will not be guided by us, but there could be others. Assuming, once again, that she wants peace, that she wants what is best for Ragona." She laughed. "Let us examine that assumption."

He wanted to say no, to stop the conversation immediately. But he knew that such a reaction was childish. They were debating the future of tens of thousands of people. If he had the power to affect this country for the good, it was his obligation to do so, no matter what his personal feelings. Wasn't that how he'd tried to always live his life?

"She is a good woman," he stated firmly. He believed that.

"Yes, yes. We started this discussion with that assumption," Sabina snapped, her voice implacable. "That she wants only to rid the world of an evil tyrant."

Kiril nodded.

"And yet . . . the first thing she asks for is power."

Kiril shifted uncomfortably, seeing where this was headed. "She was negotiating for our freedom."

"No, Kiril. She was negotiating for power."

"For the ability to make the laws, to imprison or free people justly." He said the words, but he did not know for sure if they were true. He only hoped.

"That does not sound like a woman preparing to overthrow an evil tyrant. That sounds like someone maneuvering to get more power within the existing government."

Kiril looked away. "She doesn't have many options," he said softly. "Perhaps she is just making the best of a bad situation."

Sabina released a bitter laugh. "I have no doubt of that. From the very beginning, she has shown herself to be an amateur. No plans for her hatching. No resources for after the creature was born. No training to fight the

Emperor when the time came—if that was truly what she intended. Nothing but blind faith. Tell me, please, that I am wrong. I would have more trust in you and her if you tell me she made provisions for even one of these things."

Kiril could not.

"I thought not," Sabina said. "She is crafty, I will give you that. And resourceful. But she is still an amateur in this game, Kiril. You know that as I well as I do."

"I know," he said, hating the truth as passionately as he had once hated the Emperor.

"And what happens to amateurs?" Sabina pressed. "When they go against the Emperor, what happens to the young, the naive and the innocent?"

Kiril knew the answer. They both knew, but she was making him say it aloud. "They die. They fail and they die."

"Which will land us once more back where we started: with one megalomaniac tyrant and no way to kill him."

Kiril nodded. Sabina was right.

"So, we cannot leave this up to Natiya. We must use this opportunity—this Golden Queen—to our advantage rather than to the Emperor's." She leaned forward, and Kiril recognized determination in both her tone and her body. "The question is how—how do we use Natiya to our own ends?"

He sighed, wishing once again that things were different. That he had chosen a different path from the very beginning.

"Kiril?"

"First we bathe, eat and find some decent clothes."

"And then?" Her voice was tight and eager.

"Then we have one chance, and it will be upon us very soon."

Sabina frowned, her prodigious brain working. "The hatching?"

"It is the time when she will be most vulnerable."

"But Dag Racho—"

"Will be with her, yes. In the mountain."

Sabina frowned. "The mountain. But where . . . ?"

"Yes, that mountain. Sitting inside it for so long was a boon. I learned things. I knew it was huge, but I thought it housed his army."

"It does. His very large, very considerable army."

Kiril almost laughed. He, too, had been fooled. "Yes, the army is large. But it is in the *front*. What do you think is behind those cells we were in? Behind my cage?"

Sabina shook her head. "Nothing. Rock."

"Then, what were those sounds I heard? The Emperor talking—to himself or someone else. I don't know, but I heard him. And from the way his voice echoed, the chamber was very large."

Sabina caught on. "A hatching cave? But why?"

Kiril shrugged. "Dragons are farsighted creatures with long memories. He has had a hundred cycles to think of how he would extend his life and his rule."

"By finding and marrying a Queen. We know this—"

"And we also know that the hatching is the most vulnerable time. He will take Natiya inside the mountain so that she can hatch in safety."

Sabina nodded. "Very well. But . . . how does this help us?"

"Neither you nor I saw Jaseen's hatching, but I heard. Mother and Father talked about it in whispers when they thought I was sleeping." Kiril took a deep breath, remembering those appalled and frightened words, the way his parents huddled together as if comforting themselves. But mostly he remembered that his father—his strong, unemotional, battle-tested father—had grown pale and gray when he spoke. "It is a violent, all-consuming time. There is a light and a power, I believe." Similar, no doubt, to the light and the power that had called Dag Racho to the clutching cave a little more than a week ago.

"The Emperor will be involved in that. And inside the mountain, there will be no place for his Copper to come defend him."

"And once he is killed, his heart ripped from his chest, then the Copper will be weakened—"

"He'll be insane," Kiril reminded her. "I would prefer to get the egg and poison the Copper as we originally planned."

Sabina nodded. "Very well, but how do you suppose we get in there? Through an entire army of soldiers ready to die defending Dag Racho?"

Kiril shrugged. "If I had my sword, I could find it. With it, I might be able to attune myself to the interior cave. Maybe find the entrance."

"That's a lot of ifs, even if you did have your sword."

He nodded. "I don't really need my sword, just something soaked in dragon blood. Something especially attuned to the hatching time."

She frowned, and he wondered if what he had long ago guessed was true. Now was the time he'd find out. Slowly she lifted her head, gazing into his eyes and worrying her lower lip. Finally she spoke, her voice a low throb that easily cut through the carriage's gloomy interior. "How long have you known that I have it?"

"I never knew for sure. Jaseen's armband just . . . seemed like something you would keep."

She didn't respond quickly, but when she did, he knew she was speaking the truth. "I loved him, you know. Even after, I still loved him."

"But why the armband? And how did you get it?"

She let her head drop back against the squabs, her gaze unfocused, her words soft and steeped in memory. "I won it, of course. From the Emperor, in a game of cheesta."

"What did you wager against it?"

He saw the vague outline of her smile. "Everything I had and more."

"But why?"

She shrugged. "Because I wanted to beat him in something. Because I had to prove myself capable—on so many levels."

"I never knew you were a cheesta master," Kiril remarked, awed. "When did you learn?"

She laughed. "I didn't. I cheated."

He felt his jaw go slack in astonishment, and that, of course, made Sabina laugh all the harder.

"It is a long, long story, and in the end all I wanted was the armband. You were gone at the time, searching for the Bronze, I think."

He nodded. When he'd returned, he heard rumors.

"I have it in Dabu'ut," she continued. "Do you think there is time to get it?"

He nodded. That was why he had chosen this direction in the first place. And they both had friends there, friends who were far enough removed from court to probably still be trusted. Yet he needed to know: "Why, Sabina? Why that? When it symbolizes everything you hate about the dragons, about what happened to you and to Jaseen."

She nodded, as if he had answered his own question. "That is exactly why. Because it keeps my hate alive." She sat up straighter, speaking with an extra measure of intensity. "If I could go back in time, Kiril, I would. I would kill Jaseen. I would prevent all of this from happening even though it meant I must put a dagger through Jaseen's beating heart. I would do it, Kiril."

"I know," he said, though in truth he shuddered at the vehemence in her tone, the bitterness that was dark and ugly within his friend.

"What about you?" she pressed.

"What do you mean?" he asked, very much afraid he knew exactly what she meant.

"Will you do it, Kiril? Will you cut the egg out of the body of the woman who claims to love you? The woman—"

"I love?"

"Do you?" she challenged.

"No," he lied. He'd had a great deal of time to think in prison. Away from the clutching caves, his hunger for Natiya should have faded. It hadn't. And in time, he'd realized the horrible truth: he admired her, believed in her, and yes, he loved her.

"Then, you can do it? You can kill her?"

He sighed, knowing that whatever his feelings, they didn't matter. "Natiya is dead either way. At least if I kill her, we can still make use of the egg. This way, her death will have meaning."

Sabina reached forward, stroking his cheek until he raised his gaze to hers. "Do not fail, Kiril. You are Ragona's only hope."

She was right, and yet never had his duty felt more repugnant, more evil. "I won't fail," he vowed. "She will die by my hand." He sighed. "I owe her that much. Because what Dag Racho has in mind for her is much, much worse."

CHAPTER FIFTEEN

Natiya was escorted back to her bedroom. She didn't have much choice in the matter. The Emperor had apparently indicated to her "protectors" that she would be tired after her activities with the prisoners, and so would need to rest directly after the inmates were released. She was just lucky that her bedroom was exactly the destination she desired.

She had to find Pentold's books. Unfortunately, she didn't dare look at them with the soldiers in her room. Therefore, she had to feign sleep, knowing that when lunchtime came, the guards would step out of her room to eat. She had long since established that their messy habits upset her delicate constitution.

She suspected that they spied on her through peepholes in the wall, so she remained on her guard, but at least lunch afforded a small measure of privacy. So, pretending as if she couldn't sleep, she irritably grabbed one of the books sent up by the librarian. This also had been a long-established habit of hers. She was even able, with absolute credibility, to peruse one book for a while, toss it aside, then pick up another.

It was time-consuming, but eventually she discovered what Pentold must have left for her. Money. Lots of it. Enough to buy a mount to escape on, or to bribe a guard or three. If only there was a mount for her to buy and a guard open to bribery.

She sighed, letting her head drop onto her arm. The hatching contractions were beginning. She could feel them. Tiny ones so far, like the lapping of little waves across her belly; but they were real. Whatever she was going to do had to be done now.

She absently toyed with the money, sorting through the coins, trying to think of a place to hide them. She ended up slipping them under her tunic until she could think of a better idea. And then she was once again lying on her bed, flipping through pages of books while desperately trying to think of another idea. She almost didn't pick up the last book. She almost chose to sleep, to give in to Dag Racho's will, to just relax and let whatever would happen happen.

But she didn't, and so when she opened a huge volume of epic poetry, she was rewarded by the sight of another smaller, slimmer volume compressed between the heavy pages.

She knew immediately what it was; she had a vivid memory of seeing her mother sitting on a rock or leaning against a cave wall while scribbling in this very tome. As a child, Natiya had not been allowed to touch this most important book, but she had been fascinated by it. Why was it so important to her mother? What secrets did it contain?

Nothing, sweeting. Just my thoughts, that's all.

Her mother's voice echoed through the distant recesses of Natiya's mind, a forgotten whisper nearly crowded out by the egg and all the things that had happened since she first began incubating it. But now she touched the soft leather binding. Lifting the book up, she imagined she smelled her mother's scent and crisp, salty sea air. And then, with her breath suspended in awe, Natiya opened the book.

The first thing she saw was a hastily scribbled note from Pentold.

Your mother gave this to me two days before she died. She said to keep it hidden even from my father, who probably would have sold it to the highest bidder. She wanted this to go to any of her family who survived. I think she guessed it would go badly, and even then I was sorry for her. She said I was to wait many years—for safety—and that when I was an adult, I could give it to a dragon scholar, if any still existed.

Perhaps I should have given this to you years ago, Natiya, but when you left my father's care, you left all of us behind—me included. I had hoped to give it to you on our wedding night, but I now see that that will never be. So take this and remember that I shall be here to help you whenever you need.

Signed with all my heart, Pentold

P.S. Begin reading at page 124.

Natiya read his letter, but she did not cry. She had shed many tears for Pentold over the cycles away from him, tears for an absent brother. She had missed him, but he would never have approved of the egg she carried, would never have liked the choices she made. And now, despite his signature, he had left her—though she reminded herself that she was the one who had sent him away. She could not give the Emperor more weapons to use against her.

So she was alone now, except for the whispers of her mother's words as she leafed slowly through the book pages. She read a little, knowing she needed to skip to page 124, but unable to resist the lure of scanning a few other pages, of learning how her mother had felt about her family. She had loved them as a wife and a mother should, but also, in her heart she had found them to be both a delight and an annoyance, especially since her first and primary love was dragons. Which were, in fact, the subject addressed on page 124.

The Dragon Song is louder now. Martun thinks I am crazy or trying to avoid watching the children. I don't care, so long as he lets me sit in the Queen's clutching cave. I don't know why this cave is different from the others. It could be because the Queen's clutch—with her Golden egg—is here beside me now as I write. Or it's the other way around: The clutch was laid here because of the cave's special properties. Whatever the truth, I can hear the dragons. Not in words. Just a hint of a melody and feelings, sometimes images, all jumbled together, all mismatched in my head. I have spent hours trying to refine this into words but have had little success. That is why Martun thinks I am imagining it. Besides, he firmly believes Dag Racho's Copper is the last living dragon, so how could I be communicating with a dead species?

I, of course, think he's wrong. I believe some of the creatures chose to bond with us and some did not. Which means there could be a whole world of dragons somewhere out there. That it is only the Emperor's fabricated history that suggests otherwise. In any event, Martun will allow me my "egg-watching" time, as he calls it, and I will not tweak him by saying he has spent his life documenting the fossils of a species that is not in the least bit dead.

But my thoughts are wandering, as they so often do in this cave. And that is the other thing I have noticed. The cave, or perhaps it is the dragons themselves, seem to magnify whatever I am feeling or thinking. If I am angry, I become more angry. If I am happy, I become almost ecstatic. Even my thoughts seem to echo back to me with more and more power.

I have experimented with this. On a perfectly normal day, I began thinking angry thoughts at Martun. I fabricated a reason, and put all my energies into hatred. Within moments I was in a towering rage. It was all I could do to change my mind after five beats. But I did, switching my thoughts to loving emotions. It took twice the time. Almost ten beats, and my progress was very slow at first. But by the end of the prescribed time limit—fifteen beats—Martun arrived, and I believe we shall have another playmate for the children in forty weeks. I must say that sexual feelings are the most fun to explore within the caves.

On an academic level, I have begun to wonder what would happen after prolonged exposure to this magnifying effect. Jaseen, naturally, is uppermost in my thoughts. He was such a sweet boy, and we feared he would not be strong enough to fight the Emperor to the death. But no longer. His mother noticed it first. Whatever he did, he's done it to excess. And what he has done most in the last few cycles is train in the ruthlessness of battle. All his tender qualities—of which he had so many— are now completely absent, and we fear he has become nothing but a killing beast. His mother is distraught, and I greatly fear that if he succeeds, we shall have simply replaced one despot with another. At best our lives will remain the same. The worst . . . does not bear contemplating.

I have tried talking to him about this. I asked if the egg still talked to him as it did in the beginning. Could he ask it all my questions? Are there other, unbonded dragons? Do they merely magnify our

*qualities, or do they add more? How do they com-
municate, and what have they learned?*

*Jaseen laughed at me, loudly and with much de-
rision. He said his Sapphire is simply a dumb
beast, a tool to give him strength and long life. He
worked so hard at humiliating me that I suspect I
am correct on more than one level. But I fear I shall
never know. I can only sit beside the Golden egg
and try to still my thoughts. Are you out there? I
ask. Are you just a beast, or a magnifying glass? Or
are you more? Is there a reason for this bond between man and dragon?*

*There is. I am sure of it. A purpose and an end to
the connection, though I don't know what.*

*The whispers grow louder, and I am tempted to
touch the egg. I want to. I want to join with it just to
learn the truth. But that is a step I cannot take. Not
yet. Not until we know what happens to Jaseen.
But I so want to talk to a dragon, just once. And
then, perhaps I would know how to turn Ragona
from the land of dragons into the land of freedom.*

Natiya stared at the last words her mother had ever
written in this journal. *Land of freedom* echoed in her
thoughts. Was it possible? To live without fear of a dragonlord? It hardly seemed imaginable, much less attain-
able. And yet, she wondered what it would be like. No
Copper to enforce Dag Racho's rule. No threat of swift
and complete destruction falling from the sky. How
then would people stave off chaos? Who would enforce
the law?

Her thoughts spun. An idea sprouted in her mind,
only to be crushed by another and another and another. And over all was the dawning realization of how
unprepared she was to rule. She had fought to wrest
power from Rashad, and yet she had done so more out
of instinct than idealism. If all she hoped came true—if

she was able to defeat Dag Racho in battle—then what? She had absolutely no idea. What she heard most was Kiril's words, challenging her to think beyond. What exactly were her plans for afterward?

She didn't know, and worse, even if she could decide, she was completely unprepared for the task. And she had just sent her only possible advisor—Pentold—away. Her thoughts spun back to Kiril. Then to his friend Sabina. Those two understood. They knew how to rule. But she didn't trust them, and they were long gone, anyway.

Which left her alone. She reread her mother's writing, focusing this time on earlier parts of the text. That the dragon served as an emotional magnifying glass made sense to her; she had already guessed at such possibilities. Once again, it had been Kiril who planted the seed. She had lived in such extremes—total secrecy before this began, then total lust with Kiril, then total confusion with Dag Racho. And now? Who was she now?

One last time, she scanned her mother's writing, hung up on her mother's questions. Turning her attention to her own egg, she began asking.

Do you magnify my thoughts? My feelings?

I enhance you. Whatever you are, I make you more.

Magnifying glass, then. But are you more than that? Do you think and learn and grow independent of me?

Of course.

Of course?

Of course.

The egg's tone was so matter-of-fact that Natiya was momentarily stunned into absolute silence. Then she could only re-ask the same question.

You think and live independently?

Yes.

She began to detect a measure of impatience in the egg. "But," she murmured out loud, "you have always reflected my own thoughts back to me." Well, that wasn't entirely true. Certainly the egg had reflected her mind at the beginning, but the closer it came to hatching, the more independent it had become. And it had imparted knowledge to her.

What do you know that I do not? she asked it.

I know all that you do. And I know all that I do.

A memory of the dreams of flying flashed through her mind, as well as Dag Racho's suspicion that the Copper dragon and the Queen egg communicated. She straightened on the bed, looking down at her belly in shock.

You do things I don't know about?

Of course.

Will you tell me what?

They are too many actions to name. What do you wish to know?

She didn't even know where to begin.

Do you share information with the Copper?

I am his Queen. Of course he speaks with me.

Of course, she echoed weakly. *Were you speaking with my mother?*

I was too young to speak directly, but it is possible the others were trying to communicate.

How?

That cave is a powerful location, perfectly suited for augmenting such communication. Such . . . things.

What things? Feelings or thoughts?

Yes.

Yes? To both? Natiya pressed her hand to the side of the egg, feeling the hard shell on top that was even now growing softer and more pliable as the hatching drew near.

So, you can communicate with the Copper in such a way that neither I nor Rashad know about it.

You know. He knows.

She let that comment pass. *What else can you do that I'm not aware of?*

What do you want to know?

Everything, she thought; but the egg didn't answer. So

she began with the most pressing problem. *Can you get us out of here before the hatching?*

The way has always been available. You need only have looked.

Natiya actually bit her cheek in frustration. The egg had known all along? And had not told her?

My task is not to interfere, not unless asked.

Your task? What task?

My task is my own, and it is nearing completion.

Natiya was already beginning to sense an entirely separate personality within the egg, more than she ever had. Actually, she felt stupid for not having seen it before, but until she read her mother's journal, it had never occurred to her that the egg was much more than a tool, an instrument of revenge against Dag Racho. Now she saw she had limited the egg by her own narrow viewpoint. And that dragons were both infinitely more capable and difficult than she had at first thought. Now she not only had to worry about Dag Racho's empire, but she had to deal with an entirely separate identity with unknown goals tied directly into her thoughts.

If she'd felt unprepared before, she felt completely incompetent now. But before she could allow herself to steep in self-loathing—an emotion she already felt the egg magnifying within her—she decided to force her thoughts into the most urgent task: escaping Dag Racho before the hatching.

How do I . . . She paused, then rephrased the question. *How do we escape the castle?*

You must look with my eyes.

How?

You must relinquish control to me.

And there were words to terrify her into immobility. Relinquish control? Of her body? And to an egg—a beast? And yet, even as panic gripped her, her rational mind began to argue. She already knew the dragon was more than a dumb animal. She could also assert control again whenever she wished. Couldn't she?

Of course. It is your body. I am here at your request.

I will retain control if I wish it?

Of course.

She was rapidly tiring of that particular answer, as if all answers were obvious, when the truth was anything but. Still, she had to work with the egg if she wanted to escape. And so she willed herself to relax, to give over control to . . . the thing in her belly.

It took a very long time. She had spent too many years living in paranoid secrecy to simply hand over her body to anyone else, even if she'd been taught the process in the first place. The egg gave no encouragement or discouragement; it simply waited in patience. In time, Natiya succeeded in relinquishing control of her vision.

And was stunned by what she saw.

Current. Rivers of it. Brilliant-colored waves that moved and flexed and permeated everything. The air, the walls, the furniture, even her own body seemed to pulse in a blinding pattern that her mind could not grasp.

She slammed her eyes shut.

"Well," she said out loud, just to ground herself with her own voice. "That didn't work. I saw no way to escape." Then she carefully opened her eyes, willing the return of her normal sight.

It came.

She addressed the egg. "That didn't work," she repeated. Predictably, the egg had no response, so Natiya pressed for more details, making her question silent for fear of the guards.

Why didn't that work?

It did. You could see the exit.

I saw nothing but chaos. I don't understand at all.

Again the egg had no reply, but Natiya was beginning to recognize the pattern. The egg would not tell her the answer unless she asked the right question. But if she knew the question to ask, wouldn't she already have a clue to the answer?

You understand what I saw, don't you? she asked.

Of course.

Of course it did. It was the egg's sight she had been using. Of course it would understand what it saw. Which meant . . .

You know where the exit is and how to get out.

Of course.

Of course. Natiya thought the words at the same time as the egg. She sighed, greatly fearing what she had to do.

If I cede all control to you—of my entire body—will I still be able to think on my own?

Of course.

But you would guide me out? You would work my arms and legs and body enough to get me out of the castle.

The egg took a long time answering, but eventually it did. *I believe so. I have never tried.*

Do so now, Natiya instructed, gathering her courage. *Take us out of this castle without being caught.*

You must relinquish control. I can do nothing unless you allow me to.

Of course not. And it was just as Natiya had feared: If she'd had such trouble releasing her vision, how much harder would it be to release dominion over her entire body?

I can get it back—

Any time you ask.

Very well, she thought to the egg. *Do it.*

Except, the egg could do nothing. Not until Natiya actually let it. She took a few deep breaths, consciously relaxing her body, intending to relax her mind. She tried to pull her consciousness away from her body into her thoughts and only her thoughts.

Her eyes were closed, and so it was the smell she noticed first. Her own smell. The egg's smell. Even the lingering scent of flowers, washing fluid and stale water drifted through her mind. Though she had been smelling all of it before, she realized that the egg identified and categorized all these things. Where Natiya had simply pushed them to the back of her mind, the egg noticed it all. Remembered it all.

Natiya stood without expecting to; she had been so caught up in the smells that she had relaxed enough to let the egg manage her body. But the unexpected sensation of standing startled her so much that she instinctively took back control. She snatched at her body like a child after a toy. Except, she was the toy. And as might be predicted, she fell in an ungainly heap on the floor. She landed hard enough that her teeth jarred from the impact.

This isn't working! she thought, even though she knew the reason was in her own paranoid psyche.

You do not trust me, the egg said.

I do not trust easily.

No answer; but then, Natiya did not expect one. Instead, she focused her efforts on smells again, trying to narrow her attention back down to the scents. She identified the flowery odor and decided to focus exclusively on that—forgetting to shut her eyes. So when the egg took control of her vision, she once again panicked, regaining control while she slammed her eyes closed. At least she had not been standing that time.

This is going to take forever!

No answer from the egg, nothing but a silent wall of patience while Natiya struggled to release her presence in her own body again. And again. And again.

And again.

She could not do it. She just could not give up control of her body. Not even though she wished it.

Couldn't there be a compromise here?

Of course.

Natiya did her best not to smack the egg as she

struggled to find a middle ground. *Could you tell me where the exit is?*

In the bathing chamber between the plant and the window.

Natiya walked to the specified place, pleased that she would be out of view of any guard who chose to look in on her.

Here?

Yes.

At least it hadn't said, "Of course."

What do I do now?

Press the eyelet pattern in the tiling.

Natiya did as the egg bade, and immediately a door slid open in the wall, revealing a stairway just wide enough for her to carefully ease her way inside. A lever blocked her path, and so she pushed it up, silently sliding the door closed behind her . . . and abruptly engulfing her in total blackness.

Can you see in the dark? Natiya asked.

If you let me.

That meant allowing herself to be blinded by the swirling currents of . . . what was it she would see?

Thoughts. Emotions. Power. Energy.

Of course, Natiya thought back with obvious sarcasm. None of this made any sense to her, but naturally the egg did not choose to explain. It remained silent, waiting for Natiya to release her vision to it. At least she was becoming more practiced. And since she was blinded by the darkness anyway, it was easier to allow the egg to take over her vision.

Swirling currents of energy appeared before her, and she worked hard not to focus on it. It was making her nauseated. Instead, she thought about descending the stairs one slow step at a time.

You will have to tell me when I'm about to run into something.

No answer. Apparently, she wasn't about to run into

something. She was, however, stepping in things. Dirt. Wet dirt. *Yuck.* She didn't truly want to know more. No one had used this passageway for a long time.

Rashad does, but not often. And not since you came, the egg informed her.

Where does it lead?

To the Coral.

It was a good thing Natiya was already walking extremely carefully, because this information would have made her stumble. As it was, she stopped cold, trying to understand what the egg was saying.

The Coral? A Coral dragon?

Of course.

The one bonded to Rashad's sister?

Yes.

But where is she?

At the other end of this tunnel.

Of course, Natiya thought crossly as she at last made it down to the bottom of the steps, ending in a tunnel that ran off to either side. The egg instructed her to turn right, which she did. And then she began another long trek through a passageway that was exactly like the stairway: narrow, wet and with a musky scent that made her nose itch. As she slowly waddled through a sea of colors and light—moving mostly by touch—she wondered if Dag Racho had learned how to use his dragon's sight, or if this was something she alone had discovered.

He knows. But he will not relinquish control to the Copper.

Well, that made sense, and frankly Natiya didn't blame him. This flow of energy lines was disconcerting to say the least, but she hoped she would be able to understand them given time. If only she had thought to speak to the egg this way earlier. But there was nothing she could do about it now, except to use what time she had.

She continued to travel slowly along the tunnel. Superimposing what she knew of the castle and the city, she guessed that these stairs led well beneath the ground, deep under the castle. Which meant this tunnel ran directly to the Emperor's mountain.

Of course it does, she told herself irritably. Where else could one hide a mature dragon except inside a mountain? In the distance, from back inside the castle, Natiya thought she heard a man's hoarse cry. Had her absence been discovered? Most likely. The guards never went more than thirty beats without checking on her.

Though her body was beginning to tire, Natiya picked up her pace. She needed to get away, though what she was going to do once she got into the mountain, she hadn't a clue. How much of an escape was it when one ran from a guarded bedroom into the center of the garrison for the entire army? Well, she wouldn't be any worse off, and she did suddenly have an urgent need to see the Coral.

Or was that the egg's need?

She slowed a moment, trying to sort out her thoughts. Now that she realized the egg had its own goals and desires, she needed to be a great deal clearer about who wanted what. And though she was very curious about exactly how Dag Racho had kept his sister secretly interned for nearly a hundred cycles, she didn't recognize the burning desire that seemed to pulse through her.

Are you *creating this desire?* Natiya asked.

I am magnifying your interest.

Why?

The Copper and I have been trying to revive the Coral.

Revive her?

She does not respond. We wish you to touch her. Through you, we can break the magic that restrains her.

You couldn't just ask me? You have to manipulate my desires?

I cannot ask. And I am not manipulating, I am only magnifying.

But you choose what you wish to magnify, don't you?

The egg's answer came with great reluctance. *I have some choices in this matter.*

Natiya thought so. Indeed, she was beginning to believe the dragons were a great deal more manipulative than their humans ever imagined. Which led to another question.

What will the Coral do when she wakes?

What she is required to do.

And what is that?

No answer; not that she expected one. But once this was all over, Natiya decided, she and her egg were going to have a serious heart-to-heart. In the meantime, she was still in control of her body. So if the egg wanted to wake the Coral, it would have to ante up some information. Otherwise, she was going to just bypass the other dragon, figuring that one enemy was better than two.

She is not an enemy.

Natiya smiled, though her thoughts remained grim. *She is not* your *enemy*, she said clearly to the egg. *I don't know yet if she's my enemy or not.*

We are not your enemies.

Then why are you here?

The egg took a long time to answer, and Natiya had the distinct impression it was working to phrase its response carefully.

We study you. We are scientists, like your parents. We search for the perfect human.

Scientists? Perfect human?

Yes.

That wasn't the complete answer; Natiya was sure of it.

If you are just scientists studying us, why won't you tell me what the Coral will do when she wakes?

She has been asleep for a long time. We do not know what she thinks.

You said "required." That the Coral will do what she is "required" to do. What is that?

She is required to report her experiences.

To whom?

To me.

Because you are the Queen?

Of course.

And then what?

And then I will decide.

She will take your direction?

Hesitation. And then, *Of course.*

So, Natiya realized, the Queen wasn't entirely sure of her authority.

Of course I am, the egg respond hotly. *I am their Queen.*

"You haven't even been born yet," Natiya snapped out loud. She didn't know how things worked in the dragon world, but in the human world, adults rarely listened to children. The egg didn't respond, but Natiya got the distinct impression it didn't think of itself like a child. After all, the egg had been conscious at least since Natiya began incubating it over ten cycles ago. Apparently, it felt as if it had command of the dragons beneath her.

You are sure the Coral will take direction from you? She will not kill you? Or me?

She will not harm her Queen.

There was no hesitation in the egg about that, and so Natiya decided to trust it.

I will help you wake the Coral, she told it.

Typically, there was no thanks from the egg. Neither was there any acknowledgment of Natiya's cooperation. Merely a silence that was beginning to seriously irritate her. All these years, all these cycles of loneliness, Natiya could have had a friend, a companion during the long nights of secrecy. But the egg had been silent all that time—an observer instead of a participant.

A scientist, the egg asserted.

A spy, Natiya countered.

I have not harmed you.

You haven't helped me either.

Natiya felt her irritation begin to boil into anger. She wasn't entirely sure why she was becoming so furious. So much information had hit her so quickly, she wasn't sure she was even thinking rationally. She only knew that she was angry as never before, including the moment when her parents had been killed. Back then she could rail at Dag Racho, hate him with all the pain in her young heart. But now . . . now she learned that someone—something—had been sitting in her mind all this time, watching, learning—*judging*—and never once helping.

You chose this when you first picked me up and pressed me to your belly.

Natiya felt her hands clench into fists against the damp walls. It was true, she had chosen this. And yet, she was absolutely furious.

"I have been so alone," she whispered, her voice echoing back at her in eerie hisses.

Such was the life you chose.

And as Natiya at last came to the door that would lead her inside Dag Racho's mountain, she finally saw the truth, bare and unadulterated as only the cold voice of her egg could make it. She'd chosen this life. She'd chosen to seclude herself and live in secrecy when she could have had friends. She'd chosen to go with Kiril because she wanted to know what he knew about the egg. She'd chosen to fight Dag Racho rather than accept the easy life he offered. Indeed, she'd chosen everything about her current situation, and so she could hardly complain about it.

In that moment, she made her decision.

I will help you wake the Coral. And then you will tell me how to separate from you, how to separate all of the bonded people from their dragons. Then human and dragon will go their separate ways. Can we do this? Will you do this?

There was a long moment as the egg considered Natiya's decision. Only then did it respond.

It can be done. But there is a cost.

This time, Natiya got to say the obvious:

Of course.

CHAPTER SIXTEEN

Kiril pulled on his uniform, cursing Dag Racho's symbol and red colors even as he thanked the Father that he had stored one at Sabina's place.

"It still fits," she commented as he buttoned the collar. "Not bad, considering how many cycles you've had it here."

"Prison food has been excellent for my physique," he drawled, knowing he was lying. True, he had lost weight, so there was ample room in the uniform. But he had also lost strength and speed—something he might very well need in the coming days.

"I've gotten you the fastest mount I could find. And money as well." She paused, frowning as he slipped a sword underneath his coat. "Are you sure I can't come along? You might need someone at your back."

He smiled gently at her offer, knowing that despite her fears, it was an honest one. "I need a trained soldier, or at least a man—someone who could pass for a trained soldier. You, my dear, aren't either of those things." Then, before she could offer one of her servants, he raised his hand. "This is what I do, Sabina. You cannot help me in this arena."

She sighed. "I know. But I still worry."

"That I will be caught, or that I will change my mind?"

She waited until he turned around and she could see directly into his eyes. "Have you?"

"I have not changed my mind, nor will I," he stated, pushing all his conviction into his voice. Apparently it was enough, because she nodded then held up a satchel lined with wax and a glass vial.

"Take this. If you break the egg in the process, get as much of the contents as possible."

"The contents will be a baby dragon."

"You can kill that. What we need is the liquid it rests in. As much as you can get."

He nodded, his expression flat despite the nausea roiling in his stomach. "I know what to do." Then he left, before she could ask any more questions.

He moved with a calm determination that would reassure her, kicking his mount into a gallop because he knew she was watching. He wouldn't put it beyond her to follow him, but they both knew she couldn't keep up. Even if this steed was a young, undisciplined beast.

"*D'greth!*" He cursed again as the mount fought his control. Why couldn't anything be easy? It was a stupid wish for a useless soul, but he wished it anyway, with all his heart. Because, despite his words to Sabina, he wasn't sure of himself. He knew what he had to do. Knew he would find the opportunity some way, somehow to stand beside Natiya with a sword in his hand. He knew he must kill her—quickly, cleanly—for everyone's good. After all, she was already dead; she hadn't a prayer in a fight against Dag Racho.

And yet . . .

Why had he slept with her? Why had he listened to her words, heard her declare her love for him? Why did he admire her strength of character to defy Dag Racho, and her intelligence to actually do so? Why couldn't he think that this strong, capable, intelligent, admirable woman could succeed where all others had failed?

Because she couldn't. The odds were stacked too greatly against her. And so, despite what his heart said, he would have to kill her and take her egg. So that he could make a poison. So that he could rid the land of dragons forever. But first he had to get to her.

Getting inside the castle was a vain hope; even in uniform, he would never get in. But he knew she would be hatching soon, and the only safe place to do that was inside Dag Racho's mountain. It had the same mineral that hid the clutching caves, was protected by an entire garrison of troops, and he was pretty sure there was a large chamber inside—perfect for a hatchling to spread its wings and still remain safe. All he had to do was get inside and then wait. He was bound to get his opportunity then.

But getting inside the mountain was a problem, too. He had one hope. The Father had blessed him with excellent hearing; better yet, he had spent years in court perfecting the skill, overhearing whispers that most could not. It had even been extremely useful in battle, allowing him to fight blind if necessary. But in prison, it had turned out even more so.

There had been sound behind his lonely cell at the back of the block: drips of sound, the slosh of water, but mostly the silence of stone. Except for once. He had heard a word. A command, actually, spoken with power. Magic. And then there had been a great deal more sound: of a door moving or water running or something.

It wasn't much to go on, but it was all he had. Combining that with a thorough inspection of the mountain's exterior—done over the years whenever he could—Kiril had an idea of where to go and how to get there. He would just have to pray that the overheard command word worked.

It was late afternoon by the time he arrived. His uniform and the fact that he had been officially released from prison got him through all the checkpoints. Showing up near the garrison, he knew, was just begging to be re-incarcerated, but hopefully he wouldn't be around long.

Sabina's satchel and glass vial lay heavy on his leg when he finally tethered his mount in a tiny grove of trees. The mouth of a creek was a few wispans away. Not far, but there would be no cover while he traversed it. And he stood out like a firebolt in his red uniform. There was no hope for it, however, and so he went, moving as quickly as possible.

He made it to his objective in a few beats, but as he wiped the sweat from his brow, he acknowledged that prison life had taken a severe toll. At his peak, he could have made it to this strange little tunnel in half the time.

He ducked down under a kind of muddy overhang into an even muddier channel. At some times of year this tunnel was the beginning of a stream of water. It dried up at irregular intervals. He guessed that water had something to do with the big chamber behind his cell. Ergo, this little tunnel had to lead inside the mountain. Which meant he had to crawl up inside, and that his uniform would never be the same.

The opening underneath the overhang was large enough for a man bent double. It rapidly narrowed deeper in. A combination of mud and slick rock created the side walls, and Kiril cursed as he took a whiff. Rotted vegetation was the most pleasant of the smells, and he quickly guessed he was in a sewage outlet.

Yippee.

But this was his only shot, and so he would have to take it. Except, he had one last thing to do before he began. He still needed his weapons—most specifically his sword. Sabina's cheap sword would likely break or melt from dragon fire at the first engagement. If Kiril's own weapons were close at hand, he would take the time to get them back.

Thankfully, locating them would be possible; all he had to do was focus through Jaseen's armband. Dragon blood not only attuned him and his weapons to other dragons, but it linked him with his sword. All he had to do was quiet his mind—not an easy task, given the urgency he felt to get back into action—and he would feel a tug.

Just breathe in and out, he ordered himself; then he silenced his thoughts. Or maybe he should picture his sword. Sometimes that helped.

No, just quiet your thoughts, he told himself. Jaseen's armband would automatically boost the connection. Where exactly would Natiya be at this moment? Could she already be inside?

Just silence your damn thoughts! But . . . what if this passageway led to something else entirely? There were plenty of waste rooms throughout the mountain. What if he climbed through here just to end up face to ass with some soldier taking a dump?

Shut up! Shut up! Shut up!

Kiril sighed, taking the time to calm his heart, his breath, his thoughts. He had done a great deal of this in prison—what else had there been to do?—and so he was more practiced than it seemed. He knew from his meditations in his cell that his sword and gauntlets were in the mountain, behind his cell somewhere. He just wanted to orient to them now. From this location. He just had to quiet down.

He counted out breaths—five, four, three, two, one, zero. Where was it? Where was his sword?

There! Above him. And at a bit of an angle. About where this channel originated. Which meant it was in the chamber he guessed was above this drainage ditch. And so it was time to climb in a smelly, disgusting tunnel.

He slipped and slid on his knees as he imitated a

snake or small rodentlike animal, of which there were none, thank the Father. But foul chunks of matted something were prevalent, and he truly had no wish to discover what they were because he could hardly fail to get them in his clothing, his hair, his eyes and yes, even his mouth. Until, miracle of miracles, he finally arrived at an iron hole sealed shut. It was large—big enough that he'd be able to climb through it with relative ease. But it was also shut fast, so here was where he must test the strength of his hearing.

Would the command word he'd heard in his cell work?

Taking a deep breath—or as deep as he could take in the foul air—Kiril spoke.

"Corinta sapa!"

Nothing. Perhaps he had misheard the word. There had been a thick wall of stone between the speaker and his wall; the commands had been muffled and distorted. He knew the number of syllables and was sure of the first one, but beyond that, he would have to try different pronunciations.

"Corinta sapo!"

"Corinda sapa!"

"Corina sato!"

"Corinda sapa!"

"Corinda sapat!"

Another five beats of experimentation and still nothing. He was beginning to suspect he had heard it all wrong. Or if he heard correctly, then the command went to a different door, different function, different anything. And now he was doomed.

"Corinda stapat!"

Whoosh!

There was no warning; one moment he was cursing, playing with consonants and vowels, and the next moment he was flooded in water pouring out of an opening not present a moment before. The water pressure was incredible, the deluge cold and filthy and overpowering as he lost his footing. He would have landed on his behind in the mud, but there was nothing to land on but roaring water. He couldn't even scream, as his mouth had been open, about to speak another set of words, making him choke on he-didn't-want-to-know-what.

He had no choice but to ride out the flood, his eyes blinded by the brown water, his body slammed and bounced against the walls he had just painstakingly climbed. And then, with a kind of sudden explosion, the pressure was gone and he was rolling across greenery on the side of the mountain, still pursued by the rushing water.

He coughed and gasped, but mostly he scrambled for purchase and breath and sight all at once until he finally tumbled to a stop against a bush. In time he was able to inhale without gagging, but then revulsion hit and he was vomiting up things that should not have been swallowed in the first place.

Thankfully, even as the spasms wracked his body, his legs continued to grip the bush. Its branches—hard and pointy though they were—still managed to cradle him. And when he was done, lying exhausted and wretched in the bush's not-so-tender embrace, the water still continued to pour past. Enough water to fill a lake. And all he could do was simply stare, occasionally wiping his eyes.

At least it was cleaner now. The brown filth that had initially swept him down the mountain was now flowing rapidly clearer, brighter, even pinker as whatever was above them continued to drain.

And still it continued. For another twenty beats at least. Long enough for him to struggle to a braced stand. Long enough for him to shrug out of his soggy, disgusting uniform. Long enough for him to stand shivering and naked in the afternoon sun, appreciating its warmth while the water continued to flow. At least

Sabina's satchel had come through unscathed. It was designed to hold liquid, so all he had to do was upend it, wash it out, and double check that the bottles he'd brought along were also safe.

They were. And so was his sword and belt. Not so lucky was his firestick, but hopefully there'd be light inside the mountain. All of this meant his mission could continue as planned, assuming he could find a way to swim up the deluge, so to speak. And if he ignored the being-naked aspect. He sighed, deciding to deal with that later. Right then, he needed to slowly, carefully slog his way back up to the mouth of the channel. He felt ridiculously exposed—in more ways than one—but there was no help for it. He would die of a chill if he stayed in that wet uniform, not to mention choke on the smell. If anyone questioned his naked presence, he would just say he had been out climbing—a common form of exercise for many soldiers—when the deluge caught him by surprise.

Fortunately, no one seemed around right then. In fact, he thought with a frown, things seemed especially deserted for such a sunny afternoon. But without more information, he decided to simply thank his luck while he decided what to do next.

He didn't have to ponder long, as the deluge of water began to slow and abruptly dropped to a trickle. Whatever he'd opened was now empty, which meant he could climb up and in, hopefully before the aperture closed.

He ducked in, unsure if the smell of wet, slick mud was better than the earlier rotting vegetation smell. Actually, it was better, he finally decided, which only marginally made up for the extremely slick and messy work of climbing back up to the opening. Still, he made good time, and had the added bonus of covering himself in muddy camouflage.

The aperture remained open, a steady trickle of water still draining through. It was easy work to pull himself up and inside, and—thanks to a recent diet of prison food—he had enough room to maneuver.

It was hard to hear from inside the tube beyond; his breath echoed as a low hiss that competed with his heartbeat to drown out everything. Or perhaps that was his imagination working overtime. As far as he could tell, there was nothing to hear above him, which meant Natiya hadn't arrived yet. From what his parents had said, Jaseen's hatching had been a loud, brutal affair.

He was nearing the top; he could tell because of the echo of his breath. Slowing, he judged the distance above by the sound. If he had to guess, he would say the room above him was huge. Perhaps expansively large, like a cavern. It was also blacker than pitch, which meant he would have to navigate by sound and feel alone.

He paused, taking a moment to focus on his weapons again. Quickly he confirmed his initial guess: His weapons were in the chamber above, located to his left. They were going to be his first order of business.

He crossed the last wispan to the top and slowly eased himself out of the drainage tube, careful to move with absolute silence. He still saw nothing; the cavern remained in total darkness. But as he slowly extended his hands along the slick stone floor, he realized his body was humming. Not just humming, but itching, even shaking slightly, with an energy he recognized as similar to the magic in the clutching caves. But why? He knew that the metal here—whatever it was—confused dragon senses, so why would the Emperor, the only dragonborn still alive, build something that would confuse himself?

Unless, of course, the Copper and Natiya's Queen weren't the only dragons. Kiril felt his soul freeze at the thought. He had spent most of his life rooting out the last of the demon creatures; the idea that there were more of them made him shake with fear. But that wasn't his primary worry. No, what he really wanted to know was what Dag Racho hid inside the rest of his mountain. What was so large that it must be stored here, hidden from man and dragon alike?

If only he had a firestick, he would risk a light just to find out. Meanwhile, all he could do was crawl along the floor toward his weapons, praying he didn't bump into something he shouldn't.

And just that quickly, he touched something . . . different. Wet. Leathery. And with no smell discernible from everything else. As delicately as possible, he tried to outline it, skirting the edges, but it seemed to keep going. In fact, he thought as he started to gently raise his hand, trying to gauge its height, he was beginning to think it was huge. So huge that it just might be exactly what Dag Racho needed to hide in this mountain.

Too bad Kiril hadn't a clue what it was. And damned if that energy wasn't beginning to get on his nerves. It was stronger here, much stronger, feeling more like tiny insects crawling along his skin. He'd been doing his best to ignore it, but irritation was beginning to win the war.

What the hell was going on?

"This isn't working!" a female voice snapped.

Kiril froze, stunned by the sudden knowledge that he wasn't alone. But who would be here? Without a light? And hell, he had to get to his weapons, because the woman—whoever the hell she was—could spark a light at any point and where would he be then? Naked and on his knees.

With that thought in mind he started moving faster—and quieter—around the huge, leathery thing, while still listening to the unknown woman curse in the darkness.

"I don't understand!" she continued, clearly angry. "Look, it's more important that we get out of here first. Then later, I swear, I'll come back and do whatever you'd like."

Natiya? Kiril frowned as he moved, questioning his own conclusion. He couldn't possibly be that lucky. Besides, he reminded himself, he'd been imagining Natiya in every female voice or body he'd come in contact with since first seeing the woman dance in that tacky dockside tavern. She couldn't be here, in the dark and out of Dag Racho's clutches.

But what if it was her? And just whom was she negotiating with? He'd been holding his breath waiting to hear a response, but there hadn't been any. Nothing except for Natiya's—or the unknown woman's—heavy sigh as she breathed.

"All right," she said, "but no more."

It was Natiya. It had to be. And she was talking to her egg. Jaseen had done that more and more as the hatching approached. That also explained why she was standing in the dark. Dag Racho was said to be able to see in the dark as well. And dragon sight could not be fooled.

So, why hadn't she seen him yet? He was near her, no longer blocked by the unknown object in the room. She ought to be on him like the beast she was becoming. But she wasn't, and he didn't know why.

Whatever the reason, he decided to accept his good fortune. He closed his eyes, taking a moment to refocus on his weapons. They were right in front of him. He quickly closed the last of the distance, feeling his way up the stone wall to an alcove. They weren't even magically protected, but had been dropped casually into a recessed corner. Next to a lightstick. He ignored that, focusing on his things: sword, gauntlets—even his shield, bless the Father! No saddle or tack. Just as well. He couldn't carry those and Natiya.

He paused, angered by his thoughts. He was coming to kill Natiya and take the egg; he wouldn't need to carry her. Just the egg. Just the—

His thoughts snapped shut as he felt the prickle of energy increase. It could be because he was donning his weapons. The loga wire woven through his gauntlets gave him special sensitivity to dragon activity. But the ramp-up in power was more than just better attunement. It was Natiya. She was doing something. To the big thing. And he needed to know what. Dared he risk firing up the lightstick?

That's when he heard it: a noise. A lot of noise, in fact. Coming from the front of the mountain near the barracks. Muted, distant, but with a rumble of more to come. Soldiers. Damn! Whatever he was going to do, he had to do it fast.

He would have to risk a light, if only so he could see where to swing. The power was growing stronger, setting his teeth on edge, making him honestly want to kill Natiya if only to end the burrowing power that seemed to be eating through his skin. She probably had to concentrate hard on whatever she was doing, so her reactions would be slow.

He drew his sword, doing his best to move silently. His plan was simple: spark the light, take four steps to her side, then swing—neatly and painlessly severing her head from her shoulders. A couple more moments to retrieve the egg, and then down the hatch he had entered from. He knew he had to do this, even if it roiled his stomach.

D'greth, what was she doing?

He ignited the lightstick. It blared bright—too bright— probably increased by the power throbbing in the room. He was blinded, but he'd expected that. His eyes would adjust quickly, and he knew just where he was going. He'd heard her gasp at the sudden illumination, so he had a very good idea where she stood.

His sword was raised, and he was beginning to see— at least enough to judge head and shoulders for his swing. His stomach clenched tighter than his shoulders, and he held his breath, though his mind continued to curse him for what he was about to do.

And then he saw the Coral.

A Coral dragon. Mature. Huge. Lying on the floor right in front of Natiya. Her hands were on its belly, and its eyes were open. That leathery thing he had touched? That was the wing, beginning to flutter now as it began to move.

D'greth, where had *that* come from?

Its mouth opened. Sweet *toutch*, its maw was open and he could see right down into the gullet. Though most of his brain was numb with shock, another part registered the danger. It was quite easy to see deep inside the beast's throat to the sparking light as it began to purge its built-up fire gases. After all, that was the first thing a dragon did when it woke: belched the fire out of its system. Everyone knew that.

Everyone, apparently, except Natiya, because she just stood there, weaving slightly as the power left her, her expression completely dazed. She was about to fry. And the Queen egg with her.

Kiril jumped—no thought, just movement as he slammed his entire body against Natiya, throwing her out of the direct line of fire. Thank the Father his shield was strapped to his back as the fire-belch roared above them. He felt the backs of his legs blister in the heat, but thanks to the treated loga wire in his shield, his back and head were protected. And thank the Father there was still a little water left on the ground as well. Only little puddles, but it was enough to keep them from cooking.

Was that what the Coral had been stored in? A lake?

It made some sense, he supposed. Even if the Coral woke up, it would be damn hard for it to maneuver when half submerged in a lake.

And wasn't it nice that Kiril had drained it? That way, the creature had plenty of space to toast its breakfast to crunchy perfection. Too bad the only food available was Kiril and Natiya—except for a sleeping woman he just now noticed on the other side of the cavern. Well, there was nothing he could do for her, especially as the Coral was between them.

He had to focus on getting himself and Natiya out alive. And that meant diving down the drain hatch.

Still flattened beneath him, Natiya began to stir, coming out of her daze with a murmur of irritation. Above him the Coral was becoming more alert, beginning to stretch its wings and click its jaws in hunger.

"What—?" began Natiya, and again Kiril didn't hesitate. He didn't have time to deal with a struggling woman. With one well-aimed blow, he knocked her unconscious. And then, as fast as he could manage, he began to drag her toward the drain.

Unfortunately, dragons were really good at seeing movement. Colors, not so much. Moving things—oh, yes. And Kiril felt more than saw the Coral's eyes train on him.

Then, miracle of miracles, the soldiers appeared. Normally this would have caused him to curse a blue streak, but they were young and apparently hadn't expected to come face to face with a hungry Coral. If their entrance wasn't enough to attract the dragon's attention, their full-throated screams of horror were. And then, just as if to make sure they would become breakfast, one suicidal idiot threw his sword at it.

It was a good throw—one that managed to cut a gash in the soft part of the Coral's nose. And that was the seal on their deaths. Once again fire roared through the cavern, and Dag Racho was minus a few soldiers.

Kiril meanwhile had just enough time to dump Natiya down the drain and then skedaddle behind her. It was a painful process, but with the mud coating his blisters and the threat of imminent death above him, he didn't quibble about bruises from banging left and right along the slick, slanting tunnel. His only fear was for Natiya. Sometimes unconscious lumps fared better in this type of free-fall; sometimes not. And if she broke her egg now, no way could he retrieve the liquid he needed to make the poison.

Still, there was nothing he could do about it now. Especially as he shot feet first through the drainage pipe.

He landed in an ungainly heap at the feet of an entire scouting party of Dag Racho's soldiers.

CHAPTER SEVENTEEN

Kiril groaned, more from the effort of standing than from the fact that his glorious escape attempt had just ended in ignoble defeat. Naked, mud-covered defeat.

He watched as one of the soldiers carefully assisted Natiya. She and the egg seemed fine, thank Amia, but she was still unconscious. She was also so mud-covered as to be nearly unrecognizable—except for the obviously swollen belly that outlined a pretty clear dragon egg. He, on the other hand, didn't have such distinguishing features. Fortunately, the soldiers were very young, probably recruits barely out of basic training.

He tried not to grin. Of course they were raw recruits. After all, who else would you send to cover basic mountain-guarding detail? Let the experienced ones go inside where the trouble was. The others remained outside where all they had to do was scream if they encountered trouble and others would come running. He just had to give them no reason to scream.

He spotted the one man who might be a problem: the oldest, and the leader.

"Lieutenant!" he barked. After all, he had gotten the same training as these men, some many cycles ago, so he knew just what to do. "Doga formation, now!"

As expected, the lower-ranking men responded immediately to the authority in his voice, circling around him in the most basic protective formation possible. The lieutenant even began to move, but hesitated long enough to frown at him.

"Explain your business, sir!" the man snapped as Kiril took great, painful strides to Natiya's side. Pain from his blistered feet burned through his consciousness, but that only served to make him more irritable, more authoritative.

"Defending the Empress, you moron! There's big trouble inside." He jerked his head toward the tunnel, and the Coral dragon obliged him by releasing a roar that shook the very foundation of the mountain. The roar of a mature dragon struck fear into the staunchest man's bones, even muted as it was through many wispans of dirt and mountain. This was something these recruits couldn't withstand. To a man, they fell to their knees, quaking and gibbering in horror.

Fortunately, Kiril had already been kneeling beside Natiya, so he didn't suffer the same fate. And his experience with the damned creatures allowed him to recover the quickest. Gently lifting up Natiya—*d'greth*, she was heavy—he strode to where he had tethered his mount. Well, perhaps he took tiny, staggering steps at first. But pain has a way of clearing away everything else, including the lingering horror of a dragon roar. And every step on his blistered feet became more firm, more assured.

Then the lieutenant showed his mettle, gritting his teeth and straightening his shoulders with obvious effort. Seeing the state of his men—and probably realizing Kiril couldn't outrun him on burned feet while carrying a pregnant woman—he began kicking and cursing his men. It took a while, but he got most of them on their feet. Kiril didn't give them time to reorganize. Especially as he saw his mount just ahead.

"Doga formation, now!" he bellowed again, and then grinned as they scrambled to obey. One even offered to help with Natiya, but Kiril denied him. No one was touching Natiya but him. Especially since he didn't know how long it would be before she regained consciousness. Instead, he ordered the helpful young soldier to run ahead and bring his mount to him. The other was dispatched to bring him his uniform, obligingly drying in the rapidly fading sunlight.

Moments later, Kiril and Natiya were neatly settled atop his mount. Kiril even had his uniform wrapped around them both. Though it still smelled terrible, at least he wasn't completely naked anymore. Before he rode off, he turned to the lieutenant.

"Guard that tunnel and kill anything that comes out," he said.

The man frowned. "Anything?"

"There's a mature dragon in there with a bonded human—and some dead soldiers. Don't wait. Don't ask questions. Just swing." He tucked Natiya close against his body. "I'll get the Empress back to the castle." And with that, he rode off, heading in the appropriate direction. Fortunately, the mountain was irregularly shaped, and within moments he was out of sight of the small band of soldiers. As soon as he was clear, he turned his horse and headed the opposite way.

He encountered little resistance from the soldiers he passed, but many uncertain stares. So he pulled on his wretched uniform, his eyes watering from the stench. His insignia was enough to forestall any questioning, especially since his face was too dirty to be recognizable. As he'd covered Natiya with some of his attire, she became a huge, formless lump.

He rode fast, cursing the pain as his raw legs rubbed his mount. But he had little time before Dag Racho would launch his Copper. In fact, glancing backward at the darkening sky, he thought he recognized the black silhouette of the creature circling the mountain. Fortunately the Emperor would likely be too busy containing the Coral to search for Natiya just then. Which might just give Kiril enough time to make it with her to the Clutching Mountains. Once there, the dragon field would hide them, and he would get a moment to rest and clean up. And then to kill Natiya before harvesting her egg.

A chill coursed through his body, no doubt because of the roar that rumbled through the countryside—from the Coral. Kiril was too far away for it to fully affect him. In truth, it sounded more like distant thunder, but his body clenched nonetheless. It was followed by another sound—a booming crash—and Kiril risked a glance back to see that one side of the mountain had exploded in a rain of fire and debris. Less than a beat later, the Coral soared into view.

He was already too far away to tell if the Coral carried a rider—probably the sleeping woman if anyone, he now realized. She was the most likely candidate to be the creature's bonded pair. Either way, the Coral and the Copper flew straight at one another, fire belching from their mouths.

Kiril wished he could see more. He hadn't been around to witness Jaseen's Platinum engage Racho's wyrm. A view of the battle tactics could be of enormous value.

But then he checked his thoughts. He had no reason to view any dragon battles. He intended to harvest Natiya's egg for the poison that could be made from it. There would be no Queen hatchling. No battle against the Copper for Natiya, or anyone else to fight. The Copper would be poisoned, and Kiril himself would cut Dag Racho's black heart out of his body. That was the plan to end the rule of dragons forever.

But first, he had to get himself and Natiya to safety.

He resolutely turned his back on the struggle enacted in the sky above. From the faint flashes of red light he could tell that the dragons were engaged in earnest, and he prayed that their battle would continue throughout the night. The longer Dag Racho stayed occupied, perhaps even injured, the better for himself and Natiya.

Or rather, not Natiya. Because as soon as he found the right place, she would be dead by his hand.

He clenched his legs tighter, pushing his mount to greater speeds even as he relished the pain such an act brought to his body. Pain was good. Pain cleared his thoughts. And pain was exactly what murderers like him deserved.

Kiril stripped out of his clothes and washed in a tide pool, fouling the water beyond belief, but it was the only place available where he could clean himself and watch Natiya at the same time.

It had begun. The hatching. As soon as they'd made it into the Clutching Mountains, whatever magic clung to the earth here had begun its work. She wasn't even fully conscious, but had begun moaning. Her body had twisted and writhed like a snake coming out of its skin, and it was all he could do to keep her on his mount long enough to get to a cave. Thankfully, he'd known of one near enough to the road to make it fast.

So now she was inside, the thrice-cursed magic doing what it did best: completely skrawing his plans. But it wasn't going to succeed. He still had time, albeit not a lot. He had to kill Natiya now, harvest what remained of the egg, and then—after he finished with Dag Racho—be done with this business of dragon-killing once and for all.

Once this was over, he was going to buy a plot of land and grow flowers and corn, maybe wheat—*d'greth*, weeds would be fine with him. Just so long as he didn't ever have to raise a sword again. Except, he wasn't on a farm yet. He was here, naked outside a damned clutching cave, and it was time for him to kill her.

She was awake and knew what was coming; he could see it in her eyes as she watched him approach. There was little she could do against him. Her body was no longer her own. It had been given over to the damn egg. All she'd managed to do was struggle out of her clothing, ripping it when she couldn't undo the fastening. Hell, he'd even helped her, cutting some of the worst of the bindings while they were still on his mount.

So now she was naked on the sandy floor of the cave, her entire body clenching as it tried to dislodge the damn pulsing egg from her belly. The egg was a bright, glistening gold now. In fact, if he looked very hard, Kiril could even see the dragon inside, twisting, pushing, doing everything it could to break out of its opaque shell.

But he didn't really care about it; his eyes were on her. *D'greth,* she was in agony. Her body wasn't designed to push the egg out this way. It could only writhe and twist, the contortions doing what they could to break the threads—like a human umbilicus—that connected the egg to her. When those broke, the egg would roll free and it would be up to the dragon to crack its shell—assuming the breaking process hadn't already saved it the trouble.

Damned, lazy-assed demons.

Kiril knew just how to help her—and wasn't he just the biggest bastard for even thinking it? It was plain as the ocean behind him which of her muscles needed to contract to help oust the cursed thing. Plus, she needed to contract her body in a clear pulse, one wave coming on top of the other in a systematic, powerful way. And wasn't he just rock hard thinking about it?

It was the dragon magic affecting him; he was sure of it. And yet, he couldn't deny that he had a nearly overwhelming urge to bed the woman rather than chop her head off.

She was long gone. He knew that. The Natiya he knew was dead, replaced by the beast all dragonborn became. And she was vulnerable now. Didn't it make sense—wasn't it more merciful—to kill her now instead of waiting until she destroyed half of Ragona in her bloodlust?

Of course it did. And so he raised his sword, holding it high above her head. She hadn't the breath to argue with him. In fact, she was floundering, gasping out in pain. And yet, as he watched, she began to speak, her words stuttering. He understood her nonetheless.

"The worst thing . . . that Rashad . . . has done. He . . . takes away ideals." She straightened as best she could, pushing herself upright against the cave wall as she looked at him. "When did you last try to better things? Rather than just survive? Think, Kiril. When did you . . . last believe in the goodness of your cause?"

He knew better than to listen to her. A woman as resourceful as Natiya would say anything, do anything to delay death. And yet, he could not deny her words. When *was* the last time he'd believed in what he did? When had he truly believed that what he was working for was good rather than simply not-evil? When had he last picked up his sword and believed he worked for something right? Never?

His parents had believed. And they had died for their cause. His father's conviction had burned inside him like a beacon, even when he was walking into the Copper's open maw. Had Kiril ever felt as strongly? About anything he had ever done?

No. Because from the moment Dag Racho had dropped him in the middle of court politics, Kiril had worked for survival, not success. For compromise, not victory.

And where had that gotten him? To this cave, about to kill Ragona's only hope. He felt his shoulder muscles begin to quiver, but that was nothing compared to the turmoil in his mind. Could she be the one to bring down Dag Racho? It wasn't possible. All logic argued against it.

And yet, how many people had such fire in their eyes, with the will and the intelligence and the skill to back it up? He flashed on a memory of her in the prison, facing off with Dag Racho. The dragon egg had made her body unwieldy, and she'd been surrounded by soldiers while the Emperor decided her fate. Kiril was hard pressed to imagine a more vulnerable position, and yet she had squared off with Racho as if she were the one with the upper hand.

He couldn't think of anyone with that type of nerve. That she was also a woman of poor background with the intelligence to maneuver successfully in such a situation made her remarkable indeed. More than remarkable. Absolutely unique.

He groaned, indecision making his sword arm shake. She was an amazing woman, no doubt about it. And yet, for all that, Sabina's words echoed back to him.

She is crafty, I will give you that. And resourceful. But she is still an amateur in this game.

And in games against the Emperor, amateurs died. And worse, if he didn't go through with this now—with what he and Sabina had planned—Bina would take everything. He would be penniless. Powerless. And completely lost. He simply couldn't risk everything he'd worked so hard for—his financial security, a governorship with real power, his real chance to make a difference—on an amateur, even if Natiya was intelligent and resourceful and so damn beautiful it broke his heart.

He couldn't give those things up. And so, with a curse that blistered his lips, he slammed down his blade with all his strength.

CHAPTER EIGHTEEN

Kiril cursed himself. Over and over, with every sobbing breath, he cursed himself. Cursed the dragons. Cursed Natiya for beginning this in the first place. But most of all, he cursed himself. For being a fool. For being weak. For slamming his sword down into the sand beside her head, not even close enough to cut her glorious blond hair. He couldn't do it. He couldn't kill her. And worse, he couldn't watch her suffer either.

He knew what he had to do, bastard that he was. He knew, and he didn't hesitate. Having already thrown away all of his convictions, why not go for broke? Or perhaps, having risked everything on her, why not make sure he helped her every way he could? So he did.

According to his mother, Jaseen's egg had been cut from his arm. The worst his cousin experienced was a torn muscle, which healed within a day. But Natiya had incubated the egg in her belly. Cutting the egg out of there could very well kill her. She had to push the thing out on her own. But her contortions were doing nothing. They were disorganized and weak, unable to wrench the egg from her belly. She had to have a rhythm, damn it, an overriding wave of contractions until she tossed the damn dragon from her body like so much bad meat. She had to have a frelling orgasm, and a big one. So he did the only thing he knew how to do. He dropped to his knees between her legs, using his hands to open her wide. The sunlight was fading now, bathing the clutching cave in glorious shades of red and orange. But all he could see was her. And he was smitten.

Natiya.

He kissed her. He did more than kiss her; he stroked his tongue in long, sensuous waves across her sex. He knew how to do it. *D'greth,* in some things a court education was most thorough. And thank Amia he was strong enough to hold Natiya down while he administered to her.

A kiss. A stroke. Even a hum. Everything and anything he could do to begin her contractions.

She was incredibly sensitive. Even his breath had her squirming, and not just from the damn hatching. All too soon she was crying out his name instead of just crying. And sweet *toutch,* when he pushed his fingers inside her and her flesh contracted around him, it was all he could do not to join her.

And yet, it wasn't enough. Her body was still twisting, writhing in a spastic fashion.

"More!"

He wasn't sure he had heard her at first. She had been gasping, crying, sobbing, the Father only knew what she was trying to say. Until, of course, her legs locked around his head and she reared up.

"Kiril! More!" Then, as she screamed and fell backward, one last word slipped past her lips. "Please." With every gasping breath, she kept repeating it. Over and over. "Please. Please. Please. Please."

And so he did what he knew she desired. He rolled her onto her side, doing his best to use their body weight to shove the damn egg from her belly. He spooned up behind her, his prock hard and eager.

"Yes!" she gasped. "Now. Now. Now. Now."

She arched back against him, and he thrust. He didn't even think about it; he just acted while her ecstatic scream echoed in the chamber. Cursing himself for a bastard, he thrust, burying himself so deep inside her that he didn't think he would ever come out. And then he reached down, wrapping his arms around her thighs, spreading her legs with his hands so he could slip his fingers where she needed him most.

She helped as best she could. She arched against him and writhed and sobbed. "More. More. More."

Amia, he was a bastard for loving it, but he did. She clenched him and he rammed into her, using his fingers and all his skill. At last it began—one quick contraction, followed by another and another and another. Power built inside her. He knew, because he felt each incredible wave. And bit by bit, he helped her recruit other muscles to join in the glory. Stronger wave after stronger wave. Growing, pumping, moving together until her entire body—and his along with hers—was one great fabulous explosion of power.

That kept going on.

And on.

And . . .

"YES!"

The egg sprang free, pushed from her body with enough force to crack it against the wall. He didn't know what happened after that. All he knew was Natiya was still contracting, still shuddering with him, around him.

Together.

Until they both sank into unconsciousness.

Air. Sun. Beautiful sky.

Flight, at last.

Natiya was soaring again, riding the wind while the sun beat hard and hot against her back. What joy there was in this—the flap of her wings, the cool caress of a cloud, and then the abrupt and welcome sight of prey.

Her stomach rumbled in hunger, and her wings faltered, but the prey was bound and could not run. The humans had obviously left it for her, knowing her great need so soon after the hatching. She adjusted her wings for a downward attack, but it was difficult to control her flight. She overran her target. Thankfully, she had time now to practice, and this tethered prey was useful for such things.

Below her, she heard the animal scream and was startled to realize how the sound fired her blood. She opened her mouth, instinctively wanting to purge her fire gases, but she was too young and so no flame leapt forth. No matter. She would grow, and the fire gas would come. In the meantime, she was tired of practicing. Her shoulders ached and her belly rumbled. No matter how awkward the approach, it was time to eat.

She misjudged again, but this time adjusted in midrun. She was too small to bite off the creature's head. Instead, she used her claws, narrowly grasping the creature's spine.

D'greth, the thing was heavy, double her size. Though her claws kept hold of it, the weight toppled her down onto the ground. She landed painfully on her nose and cried out, though the sound was muffled by the crash. Fortunately, the jerk of her landing had snapped the creature's back. Once her annoyance faded, she was able to feast. It was good to have food.

"Damn it! Not the mount! Oh, *d'greth*, not our mount!"

Natiya looked up, seeing the male human stumbling toward her, sharp stick extended. She frowned. Not sharp stick. A sword. And he was most skilled with it.

She opened her mouth to tell him to put it down, but her mouth was full and all she managed was a hoarse gurgle. Instead, she extended a hand to stop him, but her claws were also buried deep within her prey and her wings reached forward instead and she overbalanced, toppling onto her nose once again, gurgling in distress.

Meanwhile, she heard the man—Kiril—moan as he left her side to move back into the cave. His steps were noisy, his sword scraping the sand in defeat.

"Natiya! Natiya, you must wake!"

Natiya stirred, trying to right herself once again. All she managed was to turn her head. Fortunately, that brought the food directly against her snout, and the scent was heavenly. Warm and full. She could resume eating without even adjusting her wings. Her arms. No, her wings. But she didn't have wings.

"Natiya! Wake up!"

She opened her eyes and saw the human. She saw Kiril kneeling in the sand beside her, his jaw darkened with hair and his face clenched with passion.

No, this wasn't passion. It was . . . fear? Hunger? Anger? What was the word?

"Natiya! Can you hear me?"

She opened her mouth to speak, but instead of words she heard a loud cry, muffled because of food and sand and awkward position.

"Natiya, you are not the dragon. Separate yourself from it. Natiya!"

She blinked and tried to move, but she was already moving. Already eating. What was happening?

"Listen to me," the man continued. "You have to remember who you are. If you are only the beast, then I must kill you. I must! Show me that you are still in there. Please, Natiya!"

She heard the desperation in his voice and struggled to understand it. Of course she was still here. She was Natiya. Eating her breakfast. Except, she was not. She was Natiya, lying in aching pain upon a sandy floor.

What was she?

Again she blinked her eyes, trying to resolve her dual vision. She had an excellent view of Kiril, his eyes searching hers. She also saw her food, warm and still flowing blood, the energy fading with the death of the creature.

Energy fading? That was dragon sight.

There was no energy surrounding Kiril. Therefore, that was her human sight.

"Natiya." He was begging her now. "I don't know how long this takes. I've never stopped to question it before. I don't even know if you're in there at all. Please, for the love of the Father, don't make me do this. Show me you can hear me."

"I am here," she said. Or she thought she said. She heard only the gurgling sound of the dragon.

No, this was not right. She needed her human voice, human words. So she tried again. Another hoarse gurgle. This wasn't working.

"Natiya?"

She had to move, had to see him more clearly. And so, with her wings folded up behind her, she abandoned her food. It had been a large beast, well able to fill her belly for many days. Still, she was reluctant to leave it because the energy faded more and more after death. But it was more important to talk to Kiril now, so she left her food behind with only small regret. Then she waddled awkwardly over stone and sand until she made it to the mouth of the clutching cave.

And watched as Kiril turned away from her to stare at the golden dragon. He stood slowly, his sword tip rising slowly before him.

"Natiya? Are you in control of it? Because I swear to you, I can still kill it."

"Don't!" Again, her word came out as a hoarse cry as she continued to waddle forward.

"Natiya . . ." His voice was a low growl that made her hunch her wings. "Keep it back. Even hatchlings can kill a man. I won't let it have that chance."

She had to stop moving. She had to—

She stopped. No, the dragon stopped. No, she stopped the dragon. *D'greth*, this was so confusing.

She sat down. No, the dragon sat down. No, she sat the dragon down. And it grunted in disgust.

"Natiya? Are you in control?"

She snorted through the dragon's nose in response. And wasn't that just the oddest feeling?

"You have to try and separate yourself from it. Try and move your arm."

Her wing extended.

She looked at it, moving both her human head and her dragon head so that she got a view of herself—of the dragon wing—with both human and dragon vision. She slammed her eyes shut. Both sets.

"Work slowly. Carefully. Do not let it gain control of you."

She opened her eyes—both sets—to once again look at Kiril. Her human eyes noted that he was gloriously naked, his body in a ready stance, his sword poised but not raised. Her dragon eyes saw the strength of his energy flowing around him, coloring the air with the bright red of his aura.

The color red? When had she begun to differentiate energy flow by color and source? She didn't have an answer, nor did she need one. Instead, she began to look around, seeing the ebb and flow of energy in a rainbow of different colors as it permeated everything.

She ought to be nauseated by the sight. Her head ought to be throbbing with the strain of trying to sort through her vision, but it wasn't; somehow filtering the images through the dragon's mind made everything more recognizable.

Even Kiril.

She turned her human head to look at the Golden Queen, its short, squat body plopped in an ungainly heap on the sand. And since she could not speak with her own voice, she decided to think at it just as she had done when it was an egg in her belly.

Queen, are you there?

Of course. And then, apparently for emphasis, the Queen released a soft, purring kind of hum.

I am having trouble separating my body from yours.

Of course.

Can I release your body to you and my body to me?

Of course.

How?

You must simply do so.

Just do so. Right. Why was everything so simple for the dragon and confusing for her? And then, as if the Queen were suddenly in an expansive mood, the dragon explained further.

You have always had complete dominance over your body. But now you have two bodies. You must learn to specify which body must move, which muscles contract and relax.

She tried to do as it suggested. Once again, she raised her arm. Her human arm didn't move. Her dragon wing did.

Why does your body move and not mine?

Because I am the dominant body.

And I am the dominant mind?

Yes. For now.

As usual, Natiya detected no emotion in the dragon's voice, merely a statement of fact, and Natiya couldn't suppress a shudder at the implication. Clearly, the Queen believed that at some point she would have dominance.

Is that true? Natiya asked. *How long before you will be able to control my mind?*

Never. Unless you cede control to me.

But right now you are ceding control of your body to me?

I am sharing. As we were meant to do. It is part of the process.

Every time Natiya asked a question, the answer spawned a hundred other questions. But she didn't want to focus on them right now. Her current concern was making sure Kiril didn't kill one or both of them before she could sort out matters. So she concentrated her energies on regaining control of her body—her human body.

She began with her breathing. Inhale. Exhale.

The Queen was almost comical in the way her cheeks and belly expanded and contracted. Natiya focused more deliberately. Human inhale. Human exhale. She felt her human body respond with pain. With a lot of pain. She heard herself groan.

Kiril reacted immediately, whipping around to stare at her. "Natiya? Are you coming back to me?"

"I never left," she snapped. Of course, the Queen growled at the same time, but Natiya was sure her human body had spoken. So, apparently, was Kiril, because he abruptly dropped to his knees before her.

"Are you in pain?"

Stupid question. Now that she was beginning to separate sensations, she was able to sort through what inputs came from the dragon and what from her human body. Indeed, it wasn't all that hard. Pain was from the human. Youth and vitality came from the dragon.

Damn pleasure hog. Now she knew why babies gurgled all the time. It was a joy just being in a young body, whereas hers felt like it had just . . . had just been carrying that huge dragon around like it was a suitcase strapped to her belly. Then she'd popped it out like a cork from a bottle.

She frowned, knowing her images didn't make sense. But, *d'greth,* now that her mind felt centered back in her human body, she was in pain! Everything ached, and . . . She looked down at her naked belly where she'd once carried the egg. There was blood everywhere—dried and mixed with sand—but mostly she saw her navel with thin ugly veins drooping out of it. That was what had connected her to the egg. And all around her and Kiril, her flesh sagged, lying on the ground like the bloated skin of a fat gommet.

Sweet Amia, she was hideous!

"Well, at least I know you're in there," Kiril grumbled as he sat back on his haunches. "I seriously doubt a dragon would care what you look like. And only you could look at your naked body and make sounds of distress."

She concentrated hard, and was able to lift her human head to look directly at him.

He grinned, even as impatience laced his tone. "Yes, you are still beautiful to me. No, there aren't any stretch marks—or at least none that won't fade pretty soon. *D'greth,* Natiya, you are an amazing woman, in more ways than just your body. Now can we please get back to deciding if I have to kill you or not? Can you control your dragon?"

It was time to stretch her skills. She had mastered moving her head. She could control her vision, switching back and forth between the Queen's and her own at will. Now it was time to conquer speech.

"Frrrrreeegnoooow."

"What?"

"Frrrrrr. Nowwwww."

"One more time, Natiya. Really concentrate."

"Foooorrrrr. Nowwww."

"For now?"

She nodded.

"For now. For now what?"

She glared at him.

"Oh, right. For now. You can control your dragon for now." He frowned as her words at last sank in. "For now! Natiya, how long is now?" He abruptly stood up, his sword raised.

"Op!"

He froze at her loud tone. She concentrated harder.

"Ssssstop!"

"Natiya, I can't risk—"

"Shhhhut up! Sworrrrrrd away!"

"But—"

"Lisssten."

He hesitated, then sighed, dropping his sword into the sand. She didn't fool herself into thinking she was safe; Kiril was still lightning-fast if he wanted to be. Whatever she said now had to be good.

"Dragon nooooot evil."

He didn't answer that, and she could have kicked herself for her stupidity. This was old territory for them, an old disagreement. Just repeating the same thing was not going to change his mind. She needed another tack.

"Have plan," she lied.

"Great," he answered evenly. "What?"

And wouldn't she like to know that as well? But then she focused her thoughts away from self-pity. She did have a plan of sorts. She just needed to expand on it, figure out the details.

"Kill Rasssssshad."

He frowned. "Rashad? Who's Rashad?"

"Emperrrrror."

He grimaced. "How long can you control your dragon?"

She wasn't sure. She now strongly suspected that dragons only allowed their human pairs the illusion of control. That if the two beings truly struggled for dominance, the best she could hope for was to control her own body. Fortunately, she and her egg had reached a kind of understanding during the last few days.

"Untillll we separrrrate."

He frowned. "Separate? You mean, from your dragon? But you can't—"

"Cannnn," she stated firmly. She could. She just wasn't

quite sure she wanted to pay the price to get sole ownership of her mind back. Then again, it was too late for second thoughts. She'd chosen this path a long, long time ago.

"How?" Kiril pressed.

She knew he was asking for details of the separation, but she pretended to misunderstand. She looked at him, doing her best to bring him over to her side. Without him, she didn't stand a chance. "You must teach meeeee. To fight."

He snorted. "That takes a lifetime, Natiya. How—"

"You fight Emperor," she interrupted. "I fight Copperrrr."

He paused, obviously thinking hard. "The Copper is large and mature. Even if we can hide long enough for the Queen to grow—"

"He will not kill his Queennn." Speech was becoming easier as Natiya felt herself more and more grounded in her body. "But you must help us learn."

He laughed, a quick explosion of sound that had more to do with disdain than humor. "I don't know anything about dragon fighting."

"Then we will learn together."

"Natiya—"

"Trust me." She hated those words. They were the last-ditch plea of the truly desperate. If he didn't trust her now, begging him to believe in her would be pointless. And yet, it seemed to have an effect.

Kiril dropped his chin into his hands and looked at her before shifting his sights back to the Queen. The creature was still sitting on her backside, her large belly protruding onto the sand. In truth, she looked cute, almost cuddly. But Natiya knew there was a strong mind and an even stronger will inside that pudgy body. And if she had any doubt, all Natiya had to do was look into the dragon's golden eyes to see how closely the Queen was listening to their conversation. It, too, was making plans, though only Amia knew what.

Then, just to make doubly sure, Natiya directed a quick flurry of questions at the Queen.

Our bargain still stands, doesn't it? You will fight the Copper? Defeat it? And then we will separate as planned?

That is the true purpose of this joining.

But Kiril is right. The Copper is very large and experienced. He has won many battles.

He will not kill his Queen.

There was no doubt in the dragon's mind, and so Natiya nodded, turning her focus back to Kiril, who was looking down at the dry remains of the dragon egg.

"I have betrayed Sabina, myself, and all of Ragona," he said softly. "I know I should have killed you. I probably ought to kill you now." He lifted his gaze to look directly at Natiya. "I think the dragons have more power than you know. I think she will eventually control you, and I will have betrayed everyone for a monster."

"No—" she began, but he cut her off.

"But even so, I believe in you. And I will help you."

She nodded, but again he didn't wait for her comment.

"You understand that I will have to kill you eventually, don't you? The moment she gains control of you, I will have to kill you both."

Natiya sighed. "You don't understand. We will separate." Just not in the way he thought. She leaned forward. "Do you know why Dag Racho is evil?"

Kiril shrugged. "Because he controls everything with terror. He conquers without thought and kills without justice."

"Because he will not let the bond finish its purpose," she corrected. "Dragon and man were not meant to remain linked so long. Holding on creates madness—in both man and dragon."

Kiril straightened. "And what is its purpose?"

She struggled with her answer. She was only now beginning to grasp its full meaning. In the end, she settled for a partial truth: "The Queen was born to force Rashad to finish his bond. To end Dag Racho's reign of terror."

"I pray that is true," Kiril answered coldly, "because all our hopes rest with you now."

She stared at him, hearing the dull echo of his words but seeing something else as well. It was not her dragon sight that revealed it to her, but some part of her human self that she could not name. Some part of her heart, perhaps, that said he was feeling lost and terrified.

"What do you fear?"

He looked up at her, his heart in his eyes. "I cannot fail again," he said, his voice thick with emotion. "I cannot watch everything I love destroyed. Not again." Then he swallowed. "I will go mad," he whispered.

She stretched out her hand. Not her wing, but her hand, eventually finding his arm. He shifted his body, adjusting slowly until they gripped each other—touching finger to finger, palm to palm. "I cannot do this without you," she said. "It is so confusing. I need your help."

"You have it," he vowed, and looking at his face, she knew that he had just given her everything. Not just his vow, but his heart and his soul as well.

"Why?" The word did not come close to being the question she meant. Why would he give her such faith? Why would he risk everything for her? Why was he the man he was? And why did she need him so desperately?

He struggled with his answer, emotions flying across his face too quickly for her to read. Until, finally, he shrugged. "You give me hope, Natiya. And I have not had that in a long, long time."

She swallowed, straightening as best she could in the sand. "I will not fail you." This time she was the one who pledged her faith. She would live up to the hope in his eyes or die trying.

He brought her hand to his lips, kissing their joined fingers. "Nor I you."

In this way, they began the war.

CHAPTER NINETEEN

Preparing for war was not at all what Natiya expected. She'd envisioned endless hours in flight, drilling for this aerial twist, that winged attack. She wanted to move, to fly, to dance among the clouds.

Kiril wanted to take things slower. He wanted her to control her own body first before she controlled the dragon. He wanted her to sit her dragon still—in silence—while she stretched her aching body, while she walked or ran or even danced. And then, when her human body could take no more, he continued to make the Queen sit and watch, growing larger while Natiya practiced moving individual parts of the beast's body. One finger on the wing. Not the entire wing, just the finger. One toe of the left foot. The nose. The bellows. The tail.

War was about discipline, he kept saying. But mostly this war seemed to be about fear—Kiril's fears. Fear that the Queen would control Natiya, not the other way around. Fear that they would be discovered unless the dragon stayed hidden. Fear that Dag Racho's soldiers were even now scouring the mountains to find them. Of course, the hell of it was, he was right.

She exercised rigid discipline over her dragon,

allowing it to fly only at night, only through the darkened sky without flame, and to hunt fish when the mount was gone. That was the most glorious time for both of them: She released the Queen to hunt, only sharing in the experience through thought. Mind to mind they were, and the experience poured into her soul. She would lie down on the sand, closing her human eyes, while the Queen took control of herself, learning to control her rapidly maturing body, learning to develop her own skills.

Unbonded dragons, Natiya learned from the Queen, grew much more slowly. Part of the magical bonding process allowed bonded creatures' minds to mature long before hatching. Then, when the body at last emerged, the dragon's physical form rushed to catch up, growing as fast as it could eat, maturing as quickly as its sustenance allowed.

Each night Natiya soared with the Queen, while beside her, Kiril touched her human body, constantly reminding her that this was where she belonged, that there was glory in the human physique as well. He made a persuasive argument, and inevitably she would abandon the Queen to its feasting while she turned her attention to Kiril.

His bedroom skills were legendary at court, he confessed one night, and the things he taught her were beyond anything she imagined. And yet, he misunderstood what she valued. He believed she ached for his kisses, and he worked hard to make sure they inflamed her senses. He would shift and adjust, his every caress seeking that special moment when she began to hum, deep in the back of her throat, almost like a purr; for in this, her human body echoed the dragon's. He would then grin in satisfaction, deepening his touch, stroking her with his tongue until that hum became a groan of hunger. And when he opened her thighs, pleasuring her with his mouth as he'd done during the hatching, he pressed his hands to her hips as if trying to measure the pulsing tremors he coaxed with such quivering explosion. Only when she was sobbing his name did he at last couple with her, and then it was as if he hated himself for taking his own pleasure while she wrapped her legs around him, demanding his thickness deep and hard and most wondrously filling her.

These things he thought she valued. And in truth, she did. They were amazing, leaving her spent and filled with a contentment deep in her bones. But that was not what she cherished most.

She cherished most the moments he touched her in passing, almost without thought, because he wanted to be with her. She valued the way he tried to hide his worry from her, fearing that she would begin to doubt herself. But most of all, she loved the way he listened to her.

At first they spoke of little beyond training: what she could do, what she could control. Then they began to discuss how they could hide from the Emperor until they were ready, and in what manner a dragon fought. In this, of course, they relied heavily upon the Queen, whose inherent knowledge was surprisingly and disturbingly vast. But mostly Kiril and Natiya explored their problems together "like two blind drunks in an alley," as he often said; they talked.

And in the last few days, usually when they ate their evening meal, Kiril asked about her childhood and her dreams, about the girl she used to be and the woman she'd wanted to become. He listened to her thoughts and then shared his own past. And this she loved most of all. She hadn't known his left side was nearly as dextrous as his right, but he'd kept that a secret. Nor had she known that he loved shaping metal and clay since the first day he played in the dirt. In fact, without his loga wire, he had been reduced to carving sticks he found in the mountains, whittling them into birds or fish, insects and animals. He inevitably destroyed the things he made, otherwise their cave would be littered with carvings of all types of living creatures. And yet, she saw those sculptures as a window into his soul.

He had a great love for living things, honoring all that nature gave. And yet he was first a warrior. It hurt him, she knew, to watch beauty and life destroyed, though that too was a secret he kept well buried. Every death weighed heavily on his soul, and she believed that he longed for a time when he could at last lay down his sword.

That more than anything else pushed her to work at what he wanted her to learn. Because when this was all done, when Dag Racho was deposed forever, then perhaps Kiril could lay down his weapon and find peace in the shaping of loga wire or the carving of stone. That was her desire for him, and so she told him one night. He was sharpening his sword in the fading evening light, and she was waiting for the stars to come out while the Queen dozed near the cave mouth.

The words came easily, and she spoke softly, her vow as natural to her as breath. "One day soon you will be able to put down your sword forever. There will be no need to kill anymore; this I swear to you."

He looked up, his expression wistful. "That is a lovely dream, Natiya, but a vain hope. Do not fool yourself into believing it will ever come to pass."

She straightened, coming to stand beside him. "But after we kill Dag Racho—"

"Nature abhors a vacuum." He reached out, pulling her down beside him, and she curled naturally into his arms as he continued. "The Emperor controls so much. If we defeat him—"

"*When*," she interrupted, correcting him.

He shrugged. "When this is all over, a great many people will want his power, and most of them are just as bad as the Emperor." He sighed. "That is the one good thing I can say about Dag Racho—he kept many other evildoers in check."

"But after he is gone—"

"They will come out in force. Indeed, with his focus on us, some of them probably are already preparing."

She twisted, liking the sound of his heartbeat beneath her cheek. It seemed to combine with the steady wash of nearby ocean waves, bringing dreams of an eternity cocooned in such simple bliss. She was so content with the sound, it took a moment for her to comprehend his words. "What do you mean, 'are already preparing'?"

He dropped a kiss on her forehead, but his thoughts were far away. "I forgot that you weren't conscious at the time. Do you remember waking the Coral?"

The days before the hatching were fuzzy in places, but she definitely remembered channeling energy—only Amia knew how—into the sleeping dragon. "Rashad had kept her like that—in water—for decades," she murmured.

Kiril tightened his hold on her, folding her closer against him. "That's the only reason we escaped, Natiya. Because the Emperor was busy fighting—"

"His sister."

She felt him flinch, and she shared his horror as he spoke. "Sweet Amia, that was his own sister?" He shifted so that he could look directly at her face, and she lifted her head to accommodate him. But she did not expect the fierce anger that burned in his eyes. "I will not let that happen to you, Natiya. Decades encased in water? Whatever happens, I will not let—"

"Don't make promises, Kiril. Especially ones you can't keep." She straightened the rest of the way, pulling out of his arms. "If this goes badly, neither of us will be in a position to defend anyone." Her eyes narrowed. "Unless you have a plan I don't know."

His expression hardened, boring into hers. "My plan, Natiya? You haven't shared any of the details of your own. What do *you* intend to do?"

She was flustered. "You are to fight Dag Racho—"

"While your Queen fights the Copper," he finished for her. "I know what we discussed. But to what end do we fight? I plan to kill the Emperor. Will you kill his dragon?"

She flushed, reminded once again how much of a novice she was at this game of hiding truth, especially from a man like Kiril. He had known from the very beginning that she had other plans, and yet he remained by her side, teaching and believing in her. The thought was humbling. She tensed, knowing she would have to work hard to convince him.

"Dragons are not evil, Kiril. They are merely . . . different."

He snorted. "They are creatures of passion, Natiya. They live to hunt and destroy. They take what they want. And when they bond with a human, they gain all of our intelligence, our reason. Combine the two, and you create Dag Racho."

As if on cue, the golden Queen chose that moment to scramble up and abruptly launch herself into the sky in order to hunt up her next meal. It was dark enough now for her to be relatively safe from human eyes. Dragon eyes would see her, of course, but that was a risk they had to take.

Natiya watched the Queen glory in flight, pure joy in her every movement, but inside she felt the Queen's stomach rumble with hunger, and felt her own blood quicken in anticipation of the hunt. Natiya knew the prey would be fish and that the Queen was equally happy with the sea's bounty as she was with land-based meat, but either way, Kiril's statement had an echo of truth. The dragon's primitive drive to hunt was amazingly strong. In fact, in those first few days, Natiya had found it difficult not to become overwhelmed herself.

Only Kiril had kept her grounded in her own body. He had talked constantly, trying to keep her mind with his. Whenever that had failed, he'd resorted to his touch, his caress. Eventually, she had found a way to retain her own mind and control, even when the Queen was over-whelmed by a desire to kill or eat.

"I am not evil," she said.

"You are amazingly strong," he agreed. "And it has not been so long for you yet." He glanced at the nearly black sky. "And she is very young."

Natiya shook her head. "Our minds are completely separate at these times." She didn't want to admit that her body still hummed with the Queen's flight, the sen-sations of wind and air tingling across her skin.

"Which is why you must tell me now—without her listening—exactly what you plan and why."

She sighed. He was right. If they ever hoped to suc-ceed, she would have to tell him everything. "I think you have it backwards, Kiril. It is not the dragons who are filled with emotions, it is we humans. I think they have a plan—"

"The dragons?"

"Yes."

She knew that terrified him. Indeed, his hand instinc-tively clutched his sword, so she rushed words out quickly, hoping to make him understand. "But it is not what you think. They don't want to destroy us—"

"Only dominate us? Take control? Use us as food?"

The very thought revolted her, and yet she could un-derstand how Kiril might think that way. "I think that is Dag Racho's example, not the true path for all dragons." Then she paused, hating to ask but needing to know the truth. "How often did you see the Emperor feed prison-ers to the Copper?"

Kiril shrugged, the motion tight with anger. "Often."

"And the laws with such a punishment were tightly enforced to maintain his supply," Natiya recalled. She looked outside to where the Queen flew, playing in the waves, diving and catching fish after fish to fill her belly. She was small now, and sated by a dozen or so of the creatures. But how long before such a meal wasn't enough? How long before the Queen required a full cow or more?

"This is not how it should be," she stated firmly. "This state—this bonding—is only half the process. It has not been completed."

Kiril shifted, his eyebrows pulled down in thought.

Natiya took a deep breath. "It is the first step in a change," she said softly. "An exchange of bodies."

His eyes searched hers, and he began to speak, but she shook her head, needing to finish before he interrupted.

"That is the separation I have promised you. The bodies change. The Queen will take my body, her consciousness completely in this form." She gestured to herself. "While I—"

"Become her." He groaned. "Natiya, you cannot do this! I cannot. I won't—"

"You'll kill me," she said. "That's what you haven't told me, isn't it? Despite everything, you still intend to kill—"

"The dragon, Natiya. Your beast. Not you."

"But that *will* be me, Kiril. And so I must leave you and Ragona behind." Her gaze drifted out across the ocean, her sights focused not on the Queen but a place far to the north. "There is a land of dragons, Kiril. I'm not sure where, but I will find it." She abruptly tore her sight back to him. "There are things out there, things the dragons know that I want to learn."

"What things?" he asked, an urgency in his voice that she had never heard. "What do the dragons have that we do not? And what—"

"What do they want from us?"

He nodded.

She shook her head. "I . . . I don't entirely know."

"But you *must* know," he pressed. "Think. What does the Queen really love about you? What does she ask you to do? What does she encourage?"

Natiya thought, searching through her memories without tapping those of her dragon; she didn't want it to realize what she was doing. She spoke slowly, the process taking a great deal of time. "At first she always questioned. Why this? What does that mean?"

"Gathering information."

"Yes. But later—"

"How much later?"

"Certainly after she shared memories with the Copper. But before that, I think. When—"

"When we first came together at the clutching cave." It was not a question, but Natiya answered nonetheless.

"Yes," she said softly. "The changes began then."

"Because she was maturing?"

Natiya nodded, but slowly, because she knew there was more to the situation than that. "Because . . ." She looked around, seeing the smooth walls of the cave, the shimmer of reflective stone and the way the clutching caves were shaped like a funnel—like a cone with the large end aimed out to sea. "Because this is where she talks to the others."

"What?" Kiril was so alarmed, he jumped to his feet, scanning the cave and then the skies as if he feared immediate attack. "Others? What do they say?"

Natiya shook her head even as she, too, scrambled backward onto her toes. "I don't know," she answered, her voice betraying her agitation. And more than her voice, she realized, because just then the Queen's flight faltered. It was a small movement, barely even registering, but Natiya felt it nonetheless. And she knew the Queen sensed her distress.

It is nothing, Natiya thought to the dragon. *Kiril thinks you are evil.*

It was a ready excuse, and one the Queen easily accepted.

We wish only to search for the human. That is not evil. It is the natural progression of things.

The perfect human? Natiya pressed as she had so often before. *What does that mean?*

We mean you no harm. We search. That is all.

Naitya didn't argue. She'd had the very same discussion a hundred times with the same vague result. So she sighed, then worked to quiet her thoughts, quiet her emotions until the Queen's attention was caught by the dark shift of prey near the water's surface. Soon the beast was occupied with hunting, and Natiya could focus once again on Kiril.

He stood watching her, his sword at the ready. He stood so he could see both the Queen and her, probably trying to guess what had transpired.

"It is difficult to shield my thoughts from her. I cannot do this forever," Natiya admitted.

"She will grow too strong," he agreed.

"No," she snapped. "I am tired of it—this constant paranoia. It is part of what has made the Emperor insane. At first I thought it only a symptom, for he was an anxious child with much to fear. But now perhaps it is the other way around. This need for privacy in one's own thoughts creates a paranoia that permeates everything. If I cannot trust my own thoughts, how can I trust anything?"

"You can trust me," he pressed.

She laughed in response. "Is that why you stand with your sword in your hand? Why you still vow to kill me—"

"Not you. The—"

"The dragon," she finished for him. "Except, after the separation, I will be the Queen, and she me. What will you do then?"

He didn't answer, and she turned away from him, needing to think, needing to understand. "My mother believed the dragons acted as a magnifying glass."

She heard his gasp as he stepped closer. "I thought your mother died—"

"Many years ago, yes. But I have her journal." It was the one thing she'd brought with her from the Emperor's palace. She had tucked it in a secret pocket of her clothing, and pulled it out now, handing it to him.

He took it, but his eyes remained on her. "You are sure it's authentic?"

"Yes. And she is sure that what the dragons do is increase our feelings."

"But why?"

She looked around the cave, still exploring her theory. "I have never felt desire before. Not like—"

"Like when we are in these damned caves." His eyes grew angry. "This dragon magic—"

"Yes, magic. But it is not pervasive. It is merely an augmentation . . . of our lust."

"But Jaseen was not . . . belly-horned. Not normally. He became—"

"Violent, yes. So that is who he was. And Rashad always wanted to control, to possess. As for me, I have become more and more—"

"Curious. You want to know everything—the hows and the whys. But why would the dragons do this to us? What does it benefit them?"

"She says they're looking for the perfect human." He opened his mouth to ask the obvious question, but she held up her hand to stop him. "I don't know what that means, but she swears they aren't here to hurt us. I know you don't trust her word, but I do." She opened her arms to him. "I can read her mind as well as she reads mine, Kiril. I believe her."

He stepped forward, caressing her arms as he, too, struggled with many thoughts. Her tremors began immediately, like tiny brush fires beneath her skin wherever he touched her. Without conscious thought, she leaned into him, already lifting her lips for his kiss. And in the quiet corner of her mind where the Queen most often lurked, she felt an answering shiver of pleasure.

"This is why," she murmured. "Because they cannot feel."

His thoughts were not as clouded as hers. He was not nearly as intoxicated as she—by his touch, his scent, his presence. Or perhaps he did feel it. Perhaps he was stronger than she, maintaining better control.

"They do not feel love?"

"They do not feel anything except for a slight quickening when they hunt. They feel—nothing. Without us."

"How is that possible?"

She shook her head, already stretching up on her toes to brush her lips across his. "I don't know, but it is true. I am sure of it." And she was. "They need us—our ability—in order to feel what we do. Their lives are cold, Kiril, empty of passion, empty of everything but a daily knowledge of what they lack."

"Yet they reason? They think?"

She nodded, and the movement shifted her breasts across his chest. His hands had dropped to her hips and he drew her harder against his swelling sex. And again, in the back of her mind, she felt the dragon's attention, felt the Queen's need.

"Then they are the deadliest of enemies, because they act without emotion."

She smiled at that, allowing her tongue to trace the curve of his mouth. "Or they are the most capable of allies, swayed only by reason."

"Can it be possible?" He sounded incredulous, and she took advantage of his distraction to dart her tongue inside his mouth, teasing him before she withdrew.

"It is more than possible, Kiril," she said, and she allowed her hands to wander lazily about his toned body. "It *is.*"

He grabbed her hands, stopping her as he gazed sternly into her eyes. "Why are you doing this?" he asked. "Why are you touching me?"

She grinned. "I am testing my theory, Kiril." She twisted her hands free from his grasp. "I can feel the Queen's attention. She cares nothing for our discussion. She barely listens to our plans for the Emperor, or even her coming fight with the Copper." She let her hands drop abruptly to his hips, slipping quickly around until she released the catch of his pants. Within moments she was holding him hard and ready in her bare hand. It was like cupping power. She could not only sense the trembling hunger within Kiril, but she gloried in the excitement of how deeply he trusted her to let her touch him like this. Now. And she reveled in the knowledge of what she could do to him. What she wanted to do to him.

"The Queen wants to know what this feels like," Natiya explained, then abruptly released him, stepping backward, though it took all her will to do so. "And when I stop, she loses interest."

They stood together in silence, waiting while Natiya focused on the Queen. Only a few beats later, the dragon grew distracted by a flash of lightning far out to sea. A storm was brewing, and the wyrm wanted to test her wings against the shifting air currents that boiled around such weather.

Kiril stood back, looking from Natiya to the dark sky and then back to her. "So, what does it all mean?"

She grinned and stepped up to him, running her hands beneath his shirt and lifting it so she could kiss his velvety soft chest. "It means that we know now what the dragons want. They want our emotions—our joys and our fears. Hatred, jealousy, envy, paranoia, and—"

"Love?" he asked as he touched her face. "Do they want to feel love?"

"Yes," she whispered. "Love most of all," she said, and she began swirling her tongue around the hard disk of his nipple.

She heard his gasp of reaction even as his hands began to strip away her clothing. Then she felt the tug of the Queen's attention as a lightning bolt of desire sizzled straight to her womb.

"She likes this," Natiya whispered.

"So do I," Kiril answered.

Natiya giggled. "And I."

And at that moment, the Copper shot across the skyline headed straight for the Queen.

CHAPTER TWENTY

Kiril cursed, long and fluidly. He'd been caught belly-horned and naked once again. What was it about these cursed clutching caves that made him lose track of every shred of survival instinct? Or perhaps he should be wondering what it was about Natiya that made him forget? Either way, at least this time he was better prepared. The fight was in the air—or soon would be. His own plan required him to climb up the mountain, but he had a little time yet.

Thank Amia they'd moved to a different cave soon after the hatching. This one was high in the mountains and easily protected from soldiers. And since none of the traps he'd set up had gone off, Kiril knew he had at least thirty beats yet before anyone stormed the cave.

Glancing over, he saw Natiya wouldn't be of any help. Her gaze was completely unfocused, and he guessed her mind was locked with the Queen's in preparation of the aerial battle. She'd realized what was happening before he did, of course. The heavy stroke of the Copper's wings had barely registered in his consciousness before Natiya knew he was there, heating the air above the Clutching Mountains with his battle flame. Whether she'd been alerted through the Queen or some other dragonborn sensitivity, he didn't know; nor did he care. What was most important now was to find out if Dag Racho rode his Copper or lurked somewhere nearby.

Natiya had said that no rider could remain mounted during a true dragon fight. Of course, the Emperor was arrogant enough to attempt it, so Kiril could take nothing for granted. He pulled on his clothes, his eyes remaining fixed on the distant fires, trying to make out the silhouette of the Copper. He could only see plumes of flame, intermittent and weak, and almost all directed at the Queen. And the Queen wasn't quite old enough to have gained her full potential.

Frustratingly, Kiril could really see nothing. But Natiya could. And so, before the first of his traps triggered, he would—

A snap, then a clatter rumbled through the cave as a store of rocks and debris rattled down the side of the mountain. His first trap. Time had abruptly shortened. Which meant he had to find and kill the Emperor, now, before any soldiers reached Natiya.

He had to guide her to safety first. Gently he pulled up her shirt, rebuttoning it in a ridiculous waste of time; but he couldn't just leave her half naked for the soldiers to jeer at, should he fail. He then began tugging her, leading her to a hiding spot inside the cave. It wasn't much—just a tiny niche tucked behind a pile of rocks—but it was more defensible and might gain her a few beats. If she had any idea what was happening to her body, that was.

"Are the dragons fighting yet?" he asked. He couldn't see a damn thing.

"Not yet," she said, her voice clipped and breathy. "Soon."

"Can you see the Copper? Is the Emperor riding him?"

"Yes." Her eyes narrowed. "And no."

He frowned, needing to be sure. "Racho isn't on the Copper?"

"Not there."

Good. That meant the Emperor was probably near his troops. Which put Kiril back in play.

"I'm going now. Keep safe." Then he took another precious moment to drop a kiss on her lips. She was barely aware of him, he knew, but he wanted to touch her. He wanted to pretend that she worried for him almost as much as he worried for her. Especially since the odds of him—a single swordsman—prevailing against a troop of the Emperor's finest bodyguards made his future look extremely bleak.

It was on the tip of his tongue to say something to her; exactly what, he wasn't sure, but he held back. He hadn't the time to analyze his thoughts right then, and she certainly couldn't afford the distraction. And so he doused the fire—both in his thoughts and in the cave—since she didn't need it, and he couldn't afford it. Then he slipped into the night.

Well, he thought as he peered down the mountainside, Racho's troops obviously trusted the odds, because they certainly weren't worried. They carried firesticks and made enough sound to wake the entire country. Good. Let them be overconfident. Compared to some of the dragons he'd fought, they were nothing more than a swarm of pesky flies.

Or so he told himself as he slipped lower through the brush. Besides, the troops weren't his goal. He had little choice but to let them struggle on, triggering his traps one by one, until through sheer numbers—because *d'greth*, there were a horde of them—they overcame the resistance and marched into Natiya's cave. He hoped they wouldn't hurt her. Dag Racho had already named her his queen, and he prayed those orders would still hold.

He looked back toward the cave, unusually torn by fear. He wanted to stand by Natiya's side, defending her to his last breath. But he had a more crucial task at hand. And that meant carefully slipping through the rank and file until he found the Emperor. Fortunately, Kiril had been on many of Racho's war raids. He knew where to find his quarry. So he kept doggedly on, slipping through the underbrush toward the soldiers.

They were veterans, he noted with dispassionate annoyance. But Kiril had perfected his stealth skills against dragons, magical creatures with senses far keener than any human's. And as long as—

Kiril cursed long and fluently inside his head, hunkering down behind a nearby bush and waiting out his stupidity. Apparently, Dag Racho's men weren't the only ones prone to overconfidence. In his arrogance, Kiril had managed to slip past the primary patrol and forgot about the secondary. That meant he had just wiggled his way into the center of a double fan of soldiers. He was stuck, hunkered down half inside a thornbush while others slowly worked their way uphill.

No problem. He could wait.

Except, of course, the longer he waited, the shorter a time he would have to dispatch the Emperor before soldiers found Natiya. And, too, the idiots were about to trigger another of his rock slides. One that would happen to fall right down on top of this measly bush he was using as camouflage.

Dumb. Dumb. Dumb. He needed a distraction.

He twisted the tiniest fraction, stifling a curse as a dozen tiny pinpricks scratched his skin. Fortunately, he didn't have to shift much—just enough to see the vine that was stretched through a narrow cluster of trees. All he needed was someone to walk against it. Someone with heavy boots who wouldn't notice the vine until it was too late. And looky there, a perfect candidate was working his way right into the cluster.

He shifted his gaze to the left, watched another soldier move toward him. He had to keep them both in sight: the one about to trip the trap, and the one about to discover his hiding place. And he had to do all this without moving, without even breathing. He had to blend in with the bush. Become the bush. Stay frozen and—

Snap! The tripwire was pulled. Which tugged on the support rock, which then rolled away, which then released three long hours' worth of work piling big rocks. All were tumbling down.

Amia was with him. The front soldier had felt the vine give and called out. There was a general scramble, a chaos during which Kiril leaped free of the damn thornbush, quickly knocking unconscious the startled young man barely a wispan away from him, and then Kiril ran as fast as he could, praying he looked like just another soldier fleeing the rockslide.

Hallelujah, it worked! And he was running in the direction he guessed the Emperor would be located. Sure enough, he soon came upon a group of tethered mounts, a single campfire, two big ugly tents, and one smaller red tent behind. That was probably the Emperor's, since red was his color and there were nearly a dozen more soldiers parked in front.

Kiril took precious moments scanning the area, listened for others escaping the rockslide like himself. None? Good. That meant it was time to thin the Emperor's protection.

Moving uphill, he scrambled loudly down again toward the mounts, bellowing all the way. "Docs! And extra hands! Now!" He made sure to stay blocked from view in the darkness, a simple shadowy shape and form; then he disturbed the beasts, quickly picking one out and slapping its flank. "There's been an accident. This way!" Then he leapt on the mount and started riding it uphill.

When it neared a tree, he jumped off. Thankfully the Emperor had picked a spot with lots of cover. Kiril hoped that the soldiers didn't see his dismount, and would follow the horse uphill while he sneaked back down.

It worked. Less than a beat later, he had soldiers and medics scrambling onto the remaining mounts, riding off with all speed straight up the mountainside. His story was corroborated by other cries for help as more soldiers who'd been trapped in the rockslide appeared. Then, in another stroke of excellent fortune, someone uphill found his pit trap, falling with a maximum of noise while his buddies began cursing with a fervor that made Kiril smile. Especially since the two remaining guards of the Emperor had their eyes trained on the horizon, wondering just what was going on. Which left their backs vulnerable. A couple of beats later, the Emperor was minus his guards, and Kiril was free to slip inside that bright red tent.

He took the time to be careful, despite knowing it wouldn't make much difference. The Emperor had over a hundred cycles of fighting experience; he wasn't likely to be surprised, even if he was absorbed in the dragon fight above.

Kiril paused, listening closely for any noise before entering. He heard nothing except the harsh inhales and exhales of an angry Emperor. Glancing up at the sky, Kiril prayed the Copper was having a tough time besting the Queen. Unfortunately, all he could see were the darkened silhouettes of trees along a mountainous landscape. So he turned his attention to his task, slipping quickly inside the Emperor's tent.

The man was quick; that was for sure. By the time Kiril cleared the tent flap, the Emperor had his sword in hand and was already bearing down. But Kiril could tell from a lifetime's experience that Dag Racho's mind was on his dragon, not on the situation here.

All the better for Kiril.

Except, even with only half a mind on his attack, Dag Racho was still the finest swordsman Kiril had ever encountered. Even if he hadn't had the skill, he had a dragon's strength behind his every swing. One good blow and Kiril would be cut in half. Add to that the uncertain footing inside this pillow-strewn tent, and Kiril was in for the fight of his life.

He winced as the clashing of their swords rang loudly in the confined space. If any of the remaining soldiers heard, they would be tearing in here, and that would be the end of everything. Try as he might, Kiril could not best the Emperor.

What he did do, however, was draw more and more of the man's attention into this swordfight. That was something, at least. Though it spelled bad things for Kiril—since with more attention, the Emperor's fighting ability got better and better—it meant more freedom for the Copper to defer to his Queen and give Natiya a chance.

Kiril threw himself into the fight with renewed vigor, imagining each swing, each parry, each thrust as one more moment where Dag Racho had to be in his human body and not assisting the Copper. He managed to maneuver the Emperor around a table, backing him into the tent corner. But while Kiril was struggling to avoid tripping over a chair, the Emperor slashed out of the tent, and they were soon fighting half in, half outside.

Bad. Very, very bad. Because Kiril remained inside while Dag Racho had more room to maneuver. And if he pushed free of the tent, then the Emperor would have an open attack.

Kiril poured on the power, a furious flurry he hoped would press the Emperor back. No such luck. Racho had found a position and defended it, his mind on his Copper while waiting for Kiril to pursue. As soon as Kiril tried to push through the tent rip, he would strike a quick end to this distraction.

Just then, blistering heat ripped through the air. Even in the tent, Kiril felt the impact. Only as he was dropping to his knees did he realize he'd been hearing the beat of dragon wings for a while now. The fight must have come closer. Close enough for a fire plume to set the Emperor's tent on fire. And Kiril was trapped inside the inferno.

Natiya flinched as the Copper's breath set fire to a red tent. The sight was confusing to her, since it was filtered through the Queen's vision, but even so it made less sense than usual. The Copper hadn't even been aiming for the Queen, but had abruptly turned his head and blasted fire at something on the ground. Strangely, it looked like he had been aiming at Rashad, and that the only reason he missed was because the Queen had taken that moment's distraction to attack, throwing him off.

But why would the Copper blast Rashad? Natiya wondered. It didn't make any sense, especially given how fiercely he was fighting the Queen.

Which had been the other surprise of the night. After Natiya had been absolutely positive—thanks to the Queen—that the Copper would never attack, what had happened? The Copper had gone after the Queen like she was a tasty morsel dangled before a starving man. He had zipped through the clouds like an arrow, shooting flame that singed the Queen's wings less than a beat before he tried to lock his massive jaws around her neck. And while they were still above ocean, no less.

Natiya had been surprised by the attack, but not immobilized. After all, how often did life go as predicted? But the Queen's shock had blasted through Natiya's mind like the scream of a frightened child, and suddenly Natiya fought not just to survive the attack, but to calm the confusion that raged in her dragon's mind. Together they must do what they could to survive.

Except that, even together, they were both really bad fighters. Teeth, claw, fire and wing—all flailed to little effect, while the Copper kept up a coordinated and devastating attack. Natiya and the Queen were going to lose badly. They were going to die.

Natiya had little choice but to take over. Usually she allowed the Queen autonomy over her body, but this was an extraordinary situation and the Queen was completely inept. So, with little understanding of aerial combat or even the mechanics of flight, Natiya began issuing orders. The first being: run! Or in this case, fly! Toward land.

At least over land, they wouldn't have to worry about drowning. Just being impaled upon the trees. Much better.

Thankfully, the Queen responded, and Natiya hadn't needed to actually force wing and claw to move. She felt the bite of pain as the Copper's claws raked across the Queen's still young—and therefore little-armored— back and tail, but they were escaping, because that was the one thing the Queen had developed over the last few days: speed. *D'greth*, the creature loved to fly— hard and fast, without hesitation—and she did so now while Natiya tried to regroup.

Which was when the first inconsistency occurred.

The Copper didn't pursue. Not at first. He simply hung in the air watching, or so it seemed by the time Natiya and the Queen dared risk a glance backward.

Then the respite was over. As soon as the Queen slowed, spinning in the air to get a better view of the Copper, he abruptly attacked again—in halting, jerking movements rather than the smooth, devastating assault of earlier. Thankfully, Natiya and the Queen were able to dodge and swerve away.

So it continued, with the Copper being an inelegant, inconstant aggressor, while the Queen dodged and parried, using her smaller size and greater speed to maximum effect—meaning she stayed alive but inflicted no return damage. In fact, for a battle that lasted

so long, there seemed very few actual wounds. The
Queen rarely connected in any meaningful way, and
half the times when the Copper had an advantage, he
let it slip away.

It was bizarre in the extreme, but neither Natiya nor
the Queen had the time to reason it out. And right there
was the main problem: time. Or the lack of it. Because
while the two dragons exhausted themselves in the air,
the Emperor's squads were making steady progress up
the mountainside. Kiril's traps would only slow them so
long, and by the time Natiya calmed the Queen enough
to return control of the aerial battle to her, soldiers were
gripping both of Natiya's arms and dragging her out of a
place she couldn't even remember hiding in.

She didn't even put up any resistance. Now she was
being firmly escorted down the mountain.

That was when she came back enough to her own
thoughts to remember Kiril. She knew what he was
doing—or at least what he'd planned. His intention was
to kill the Emperor in a swift, surprise attack. But they
had been the ones surprised, not Rashad. Which meant
Kiril and the Emperor were likely right now fighting for
their lives. If Kiril still lived.

Natiya suppressed a quick surge of panic at the
thought, reassuring herself that he was an experienced
fighter. Surely he could hold his own. But against the
Emperor and his bodyguards? Not likely. Which
meant—

At that moment the Copper twisted its head, shooting
its jet of fire at Rashad but catching the tent instead.
Natiya wanted to make the Queen look around, find
Kiril, but knew she couldn't risk it. The Queen was busy
enough without distractions.

That was when Natiya at last understood the Copper's
inconsistencies. She'd thought all along that Rashad
seemed at odds with his dragon. The man's strength of
will was legendary, but could it be that dragon and man

were so at odds that they fought constantly for control? That, whenever Rashad was distracted, the Copper took enough control to stop fighting the Queen?

It was certainly possible. That would explain the Copper's actions: one moment viciously brutal, the next moment hesitant. If Rashad and the Copper had different goals, different agendas, then she would see the Copper's plan in the moments when Rashad was preoccupied. Which meant—

He will not kill his Queen.

Natiya acknowledged the Queen's comment, even as she urged her dragon to pay attention to the fight at hand. Especially as the Copper was rearing up for another attack. Which meant Rashad was in control again, his distraction gone. Which meant Kiril was . . . She couldn't finish the thought.

She and her escort broke through the trees, at last allowing Natiya to see what was happening with her own eyes. Thankfully, the darkness wasn't a problem. Not only did the soldiers carry firesticks, but the clearing was blazing with firelight—from the tent, from some of the nearby trees, from small brush fires in the ground cover. How odd that she had no fear of the fire—a carryover, perhaps, from the Queen. She was able to remain quite dispassionate when viewing and walking straight into the blaze.

But then she saw a man—Kiril!—fly suddenly out of the side of the burning tent, straight at Rashad's upraised sword. A grazing blow, and Kiril's chest gouted blood. Yet he continued to fight, continued to press his attack, while half the soldiers around her ran bellowing forward. Kiril didn't stand a chance.

Neither, apparently, did the Queen, because at that moment the Copper found his opening. He locked his jaws around the Queen's neck, then angled his claws up and around the top bone of each wing. Belly to belly, they tumbled through the air, the Queen's weight

too much for the Copper, especially as her claws raked
at his underbelly.

But the Copper hung on, his massive weight bearing
the Queen down as they plummeted toward the
ground.

Unable to help Kiril, Natiya did what she could to
calm her dragon, to find a way out, to . . . Natiya paused,
her thoughts reeling with shock because the Queen
wasn't interested in fighting. She wasn't even interested
in listening, for a wave of conflicting lust and terror
brought Natiya to her knees.

And in that suffocating moment, when awareness
connected with understanding, Natiya discovered the
truth. This wasn't a fight to the death. This was a fight
that preluded copulation. And yet, it couldn't be. The
Queen was too young, the Copper too large. It wasn't
her time yet, and the Queen would likely be killed.

But, how to stop it? How to prevent the Copper from
finishing what he'd begun? Especially as the two wyrms
finally crashed to the ground—the Queen taking the
brunt of the impact, the Copper landing on top of her
with wings spread, belly-horn ready.

"No!" Natiya screamed, the action doing a great deal
to separate her mind from the Queen's, which was
stunned and nearly unconscious. She scrambled to her
feet, running forward—but not to the dragons. She
hadn't enough physical strength to prevent what was
about to happen there. No, she ran to Rashad, who was
now fighting a losing battle with Kiril, because his mind
was similarly overwhelmed by the Copper's lust. Thank
Amia the Queen had been stunned from the impact
with the ground; otherwise, Natiya would be equally
impaired.

"Stop!" Natiya shrieked, speaking to everyone at
once. It was all going too fast, and in the wrong ways.
"Kiril, stop!"

She hadn't meant to single him out, and yet he was the one person she knew would listen. Except he didn't. He took the moment when Rashad was slow and uncoordinated—surely struggling with his Copper's emotions—to finish the battle. Though cut in half a dozen places, Kiril slammed away the approaching guards to spin around behind Rashad, hauling them both back against a boulder while he held his sword to the Emperor's neck. Then, and only then, did he take the time to glare at Natiya through the fringe of his sweat-soaked hair.

"What?" he snapped.

And that was when everything froze into a tableau of shock. Kiril held Rashad hostage, his sword at the Emperor's throat. The soldiers hovered nearby, waiting for their opportunity. And the dragons . . . Natiya shifted her attention to them.

The Copper had not completed his intent, but seemed to wait, his glittering eyes focused not on the Queen but on Rashad. What was going on? What was happening in this silent war between dragon and Emperor?

Natiya slowly walked forward, stepping gingerly in front of the Emperor. "What is happening, Rashad? Why do you fight your own dragon?" she asked.

The Emperor turned his furious glare on her, his teeth grinding even as he spat his answer. "You see what he is going to do. He is going to kill her."

Natiya turned her head, only now processing how close the two dragons were. The Copper needed only extend his head just the tiniest bit for the Emperor and him to touch.

"You see?" Rashad snapped. "He will *kill* her."

True, the Copper was still poised, his body ready to force an act that would, if not outright kill the much smaller Queen, certainly injure her severely. Certainly he would not accomplish any reproductive goals; this would be more an act of violence than biology. The Queen was beginning to come back to herself, was struggling, though she had little maneuvering room.

Natiya frowned, trying to understand what she was seeing. She even ordered the Queen to remain still, to gather her strength and wait until Natiya better understood the situation. The Copper was poised, ready to harm the Queen, and yet, he had stopped. His head was turned away from the Queen to stare directly at Rashad.

"What does the Copper want, Rashad?" Natiya asked. She took another step toward the Emperor. "He knows, doesn't he? He knows that it is time for you to move on. And he is willing to kill the Queen to prevent your success. He is willing to do anything to destroy your plans."

Rashad didn't answer. His face had become a stubborn mask of anger. Kiril, on the other hand, received the news with a gaping jaw. His gaze darted between her, the Emperor and the Copper.

"Yes," Natiya continued, "the Copper knows it is time for you to complete the process." She let her voice drop to a more compassionate level. She knew exactly how frightening the prospect was: to give up everything and become something completely different. Something completely foreign. But it was what had been started the moment both she and Rashad had picked up their dragon eggs and begun the incubation process. "The blending is only supposed to be temporary," she said. "It is time to complete the switch."

"Natiya . . ." Kiril began, a low throb of warning in his voice. But his next words were cut off by Rashad's bellow.

"No!" the Emperor screamed, erupting in a fierce struggle to escape Kiril's restraint. But Natiya's dragon-hunter was strong, even if his arms dripped blood, and he held fast. There was nowhere for Rashad to go, and bit by slow bit the Copper extended his head, angling his forehead to touch Rashad's.

Still the Emperor fought. "I won't! And he can't force me!"

Natiya had reached the Emperor's side, though she stayed opposite the Copper. "No one can force you, Rashad, but think a moment. What has being human gotten you? Your people despise you, kept in check only by an army you don't trust. The bordering countries are allying against you, and even your mind is not your own." Instinctively Natiya shuddered. It was difficult enough to share mental space with the Queen, and they had formed an alliance of sorts. Cooperation, not domination. How terrible would it be to exist in a constant mental war, every day, every night? Constantly having to exert massive force of will to keep the dragon under control? She couldn't imagine it, and yet the struggle had become so fierce that the Copper was willing to kill his own Queen just to find a means of escape.

"This is not the life you wanted, Rashad. This is not the way to get what you need."

The Emperor's eyes turned tragic. He gasped out her name, whispering his words even as he fought tears. "You love me, Natiya, I know you do. I have felt it. In our dreams."

She hesitated, wondering what to say. He was correct. She did feel a kind of love for the Emperor, a sympathy and compassion that encompassed the boy Rashad and extended to the torn and tortured Dag Racho. But was it love?

Her gaze passed beyond the Emperor to Kiril. He was the man who had challenged her at every turn. He was the one who'd once vowed to kill her, and who even now remained with sword at the ready if she relinquished control to the Queen. And yet, he was the one she turned to when she looked for truth. And for love.

No, she didn't love Rashad. Certainly not the way he wanted. Her heart belonged to Kiril.

She saw the realization hit both men at once. She watched Kiril's eyes widen with wonder, while, trapped in his arms, Rashad crumpled, screaming out in his soul's agony.

"No!" he cried, and Natiya started at the sound. "No!" he said again, only this time fury was replacing his pain. "I gave you everything, *forgave* you everything. You cannot want him!"

She looked at the Emperor's frenzied expression, his desperate struggles, and she finally understood the truth. "You have been at war in your mind so long, all your emotions are confused. You don't love me. You love the dream of a Queen and a dragon army. You think you can threaten, manipulate or force love—from me, from your people—but it doesn't work that way. Everything has gone wrong, Rashad, because you would not finish what you started."

"No!" he screamed again . . . just as the Copper struck.

She wouldn't have believed it possible if she hadn't seen it with her own eyes. The Copper released a narrow jet of fire, pinpointed on its target. The blast engulfed Rashad and Kiril, and left her virtually untouched.

This time it was Natiya who screamed, Natiya who tried to rush forward. "Kiril!"

But it was too late. Rashad was a smoking, blistered and charred mass; though somehow he was still breathing, his every inhalation a wheezing and continuous silent scream. But Kiril? She didn't see him. Where was—

There! Alive. Bald and blistered, but alive. And much better off than Rashad. Natiya wept with relief even as she dropped to her knees beside him and the Emperor. She tried to speak, but her throat closed around the words. The shock and horror still rippled through her mind, clouding her emotions and silencing her. Even the Queen was dumbfounded. And the surrounding soldiers. So Natiya simply sat there, reaching for and finding Kiril's hand while the two of them looked at the Emperor.

As they did nothing, the Copper moved. He rolled off the Queen, extending his head so that his forehead connected with the Emperor's once more. And at last Natiya understood.

"There is no other choice," she said softly. "Not if you want to live, Rashad. You must switch bodies with the Copper. Otherwise—"

"No, Natiya!" Kiril snapped, his voice tight with pain or fear. "Let him die!" He began to struggle to his feet, but he was pinned under the Emperor's body. "You can't let him become a dragon. Think what damage—"

"He's not evil," Natiya interrupted. "He doesn't want to hurt people, do you, Rashad? And even if he did"—her gaze lifted to indicate the score of dragons one by one landing in the trees, on the ground around them— "they wouldn't let him. That's not what this is about."

She heard Kiril gasp in horror as the stately creatures surrounded them, landing haphazardly here and there, all eyes trained on the Emperor and the Copper. But she didn't have time to soothe his fears; and, in truth, she thought he was beginning to understand. It was Rashad who needed help, and it was to him she spoke.

"This is about moving on. About not being stuck or afraid."

She saw anger flash in the Emperor's eyes at her comment, but there was little time for more, for the Copper pressed his head to Rashad's. The wyrm's glittering brown eyes closed, and Natiya knew he simply waited. Rashad had to willingly choose to complete the process—to take dragon form—and Natiya marveled at the length of time it seemed to take for the Emperor to make the decision. Especially since his other choice was death.

"You will be in control of your own mind again," she urged. "No more fighting someone else's thoughts, no more hiding even within your own mind. You can be who you are without fear, without anger or dissension. Surely that is better than dying. Release your fears and become whole again."

Whether because of her words or his pain, Rashad finally made his decision. She watched his eyes close, and his breath eased out with a final bitter wheeze. And then the magic began.

Natiya saw the transfer more than felt it. The Queen's sight gave her a view of the power, growing and pulsing around both man and creature. And it was in that first enveloping of energy that Rashad's human body healed. But then the power tightened. It drew together, growing smaller, harder and much, much brighter. She was seeing their souls, or so she guessed, and she marveled at how completely the spirit saturated one's every cell. But both lights were tightening, drawing into themselves, pulling together at that one point where the foreheads touched.

It began slowly, the shrinking barely measurable. But then it grew stronger and faster, the power bright enough that she saw it with her human eyes as well as the dragon's. Then, with a crash she felt more than saw, the two lights seemed to explode against one another. The power was so strong it knocked her to the ground, blinding both her human and dragon sight. She heard Kiril grunt with pain, while behind her the soldiers toppled, their weapons dropping with a loud clatter onto the ground.

And when her vision cleared, she saw the man she'd once called Dag Racho blink shimmering copper eyes. He was the Copper now, in human form. Twisting quickly, she saw the dragon roll to the ground, clearly stunned, his darker, more humanlike eyes blinking in dazed confusion.

Natiya struggled to her feet, intending to say something to Rashad, though she didn't know what. Meanwhile, Kiril sighed as the Emperor's body at last rolled off of him, and Kiril began awkwardly gaining his feet.

The now-human Copper seemed to be adjusting to his new body quickly, stretching and moving with more and more control. Rashad, on the other hand, moved weakly and in a chaotic fashion, one moment twitching his wing, the next moment twisting his head while shifting his tail. It would be a difficult road for Rashad, learning the basics all over again.

Natiya turned back to the Copper, seeing a focused purpose in the way he practiced his balance, shifting his human weight from one foot to the other. He was even rolling his shoulders, learning the finer differences of arm and spine.

He was smart, she suddenly realized. Smarter, surely, than she initially gave him credit for. He had a hundred years of experience, plus whatever knowledge was shared among dragons. And he had an agenda. He had to. Everything about this incident indicated a plan. He'd awaited an opportunity—which she and Kiril had provided. All so he could take human form.

But why?

She shifted, turning her attention back to Rashad. Would he know? And would he tell?

She stepped forward, gently resting her hand on the dragon's neck. He smiled at her, or at least she wanted to believe he did: he bared his teeth. She directed her question to the Queen, whom she hoped would ask Rashad.

Why does the Copper want to be human? What are his plans?

The Queen acknowledged the questions, and Natiya knew the Queen had turned to ask Rashad; she could see the energy shift. Rashad was able to turn his dragon head toward the smaller dragon beside him.

But that was all he could do, because a sword suddenly sprouted from the vulnerable soft flesh beneath his jaw. Natiya barely registered the movement out of the corner of her eye, and then she saw that Kiril's sword was embedded straight through the lower flesh and up into Rashad's brain. He shuddered, his massive body twitching the tiniest bit before his head crashed to the ground. Dead.

Natiya spun around, unbelieving and angry. But one look at Kiril and she saw it hadn't been him who'd thrown the sword. He was as stunned as she, though mixed emotions warred in his expression. It had been the Copper—in Rashad's old body—who had delivered the fatal blow. How he had managed to coordinate himself enough to throw the blade so well was beyond her, but he had. And now he was stumbling, trying to regain his balance after so powerful a throw.

"Why?" she demanded, the sound more a gasp than a word.

Kiril had made it to the Copper's side, grabbing hold of the man's arm to both balance and restrain him. And so the former dragon was able to focus on speech, carefully forming each word.

"Heeee could not beee a drrrragonnn."

Natiya took a step forward, unreasoning anger flowing through her. "Why not?"

The Copper shook his head. "Tooooo laaate." And then, despite Kiril's hold on his arm, the Copper crumpled, dropping to the ground with a thud.

Natiya turned to her own dragon, at last fully extricated from beneath Rashad.

Do you understand this? she demanded.

The Queen shook her head—a surprisingly human gesture that conveyed the same horror and confusion that reverberated through Natiya.

And then another shock rolled through Natiya's system, this one expected but no less powerful. The Queen waddled forward, her body slow because of her recent fight, and because she moved to avoid the body of Rashad the dragon.

I am ready, she said to Natiya. *We can complete the process now.*

CHAPTER TWENTY-ONE

"What are you doing?"

Kiril's voice cut through Natiya's thoughts, freezing her in place before she reached the Queen's out-stretched forehead.

"Natiya! Stop!" She could hear the panic in Kiril's voice, and she smiled, startled to realize she found humor in the situation. He was feeling panic? She was the one about to become a dragon. And yet, even as she smiled, she felt her eyes tear. She didn't even want to look at him, to see what she was leaving behind; but he made her. He reached out and pulled her face to his.

"What are you doing?" he repeated, his expression fierce.

"What I promised." How she kept her voice level, she hadn't a clue. But she did, swallowing down her dread as she tried to force herself to turn back to the Queen. Instead, she found herself kissing Kiril, her lips, his mouth, their entire bodies abruptly crushed together as if joined.

But in time, they had to separate; they had to pull back and look into each other's eyes.

"I promised I would go when this was done. I promised—"

"I don't give a damn about your promise," he interrupted, his grip firm on her arms. "You love me!" It wasn't a statement so much as a command.

"You think I'm evil."

He ground his teeth. She could hear it, and yet he'd never seemed sweeter to her. "You're not evil. Natiya, I trust you."

Never had those words touched her more, and yet she knew Kiril was suspicious by nature. "I can't live with you constantly watching me, wondering if I'm suddenly going to start killing people or destroying the good that you desire. Besides," she began, as she forced herself to pull away from him, "the Queen's much smarter than I am. She'll be a good ally for you."

"A dragon ally?" he snapped, clearly horrified, and she looked away, her other offer dying on her lips. Except, when she looked away, her gaze landed on the carcass of the Copper. And then on the dragons around them, all waiting patiently throughout the clearing. What would it be like to be with them? Would she remain herself, or would her personality change?

"I'll make sure they leave," she said, unwilling to think about the questions and doubts that swirled through her. "I don't know how much influence I'll have, but I'll keep them away. You'll have enough problems without . . ." *Without me making things worse*, she almost said. She had been unprepared and unthinking throughout her entire life. She wasn't the asset he needed.

"Is this what you want? Natiya!" When she didn't answer, he pulled her face back to his. "Is this what you want?"

She stared at him, not knowing what to say. "I promised—"

"To Frith with your promise!" he snapped. "What do *you* want?"

She swallowed her tears, confusion making her voice clipped. "You don't want dragons in Ragona anymore. Changing is the only way—"

"And what if I'm wrong? What if—"

"But you've never been wrong!" she exclaimed. "Don't you see? Everything you said—that I was unprepared, naive, too stupid to think beyond the obvious— all of that is true. Everything I've done from the very beginning has been wrong. It led to this."

He shook his head, his grip tightening as he spoke. "You haven't been wrong. Just not completely right." He grimaced. "*D'greth,* Natiya, why do you think I didn't kill you during the hatching? Why do you think I've been chasing you around like a lost puppy? Why do you think I've given up everything I have, everything I know, just to follow you?"

She bit her lip, the enormity of what he had done crashing in on her. Everything he'd risked—his life, his future, his entire rebellion—on her. When she'd been completely unprepared for any of it.

"I believe in you, Natiya. I don't know how, but you see things, you know things that none of us have figured out."

"I've been guessing—"

"And you've succeeded. Natiya, don't you see? From the first moment I saw you dancing, I knew you were different. I knew you had the answers." She could feel his body tense as he tried to explain. The words weren't coming easily to him, but she saw truth in the fierceness of his expression. "That's why I took you to the caves. And that's why I risked everything to get you out of the Emperor's mountain. And that's why I've been helping. Against all logic, against all reason, you"—he swallowed—"you find the answers when no one else does. And you don't stop until you have them."

"But I don't know what I'm doing."

He shrugged. "Neither do any of us. But you succeed. I don't know how, but you do."

"But I can't—"

"I love you, Natiya," he interrupted. And when she stared at him in shock, he repeated it again. "I love you. I always have. You"—he frowned as he fought for the words—"you inspire me. You can't leave me now." He reached up and touched her face. "I need you."

She felt her heart squeeze tight in her chest, his words flowing over her in the most wonderful and painful of ways. He loved her. And yet . . . "It doesn't make sense. Kiril, you're the one who told me to think, to reason out the consequences." She stepped forward, at last giving voice to her offer. "If I change, if I become a dragon, I can help. I can stay with you for a while. If you want—"

He smiled, though she knew the effort cost him. "Is that what I've taught you? To look for logic?"

"It's not a bad thing."

He laughed, though the sound was brittle in the thin mountain air. "I was wrong," he said. Then she watched him visibly steel himself before he turned to the Queen, who regarded him calmly, her golden eyes glittering in the torchlight.

"I don't trust you," he told her. "I think you have an agenda that none of us understand." Then he glanced back at Natiya. "But if I have learned anything these last weeks, it's that everything I thought I knew is wrong. Or not entirely correct."

I do not understand his fears. My presence here was to help the Copper.

"And?" Natiya prompted the dragon. "There is more."

The Queen dipped her head in a nod. *We search for The Human.*

Natiya blinked. "The Human? The Human what?"

The Human who will be a bridge between us and you. Rashad was not that man.

She frowned, trying to understand. "A person who can be both dragon and human? But why?"

Do you not wish to evolve?

Kiril shifted uncertainly between dragon and Natiya. "What? What is she saying?"

"That they are searching for a way to bridge human and dragon. That they look for a way to better both species."

His eyes narrowed as he looked from her back to the Queen. "Is that possible?"

Of course.

"She says yes," Natiya translated.

Kiril shook his head, clearly struggling to understand. "Will she explain this to you? Can she answer my questions?"

Of course.

Natiya smiled. "She will answer whatever you like. But dragon answers . . ." She shook her head. "Sometimes they are confusing."

Kiril sighed. "Of course they are." He turned to face Natiya directly. "But I can't do it alone. I need *you* with me." He reached out, his hand trembling as it touched her cheek. "I love you. Please stay."

She hesitated, torn between what her heart wanted and what her head told her to do. "But I will still be bonded with the Queen."

"And I will still believe in you. I will still love you." He touched her chin, tilting her face up until she looked directly into his eyes. "Do you love me?" He spoke in a whisper, anxiety radiating from every line of his body.

She said the words without thought: "Of course I do! I have from the very beginning, but—"

He was kissing her. Even when she struggled against his mouth, trying to voice any of the hundreds of objections in her thoughts, he kept her silent. And soon, she had no more thought but him in her arms, his body with hers. Their love protecting them both.

Except, it couldn't. It hadn't. Love hadn't protected anyone, ever.

She pulled away. "Kiril," she whispered. "What are we going to do?"

"We're going to keep working. We're going to build a kingdom. And we're going to find a way to protect ourselves against all those neighboring countries that Racho allied against us."

"But how?"

He grinned. "Didn't you have plans for the justice system? Didn't you talk about restructuring the laws?"

"Of course I did. I have lots of ideas, but—"

"We can do it now. You still control the Queen, don't you?"

She glanced over her shoulder, startled to see that one by one, the other dragons had started to fly away, lifting into the air, heading back to their home, wherever that was. And yet the Queen remained, her golden eyes calm as she looked at Natiya and Kiril, answering the question before Natiya could ask.

I still have much to learn in the human world.

Natiya turned back to Kiril. "We cooperate. And yes, she is willing to remain here with us." *With us.* The words echoed in her thoughts. Could this really be happening? Could she suddenly—abruptly—have everything she'd ever wanted? A man who believed in her? The power to change her world?

"I have ideas too, Natiya. And allies. Sabina, for one. And—"

"Pentold and Uncle Rened."

He nodded, his expression lightening. "So the financiers are on our side." He turned, looking toward the soldiers that surrounded them. "And I think the military could be persuaded, especially since we still have the biggest weapon at our disposal." He gestured at the Queen.

To their left, Natiya watched the leader of the Emperor's guard nod in slow approval. Yes, he would support them. And with him, the rest of the military.

"What of the Coral?"

"Gone," the man said. "She flew as far and as fast as she could. We don't know where."

"We can do it, Natiya," Kiril pressed. "But only if we do it together."

"I think," she began slowly, her thoughts falling piece by piece into a beautiful order. "All this time I've been asking the wrong question. I've been asking everyone what they want from me. I should have been asking myself what I want."

"And what is that?"

She grinned. "I want justice. I want happiness. I want a chance to help Ragona by finishing what I started. But mostly," she said as she wrapped her arms around him, "I want you."

He planted a large, loud, wet kiss on her lips. "Then there's nothing that can stop us."

EVE KENIN

*The Award-Winning Author
of DRIVEN Brings You...*

HIDDEN

Tatiana has honed her genetic gifts to perfection. She can withstand the subzero temperatures of the Northern Waste, read somebody's mind with the briefest touch, and slice through bone with her bare hands. Which makes her one badass chick, all right.

Nothing gets to her. Until she meets Tristan. Villain or ally, she can't be sure. But one thing she does know: he has gifts too—including the ability to ramp up her heart rate to dangerous levels. But before they can start some chemistry of their own, they have to survive being trapped in an underground lab, hunted by a madman, and exposed to a plague that could destroy mankind.

AVAILABLE JULY 2008

ISBN 13: 978-0-505-52761-5

COUNTDOWN

MICHELLE MADDOX

THREE

Kira Jordan wakes up in a pitch-black room
handcuffed to a metal wall. She has 60 seconds to
escape. Thus begins a vicious game where to lose
is to die.

TWO

The man she's been partnered with—her only ally
in this nightmare—is a convicted mass murderer.
But if he's so violent, why does he protect her?
And stranger still, what is it behind those haunted
sea-green eyes that makes her want to protect him?

ONE

No one to trust. Nowhere to run. And the only
hope of survival is working together to beat the
Countdown.

AVAILABLE AUGUST 2008

ISBN 13: 978-0-505-52755-4

These Boots Were Made for STOMPING

Award-winning authors Julie Kenner, Jade Lee, and Marianne Mancusi

Yes, there are the right shoes for the right situation, and not every moment calls for Manolos. Sometimes a woman's gotta be fierce as well as feminine, fiery as well as fragile. And when the legwork required is a roundhouse, when a girl's mantra has to become "I am woman, hear me roar," those are the times it's good to know there's magic in the world…because in super-powered pumps, the shrinking-est Violet or the nervous-est Nellie can do anything. Every step in magic shoes is sure to be a big one.

After a single trip to Hiheelia.com, our heroines are safe. Their hearts are not.

AVAILABLE APRIL 2008

ISBN 13: 978-0-505-52760-8